TEARS
OF THE
SUN

Kelly King has worked primarily as an advertising writer/producer and as an occasional writer/producer for radio and television. She lived in Japan during the 1960s and 70s and, since then, has visited Japan to see family and to research *Tears of the Sun* and its forthcoming sequel, *Sea of Dreams*. She has also travelled extensively throughout Europe, Asia, England and the South Pacific, recently completing her research for this novel in Hawaii.

TEARS OF THE SUN

KELLY KING

ALLEN & UNWIN

Copyright © Kelly King 1998

All rights reserved. No part of this book may be reproduced or transmitted in any form or by any means, electronic or mechanical, including photocopying, recording or by any information storage and retrieval system, without prior permission in writing from the publisher.

First published in 1998 by
Allen & Unwin
9 Atchison Street
St Leonards NSW 2065
Australia
Phone: (61 2) 9901 4088
Fax: (61 2) 9906 2218
E-mail: frontdesk@allen-unwin.com.au
Web: http://www.allen-unwin.com.au

National Library of Australia
Cataloguing-in-Publication entry:

King, Kelly, 1941– .
 Tears of the sun.

 ISBN 1 86448 334 2.

 I. Title.

A823.3

Set in 10/11 pt Times Roman by DOCUPRO, Sydney
Printed and bound at McPhersons Printing Group,
Maryborough, Victoria

10 9 8 7 6 5 4 3 2 1

To my mother, Josephine,
and my father, Geoffrey Ingleton,
with love.

It's the promise and our pursuit of peace
which sets us apart.

'There's nothing so strange in a strange land,
As the stranger who comes to visit it.'

(Anon)

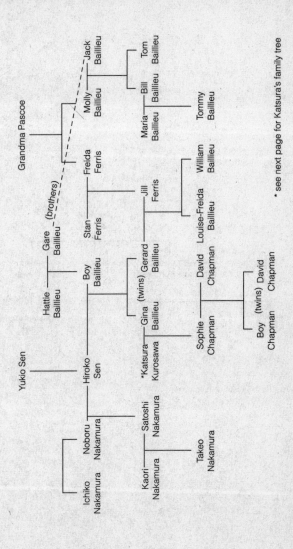

* see next page for Katsura's family tree

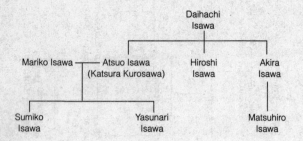

PRELUDE

DREAMTIME—QUEENSLAND, DECEMBER 1971

From a distance through the haze, it looked like a tiny speck dancing a frenzied tattoo. The shimmering layers of hot moist air imbued the endless stretch of land with an almost dreamlike quality, a mirage effect. The speck persisted, became larger, arms reaching out as if to pull by sheer momentum the weight behind them. Legs moving like pistons, leaping forward in thrusting strides, beating time to the panting, wrenching breaths that rose and fell on the stillness. Every now and then, as though from another dimension of time and space, a half-strangled cry shattered the great silence.

* * *

He emerged from the surf, removing his goggles, then flippers, shaking off the excess water. The sea was so warm. It was almost like swimming in the heated springs at Atami. Except there was no smell of sulphur, or the sight of crowds enjoying the steam and medicinal promise of the springs.

This was the thing he couldn't get accustomed to. Where were the people? It was amazing, like a scene from 'The Lost Planet.' Stretches of almost totally uninhabited sand, sea and land. Here one could truly blend with the elements, and never be missed. It was wonderful and it was frightening, this unnerving sense of aloneness that he'd never experienced before.

Here he was, sitting on this rocky outcrop in a land that felt as old as time, his shiny new snorkelling gear strangely out of place. The moulded plastics, vibrant colours clashed with the soft browns and greens of trees weathered by an ancient past, a sea of silvery spinifex that shone under an unrelenting sun which hit the sand like a hammer on an anvil.

The sky stretched forever, and for some time he sat meditating in the sparse shade of a melaleuca tree. He thought of the sweet face of his girlfriend. He would have to bring her here, to this place, in two years maybe. Shading his eyes against the intense glare, he could see in the distance the launch his group had hired riding at anchor close to the reef. He had decided to stay ashore and snorkel around the rock shelf, and later jog the two kilometres back to the hotel.

A sudden inexplicable sadness descended. A cold feeling of loss spread through his body, despite the heat of the day. He shivered and stood up quickly, trying to throw off this dreaded mantle of depression that had crept up on him. Every intuitive sense seemed to be saying something. But what?

Now, here in this place, completely alone, he was totally aware of it. It bore down on him relentlessly, and he decided he wouldn't wait for the others, but would return to their hotel. He had an almost overwhelming urge to get back quickly and put a call through to Tokyo. He could still see the boat bobbing about further out on the reef. He called out and caught their attention, and waved, indicating his intention to go. It was then he noticed a bank of dark cloud moving across the sky from the north.

He wished that he'd stayed with his friends on the boat. This sense of isolation was almost overwhelming. Images of their brief time in a local hotel the evening before came crowding in to fill the surrounding emptiness. He recalled the stares and sudden hush when they'd entered the public bar. Even now he could still smell the sharp sweet tang of beer as it spurted in an amber froth from stainless steel taps into long glasses lined up along the counter. Its smell mingled with that of the sweat of men standing staring hard at them. Mindful of the sudden air of hostility that had greeted their arrival, they'd moved quietly to the bar. His friend, Hideyoshi-san, had ordered for them all. And he recalled with a rising anger how the barman, his face coarsened and sun-cracked, had cast a knowing look to others at the bar and had made Hideyoshi repeat his order three times to the accompanying sniggers of the bystanders. Hideyoshi had turned on them and hissed his displeasure in a gutteral curse, then before they'd known it one of the younger men, large and raw-boned, had sprung across the room, towering over him.

'You got anything to say, you say it to me, you little Nip mother-fucker.' He'd spun Hideyoshi around, and as quickly Hideyoshi had kicked out, aiming high at the man's chest, felling him in an instant. There was a roar of anger as the men at the bar crowded in, hauling Hideyoshi back and punching into him at random.

His friend had put up a good fight he recalled with a renewed sense of pride. He was the true son of his father, the esteemed war hero, General Hideyoshi Ueda and had trained from an early age to be skilled in the martial arts and well able to rise to this or any other occasion. Even when so outnumbered his friend had fought back, and only the arrival of the local police had put an end to it.

The sudden harsh cry of a bird flying overhead shattered the stillness and returned him to this desolate place. Turning away from the beach, he walked back along a rough track winding among the paperbarks they'd been driven through earlier that morning. Although a quick glance at his Seiko told him it was still only 11 a.m., it seemed they'd been there for months or years, not a few brief hours. Already the heat was intense, the air so still. The trees were getting thicker now and threw a welcome shade as the track wound around the mouth of the river flats.

He was hot and felt overwhelmingly tired, and decided to rest for a while at the side of the river. He leaned back against the trunk of a mangrove, his feet dangling in the blessed cool of the water. The sadness was still with him, and a sudden picture rose before him, of his mother and father, sitting at the kitchen table in their tiny apartment in Shibuya. She was quietly listening to his father with the intensity and slight lilt of her head that he so loved. She was laughing delightedly, as if he'd said something very amusing. His father reached across and touched her arm, and they both laughed. It was an intimate moment, and he felt, as he had so often as a boy, that he had no part in their private world.

His mother turned suddenly, and he saw himself entering the room, running to her, his tiny *yukata* trailing on the floor behind him. She smiled at him, and lifted him onto her lap. He nestled into her as her arms went around him, looking across at his father, feeling completely safe within the circle of her warmth. With eyes closed as he drifted in the comforting memory of that moment, he heard her sweet high voice softly singing the song she often sang to lull him to sleep.

Kibo to, yu na no anata o tasunete
Toi kunieto mata kisha ni noru
Anata wa mukashi no watashi no omoide
Furusato no yume hayimete no koi
Keredo watashi ga otona ni natta hi ni
Damatte dokoka e tachisatta anata
Itsuka anata ni mata aumada wa
Watashi no tabi wa owari no nai tabi.
I board a train again, heading for a distant land,
Searching for you, whose name is Hope.
You are my memory of former times,
My dream of home, my first love.
But on the day I grew up
You went off somewhere without a word,

And my journey will never end
Until the day I meet you once again.[1]

Almost without realising, he sang her song, the words falling for the first time on the air of this totally alien place. He didn't see the flecked golden eye suddenly blink open and gaze in timeless intensity, unmoving, contemplating, suspended in somnolent cunning.

A sharp sting of a mosquito on his arm roused him, and he slapped at the offending mite. His movement coincided with the sudden lunge of the crocodile. It was like a large dark branch shooting across the river bank at incredible speed. He saw the movement, then felt the jaws close tightly around his chest.

He was dreaming. He must be dreaming. For a split second that seemed an eternity, everything in his body seized in a catatonic spasm of fear. Then it hit him with the force of a locomotive—the overwhelming agony, the smell and feel of the beast, the incredible desire to tear himself free from this monster. It couldn't be happening. It couldn't be. He screamed and screamed, the sound rising with as much effect as a moth's wing brushing the air.

At the sound of his screams, the beast's jaws relaxed, and he pulled himself away, clawing at the mud and mangrove roots, frantic in his effort to break free. Then he felt a searing sensation as those jaws closed tight around him again, and with a speed that seemed impossible, he was carried roughly through the shallows, his body buffeted and knocked without mercy against what lay in its way.

He could hear himself screaming. It was all around him, the sound of his screaming. Was it his? It must be. It was. He tried, with renewed desperation and strength, to free himself from the steel tap that held him, but he couldn't move. As he tried, the teeth tore at his flesh, pinioning him deeper into the maws of the beast. Red blood of pain suffused his eyes, his mind, his thinking world. He could see only red, the red of the sun, then in a brief flash of recognition, the sky, clear, tranquil and unmoved above him.

A flash of golden sunlight followed him down as the beast submerged in deeper water, carrying him tightly locked in its massive jaws. As if in a dance of love with its resisting partner, it did a slow roll, then another and another as it carried him into the darkening depths of the river. The water rushed into his screaming throat. Instinct based on years of deep-water diving made him hold his breath, then he felt himself borne aloft, rising phoenix-like from the watery grave of agony and fear as the creature surfaced, and for one brief instant, he had a final precious sighting of his golden sun-filled world.

A strangled cry as the teeth bit deeper, and he never felt the bloodied waters as they closed over him once more.

* * *

The jangle of the phone barely broke the surface crescendo of cicadas, cutting the air with their shrill vibrations.

'Yeh?' Sergeant Sid Carpenter sighed as he added almost tokenly, 'Reef Cove Police Station . . . What? You'll have to speak up, can hardly hear you . . . When? Say that again?'

Sid heaved his huge bulk from one side of the chair to the other and felt the rivulets of perspiration changing course. Overhead, the ceiling fan sent a slow-motion wave of warm air flowing over him, ruffling the papers on his desk. They flapped from underneath assorted stones, beer cans, old scissors and paper clamps. 'You what? Look, I can't bloody hear a thing you're bloody saying.' Sid looked up as the fly-screen door to his office swung open, and a tall washed-out woman entered. She carefully placed a mug of tea in front of him, leaning over to catch the excited, high-pitched voice on the receiver. Sid motioned to her to sit down. 'Thanks, love.' He took a long gulp.

She gazed through the gauze-screened window behind him. A delicate mauve haze of jacaranda framed the window, with the flame of coral trees behind. The clear blue backdrop of sky disappeared into a luminous distance. It really is beautiful, she thought. Sometimes almost worth the heat, flies and monotony of timeless days, merging, each almost a replica of the one before. It seemed a lifetime since she and Sid had come with the kids to Reef Cove, yet it was barely three years ago.

'A croc, you say?' Sid's voice rose slightly. She looked at him expectantly. 'When?' She heard words crackling from the receiver, high, insistent staccato, like morse code from some disabled ship. 'Now listen, slow down. If you want me to help you, mate, I've got to know what the hell you're saying.' Sid raised his eyes to his wife. 'Now start again. You were off to do a spot of fishing . . .' he paused, listening. 'You took a short cut—where? What, through the mangroves? Hell! This bloody line!' He shook the phone, then listened again.

'That's better. You found his what?'

She felt those cold prickles of fear at the thought of some poor devil being dragged through the waters of that no-man's land.

'There was lots of what? Bloody hell!' Even Sid's usual calm registered a look of horror and disgust. He went on, his voice placating the unseen caller. 'No, no, of course you had to. Look, calm down. Get yourself a drink. I'll come out and see what's up.'

The voice continued at the other end.

'Yeh, as soon as I can . . . yeh, yeh. Look, calm down.' He hung up, then let out a long slow whistle. 'Jesus, another bloody croc attack!'

'There'll be others.' It was almost an accusation.

He looked at her. 'Yes, love, if we don't act quick. I'd lay ten to one on it being that old bugger, Titan. They thought they'd bagged him last week till he took off like a drover's dog.'

'What's happened just now?'

'Who knows? This poor bugger's pretty upset. Seems

he ran over a mile to get to that old phone up near the breakwater. One thing's for certain, though. The young bloke's a goner, and it'll be that old saltie, Titan. We'll get him though.' He paused, whistling softly through his teeth, a mannerism she knew meant that his mind was already considering the problem.

'Seems he found a passport near the remains. It's a tourist, a Japanese.' Sid continued, 'This won't make things look too rosy for those guys taking the Nips and Yanks out to the reef.'

She sighed. It all came back to business in the end. 'It's horrible, just horrible,' she said.

Sid was moving around his office, collecting pen, notepad, his gun and hat, then rummaging around in a mess of papers, old biros and screwed up bags in his drawer, pulled out a crumpled packet of menthols. He smiled across at her.

'Might be a bit late back, love. But don't worry, you can hold the fort till then, eh? I'll have to take a gander at where it all happened.' He bent to kiss her as he passed. 'See you later, love.'

She watched him heave himself into the big blue Toyota four-wheel-drive, windmilling his arms around his head as he did to ward off the black swarm of flies which descended the moment he was outside. He slammed the car door to cut off their access, and within seconds was roaring over the dust and out onto the arterial road, taking him ten kilometres out towards the coast, then onto the Northern Highway. He noticed the sky ahead to the north was looking ominous, with dark clouds hurrying towards him, cutting across the clear blue in a straight black line. But any thoughts of storm warnings were pushed aside for the business at hand.

Jesus, he thought, what on earth gets into these people, sitting around those mangroves at this time of the year. If that poor bloody Jap wanted to commit *hara-kiri*, then there were easier ways to do it.

PART ONE

1

YASUKUNI SHRINE
TOKYO, JULY 1921

With a growing sense of urgency, Hiroko-san made her way towards the Yasukuni shrine, up the steep climb to the top of Kudan hill. Her breath came in light rapid bursts as she hurried to get there.

Hardly noticing the flowering rows of cherry trees, like swarms of huge pale pink butterflies fluttering their velvety wings as they alighted at either side of the broad stone drive, she bent her head as if in silent prayer, resting momentarily to try and still the thudding of her heart before passing under the towering *torii*. She paused and turned to look for her father's servant Ume who had accompanied her and had now fallen some way behind. She knew that Ume would settle herself patiently at the entrance, waiting for as long as it took her young mistress to pay her respects.

At the side of one of the gates, an ancient stone fountain of running water caught her eye. She went across, and leaning forward, picked up the wooden pitcher, scooping deep into the pool, pouring the water over her hands—first one and then the other—before raising it to her lips and rinsing her mouth. Taking out a white cloth that lay tucked into her *obi*, she wet a corner, then patted her face with a short intake of breath as the icy water touched her burning cheeks. Closing her eyes, she felt for the first time in months a sense of *wa* descending. Tears welled up and spilled slowly down her face, not in sadness, but from a long pent-up cleansing away of grief.

Her young husband had died one year ago while on a tour of duty with his small army contingent in China. His unexpected death had at first left her numbed, just drifting from day to day, absorbed only by their four-year-old son Satoshi, but with a growing sense of alienation from the demands of her husband's family. Her place as a widow, rather than as a wife, with all its disempowering connotations brought home more keenly her increasing isolation. But even now in this holy place, she could still feel Noboru's strengthening presence as clearly as if he had only that moment left. And she ached to feel his arms around her, assuring her once more that he would protect her and her status.

But with each passing day, this knowledge that his influence and protection were still there for her within his family was fast diminishing. He, their beloved and only son, had now taken his place in the family's own shrine as a revered hero. She was merely his wife, now widow, an encumbrance, there only to serve their needs. Even her precious son Satoshi, as if to replace his father, was being taken over as their own child, while she was made to feel that her place in his life was being constantly undermined. She was becoming less and less important to his upbringing. A cold hand gripped her heart at this thought, and she straightened, steeling herself to believe that come what may, they would never take Satoshi away from her and she would keep her rightful place in her son's heart.

A sudden gust of wind blew some blossoms into her lap. They made her think of the glorious abundance of blossom in the Hama Rikyu, the Hama Detached Palace where the Empress would often spend some weeks late in spring to enjoy the breezes that blew in fresh from the sea. Hiroko's mother had once taken her there as a small child to see the blossoms and the ducks, and she could still remember listening to the ebb and flow of waves against the strong stone walls at the foot of the gardens.

Rousing herself from her reverie, she continued her way though the spreading Yasukuni grounds from *torii* to *torii* until at last she arrived at the shrine itself. The soft glint of gold from the large *kiku* stopped her momentarily, and she looked at its sixteen spreading petals, comforted by the familiarity of this sacred symbol with all its associations.

Here enshrined were the spirits or *kami*, the souls of the dead warriors, now guardian gods of their country, waiting, ready to rejoin the living in times of battle. Hiroko bowed her head, feeling the spirit of her husband close at hand.

'Noboru. Noboru.' She repeated his name in an inward chant of invocation.

The movement of someone passing close beside her brought her back to the reality of the moment. She knelt now quietly, watching people as they passed in and out of the shrine, with a feeling of sharing with them something special in this sacred place.

She was alone, yet not alone—Noboru was here with her. Like so many of the others now gone in living form, but still there in spirit, he was elevated to a *kami*, having died a hero's death. She saw him in her mind's eye. His face was clear, but his body hard to define, enveloped in a haziness of white and gold light. Closing her eyes, she felt herself floating up to meet him, their bodies dissolving one into the other, vibrating to the same rhythm as if embracing at the height of sexual passion, enclosed in that warm world of personal intensity that precluded all others.

The sudden strident chanting and clapping of the monks on the far side of the shrine made her look up, and she noticed a fair-haired man staring at her from across the outer courtyard. She lowered her eyes, but not before a twinge of familiarity—as though in recognition—ran through her. The noise of the chanting and smell of incense made her feel light-headed and weak.

Apart from a small bowl of rice and miso soup, she hadn't eaten since early yesterday.

She took another quick look at the golden-haired young man. He was now moving towards her, smiling a slow shy smile, and she saw in surprise that it was the angel god of her childhood dreams. Her head spun, and she suddenly swayed as if to faint.

He leant down and reached out to steady her. His face was radiant, and she felt drawn to him. Rising to her feet, Hiroko bowed, murmuring her thanks, then in some confusion, turned and quickly moved away.

Rather unsteadily, she walked out of the shrine and through the *torii*, then made her way towards a wooden bench beneath one of the cherry trees. She sat awhile, still feeling dizzy and confused by what had just transpired, then reaching into her *furoshiki*, she took out a purse and from it a holy card, now creased and softened from years of handling. She ran her fingers gently over the face of the angel on the card. As she looked at the angel's blue eyes and their expression of concern for the small figure it was guarding, her mind drifted back to a night seven years ago. Nervous with anticipation, and with downcast eyes, she had followed her father into the spacious forecourt of an imposing diplomatic residence.

* * *

Guardian angel—Tokyo, 1914

Lights flared at either end of the forecourt, imbuing the mansion with an air of openness and foreignness that at once mystified and excited her. Hiroko could still hardly believe that she had been allowed to accompany her father to this place where he'd been invited, and was at a loss as to why, although not for an instant would she have questioned him about it. She was there, and that was all that mattered.

Raising her eyes a little, she surveyed the long courtyard with its gracefully raked white pebble garden leading to a fountain playing against a natural rock wall. As they moved into the immense foyer, the sounds of music, voices and laughter spilled from a chandelier-lit room that loomed through a curved archway to their left.

A tall distinguished man—an American diplomat with the delegation her father had told her about—came forward to warmly greet Hiroko and her father. She felt a little taken aback by his easy manner, but pleased that her English was almost a match for his. Her London-born tutor, Miss Giles, who came to their house every day to instruct her in English and French, found her a gifted pupil with a natural ear for language. Words came easily to Hiroko, and she worked hard to please her father. She loved to excel in whatever she did, and she thought tonight may be a reward for an almost perfect translation of Milton's 'Paradise Lost'.

Behind their host, a girl of fifteen, her own age, stood smiling at her. She had the longest fiery red hair, unlike any Hiroko had ever seen before. To Hiroko's surprise, she barely waited for her father's more formal introductions before moving forward and taking Hiroko by the hand.

'Forget the Priscilla, I'm Cilla,' she announced with a smile. 'Would you like to come with me?' With a backward glance to her father, who nodded, Hiroko followed Cilla across the foyer and up a wide oak staircase to the top floor, then down a long hallway with rooms appearing at either side.

'This is the most important place in the house,' said Cilla with a flourish, pushing open a door. 'My room!' She laughed, drawing Hiroko inside.

Hiroko gazed around in surprise at a room filled with dolls, tennis rackets, skates, clothes, books, objects of every description packed into deep white shelves that ran around the walls. Everything was so large. There was an enormous bed with its frilled flowery satin cover, matching canopy, lots of white lace-edged cushions, velvet easy chairs, a desk and dressing table with a tall curved mirror and matching wardrobe, in white and palest pink.

Cilla led Hiroko to a chair near a fire crackling behind a brass-netted screen. It was all so different and exciting. Wherever you looked, there was something new to see.

'How do you like my butterfly collection?' Cilla asked, pointing to the vaulted ceiling, from which hung multi-coloured paper butterfly kites of every shape and size, some with long floating tails. 'Da-da daaaa! The show begins,' she cried, blowing out the lamps, then flicking a switch so that one soft spotlight shone on the kites, and an overhead fan's heavy wooden blades slowly rotated to bring all the butterflies to life.

Hiroko stared, transfixed. It was wonderful.

'But wait,' said Cilla, 'that's not all!' and lifting the lid of a bright red box, she wound a handle on its side, then moved a silver arm with a needle at its tip across a rotating black disc, carefully placing the needle onto the disc. There was a loud scratching noise, and then the notes of Strauss's Skaters' Waltz rose in accompaniment to the floating butterflies above, which swayed and fluttered on their strings in a fantastic dreamlike dance.

Hiroko sat entranced. The music, the movement above . . . it was like a heavenly puppet show. The two girls watched for some minutes, and then Cilla lit the lamps once more.

'Show's over. No, stay,' she said, as Hiroko rose to leave. 'We'll make our own fun here. That party below's too boring for words—no boys at all.'

'You like boys?' Hiroko asked shyly.

'Of course, I have dozens of boyfriends back home in Washington.'

'Really?' Hiroko was intrigued.

'Mother said we'll be returning there in two years anyway, so then I'll take my pick of them.'

'Your parents won't choose a husband for you?'

'Are you crazy?' Cilla laughed. 'Maybe that's how you do things here, but not us.'

Seeing Hiroko's hurt expression, she added quickly, 'Of course, everyone has their own way of doing things.'

She paused. 'Will you show me how to wear a kimono and tie the *obi* properly?'

'Yes, please,' Hiroko nodded, smiling at her. 'I would like to give you one for yourself—your own kimono.'

'You will? Then I'll give you something.' Cilla rummaged through the drawer of her dressing table and produced three small postcards.

'These are my holy cards,' she remarked, spreading them over the table. 'Sister Scholastica gave them to me before I left the convent back home and came here. They're very special. You can choose one if you like.'

Hiroko leaned over. They were hand-tinted illustrations, and different to any she'd ever seen. One depicted a mother with a plump naked baby sitting on her lap. He had a shining circle of light around his head. The mother's face was very composed and somehow sad, as she looked down at her baby. A blue veil partly covered her head, and fell about her shoulders. 'Our Lady of Mercy,' said Cilla.

The card was beautiful. Hiroko touched the woman's face gently with her fingers. She thought of her own mother who, after a long fight with cancer, had died one year ago, and a lump rose in her throat. She felt close to tears, but forced them back. Her eyes went to the next card. A man, naked to the waist, stood bowed down by a heavy wooden cross he was carrying on his back. His face looked so haggard and drawn, and around his head a circlet of thorns dug cruelly into his skin, blood trickling from his wounds. She sighed, and glanced at the next picture.

A small child was bending over a stream, reaching out to pick a bullrush growing towards the middle of the water. Behind her, a tall figure dressed in white with outstretched wings, hovered protectively behind the child. He was handsome, with blue eyes and golden hair, and an expression on his shining face that made her draw in her breath.

'The guardian angel, Gabriel,' said Cilla, watching her.

'Would you like that one?' Hiroko nodded, too overcome to speak.

'Then it's yours,' Cilla smiled, handing the card to her. 'I've organised our own supper,' she said, ringing a bell. A maid brought in a tray of hot buttered toast fingers, some tiny cream-filled cakes with icing-dusted butterfly wings, slices of dark chocolate cake, a bowl of striped bon-bons and a large silver pot of coffee, with a jug of cream.

Hiroko ate a little of each. She didn't like the chocolate, but her first sip of coffee through the delicious layer of sweetened cream that Cilla had spooned across the top was the foretaste of many new things to come.

Hiroko remembered now how, as they had chatted away, Cilla's open friendliness had soon worn down her own shyness and reserve. So much so, she had even brought herself to talk a little of her sense of desolation following the death of her mother. She felt tears well up as she recalled how Cilla had reached out and hugged her in a sudden show of affection and concern.

Later that night, as she and her father had driven home, she had kept peering at the card Cilla had given her in the flash of passing street lights, with a warm feeling that a lucky talisman had come into her life. And with it came the awakening of a fascination for a world quite outside her own.

* * *

Boy—1921

Hiroko felt a movement beside her, and looking up, there he was smiling down at her. It was the man who had helped her in the shrine, the guardian angel of her holy card.

'I hope you will forgive me,' he said, 'my Japanese is not the best. Are you all right now?' She didn't answer, but stared at him as if in a dream. 'My name is Boy

Baillieu,' he continued, holding out his hand to reassure her.

She stood now, and looking away from him bowed low to hide her confusion. 'Oh, yes, forgive me, please,' she murmured, bowing again. 'My name is Hiroko Sen.'

As he shook her hand, the holy card fluttered to the ground. He bent to retrieve it, and feeling embarrassed, she hastily took it from him and pushed it out of sight back into her *furoshiki*. 'Perhaps I might walk you home?' he suggested, smiling at her once more.

'Thank you, but I am fine now, and my father's servant is waiting. Please don't worry.' But he insisted, and together, with Ume following, they walked down the hill to her father's house. Sensing somehow that he could be trusted, Hiroko told him that her father was not well, and that she had come from her in-laws' home to be with him for a few days.

'And your husband doesn't mind your going?'

Hiroko looked down, saying nothing for a minute, then in a low voice, 'My husband is not with us any more.'

'I'm sorry,' he said.

'That is why I was at the shrine today, to pay my respects,' she said gravely.

'I see.' He looked long at her, taking in the sadness in her face, and deciding it was not a good time to pursue its cause. After some deliberation, he went on, 'Maybe you can help me.'

'Help you?'

'Yes, I only have a short while left in Tokyo. Can you suggest what is best for me to see?'

She looked away quickly. He was so beautiful—she could hardly believe they were walking and talking together. It was all so unexpected, and yet he didn't seem a stranger. At the same time, she felt uneasy, a shadow of premonition clouding her thoughts as she imagined the dark, disapproving face of her sister-in-law Michiko.

As if to dispel such thoughts, she suddenly laughed. He glanced at her in surprise. Feeling that she had been impolite, and to cover her lapse, she said formally, 'There is so much to see and you're here for such a short time, Boy-san. I will talk with my father first, and we will speak then.'

They continued mostly in silence for the rest of the walk, with Hiroko stealing occasional sidelong glimpses at the handsome young man at her side. It *was* the angel of her holy card. Maybe Noboru had sent him to her. Could that be possible?

As they moved through the narrow streets leading towards her home, passing small shops with their *noren* hanging fluttering in the breeze proclaiming their different wares in bold *hiragana* characters, the wailing of a flute floated towards them. On a street corner, dressed in sombre black, his head covered by a densely woven basket, stood a mendicant monk playing his long bamboo *shakuhachi*, the notes rising in plaintive reedy sound.

They stopped, and as Hiroko listened to the melody, it spoke to her as if in confirmation. Yes, this golden-haired stranger had been sent by the *kami*, and all would be well now. She smiled at him shyly.

'I must hurry,' was all she said. When they eventually arrived at her house, she bowed, thanking him, and he told her where he was staying.

'I will speak to my father and we will send a message to your hotel in the morning.'

'Till then,' he said smiling.

Later that night, he was awakened by a familiar rumble and shaking that moved with a relentless shudder through the building. He lay in bed motionless, hoping it would cease. After a while, everything stilled once more. Wet with perspiration in the oppressive heat, he arose, reaching for his *yukata*. Tokyo in July was the last place one ever wanted to be. He went over to a table where his sketches of the different shrines and buildings which had taken his fancy on this trip now lay scattered from the quake's tremor. Even though freely drawn, they had captured a certain essence of this unique architecture. The tilted roofs and the simplicity of line revealed the minimalist restraint and beauty he'd always admired. His detailing on each sketch was not bad, he thought. It would help when he designed and built the house of his dreams on the lush piece of land he'd already chosen on Maui at Maalaea, overlooking the Bay to Mount Haleakala rising majestically in the distance.

He'd like to have drawn more, he thought, but he'd be gone soon to France, then back to Honolulu and to Grace. Pouring himself a tonic water, he drank slowly, thinking of the fair Grace gazing at him with clear eyes.

'We will marry in the spring,' she had told him with her usual directness, as if no-one could question it otherwise.

'You'll have that all organised?' he'd answered with a faint smile.

Ignoring any hint of irony, she'd replied, 'Why not, darling?' looking up at him appealingly, using her eyes in that way she had.

As he thought of her expression, her face was replaced with that of another, the lotus beauty of the woman at the Yasukuni Shrine. He thought of Hiroko, then returned to Grace, but each time he pictured Grace, the fragile Eastern face and figure swam into his mind, superimposed on the other's image, blotting it out. He lay back, thinking of them both, but only the dark-eyed girl positioned herself firmly in the mirror of his mind. Even as he drifted into sleep, she remained there, a haunting persona anchored in, floating with and around him.

2

ALONG THE TOKAIDO

We met at a time of death and through death, Hiroko thought, and this is why it haunts us now. Remembering the face of the golden angel of her dreams, she wept.

The next day, she sent a message with Ume as arranged, and wrote, 'Tomorrow, Boy-san, we will go to Hakone and stay at our summer house on Lake Ashimoko as it will be cooler there for my father. He has said you are most welcome to come with us. Please let Ume know if this suits you.'

Her father, after some deliberation, had agreed to this, but had cautioned her first.

'He has been sent by the *kami*,' she'd said.

'Perhaps,' Yukio answered, seeing her now shining face, the shadow of the past year somehow lifted. 'But be very prudent, Hiroko-chan. It is best that you don't mention any of this to the Nakamuras.'

Early the following morning, the cobbles of the street still wet with mist, Boy had arrived in a chauffeur-driven Packard, slowly and conspicuously nosing its way through the narrow street. He grinned at her surprise.

'We'll ride by chariot and go along the great Tokaido road. I've got it all worked out, so you can tell me about everything as we go.' She smiled, responding to his enthusiasm.

'That will please my father. He was a professor in world history at the Kanda university, and is now a director of many of our historical records.' She led him inside to meet Yukio.

Following their first somewhat stilted introduction, the older man had warmed to Boy's eager talk about the Tokaido. Little Satoshi stared, fascinated by the man's golden hair, pale skin and blue eyes. Hiroko gently pushed his bristly black head forward in a small bow when she introduced him to Boy-san. After a light breakfast of miso soup and vegetables sprinkled with seaweed, they set forth—her father and Boy with the chauffeur in front, and in the back, Ume and Hiroko with Satoshi sitting wide-eyed on her lap.

The heat of the night before had subsided. As they drove, a fresh early morning breeze cooled their cheeks, and overhead the sky stretched, clear blue with clouds massed in uneasy puffs in the distance. Hiroko felt the light-hearted anticipation that only the start of a new journey can bring. For Boy, the restless mood of the previous weeks had lifted, swept away by the winds of change he now felt entering his life. For the first time since arriving in Japan some weeks earlier, he felt a sense of belonging.

This woman entranced him, her beauty so contained, every movement perfect, and yet without guile. Rather, she possessed a freshness and sweet candour that was disarming. And as the day wore on, her awareness and interest in all around her, along with her depth of knowledge, constantly surprised him. She was truly her father's daughter.

The landscape slipped by as they drove along the Tokaido from one famous staging post or station to the next. It was like a ride back into history, as Yukio Sen and his daughter recounted tales of the highway's feudal past.

As they drove through Nihonbashi, Yukio told Boy of the enormous wooden gates that once stood at the entrance to Edo, as Tokyo was then called, and of the high curved bridge which spanned 226 feet, taking the canal out of the city. There, the gates would open at four in the morning, when travellers first set foot on what often proved to be a perilous and sometimes fatal journey—usually with little knowledge of what lay ahead in the territories through which they would pass.

'It was a trip into the unknown,' Yukio said. 'Many would die along the way, from sheer exhaustion, or at the hands of bandits.'

They passed through the densely housed streets of Shinagawa.

'This was once a seaport,' Yukio said, 'but the land was later reclaimed for housing. It was the first station of the Tokaido, famous for its cherry blossoms and the *yu-jo* who entertained travellers about to begin their long journey.'

Just as we are, Boy thought, and looking back over his shoulder at Hiroko, smiled.

Added Hiroko, demurely, 'And the mendicant priests, like the one we saw, prayed and pounded on gongs to ward off evil spirits as the travellers set out. And from the top of the bridge, Mount Fuji-san could be seen away in the distance, beckoning them along the 326-mile-long Tokaido to the Sanjo Bridge in the ancient city of Kyoto. We usually go right after the Star festival on July seventeen, but because my father is not well, we were delayed this year. There's been no rain, so that's not good.' She paused. 'You see Boy-san, rain is the tears of the princess, and is a good omen if it falls at this time.'

'The princess?' Boy asked.

Hiroko told him of the Star festival, and of the two lovers who lived on opposite sides of the Milky Way, or Celestial River.

'She was the daughter of the King of Heaven, and when she met and fell in love with a local cowherd, they spent so much time together, she neglected her weaving and he let his oxen stray. Her father was angry, and separated them to live on opposite sides of the River of Heaven, allowing them to meet only once a year.' She hesitated.

'And what then?' Boy prompted.

Hiroko looked at him, and then away.

'When they came to the bank of the river, there was no bridge, and in despair, the princess wept so bitterly that the magpies took pity on her, and flew together so that their wings formed a bridge, over which she lightly ran, and into the arms of her lover.' Her eyes met Boy's reflected in the mirror, and she glanced away quickly to Satoshi.

The child was unusually silent, but every now and then she caught him staring at Boy's golden hair and face whenever he turned to look at her, and when he did she felt the child shrink in closer to her, clutching at her kimono. He seemed almost fearful of this stranger.

As they talked, it soon became evident that Boy's Japanese was a lot more fluent than he'd initially admitted. 'We have many Japanese families living and working on our plantations,' he said. 'As a boy, I made friends with Kenji Seki, the son of a Japanese teacher and his family, and somehow over the years, a little of the language rubbed off.' He gave a self-deprecating smile, and then with Yukio's urging, explained that he was an architect, and had come to Japan to study some of the shrines, before travelling onto France and then returning to Hawaii. He told them a little of his island home in the South Pacific, and she listened, absorbed, as he spoke of his parents' sugar plantation in Maui, describing the seasons, the skies and seas, the ever-changing patterns of a luxuriant countryside, undulating from mountain to sea, light to shadow, the beaches' sultry warmth to the deep green cool of the forests and streams. And everywhere, he said, were the sounds of singing birds and the perfumed brilliance of the flowers.

He spoke of the storms rolling across the islands from the windward shores, racing over the south coast canefields and disappearing as fast as they came, leaving the scent of damp earth and salt from the blue-green waters of the restless Akua Lapu channel. And how the blue sky sliced across horizons of vivid green and yellow terraced taro fields. And Mauna Paele, the mystic mountain rising 'like Olympus' to survey the four islands set like emeralds in an aquamarine sea.

'Mauna Paele,' Hiroko repeated softly. 'It's *sodai* . . . great,' she added. And they talked also of *shibui*, the beauty that is seen, yet unseen, a powerful presence that transcends the ordinary. It was indeed *shibui*, Boy agreed.

They drove along in silence for a while, and then quietly at first, but with growing intensity, Boy began to sing.

> *Lei of Mauna Loa, beautiful to look upon,*
> *The mountains honoured by the winds,*
> *Known by the peaceful motion,*
> *Calm becomes the whirlwind.*
> *Beautiful is the sun upon the plain,*
> *Dark-leaved the trees in the midst of the hot sun,*
> *Heat rising from the face of the moist lava.*
> *The sunrise mist lying on the grass,*
> *Free from the care of the strong wind,*
> *The bird returns to rest at Palaau,*
> *He who owns the right to sleep is at Palaau,*
> *I am alive for your love—*
> *For you indeed.*[2]

Both Yukio and Hiroko were too touched by the strange beauty of the song to speak for a moment. Then Hiroko leaned forward, and smilingly bowed her head, saying simply: 'Thank you, Boy-san.'

Her father went on to tell more of the Tokaido, of the hardships experienced by the early travellers as they traversed the eastern seaboard, moving from the gentle patchwork farming plains past lakes and seashore, through undulating hills to the treacherous mountain passes with their slippery mist-bound tracks perched high over deep crevasses. And always with them was the fear of confronting bands of cut-throats, thieves and brigands who often lurked in the forest and mountain passes.

'But always they must remember,' Yukio said, 'to keep

to the left of the road to make way for the passing retinue of the Daimyo and his retainers.'

'Our *samurai* ancestors accompanied the great feudal lords or Daimyo,' Hiroko continued. 'They carried their long heavy bows, spears, scimitar and standards in magnificent trains of horses and palanquins, along with many pages with parasols and bearers with their red lacquered boxes of luggage.'

Boy laughed. 'It must have been quite a sight.'

She smiled shyly at him and told him how the Daimyo's entourage made way only for other more important and powerful lords and the *hikyaku* messengers who ran, briefly clad, holding aloft the lacquered boxes containing official edicts, letters and money. 'They would often push ordinary travellers aside in their haste to cover the distance, over three hundred miles, in three days, flashing their wooden licence tablets to give them fast and free passage through the numerous check-points along the way. At night they carried paper lanterns with *go-yo* written on them, to light their way.'

'Ordinary travellers would take over two weeks to travel the same distance,' said her father.

'And always,' Hiroko gently broke in, 'as if acting as their guide along the way were glimpses of Fuji-san, the sacred mountain, rising as a perpetual beacon to the weary traveller.'

As the car rounded a corner at Kawasaki, the second station along the road, they had a sudden sighting of Fuji, its white-tipped cone floating in a sea of clear blue sky, contrasting with the passing flash of pink and white cherry and plum blossom trees.

'This is where the Meshimori girls served rice with hot tea and cherry blossom pickled in salt,' Hiroko said, and she told them about the Meshimori and Yu-jo girls and the lure of the inns and tea houses that sprang up along the way around the fifty-three stations to provide food, accommodation and comfort to the travellers. These varied in status and amenities offered, from the simple lodging house to the luxurious *waki-honjin hatago* for high officials and feudal lords, with their hot baths, masseurs, warmed sake and pleasure girls waiting like brilliant fluttering butterflies to beguile, serve and entice the weary traveller who could afford their services.

'Many of these girls,' she said, 'were great beauties to rival even those of the floating world of Yoshiwara.'

'I have seen them in the Ukioe paintings,' Boy commented, thinking how Hiroko's face, the creamy colour and texture of her skin, reminded him of the languorous beauties in his first brief glimpse into Yoshiwara's floating world of pleasure which catered to every sensual desire. He recalled the explicit love-making in the Ukioe and Shuncho *shunga*, their elegant and often formal settings a stylised contrast to the abandonment of the couples involved. The pretty *ichiya-zuma* were there to be 'married' and to give satisfaction to their clients in one night of torrid love. Their carefully made-up faces, he remembered, seemed composed and contained, their vividly printed and embroidered kimonos were meticulously draped, yet parted to reveal their genitals, enlarged to highlight all sensual focus on these instruments of pleasure.

Memories of such salacious invitations intensified his sense of longing for this woman he'd only just met, yet with whom he already felt somehow bonded. He felt a growing urge to take her in his arms and recreate those sensual images. To still and control his feelings, he focused on the fields moving past them.

Her father's voice raised in question made him turn. 'I'm sorry—you were saying?'

'Have you seen the Hiroshige woodblock prints of his journey along the Tokaido?' Yukio Sen asked.

'Only one that I remember,' answered Boy. 'It was of Fujiyama rising from fields of rice paddies, with some travellers in the foreground.'

'That would probably be the one he did at Hara.'

'I could take you there tomorrow,' said Hiroko, her face alight with pleasure at the prospect. 'It's not too far from where we'll be staying.'

To Hara

Obon, the Festival of Souls. Who would have thought that a lighting of the way for the dead to and from their spirit world, would be the same guiding light that would lead her away from her old home to the beginning of a life on the other side of the world? And this, Boy felt, is how it was to be.

The past day had transported him to another time and place of which Hiroko was very much a part. Finally he was at rest in his room upstairs in the Sen's summer house set high in the pine forest with its silvery glimpses of the lake below. His mind was racing with all that had happened that day, and as to how he could persuade Hiroko to be part of his life. For he knew he must. Her delicate beauty veiled a strength and certain mystique which drew him to her. But what were her feelings for him? He'd sensed an attraction, and wondered if she would ever consent to leave Japan and go with him. And what of the boy? He was a quiet strange little kid, but she loved him and so naturally he would be part of any decision. He lay back planning how he could talk with her and her father, and somehow win her over to the idea. He was being impulsive, he thought, but hadn't that always been part of his nature? No, this was more than just impulse.

He felt at once excited and apprehensive, a part of him still disbelieving that things could happen so swiftly. His thoughts went to Hattie and that hot summer morning six years ago on their plantation in Maui. He knew now that his mother's premonition was coming true. They had been sitting at breakfast, and he'd looked to see her staring at him with an expression of sadness. He felt a chill as he remembered her words and her face.

'What is it, Hattie?' She had always been Hattie, somehow never Mother.

'Oh, nothing, honey—just a feeling that you'll soon be on your way.'

'What do you mean?' he'd laughed. 'My life's here. I love it here,' he said as if to reassure himself.

'That's true,' she answered, 'but often forces stronger than ourselves have some say in the matter.'

That was so typical of his mother, he thought now. He'd been aware of her sense of the 'other world' since a tiny child. The Irish would call her 'fey' and in touch with the little people. She was almost a pixie herself with those clear blue eyes and long hair turned prematurely white, coiled like a silver halo high upon her head. Far from the elite Philadelphian background and the brownstone mansion where she had grown up, Hattie was now happily at home with her husband Gare, running their sprawling sugar and pineapple plantations in Maui.

'I suppose you could call college being away,' he'd said, still anxious for reassurance.

Hattie had smiled at him and replied simply: 'Not college, Boy, but another world, another time will become part of your life. You will see it, take it and make it yours.' She had paused, and he recalled the shadow that passed across her face. 'Great happiness and a sense of truly belonging, often these things come with a price.' She reached out and took his hand, not saying anything for a moment, as if looking beyond him to something that only she could see. 'It will affect us all. On the one hand, a gift, and on the other, something lost. Just what, I'm not sure. Maybe that's for the better,' she said laughing suddenly. 'It's not always good to know what fate has in store for us.'

She patted his hand. 'My golden boy . . .' She hesitated, then closing her eyes, murmured, 'I see a red sun, so red, suspended in a washed-out sky. And a mountain, like our beautiful Haleakala.' She shuddered a little, then opening her eyes, said firmly: 'You must take the warrior way, like the Hawaiian boy Maui. You remember his harnessing of the sun?'

He'd nodded; his young life had been filled with the legends and folklore of their island home. He remembered the story of how, in a time when the sun made only a brief and hasty passage across the sky of the island. It was insufficient to provide the warmth and light needed by Maui's mother to dry her hand-woven sheets of kapa cloth, and Maui had decided to do something about it. He had gone to the north-west of the island and climbed the highest ridge of Mount Iao, and observing the course taken by the sun as it passed over the islands, saw that it rose far to the eastern side of Mount Haleakala.

Crossing the plain that lay between the two mountains, Maui had climbed to the top of Haleakala, an enormous extinct volcano, and watched as the sun rose from Koolau chasm at the side of the crater, and thought, *There I will catch the sun.*

On his way back, he met a man, Moemoe, who ridiculed him in his quest, and Maui vowed to return and vanquish him, just as he would the sun. When he told his mother of his plan, she presented him with fifteen strands of plaited fibre rope, and suggested that he obtain the rest of the things he needed for his conquest of the sun from his grandmother who lived in the crater. 'That is where the sun pauses to eat the bananas she cooks for him,' she said. 'Go to the place where the large Wiliwili tree stands, and when the rooster crows three times, watch as your grandmother prepares the fire and the food. As she does, take away her bananas. She will then look for them, and ask who you are. Tell her you are the son of Hina.'

Boy remembered how Maui had done these things, and how the old lady, upon hearing who he was, had given him a magic stone to make a battle axe, and one more rope. She had shown him how to catch the sun as it came shining over the crater's edge.

One by one, Maui had caught the sun's legs with his fifteen ropes as they came spilling over the crater's ridge, until only one leg was left hanging down the mountainside. At last, it too came trembling over the ridge, and was caught and held by the last rope given to him by his grandmother. He had then pulled and pulled until the large round body of the sun rose above the mountain. Then taking his magic axe, he had begun to strike the sun until, fearing for its life, it begged him for mercy. Maui had talked with the sun and told him of his mother's plight, and the sun promised the youth that he would give longer hours of sunshine and that he would traverse the sky in a regular journey of longer days for summer, and shorter days for winter, and so spread the precious gift of sunlight to be shared by all.

On his triumphant return home, Maui met Moemoe and they fought fiercely right across the island. At last on the seashore of Laihana, Maui slew his foe and the body became the long black rock, still there, and the scene for many of Boy's childhood picnics.

'You will be like the warrior Maui, and harness the sun,' Hattie had said that day, 'but always remember we hold something precious only for so long as we're given.' The shadow flitted across her face once more.

Boy sat up on his *futon*, now wide awake, remembering that morning with his mother in Hawaii long ago. It was all starting to happen just as she'd said. The mountain, the red Japanese sun, and Hiroko. She would be his, he knew. He thought of Hattie's cautioning words. Well, this wouldn't be an elusive thing, this happiness they would share. He would take her and the boy Satoshi back to Hawaii, and to a new life.

The sighing of the wind outside brought with it the smell of pine-scented mist from the forest around them. Somewhere below, the sweet sound of a *koto* rose with the wind and soon lulled him into a deep and dreamless sleep.

The next morning he came down into the main room. Hiroko was there alone, placing upon the lacquered wood shelves of the Buddhist altar ceramic containers of fruit and small rice balls, along with eggplant and melon cut in the shape of horses to carry the gifts to the spirits in the other world. Incense smoke coiled lazily to the ceiling. Clasping her hands, she bowed her head as if in prayer.

He watched her for some minutes, then as she became aware that someone was there, she turned and jumped up, smiling brightly. Hastening across the room, she greeted him with a small bow.

'Good morning, Boy-san, everything is ready now.'

'Ready for what?' he asked.

'Our trip to Hara. You still want to go?' she asked, looking up at him, now doubtful. With a teasing expression as if to prolong her uncertainty, he paused, then laughed.

'Of course,' he said, 'I'm happy to do whatever you suggest.' She smiled and ducked her head, her pleasure barely veiled.

'My father has taken Satoshi to the lake so we'll go when you are ready.'

Later, as they drove away from the house through the towering pine and cryptomeria cedar trees, he felt a sense of exhilaration that at last they were truly alone together, and that this day was to be theirs. She kept sneaking glances at him as he drove purposefully onto the Tokaido. This morning, there seemed to be a golden aura surrounding him, his hair so fair in the sunlight, those eyes like the deep blue of the lake, while his smile made her think of the brilliance of the snow on the peak of Fuji. He is truly magnificent, she thought. She added aloud, 'We will stop soon, Boy-san, and I will show you one of our very old tea houses.'

They parked nearby and walked up a road of rounded stones through an avenue of maple trees forming a leafy canopy of green and gold overhead. The smell of wood smoke drifted down to greet them.

'This was part of the original Tokaido road, and my ancestors trod these same stones over two hundred years ago,' she told him. 'I feel almost as if I'm in touch with them here, especially during the Obon.'

She chatted on, talking about the different members of her family who had traversed the route over the years, including one honoured great-grandfather, a *samurai* who had committed *seppuku* (*hara-kiri*) not far from where they now stood. 'It was a matter of *bushido*—family honour. He was a great man.'

'And your mother?' Boy asked.

Hiroko hesitated, then in a low voice, 'She was taken from us many years ago, Boy-san, but really she is always with me.' She smiled at him, but he noticed the long-felt sadness in her eyes.

'She would be very happy with you,' was all he said, and she flushed at this indication of his approval.

They arrived at the Tea House of the Maple Leaves and sat enjoying the hot *amazake* wine and small steamed rice cakes, wrapped in rice paper and tied with noodles. 'Not far from here,' Hiroko said between sips, 'is where the first check-point to the Tokaido road lay. Travellers gathered here, often fearful of the guards who were very fierce and strict as to who they allowed through. The Daimyo and his entourage and even his horses had to have their own permits to go through this notorious place.' She pointed out the spot where travellers had knelt with their hands on the stone ledge while officials searched them for their papers. Anyone trying to escape or get through unchecked were caught with frightening spiked instruments and pinned by the throat to the wall. Others were often caught by barbed hooks clutching and tearing at their ankles and legs as they ran.

Far below the check-point, mirrored in the clear blue of Lake Ashimoko, was Fuji, gazing Narcissus-like at her perfect reflection of icy white against the blue. 'She is Mirror Fuji here,' said Hiroko. Clusters of small Buddhist temples and Shinto shrines were dotted like groups of children around the lake. 'That's the home of Jizo, the gentle god of mercy. He was beloved by travellers, and appealed to in their prayers along this treacherous route. Jizo waited to take those who died along the way in his arms into the lake, and into the next world.'

She placed some small rice cakes at the feet of a statue nearby and strung a necklace of white paper cranes around the neck of another, reminiscent of the Hawaiian *leis* of white frangipani and star orchids, Boy thought.

'Many small children and babies died on this road,' she said. 'It was very hard for them.' She looked so fragile and beautiful as she stood silently contemplating the shrines, and he wondered what she was thinking. Without forethought, he heard himself saying, 'You will like being in Hawaii. You'll be happy there.'

She looked up at him, not in surprise, but as if she already understood. 'And Satoshi?'

'Satoshi too,' he answered. She looked away, and didn't say any more, and he felt a ripple of unrest enter their perfect lake.

* * *

As they drove into Hara, they rounded a corner and he drew in his breath, slowing the car and pulling off the road, for there, rising majestically out of a jade sea of rice was Fuji, at once so close and attainable. It was as if he had stepped into the Hiroshige depiction. Only this was no mirage, no fantasy of the mind, but a reality he could reach out and feel. He could smell the earth, the paddy fields, the wind riffling across the stalks of rice towards them.

Farmers in their loose blue and white cotton work clothes, with white draped scarves beneath their peaked straw hats, bent towards the earth in the timeless tending of their fields. A sudden rush of wild duck taking flight from a nearby marsh startled them, and the two laughed in delight as they watched the birds fly low over the fields, then ascend, high against the sky, flying towards Fuji.

For Boy, it was an instant that reflected a sense of homecoming to his own Hawaiian Haleakala. His spirit winged with them in imagined flight, wanting to explore and surmount this sacred place and bring him closer to this woman who was part of it. With a new-found sense of elation, he turned, and lifting Hiroko off her feet, swirled her around and around, calling out 'Come, we will fly with them, my darling.'

She laughed, and as he gently put her down, he stared deep into her eyes and said, 'Hiroko-san, I want to . . .' He hesitated, fearful that even now, despite his certainty, she might still reject him. 'Will you . . . will you be my wife?' His voice was low and firm. She looked down, but he sensed her happiness. She felt his eyes on every part of her like the soft brush of wings, and the loving energy and spirit that flowed from him bathed her in a warming light, stilling any uncertainties. She drew in her breath; the *kami* were surely blessing her. She pushed away the small quiver of unease that arose momentarily within. She felt she was being lifted into the arms of something strong and powerful that would take her away from the petty triumphs of her sister-in-law Michiko and her world, to a wider landscape of her own making.

She looked up at him. 'I must speak to my father first.'

'But you will?' he persisted.

Hiroko nodded slowly then looked up at him, 'Yes, Boy-san, I will.'

Boy let out a shout of delight, then with a series of loud whoops, he ran off along one of the tracks snaking through the fields and up towards the mountain, swinging his jacket like a lariat as he went. Hiroko watched as he passed the startled farmers who stood up from their work to stare at this golden-haired young man in his bright blue shirt, his coat held high and flying behind him like the tail of a kite, and who barely stopped for a brief salutation as he passed. His figure receded towards the mountain, and she felt suddenly alone as she watched him move further away, as if to scale in one almighty leap the steep slopes of Fuji.

Some forty minutes later, when Boy returned, she was sitting on a cotton quilt on a small rise under a spreading maple tree. Still panting from his run, he threw himself down beside her, gazing up at her face framed by the tracery of leaves.

'One day, we will go to the top, to the very heavens,' he smiled at her.

Producing a damp cloth smelling faintly of pine, she cooled his face, then handed him another for his hands.

'We will eat now.'

Hiroko unpacked the *bento* box, first untying the red silk tassels, then removing its shiny wooden compartments. She laughed at his expression as he saw the bright array of *sushi* emerge, tiny rice balls, dried fish, seaweed-wrapped egg and rice, pickled plum *umeboshi,* tofu wedges and a small container of dipping *dashi* sauce. She placed paper-wrapped wooden chopsticks neatly alongside. They ate in silence, drinking in the beauty and peace around and within them. It was an unhurried time, almost as though it were to give them both a little longer to dwell in this moment of their shared joy.

Obon

Like jewelled butterflies, the vibrant patterns on their white kimono moving in an ever-changing kaleidoscope of candlelight, the women went from temple to temple, pausing only to light a candle here and there and another stick of incense. The flickering lights briefly illuminated the quiet repose of their faces as they paid homage to their ancestral spirits in the Obon All Souls ceremony.

Boy watched as Hiroko and Ume helped ignite their string of lights, feeding the pools of flame. The perfumed incense lent a mystical yet strangely comforting dimension to the scene. There was, he thought, a familial sense in this conscious merging of the living with the dead. It was an accepted meeting of past and present that softened the finality of death, imparting a timelessness and continuity to the pattern of their lives that he envied.

Later that day, they descended to Lake Ashimoko with Satoshi running ahead, and Boy helped Hiroko carry a woven straw boat. In it, she had placed tiny bundles of fruit, *sashimi* and rice together with a small lantern in its prow. She had been busy writing messages to the departed ones. She felt that this was to be a special voyage of the spirits' return to the other world, and her heart was light with happiness, as she had written a message to Noboru, thanking him for sending Boy-san to her. To her mother's spirit, she wrote that she would like to go with Boy-san to his home in Hawaii, and to please forgive her for thinking of leaving her father at this time, but he seemed much better now and she would come back often to visit, and maybe he could join her there.

As she wrote the messages, she felt a pang of anxiety. Should she write to Noboru and ask for his blessing in taking Satoshi so far away? She decided it was too difficult to explain fully, because each time she'd started to write, the thought of Michiko's scornful face blotted out any powers of expression.

From when she had first met Noboru, his sister Michiko had always been a dark presence in their lives with her barbed comments and disapproval. Although theirs had been an *omiai* marriage, arranged by their parents rather than a *renai* or love marriage, she had been lucky in that Noboru was often there to intervene on her behalf. Yet when she'd tried to explain how Michiko was creating difficulties, he'd laughed and tried to push her worries away as nothing of importance, but merely Michiko's spirited ways.

'My sister is born in the year of the fire horse which is unfortunate for a girl, and that's why she's so strong,' he explained. 'You just have to learn how to handle her.'

'That's easy for you to say, as she would never oppose you. And I do try to understand and please her.' Hiroko felt angry even having to explain this and to hold back the fact that what she was dealing with in Michiko went far beyond mere strength. Michiko seemed to have more than a normal love or sense of obligation to her brother.

At first she'd cast such thoughts aside, but gradually as she became aware of Michiko's obsession with Noboru, she saw how in a multitude of ways Michiko was trying to damage her in his eyes, and she knew then that she was dealing with a jealous and dangerous woman. One who was determined to replace her.

Then to confirm her suspicions, only weeks after her marriage, she had discovered Michiko soaping Noboru down in the family bath house. She had entered quietly, to see Michiko stripped to the waist and partly turned away from her, kneeling behind Noboru with her arms around his wet soaped body sliding her breasts against his back, her hands working down his stomach and between his legs. She'd watched transfixed at first, not believing what she was seeing, then his low moans of pleasure confirmed what she thought was happening. She'd gasped and they'd turned swiftly, Noboru hastily covering himself, but not before she'd seen Michiko slowly slip her hands from his huge erection. Smiling at her, Michiko left quickly. With a sense of betrayal, Hiroko had stifled a desire to scream and turned to run from the room. But Noboru had leapt up, grabbing her, she remembered, and cajoling softly, had forced her down onto the tatami, and tearing aside her kimono had quickly entered her. Stifling her sobs with his mouth and tongue as they worked hers to respond to him, he'd thrust into her with a passion she'd never before experienced. His desire had seemed to last forever and gradually at first, then with mounting passion, had ignited hers.

It was that night, she recalled, that she'd conceived Satoshi. It was then, too, as she glimpsed Michiko's face barely concealed behind the *shoji* screen, that she realised Michiko was watching their love-making, and probably had before and would again.

She had never caught them together again. Somehow, Noboru's sense of authority within the family had precluded any open discussion. She could never bring herself to talk about this aspect of their life without a shamed sense that in some way, she had not fulfilled her role as a dutiful wife, providing him with all that he needed. Any resentment she felt, she lay at Michiko's door.

And then he was gone forever from their lives, and now Michiko was pouring all her energies into Noboru's son, almost as if, in some sick way, Satoshi was hers and

Noboru's own child, the result of that night in the bath house.

To Boy earlier that day, Hiroko had spoken briefly of the difficulty she felt sure lay ahead with her sister-in-law and the Nakamura family.

'They will not understand my going, nor my wanting to take Satoshi. It could be very difficult.'

'But why, when you're the boy's mother? What is there to understand?' he'd asked, mystified by her hesitation and inability to be confident in her claim to her son.

'It is not easy, Boy-san,' was all she'd said. How could she explain the intricacies of a way of life that seemed so different from his own, or the sense of *giri*: obligation one felt to one's father, and to her husband's family. Now that Noboru had passed on to the spirit world, Satoshi belonged to his father's family. As Noboru's older sister, Michiko had made it quite plain that Hiroko—a widow— would play only a very minor role in the Nakamura household affairs from now on. And that included the raising of her son. Having been so obsessed with her brother, Michiko was increasingly committed to taking over what remained of him.

Without some loss of pride, it was difficult for her to explain exactly how her status within the Nakamura family had changed so dramatically from the days when her husband had been alive. She was now relegated to the position of 'cold rice relative', subservient to Michiko and other members of the family, and spent whatever time she could visiting her father's house to escape the demeaning pressures put upon her by the Nakamuras.

Often, Hiroko would meet up with her old school friend, Suzue, whose son was much the same age as Satoshi. But despite their closeness, the fact that Suzue still had her husband and the role of a young committed wife made Hiroko's widowhood all the harder to bear. Hiroko wondered what Suzue would think of Boy-san, and her plans to go away. Should she go, after all? Her sense of filial piety and duty to her father was strong.

But Yukio liked Boy-san and would want to see her happy, she knew. And Michiko? Somehow her sense of failure in getting the better of this woman made it impossible to explain Michiko's dark resentments, jealousies and betrayal to Boy-san. Her pride would not allow it. And why burden him now, and cast further doubts on this happy time together? After all, he was her lucky talisman, her guardian angel, and had come to change her life. If she left with him, all unhappiness would soon be behind her.

She felt sure in her heart that Noboru would want what was best for herself and his son, but she needed his blessing. So, before they pushed the little boat out from the shore, she simply wrote 'Please, dear husband, give us safe journey on our voyage through this new life', and carefully stowed it with the other prayers and offerings.

Watching the flotilla of frail craft sail out with the current across the vast lake, heading towards their far distant destination, each one carrying its glowing lantern to guide it on its way, Boy experienced the sadness of leave-taking. It was as if the ancestral spirits, now hastening to their home in the other world, reminded him that he too must go. Somehow, an air of uncertainty now hung between Hiroko and himself. No more had been said about his offer of marriage. Sensing her conflict, however, he felt that he must wait until she brought up the subject again. But there was so little time. He wanted them to marry before he left, so she could accompany him to France before they returned to Hawaii.

As they watched the flickering lights from the receding boats now far out on the darkened lake, he said, 'I will probably be returning to Tokyo tomorrow as I have many things to arrange.' She looked at him, and he sensed her disappointment. For a minute she said nothing, and then in a low voice, 'We will speak tonight, Boy-san.'

After they returned from the lake, Ume prepared the water for his bath, and as he washed himself down on the small wooden stool beside the steaming tub, he glanced out through slits in the screens to the darkened garden, and thought he'd seen a passing figure. But the light from the oil lamps outlined only the stone lantern and bamboo fence. When he'd first stepped into the small timber room of their bath house, he was touched to see that Hiroko had laid out a fresh cotton *yukata* and white towel and on it, in a carefully arranged spray of mulberry leaves, lay an exquisitely carved *netsuke*.

As he picked it up, he saw that it was the figure of a small child in ivory, with inlaid eyes, resting in its mother's lap. Its dark, steady gaze reminded him of Satoshi. He thought of the boy, and how, whenever he came near him, Satoshi would stop what he was doing, and stare expressionlessly at him. Boy had tried to play, to win him over, but when Satoshi saw him, it was as though all movement and life stopped. He would become still like a young animal, waiting, watching, wondering which way to move next—and then taking hasty refuge in the skirt of either his mother or Ume, or leaning in close to his grandfather.

Earlier in the day in an attempt to play, he'd tried to lift the boy and whirl him around. Satoshi's little body stiffened as if terrified, then kicked out at him while crying out to his mother. No attempt at blandishment or jollying him along seemed to work.

'He is shy, still,' Hiroko had remarked. 'He will make friends soon, Boy-san.' But she did not urge or hasten it, as the shadow of Michiko seemed to hang between them.

As Boy sank into the tub, the water so hot that he gasped, a sudden feeling that he was being watched caused him to look around the room again. No-one was there. He closed his eyes, feeling the tensions in his body ebb as he savoured the water's warmth. A sharp whirring above made him look up, and there sitting on the wall was a large cricket. As he looked at its black bulbous eyes, he laughed: so there was his uninvited guest! Later, feeling warmed and refreshed, he went in to eat. His hands cupped before him, he walked over to Satoshi and opening his fingers a little, said, 'I have a gift for you,

Satoshi-chan. Would you like to see it?' The boy, looking solemn, said nothing.

'Look,' Boy said, 'it's in there—go on, look!' He brought his hands right up close to Satoshi's face, opening his fingers a little more. A faint whirr came from inside.

'*Kirigirisu?*' the little boy asked. Boy nodded, and the small hands reached out eagerly, his face lighting up. Gently transferring the insect's fragile body to the child's cupped hands, Boy looked across at Hiroko, and their eyes met in mutual joy.

* * *

We will speak later, she'd said, but nothing had transpired. The evening meal had passed with an air of festivity. After a hot, clear *suimono* soup, Ume had served a grilled silvery Ayu fish, artfully skewered, so that it appeared to be almost swimming across the plate, and with it came tea, rice and pickles. As he dipped the hot succulent fish into the fresh ginger sauce, its sweet flavour seemed to merge with the conviviality of the evening, and Boy warmed to the feeling of being further accepted into this small family. He hoped that this would be far from their last supper together.

Satoshi had at length gone off with Ume to find a box for his cricket, and when her father retired from the table, Hiroko had followed not long afterwards, bidding Boy goodnight. He had waited a while, but then had given up, and with a bitter sense of let-down had gone up to his room.

Later, lying sleepless on his *futon*, he thought of all that had happened between them. He decided that he would leave in the morning, but not before speaking to her father. He hoped they would come to some agreement, and surely this would help hasten her actions.

A strong wind had blown up, and the solitary banging of the wooden shutters against the wall outside added to his sense of loneliness as he lay reflecting on the day's events and his growing need for Hiroko. A swishing of the *shoji* screen sliding back against the wall made him sit up, every sense alert. He stared as Hiroko entered his room. In the soft light filtering through the window, he saw that she was carrying a tray loaded with some jars and folded cloths. She lit the candle in a small white paper lantern with its red crane in flight and hung it near the bed, smiling at him. She then placed a long-stemmed ginger flower in a vase by the window, so that the heavy scent wafted in on the night air.

He sat watching her, not speaking, as she moved around the room, arranging and organising. Her hair, usually coiled at the nape of her neck, hung loose, swaying like a long silken curtain. She had changed into a light kimono, loosely tied, and he could see the line of her naked body beneath it. Kneeling beside his futon, she poured some warmed *sake* from a flat earthenware teapot into two small cups and passed one to him with a slight bow. They sat sipping the wine, then taking the cup from him, she placed it back on the tray.

He started to speak, but she put her fingers across his lips. Moving closer to him, she loosened his gown, and gently pushed him back onto the *futon.* Pouring a little oil from a phial, she started to massage his chest and neck with sure deft movements, her hands light and cool. Then, turning him, she worked on his shoulders and back with a practised *shiatsu* technique and a strength he found surprising in one so small. Every muscle in his body was being stimulated in a rhythmic flow, so that it was hard to define the different motions of chopping, slapping and pinching as they dissolved into one another.

Hiroko felt him responding to her every touch. Since she'd first peeped in on his bathing in the bath house earlier that evening, and seen his body so strong and fair, she had experienced a surge of passion, causing all other considerations to disappear. She sat lightly astride him, and he felt her smooth thighs slip around his waist, the tremors of her body signalling her desire. He turned, and taking her in his arms, yielded to the passion that had been uppermost in his mind since first they'd met.

3

ACCIDENT—TOKYO, NOVEMBER 1921

Could a time have been so perfect, she wondered, and yet still contain the seeds of a sadness that wouldn't let go? I paid for my time of happiness.

When Hiroko arrived at the hospital, he was in a coma. He was lying so still, in a sleep from which she knew he'd never wake. Just once, Boy stirred, like a passing ripple on the surface of a lake, a movement so faint that only the most watchful of eyes could discern it. She reached out and touched his cheek. His skin was pale and chilled, of someone else, not of her vital golden husband.

How could a life force cling to a body that was now so broken? He will never walk or move again, they had said. He will be lucky to last out the day. Lucky? She wondered at the meaning of such a word. Lucky! She sat now, keeping a vigil for a man who would soon be dead. No more her lover, her husband, but someone who had already entered the spirit world.

It seemed a lifetime, not hours ago, since he had gone to collect Satoshi, as they'd arranged with Michiko. And then, the message from the hospital. A car driving at high speed had hit him as he crossed the street, coming from behind, they'd said. It was all over so quickly, no-one could be sure of the details. These things happened. No, the police had not yet found the car or the driver. Each fact, as they told it, slipped neatly into a place that had no reality for her. She had asked tremulously, 'And the little boy? There was a little boy, my son. Where is he?'

'Your husband was alone. There was no little boy with him,' the police replied.

She sat without movement, her whole being numbed. Was it only ten days ago that they had returned to Japan after their brief few months together in France? I've been made to pay for leaving my child, she thought, gazing at her dying husband.

Before leaving Tokyo after their wedding, she had returned Satoshi to the Nakamura household to stay while she and Boy had honeymooned in France. Satoshi could visit her father and Ume often, and he would be happier in a familiar enviroment, she reasoned, as he still wasn't at ease with Boy. Besides, it gave her that precious time alone with Boy before they returned to a family life, and then all made their way to Hawaii. And this time there was to be no Michiko, no one to cloud the intimacy she and her new husband would share.

Their time in France had been as if a life apart, separate from anything she could remember, culminating in her joy at discovering she was carrying Boy's child. He had arranged a special radio-telegraphic link-up, so she had spoken twice to his parents, Hattie and Gare, once on their wedding day, and later from Paris when they told them about the baby. They had sounded far away and strange, she remembered, but Boy's love for her and his glowing descriptions of his bride had won them over. She was welcomed as part of their family, a long-awaited daughter. But what would happen now?

Hiroko and Boy had returned from France earlier in the week and, anxious to see Satoshi, she had rung Michiko from Boy's hotel, feeling a sense of apprehension as she waited for Michiko's cool voice.

'Satoshi is not here,' she had said, almost at once.

'Oh, I see. Well, then, I'll come and get him later.'

'That will not be possible,' Michiko answered. 'He is away with my mother, and does not return until Sunday.

We weren't expecting you so soon,' she added coldly, with no hint of welcome. Hiroko's heart sank.

'I will call on Sunday, and collect him then,' she said.

But on the Sunday when she went, there was no-one there, and the maid said the family was away, and were not returning until the end of the following week.

Feeling downcast, and increasingly uneasy, she had gone with Boy to a small hotel at Miyanoshita. Their few days there had been blissful, each totally caught up with the other and the shared passion they felt. Her husband had led her into a world of heightened sensuality, their love-making carrying her on a wave of new-found awareness of the sexual power of their bodies to discover and delight in each other. All memories of a former life with Noboru were swept aside by Boy's need and love for her.

Although only four months pregnant, her breasts and stomach were beginning to burgeon, and often at the height of their love-making as Boy suckled her nipples as he entered deep into her, she could feel the faint flutter of the baby's movements, a quickening of the life growing within her as though in response to the one who had planted it there.

Theirs was truly a *renai*. Boy's imprint was cast on her forever. There was only the absence of Satoshi to haunt her, and a growing anger that yet again Michiko was controlling the situation through her son.

'I will get him for you,' Boy had promised. 'She can't keep him—don't worry, darling.'

'But you see how it is with Michiko and the Nakamura family. With Noboru gone, they now consider Satoshi their son and heir.'

'Maybe so,' he'd said, 'but you are the boy's mother, and he will come home with us—I'll see to it.' But the dragging feeling in her heart and a strong presentiment that things were not as they should be, did nothing to convince her that he was right. Outwardly, she responded to his optimism, but had insisted on returning to Tokyo ahead of him.

'It may be better if I try to see them alone,' Hiroko

told him. She didn't say that their dislike of Boy as a *gaijin* or foreigner would only complicate matters and further impair her claim to her son. Her resentment of Michiko grew with every day that Satoshi was kept from her. Any happiness at the approaching birth of Boy's and her child was clouded by her son's absence.

She had not long arrived back from Miyanoshita when, unexpectedly, Michiko had brought the boy to her with profuse apologies; most out of character for her. Her mother had been sick, Michiko explained, and they had stayed away longer than expected.

He ran to Hiroko, and she held him fast. Michiko stood by watching, coolly appraising their reunion. Satoshi seemed subdued at first, then as she laughed, whirling him around and around, his face broke into smiles as he clung to his mother. She felt Michiko's eyes on her rounded stomach, barely concealed by the light dress Boy had bought for her in Paris. But she refrained from saying anything about the baby to her.

'What do you plan to do now?' Michiko inquired, an edge to her voice.

Hiroko hesitated, fearing a confrontation. 'It's not certain, yet.'

'Well, are you going to America or not?' Michiko asked.

'In a little while, maybe.'

'I see.' Michiko looked down at Satoshi still clinging to his mother, her expression conveying more of her disapproval than if she'd spoken. Hiroko was glad Boy was not there to see how badly she was handling the situation. 'And Satoshi?' Michiko asked.

'Well, naturally, I had hoped that he . . .' pausing, then gathering courage '. . . he will come with me.'

Michiko said nothing—just looked at her appraisingly. Hiroko felt her heart sink, knowing she was not at this moment brave enough to face the tirade that would surely ensue. To her surprise, Michiko said no more, but rose as if to go. As she left, she turned and said, 'By the way, my family was hoping to see Satoshi again for the day on Saturday. I will pick him up early in the morning.'

She bowed, and Hiroko, not daring to create a fuss in front of her child by denying her sister-in-law's request, bowed slightly in return. 'But of course,' she murmured.

How could she have been so foolish? She should have known; every instinct had forewarned her that Michiko would play some trick. She remembered the words of the great nineteenth-century warrior, Takamori Saigo, inscribed on a wooden tablet given to her by her teacher years ago when she was finding it difficult to study after the loss of her mother. They'd read: *'In times of great difficulty, one must not fail to create the opportunity.'* But that is just what I have done now, she thought in despair.

On the Saturday when Satoshi had not returned from his visit as arranged, she went to the house. It was shuttered and no-one was there. Boy had been furious.

'He is your son—our son now,' he added as she wept in his arms. 'We will get him back—don't worry darling. I've made a booking for us all to leave for Hawaii before the end of the month, and nothing will stop us. By the time Michiko and her family find out, we'll be far away and Satoshi well out of their clutches. Don't be frightened.' He had set in motion his plan to regain the child.

Then, two days, later, there was an unexpected message from Michiko asking them to come and collect Satoshi at the Nakamura home. Hiroko had felt sick with anxiety, so Boy had offered to go, and against her better judgement, she agreed. She had waited for their return, almost counting the minutes. But the time for their arrival home had come and gone, stretching first to one hour, then two, three. And then, the message from the hospital.

She sat gazing at him now, as he lay motionless. Everything had stilled and was so quiet, she imagined she could hear the ticking of his watch which they had removed, still intact, from his broken arm and she had now placed on her own. She glanced at it, mesmerised, willing the tiny hands to stop in their passage of time, and give her Boy back for that much longer.

When his spirit finally took flight, she was not even aware that he had gone, until the doctor gently informed her.

Mechanically, Hiroko organised the cremation and small Buddhist funeral service, with only her father, Ume and herself in attendance. Again and again, she called on Michiko, trying to make contact, but no-one was ever there. She felt humiliated and angered. Her grieving for Boy and the absence of Satoshi left her numb, suspended like a moth, caught and held in Michiko's web of deceit and hatred. She had stepped outside that family, and it seemed its doors were closed to her forever.

The final onslaught came two days before they'd been due to sail. A message came from Michiko, each word chiselling its way into her heart.

'I hear your husband is dead', it ran, 'so don't mistake what I say to you now'. Hiroko was mesmerised by the menace of its tone. 'Never, ever try and take Satoshi again, or you and the boy will surely die. His life, and yours, depend on it'. Hiroko felt she was listening to Michiko's measured breathing. 'If you want him to live, go away. Go far away. Come for him, and you will both die'.

Later that day, after many long and anguished discussions with her father, Hiroko made her decision. Her broken tearful call to Hattie and Gare in Maui, telling them a little of the terrible events, confirmed it. 'I will bring Boy home to you,' she said. She was their daughter now by her marriage to their golden Boy, and she owed them that. And Yukio, fearful for her and aware of what the Nakamuras could do, urged her to go.

As soon as she could, she would return to her father and fight for her son. She would never finally relinquish Satoshi to that woman. But she didn't dare jeopardise his life at this time while feelings ran so high. Her life seemed of little value now that Boy was no longer there for her. But she would go to Hawaii for a short while, to pay her respects to her husband's parents and return their son to them.

Like the ashes of the fallen warriors of old when brought back in honour to their grieving parents, she carried Boy's ashes in a small box enclosed in a white cotton *furoshiki* which she hung around her neck.

And it was with Boy's ashes tied to her that, two weeks later, she first stepped onto Hawaiian shores.

4

THE BIRTH—HONOLULU, 1922

'Two for joy,' Hattie whispered as she looked through the glass window at the two tiny forms lying peacefully sleeping. 'Thank you, heavenly Father for sending us this blessing,' she prayed, crossing herself as she gazed at the babies. Something in her heart stirred, and for the first time since that terrible call from Japan, she felt a renewed flicker of hope. These were Boy's gift to her, to all of them, she thought. And Hiroko had brought them to her.

'Two for joy,' she repeated. A boy and a girl. How perfect. They had arrived earlier than expected at two o'clock on the morning of the seventh of March. Pisces twins. She must chart their horoscope, but that could come later. Pisces was not an easy sign, but at least it came with the innate wisdom of an old soul. Maybe they would have an Aries ascendancy, she thought, and that would give them the strength to cope with whatever came along, and so not lose themselves in the altruistic meanderings that often beset the sign of the fish. Pisces' grasp on the practicalities of life was often shaky, but its Neptunian imagination and charm would more than compensate. Whatever happened, life won't be dull for our Pisces two, she assured herself.

They were so pretty, with their ivory skin and dark, downy heads. The girl, tiny fists curled beside her face, seemed more rested than the boy. He stirred, and the curve of his long lashes fluttered and opened, and she looked into dark blue-black eyes. They were not her Boy's eyes, she thought, contemplating him, the child and his grandmother locked in each other's gaze.

'Oh, Boy, why aren't you here too?' she whispered, feeling a stinging in her eyes. Tears dropped onto the mass of white orchids and roses she had brought for Hiroko.

'Would you like to go in and see the babies, Mrs Baillieu?' She turned; it was the nursing sister. 'No, no thank you, Sister,' she smiled. 'I'm just popping in to see my daughter-in-law first.'

As Hattie opened the door, Hiroko was sleeping. She looked so defenceless lying there, her hair pulled back, her face without makeup, childlike in repose. Laying the flowers on the bedside table, Hattie sat quietly, wondering what strange turn of fate had taken her son away, only to replace him with this young woman and now her two babies. His babies.

Soon after meeting Hiroko, Boy had written a long letter to them, and she thought of it now. He had told her of his first meeting with Hiroko at the Yasukuni shrine. 'I knew in that moment,' he'd written, 'that it was like linking myself with the soul-mate of my dreams. I just knew that this was it.'

She had read that first letter to Gare at breakfast, and he'd listened, elbows propped on the table, and his chin resting on his crossed hands, gazing out to the ocean while she spoke. Boy had talked of their trip to Hara, the whole letter full of his awakening to this new experience in his life. He described Hiroko's father, Yukio, and their delight in his recounting of Hawaiian life and legends.

But when speaking of home, there was no mention of Grace, and Hattie wondered if it was her place to tell her. She sighed. Boy had always been impulsive, and she, Hattie, had always been there to help pick up the pieces. But then again, she had often felt that Grace with her domineering ways was not for him. There had never been any talk of marriage or a real involvement, as far as she knew.

Boy had spoken of the child Satoshi and in his last letter, his determination to bring the boy to Hawaii.

'But it's not easy. There's a former sister-in-law and her family who won't let him go. They seem to have some prior claim', he'd written. How could that be, Hattie had wondered at the time, when he's not even their child?

'Hiroko's just so right for me, Hattie', Boy had continued. 'You'll love her, and Dad will, too'. The letter had been followed by their call to Hawaii on their wedding day. 'We couldn't wait. Seems there won't be that big white wedding after all, but I don't think you'll lose any sleep over that.' Hattie imagined Boy laughing. 'Now, don't have a fit, Hattie, but we've had a Shinto and a civil ceremony. The cathedral service can wait until we return, so don't worry—you'll still be at our wedding.' He added, 'We drank our marriage toast in sake, and I wish you could see her in her red kimono—she's beautiful! I feel so happy. So very happy and complete now.'

There was the call from France. 'How would you like to be an even grander mother?' Boy asked. And Hiroko's voice, sweet and polite, speaking to them briefly, but with the static on the line making it difficult to hear her clearly.

Then that last unbelievable call. Hiroko's voice, miles away, shaking and hushed. '*Gomen-nasai* please forgive me,' she'd whispered eventually before hanging up. '*Gomen-nasai.*'

Three weeks later, Hattie had stood with Gare on the wharf in Honolulu harbour, concentrating her attention more on the unloading of the freight than on the passengers descending the gang plank. She was waiting for the long familiar shape of a coffin swinging its way onto the wharf, bearing the body of her son.

'I think that's our girl,' Gare said quietly.

She looked around, and there, standing at the top of

the gangplank, her face impassively gazing at the noise and activity below, stood a slight figure dressed in a black silk kimono, a small white box-shaped sling around her neck. She stood motionless, waiting to step into another world. Hattie looked at the young Japanese woman, and felt a tremor pass through her. Without a word, she had gone forward, carrying the sweetly perfumed *lei* of welcome. As she placed it around Hiroko's slender shoulders and across the white sling of ashes, it became the wreath she cast upon the body of her son.

The young woman had bowed in deep obeisance, then removing the sling with its container and bowing again, had handed it to Hattie. Hattie had held it, not knowing at first, just staring at Hiroko, then as realisation dawned she'd opened her mouth as if to scream. Gare's hand tightened on her arm, his grip forcing her to take hold of herself. He then put his arms around them both, and shepherded them to the waiting car.

Driving home, hardly aware of the passing scenery, Hattie knew that in the cloth-covered box now resting on her lap was all that remained of Boy. 'They are only ashes, Heavenly Father, no body to deliver to you, only ashes to cast like dust upon the wind,' she thought, feeling cheated, deprived of a mother's hope for that one last look, a glimpse of the face that had brought her so much joy. But it was not to be. She had sat, stonelike, while Gare chatted, attempting to make Hiroko feel welcome.

As if in gentle tribute to the return of a lost son, the day had been overcast on that early December morning, a fine misty rain sweeping in from the ocean and Kaiwi channel, curtaining the brilliance of their island in a soft mantle of mourning. Soon it would be Christmas, and already small tokens of childlike expectation were decorating the shops and houses as they passed. Hiroko had brought very little luggage, and they decided that they would spend the first night in the house in Honolulu, before taking the boat to Maui the following day.

Gare had been adamant. 'Hiroko will take the place

she would have had if Boy had been with her. Her rightful place is in the heart of our family now.'

Hattie watched now as Hiroko stirred in her bed, then sat up, half-awake and confused.

'Hattie-san,' she said with a shy smile.

'The babies are beautiful,' Hattie told her. 'Thank you, thank you for bringing them home to us.' She put her arms around the young woman, and for the first time, really wept.

* * *

Later, after Hattie had left, the twins were wheeled into Hiroko's room to be fed. She nursed Gerard first as he was awake. She felt the surge of milk as he pulled hungrily at her nipple, and looking at the soft curve of his cheek as he nestled into her, she thought of Satoshi.

Now she had another little boy, but how different this birth had been, she thought, as she took in the clinical whiteness of her room, and felt for the first time since arriving, quite alone. She missed the hum of the Nakamura household where she had given birth to Satoshi, and nursed him surrounded by family and servants. At the thought of Michiko, she felt a surge of anger. Satoshi was gone, and Boy. Forcing these thoughts back, she tried to remain calm.

Hattie and Gare had been so good to her, but had been insistent when she suggested that she would like to have the baby at home.

'It's just not possible, honey, it's not safe or hygienic. Hospital's the only place to go.'

Naming the twins had been easy. Boy had told her his two favourite names when they'd first learned that a baby was on the way.

'Who knows what we'll have?' he said. 'If it's a girl, I like Gina, and if it's a boy, why not David or Jerry.'

'Jelly?' she'd asked. He laughed uproariously, and she'd felt abashed that those 'r's even now still posed an occasional problem to the fluency of her English.

'Jerry is short for Gerard,' he said. 'It has a kind of individual ring to it, don't you agree?'

'Gerard,' she repeated, pronouncing it perfectly this time. Boy smiled at her, and held her close. 'I like Gerard,' she said, cuddling him.

Now she looked at Gerard as he suckled hungrily, and she wished he wasn't so demanding. She worried that there would not be enough milk left for Gina. His little hand flexed against the fullness of her breast as if trying to burrow his way back into her, and she felt a sense of wanting to distance herself from these new demands upon her. She wasn't yet ready to give in this way, and wanted to withdraw into her own safe shell to escape.

She took him off her breast before he was fully satisfied, and he cried lustily, his tiny face reddening in frustration as she placed him back in his cot. Soon he quietened, taking comfort in sucking on his small thumb. She started to feed Gina, who seemed only to want to sleep. Tickling her gently under the chin to wake her and get her going, Hiroko thought how much more relaxing it was nursing this little one.

She had just placed Gina back in her cot, and settled back, when there was a light tap on the door. A tall, striking blonde woman in her early twenties came into the room.

'Hi!' she said. 'I'm Grace Lawrence, a close friend of Boy's. I've been meaning to pay a call.' She carried a large bunch of American Beauty roses which offset her golden sheen of glamour. Hiroko nevertheless detected a certain edge of antagonism.

'I was so sorry to hear of . . .' Grace paused '. . . to hear about everything.' Her eyes didn't quite convey the same sentiment.

There are shades of Michiko here, thought Hiroko. She sat up straight in the bed.

'Please, Grace-san, will you take a seat?' She smiled as she took the flowers. 'They are very beautiful, thank you.' A thorn on one of the long stems scratched her, and she saw a drop of blood fall onto the white counterpane.

'Twins—aren't you the lucky one,' said Grace, looking at the babies, thinking they were like little mice, and not unlike their mother. How *could* Boy have left her for this? How could he have done this to her?

Hiroko smiled disarmingly at her. Grace was beautiful, but carefully groomed and put together. She reminded Hiroko of the high-ranking courtesans in the floating world of *Yoshiwara*, with their elaborately coiffeured hair, their painted faces, their colourful kimonos, skilled in the world of artifice, entertainment and illusion. But Grace hadn't come to entertain her, so what lay beneath the golden sheen, and why had she gone to so much trouble to see her? She sensed an anger, barely veiled, and remembered her father's words.

'Never underestimate anger. Win over your enemies, defuse what could be a future explosive situation,' Yukio had advised. 'Disarm them, reassure them, cajole and smooth away their fears. Anger is usually based on fear—fear of some kind.'

Glancing at Grace, Hiroko could see that every polished inch of this woman was barely concealing her dislike and resentment. She didn't want another Michiko causing trouble. She had failed in Japan, but she would have to win this one over.

'Boy often spoke of you.'

'Of me—really?' Grace said, looking wary.

'He said you were a wonderful friend,' Hiroko continued.

'Did he?' The other woman faltered.

'Yes, in fact, I was quite jealous. He often said how special and talented you were.'

'But he married you,' Grace put in quickly.

'Yes,' Hiroko said. 'We married, and now he's gone.'

'He should never have gone to Japan—I told him so,' Grace said, not bothering now to hide her feelings.

'Who knows which path we should or shouldn't take? It's not always ours to choose,' murmured Hiroko, looking down at the flowers, the colour of spilt blood. To steer the conversation away from further recriminations, she added, 'The priest tells me that when the twins are baptised soon, I will need to choose godparents. As you were both so close, I know Boy would have liked you to be their godmother. Will you do me that honour?' She looked appealingly at the other woman.

Grace, surprised, fumbled for words. 'Oh, I . . .'

'Please,' Hiroko requested. 'I would very much like you to be my friend, Grace-san. Boy said that you,' she paused, 'that you know this place inside out.' She tried to use one of his phrases, although it had never been said in reference to Grace. His only mention of Grace had in fact been brief. 'She's a great girl, but not for me. She tried to get us married, but somehow I've always held back. It wasn't fair to her, I guess, but that's how it was.'

'Did you feel much . . .' she'd hesitated, not wanting to cloud her happiness.

'You mean, did I love her? No, I never knew until now what that feeling really meant.'

Looking at Grace now, Hiroko went on, using another of his terms. 'I need an ally, a buddy. You will be my buddy, please, Grace-san?' She looked up at Grace, waiting for an answer. Grace gazed back at her, at a loss with this turn of events. Hiroko was really rather pretty, she thought grudgingly. Small bones, a smile that was somehow appealing, and anyone who could look that good without makeup . . . She could see a little of what had attracted him. But the thought that Boy had chosen this woman instead of her still grated, and her heart ached with a hurt that wouldn't let go. She said nothing, and Hiroko, laying aside the flowers, got out of bed, went over to the cots and picked up Gina. Turning, she placed the tiny bundle in Grace's arms.

Grace was not used to holding a baby, and was momentarily taken aback. The child woke and looked up at her, and for an instant, Grace saw a flash of Boy's face. She looked across at Hiroko, her resentment slowly receding, sensing that through this child, Boy was reaching out to her. He'd always needed someone to organise him she thought, and maybe now, here was a chance to still have some link to him through his children. But she found it hard to reconcile herself to the fact that in the final count he had chosen to marry another. Well, that would take time.

Gina's little hand reached up and touched her and she felt a twinge of warmth for the child, and a sudden certainty that Boy hadn't completely gone from her life.

'Please, Grace-san, will you be her mother too?' Hiroko asked. Grace, her eyes misty, felt that she'd break down if she spoke a word. She nodded. Hiroko smiled. 'I feel I have found a buddy here now. Thank you, Grace-san,' and she bowed as she spoke.

And it was Grace who came into their lives and helped familiarise and establish Hiroko in the ways of island society. She became 'Aunty Grace' to the twins and Hiroko was her matron of honour when she married a dashing young naval lieutenant, Jimmy Cottington, the following year. Eighteen months later, Grace moved back to the mainland with her husband and baby daughter, Mardi, and they didn't return to Hawaii to live until the twins were in their early teens. But by then the bonds of friendship, augmented by visits and letters, were strong enough to withstand the many separations.

Two weeks after their first meeting at the hospital, Grace stood alongside Hiroko, Gare and Hattie in the cool nave of the coral-built cathedral of Our Lady of Peace at the top of Fort Street, and became the twins' godmother. Hiroko, looking across the pews to a plaque on the wall, saw a gold-lettered passage from the scriptures that Jesus had taught his disciples so long ago.

'Suffer the little children to come unto me, for I am the kingdom of heaven', she read, touching the simple gold cross she now wore at her throat. She thought of the day she had first come to this church some months before. The Sunday after arriving in Hawaii she had gone to Mass at Hattie's invitation. The ordered ritual and symbolism of the service had given her comfort and a sense of belonging, and helped dispel the untethered feeling she had experienced since leaving Japan.

The words of the Mass had given Hiroko new heart and hope. 'We believe in our Lord, Jesus Christ, the only Son of God eternally begotten of the Father, God from God, Light from Light, true God from true God, begotten, not made, one in Being with the Father.'

Hearing these words, she felt that if she could accept them, she would become part of the holy family. Boy would have wanted that, and it was only right that as the mother of his children, she should bring them up in his faith.

It was then she had decided to embrace Catholicism. A priest had come to the house and she had started taking instruction in the catechism. As with anything Hiroko had ever undertaken, she threw herself into absorbing and learning with a dedication and concentrated effort that surprised even Father O'Flannery. It helped to fill the void that Boy had left behind. She devoured the scriptures, feasting on their spiritual sustenance.

'I am the way, the truth, and the life,' she read. 'No one comes to the Father but by me.' And his promise 'I am the light of the world; he who follows me will not walk in darkness, but will have the light of life,' filled her with a sense of renewal and joy.

The ritual, the lighting of the candles, was only a step removed from such she had learnt in her Shinto and Buddhist teachings. Now Jesus was her *kami*, her link to Boy, and the cross a symbol of hope. Her small Buddhist altar in Japan became her Christian altar in Hawaii. On the altar, she placed a simple antique mirror that her father had given to her as a child. It symbolised the embodiment of the fidelity of the worshipper, and was a link with her homeland. It was also the bridge she felt from Amaterasu, the Sun Goddess from whose tears the eight Islands of Japan had sprung and from whom the Emperor was descended, to her new-found father, the Holy Trinity.

She remembered the lines written on rice paper that had come with the mirror.

The mirror hides nothing. It shines without a selfish mind. Everything good and bad, right and wrong, is reflected without fail. The mirror is the source of honesty because it has the virtue of responding according to the shape of objects. It points out the fairness and impartiality of the divine will.[3]

And this divine will was now transferred in her mind to the Holy Trinity. The mirror, too, made her think of the Great Mirror, a gift from the Emperor Meiji, which stood before the inner sanctuary of the Yasukuni Shrine, where she and Boy had first met.

A week before the birth of her twins, Hiroko became a 'Child of Light', by the one God, in whom dwelt Father, Son and Holy Spirit, the blessed Trinity. She took comfort from the scriptures, 'In Christ, all will come to life again.' Now she had embraced no ordinary man, but the Son of God into her life, as she repeated the Profession of Faith. When the day came for the twins' baptism, Gerard had been dressed in Boy's own white christening robe, with a similar finely worked white lace and lawn dress for Gina. Holding the babies to her, Hiroko experienced a sense of true spiritual fulfilment. Gravely, she looked at the priest as he turned to her.

'You have asked to have your children baptised,' he said. 'In doing so, you are accepting the responsibility of training them in the practice of the faith. It will be your duty to bring them up to keep God's commandments as Christ taught us, by loving God and neighbour. Do you clearly understand what you are undertaking?'

Her 'I do' was drowned by a sudden wailing cry from Gerard, and she had to repeat it clearly for all to hear.

Gare, who was to be the twins' godfather, took Gerard from her and handed him to the priest for the wetting of the baby's head. 'I baptise you in the name of the Father,' he intoned as he trickled the holy water onto Gerard's forehead. The baby cried again as if in total rejection of all that was happening.

'. . . and of the Son and the Holy Spirit,' the priest

continued, amidst Gerard's wails. Hastily, he handed the angry baby back, and turning to Grace took Gina into his arms for her turn and, unlike her brother, she smiled up at him throughout the whole performance. The priest smiled back at her. 'Ah, the little lamb, a willing follower already. But the other one!' he thought and shook his head.

Then Hattie lit one candle and Gare the other from the Easter candle for the children, and Hiroko took comfort that now they would always walk as 'children of light', and that at the priest's bidding, she would do all that she could to ensure that they kept the flame of faith alive in their hearts.

As the sounds of the pipe organ rose and resounded through the holy place, Hiroko thought of Satoshi with the sense of anguish she had felt so many times, and longed to hold him and make him part of her new life. Remembering Michiko's threats, and despite a new-found confidence in her faith, she still feared for his life and her own.

And now only the *kami* and her Holy Father were to know how or when she would see her son again.

5

SATOSHI'S SUMMER—TOKYO, 1922

He lay in the long summer grass, pressing himself close to the ground as if to burrow into its welcoming warmth. The full heat of the sun had penetrated where he lay, and he stilled his body and breathing, waiting for the footsteps he knew would be following.

Soon he heard them, and froze, trying to merge into the landscape.

The loud crackle of dried grasses as the steps came closer filled him with a new fear, and he whimpered softly. 'Mamma! Mamma!' His tears flowed into the ground and he stared at the tiny wet circles as they fell on top of the soil, hardening in the heat.

The swish of a stick parting the grasses approached, and he lay now shivering, despite the warmth. Then two strong brown arms reached down and hauled him to his feet.

'Aaagh. Naughty boy, Satoshi-chan!'

And he heard the whistle of the stick as it sliced through the air, then a sudden pain as it hit his shoulders. 'I want Mamma, Mamma!' he screamed.

Again and again the stick came down, and he could hear his Aunt Michiko's laboured breathing, and her words with every blow.

'She's gone! She's gone! She's gone!'

He struggled and fought to free himself, flailing at her with his arms and legs, but her grasp was strong and his small *yukata* was slipping from his shoulders and the stick was hitting his bare skin with a white hot pain.

A voice called out to her, and she stopped. As her grasp relaxed, he was away like a young deer, flying back towards the house with her following hard behind. She caught him just as he arrived at the door, and he stood still waiting for her to hit him again. But she didn't, instead smiled as if to comfort him.

'Now, now, Satoshi-chan—you be a good boy, and go inside quietly, and we'll see what a nice surprise I can get for you, *ne*?'

A man came forward and she bowed low. Satoshi had seen him many times before at his aunt's house, and he could feel the man's keen eyes passing over his tear-stained face then looking back across to his aunt.

'Aaaaah, Daihachi-san, welcome, welcome!' Her voice took on a deferential note. She pushed Satoshi's head down in a deep bow, holding it till it ached. As he slowly raised his head, he noticed the dark swirling tattoos on the man's muscled arm, and that the top of his index finger was missing. He wondered about that.

His aunt was fussing and smiling about this person. As she pushed Satoshi from the room, he saw the man reach out, his hand sliding inside the top of his aunt's kimono. She laughed coquettishly up at him, pulling away like a young girl, but he came in closer towards her as she slid across the *shoji* screened door, shutting the child out. Satoshi could hear the man's harsh voice and sudden laugh, and his Aunt Michiko, speaking in quite a different softer tone, then her high laugh and commands as the servants hurried in to wait on them.

He sat cross-legged in the corner of their kitchen, feeling the young servant girl's hands as she bathed the welts on his shoulders and back.

'Ahhh, chchchch! Poor 'Toshi-chan,' she clucked in sympathy as he flinched whenever the soft cloth touched his tender skin. He sucked at a sweet nashi fruit she gave him, remembering the treats his mother and Ume always had waiting for him whenever he was hungry.

'Mamma, mamma,' he whispered, hot tears of loneliness and self-pity coursing down his face.

Where had she gone? Why wasn't he with her? And with Ume and his grandfather Yukio? His mother must come for him soon and take him away from this hateful place.

'Your mother's a very bad woman and gone far away and left you forever. This is your home now.' His aunt's harsh voice always gave the same reply whenever he asked her and soon he stopped, for her answer never changed. He would run away and find his mother—that's what he'd do. Every fibre in his five-year-old body rebelled against staying here.

At first he'd tried to get away and see if he could somehow find his grandfather's house, but his aunt Michiko always found him. She seemed to know just where he would go, and delighted in hitting him in reprisal. With each attempt to escape her, the beatings were getting worse. One time when his screams for her to stop were resounding through the house, he'd heard her father, the grandfather who was hardly ever there and more like a stranger to him, come out and scold her. A harsh argument had ensued between them.

After that she only ever hit him when they were far enough away from the house for his cries not to be heard. Her eyes would glaze and fill him with an unspeakable fear. Then after the punishment was over, she would smile, and speak in a honeyed voice.

'She's gone. I'm your mother now, 'Toshi-chan. I'm your mother now, *ne*?' She would pick him up, pulling him in close to her and he'd feel the heat and different smell of her, and recoil, hicupping and sobbing quietly, a sense of confusion and loss overwhelming him.

A shaft of sunlight highlighting some yellow persimmons on the kitchen table reminded him suddenly of the colour of that man's hair who had come into his mother's house last year.

He felt a surge of anger as he remembered that it was then that everything seemed to change. His mother was always smiling at this person with his loud strange voice and white skin. He was so different, almost scary, and Satoshi didn't want him there with them. And then they had gone away and left him. He had a sudden memory of his mother crying. Why was she crying? But as quickly as it came, the fleeting picture dissolved.

Little chinks of memory came and went, and he clung to them as if for sustenance. He recalled how only Ume seemed to understand his feelings and when she carried him to his *futon* at night, had made more of a fuss of him, and had even let him take some special sweets with him to bed. But later, his mother would come in and stroke his forehead as he drifted into sleep. The thought of those soft hands filled him with a longing and anguish almost too hard to bear, and he put his head to his knees and sobbed for her.

'Aaaah, 'Toshi-chan, hush, hush,' the servant girl murmured in sympathy, and she got up, then reappeared a moment later with his doll. It was one his grandfather Yukio had sent earlier in May that year for Boy's Day. He'd wanted to see his grandfather but Michiko had forbidden it. Then, to soften the blow, she had allowed Ume inside the door for a few minutes when she came to see him and give him his grandfather's gift.

He'd run to her and clung to the skirt of the maid's kimono. Gently, she had removed his hands and held them as she knelt before him, then reaching into her *furoshiki*, handed him the doll. 'Where's Mamma, I want to see Mamma!' he'd cried. But Michiko had picked him up, bundling him from the room, and he heard their raised voices as she dismissed Ume from the house.

He stared at his doll now. It was a *Samurai* warrior, its brightly coloured battle armour intricately crafted from woven black and gold leather, reflecting the *Domaru* style of the late fourteenth century. He ran his fingers gently along the doll's elaborate helmet of the same gold and black with a sharp pointed decorative piece on top which he often thought looked just like the claws of a crab.

Visions rose before him of large brightly coloured banners shaped like carp fish fluttering from the pole his grandfather had erected over their house, for *Tango No Sekku*. When he had seen them, he'd jumped up as high as he could, laughing aloud and trying to reach up and catch the banners as they swooped in the wind, calling out to his mother to come and watch.

Remembering the happy time, he smiled through his tears.

'Good boy,' the servant girl said, pleased to see him recovering. 'Now listen 'Toshi-chan,' she went on, kneeling down close to him. 'I just heard them say that they are going to get you a special *sensei*. Daihachi Isawa was telling your Aunt Michiko-san that he will organise for a very good sensei who will make it all different for you, and very soon. But it's our secret, *ne*?' She put a finger to his lips, cautioning him to silence. Satoshi nodded, wondering who this person would be. Maybe he would change everything and make it all better for him by helping him to get away and be with his mother again.

6

RE-AWAKENING—MAUI, 1930

Why is it that the very thing which is withheld or taken from us, is the one we most aspire to, and that which we long for?

Hattie, gazing across at her daughter-in-law listlessly staring out to sea, knew in that moment that Hiroko was still fretting for the child she'd left behind in Japan. She had seen that expression many times in the eight years since Hiroko had first arrived at their home.

Her slight figure was almost lost in the reclining canvas chair at the edge of the lanai, only her legs swinging nervously—one across the other—gave any indication of the tension she was feeling.

Are our mothers' hearts forever bonded to the being that has lain within our body, to be born, suckled and nurtured with all we can give—only finally to leave us? Hattie wondered. Even now, there was the shadow play of her own Boy as a baby, his face upturned to hers, smiling, always smiling. She could still feel the silky softness of his skin. Smell his warm baby smell.

The dull ache whenever she thought of him receded as she caught sight of Gerard chasing Gina across the lawn, whooping and shouting. Seeing his mother, he changed direction and came running to her, throwing himself into her lap. Hattie watched as Hiroko loudly chastised him, pushing the boy away, and turning from him to the letter she had been reading. He stopped still, like a young stag, staring at his mother. Hattie could see the hurt and anger in his dark eyes as he waited silently for Hiroko to notice him. But her face remained averted. Why doesn't he cry and scream, Hattie thought, and break through to her? Claim what is his?

But a mother's love is divisible, she mused, and Hiroko's was mostly with some far-away phantom, rather than with the here and now.

She sighed. Gerard was a demanding and difficult little boy and always had been, but it was intensified by Hiroko's indifference to him. If only his father Boy was still with them, things would be so different. He surely would have given his son the love and attention he craved. She could still hear Boy's sudden laugh and see the way he had of winning over whoever or whatever he wanted. But she pushed these thoughts of Boy away, knowing that all her wishful thinking could never bring him back.

Now seeing the excitement of their game receding, little Gina had reversed the rules and run back after her brother. He roughly pushed her aside and ran into the house. She started to cry, and Hattie got up, calling to her, 'Gina honey, come we'll go inside, and get something nice to eat.' The little girl's pixie face lit up. 'Can we Gran, can we . . . and later go down for a swim?' Hattie lifted the child, wiping away her tears.

How many times she'd watched as Hiroko rejected the boy. Yet with Gina, she was often affectionate, but then Gina was more self-contained and never demanding. She simply saw and quietly took what was given. The hunger and need within Gerard to demand and take everything he wanted, then face the pain of denial when it came, seemed to have passed Gina by.

Hiroko half-listened to the sounds of Hattie and Gina as they went inside. She felt a slow scream build within her, then as always, she forced it back, willing herself to be calm.

Staring out over the bay, she could see the sea starting to ruffle as the wind moved in across its surface, highlighting the cobalt blue and aquamarine water with curls of white foam as the waves began to build. She recalled the waves in the *Tosa* School, Sun and Moon landscapes of the anonymous screen painters of the sixteenth century *Muromachi* period in her father's collection of screens and scrolls. Their stylised curl and contained strength, imparting the power and mystery of the sea, rose before her.

She felt a longing to be back there with her father in their summer house at Lake Ashimoko, with Satoshi in her arms, and Ume quietly there to care for them. Her frustration and homesickness were more often with her now than not.

Try as she might, she could not reconcile herself to the loss of Satoshi, and the anger which would not subside whenever she thought of Michiko and the Nakamura family, and their treatment of her and her father.

Hiroko looked down at her dress, its fine pleats now crumpled by Gerard's boisterous actions, and she felt a further irritation at his sudden unwanted intrusion. Her father's letter was now creased too, and a surge of anger towards her son fanned her sense of resentment. If only it could all go away, and once more she could be in the arms of her Boy, with Satoshi there beside them. She lay back on the chair closing her eyes, picturing Boy's face moving down to meet hers, his lips reaching for her, their bodies merged in a film of sweat and sandalwood perfume. Every part of her ached to be with him. Even now with all that had happened, her emotional life had lingered in the time they were together—locked into a landscape that was no longer part of her life.

Forcing herself back to the present, she sat up and opening her father's letter, once more skimmed his words.

The days are getting longer here now, daughter, with the heat of summer soon to be upon us. Of course, we shall journey to Hakone again and take refuge in the cool. But it is never quite the same without you and

Satoshi there, although my writing keeps me busy. But the energy I once felt is receding with age, so small compensations take on a larger importance in our lives. The ni-ju seki nashi are in season, and I can't get enough of them.

Hiroko smiled at this, her father, always the academic and philosopher who took refuge in the world of books and art. Even as a child he'd imbued her with his love of the Greek philosophers and their teachings. Strange that with all his Japaneseness and sense of containment, he lacked the national insularity, and so looked beyond those shores for much of his guidance.

He had been trying to get in touch with Satoshi for her.

His visits here now are even fewer than before. When I send Ume to get him, often he is not there at the Nakamura house, and there's not even an excuse or apology given. They have made it very difficult. Once again, I have sought legal advice, but there is little we can do in the circumstances. I have heard that Michiko's father is now very high up in the Zaibatsu *and has much influence. I have tried to speak with him about Satoshi, but with little success. Indirectly, I received a message through his colleague, Daihachi Isawa, to the effect that it would be better for Satoshi if we do not try to make contact at all, as it can only lead to trouble for everyone. You can read between the lines.*

Hiroko drew in her breath. As clearly as if it were yesterday, she recalled Michiko's promise of certain death to her son and herself if she tried to take him. She knew that the threat was still there, as strong as ever. And now it seemed they had brought in the Isawa family, whom she'd heard were linked with the *Yakuza,* to deliver this message. The sinister nature of this could not be discounted. Her heart grew cold at the thought that

Satoshi was in the control of this family who had behaved so dishonourably, and that he now seemed even further from her grasp.

A sudden breeze fluttered the other letter in her lap, and she reached for it. It was from Grace, and she opened it with a sense of anticipation. As always, it was short and to the point.

Hi there Hiroko,
   Just a quick note to say that we'll be over there in two weeks' time, staying for a month, and I'm just dying to see you and catch up with everyone.
   It's my 30th birthday on the 29th, and we've decided on a really big party at the new 'Pink Palace' so you must come. There'll be a band, lots of booze and Jimmy's naval friends will be there, so get yourself a gorgeous dress and help us celebrate.
   It will be nice for Mardi to catch up with Gina and Gerard, and we're all looking forward to seeing you. So please, don't duck out on me this time. There's lots to tell. See you soon. With love from Grace.

She missed her friend. Next to Gare, who had become a substitute father to her on the island, the person she had most grown to depend upon in her first years there was Grace. Since she'd gone to live on the mainland, letters and occasional visits had had to suffice. With each visit, Grace urged her to find another husband.

'Time's slipping past so quick, honey, and while you still look great, you should get out there, before it's too late.'

'Oh Grace-san, I don't want another husband. I've already had two,' she would laugh, never quite confiding that no-one could ever replace Boy in her heart. Still, it would be fun to dress up and go to a party. She would soon turn thirty herself in November, but somehow life spent mostly with Hattie and Gare had made her feel almost middle-aged. It would be good to feel young again, if only for a night. But she wondered if that were possible. Once more, her thoughts, like swallows, flew back to her father's letter and the hopelessness of retrieving Satoshi. She sighed, picking up his letter to go through it again. There must be a way to get him out, she thought, there must.

* * *

'How can they keep him away from her, Gare?' Hattie asked as she had so many times before. 'I still just don't see how it works. I mean, if she was here and had had Satoshi in America, there's just no way that family could have taken him. It's a strange custom, that's all I can say.'

Gare sighed, and thought, if only they'd all let up on the boy.

'And it's really affecting the way she treats Gerard,' Hattie persisted. 'Because of all that's happened, Hiroko just can't seem to relate to him. It's almost as if she resents the fact that he's here, and not Satoshi.' It was so like a Scorpio, she thought to herself. Always the sting in the tail, and that self-destructive urge. It was the sign Hattie liked least, although her largely altruistic nature tried to stifle such thoughts.

'Well you've got to hand it to her, Hattie, she's really thrown herself into our life here on the plantation. She's becoming a really good little manager,' Gare answered, thinking how bright this woman was. Hiroko seemed to know that she needed to fill the place of their lost son, and to help administer their thriving sugar and pineapple plantation. She was even coming up with ideas for expansion, and they made good economic sense, he thought.

Despite this, there was a distancing between Hiroko and his wife. Hattie still linked Hiroko with Boy's death in Tokyo, and couldn't bring herself to fully forgive her. It was never stated, but it lingered between them. But Hattie more than made up for the lack of any real affection there in her devotion to the two children, particularly Gina, who adored her grandmother. Gerard by comparison. It was like stepping from the subdued sepia tones of Tokyo into a lush brilliantly coloured landscape, with its almost surreal mythic intensity. Boy would have wanted her to stay and help his parents on the plantation. And she had. And one day, her father would decide to come and be with her. But only if they could get Satoshi. In the meantime, he needed to be there for her son, just in case.

She stood, and slipped the satin dress off its hanger, stepping into it. After years of wearing a kimono, it still seemed strange to wear Western dress and this was a little too fitted and cut lower than those she now usually wore. But it glowed, lending colour and sparkle to her eyes. Pausing before the mirror she touched her gold cross resting on the swell of her breasts, then hurried downstairs to await Grace and Jimmy's arrival.

* * *

It was so hot.

The heat of the night made her feel dizzy. Perhaps, she giggled, it was the champagne. Champagne? She hardly ever drank. There had been a time in Paris, with Boy, but so long ago. She looked up at the face above her. His smile was like Boy's, but it was not Boy's. They moved well together, and had been dancing for what seemed like forever. His arms around her held her tight, made her feel so light, almost floating.

She looked across at Grace, laughing and dancing the Charleston with Jimmy, to an up-tempo 'Putting on the Ritz' beating out from the big hotel band. She closed her eyes, and wondered why she was here. It seemed so cut off from everything she knew. But it was wonderful, just to float and be part of it all.

'Hey, Hiroko honey, you OK?' he asked.

She nodded.

'I'm so hot,' she said.

'We'll go outside and cool off.' He laughed.

Grace's face appeared in a blur as she passed by and

she stumbled a little. The man's grip tightened and then they were outside in the hotel courtyard, a warm breeze riffling the palms and the sound of the waves breaking on the beach seeming louder than ever before. She swayed back against him.

'Hey, I think we'd better get some more champagne,' he said. 'Sit right here honey, and I'll be back.'

She leaned, resting her head against the palm, and then he was back with a bottle and brimming glasses. She reached for it, wanting the coolness, and drank quickly, feeling some of the bubbles spill down her chin and neck into her dress. He leaned forward, licking the top of her breasts as the champagne slid into her cleavage.

She pulled back trying to focus on him. The white of his uniform glowed in the party lights and his face stared down at her with a look she hadn't seen for so long. His features became blurred and she felt dizzy.

'I don't feel so well.' She hesitated. 'Maybe I should go home now. But Grace, I should speak to her first and . . .'

'No, no,' he broke in. 'I'll organise everything—you just wait here.'

It seemed only an instant and he was back, lifting her and carrying her along the beach, her arms around his neck. She drifted into sleep, dreaming. It was Boy carrying her at Hara and she could see Fuji hovering in the distance. They moved swiftly towards it like the wind, yet it never seemed to get any closer.

She felt herself falling back, and it was so nice and soft to lie down.

The slam of a door roused her and she awoke fully and was surprised to find that she was lying on her bed, and he was bending over her, but the white of his uniform had gone. His breathing seemed to fill the room, then she felt his naked body slump onto hers.

'Hey come on, come on, that's the girl—now wake up honey. This is what you want, eh. This is what you want.'

There were hands reaching between her legs and she stiffened, trying to focus on what was happening. Her dress. He was pulling it off and she could hear it tear. She cried out. '*Ie Ie*!!'

But he was intent on what lay beneath him, his whole body enveloping her, his hands and mouth laying claim to every part of her.

'Hey, you little *Nisei* bitch, you're hot for it.' All his weight was on her, and she couldn't move. She pushed against him and cried out, but this only seemed to urge him further.

'This is what you want, eh? This is what you want, you hot little *Nisei* bitch!'

The sudden pain as his penis pushed into her made her cry out again.

It was as if he would never stop, like a sword slicing away at her. She was the *yu-jo* girl, there to service him. She scratched viciously at his back. And he laughed, 'God, you're wonderful, wonderful!'

'Boy! Boy!' she moaned. But this wasn't Boy. She screamed, as she felt him roughly turn her over. Then the sweat and heat of him was on her back as he rammed into her again and again. Suddenly she was back in the bath house and it was Noboru, spreading her legs and forcing his way in. The bath house had been his favoured trysting place. She had begun to dread going there when he was there, armed with the knowledge that he would grab her and push her face down over the bench, and come into her from behind, grunting and shouting as he climaxed inside her. She'd submitted, but there was always the feeling that Michiko was there behind the screen to watch.

Now this stranger was upon her. She could feel his body stiffen, then tremble—ready to uncoil—and knew the signs that he was coming. But not inside her. Please dear God, not inside her! She squirmed, fighting to force him out of her and she cried out with pain as his hands clamped into her breasts, pulling at her nipples as if to tear them away.

She didn't want his seed in her. She was panting in her desperate and futile bid to force him out, then screamed as the red hot flow of semen shot deep into her and she felt him shudder and heard his moans. She was aware of his moving away, as she drifted into unconsciousness.

* * *

When Hiroko awoke, she was alone. A faint glow filtering into the room bathed its disarray in dawn's soft light. She lay unmoving, her head and body aching and an acid feeling rising in her throat. She was home, yet something was wrong. But what? Then the horror of the night came rushing back, and she sat up reaching for the light switch and stumbling from the bed. Her ripped dress lay across the floor. A champagne bottle on its side pooled its contents on the tiles beneath her feet.

She staggered to the mirror, and stared in silence as the face of another woman stared back at her. A redbluish bruise was beginning to spread from her eye to her mouth, which was cut and swollen. Scratches and darkening bruises across her breast spoke their silent reproach. She looked down, and felt a stickiness move slowly down her leg to her stockings, which were still pulled up in their garters, their ladders mute testimony to assault. Slowly, almost fearfully, her fingers reached down and moved into the soft hair between her legs, feeling the sticky wetness within the swollen lips. A sob rose in her throat, becoming a low moan.

'*Ie! Ie! Ie!!!*' Nausea rose like a revolt and she ran to the bathroom to rid herself of everything within her.

The water was near boiling, yet she lay barely noticing the burning that seeped into every pore and crevice. She lay back, inhaling the steam, half floating, pushing those phantoms of the night from her consciousness. She could still feel his hands, his breath, the heat of his body devouring her. 'Oh holy Father, holy Father,' she moaned. She reached for her cross, then froze. Her cross was gone.

She staggered from the bath, then crawled into the

bedroom, her eyes scouring every part of the floor, sobbing as she went.

There was a tap on the door and Lalana entered, taking in the scene at a glance. Grabbing a large towel she hurried across the room, scooping up the girl in her strong arms, clucking her concern.

'Oh, Miss Hiroko honey, you just hush there now, it's all fine, everything's going to be fine.'

Gently, the maid laid her on the bed, pulling up the blankets.

'You just rest up and I'll get you something to make you feel a whole lot better. Just rest up now, you hear,' she crooned in her soft Island voice. 'And don't you worry about those bruises, I know just how to make them better.' Then, reaching into her pocket. 'Is this what you were looking for, honey?' The cross on its fine chain shone like a golden beacon as Hiroko reached out for it, then closed her hand around it, as if to never let go.

* * *

'Please, I would rather not talk about it, Grace-san.' Hiroko turned her face as if to hide any tell-tale marks which, though only days later, still faintly darkened her skin.

'Well, something must have happened. I mean you two left so early. He seemed really smitten. Are you going to see him again? Come on, 'fess up,' Grace urged, turning the full power of her blue eyes on her friend.

Hiroko moved away, feeling her heart start to pound.

'There's really nothing to say,' she said, willing her voice to sound off-hand.

'Well, he took off like a blue-tail fly the very next day, right back to the mainland. So something must have happened.'

Hiroko looked at her friend, feeling a distancing. Surely she could see that she had no intention of taking it any further.

'Well, honey, if you can't talk to me, who can you

talk to then?' Grace pursued, a note of irritation entering her voice. 'I mean, he's gorgeous, and the two of you danced together all night. Maybe he'll be husband number three?'

Hiroko felt herself start to shake, and a pain build up deep inside her chest.

'You really couldn't do any better,' Grace was really warming to the idea. 'I mean, he comes from a top Philadelphian family, and he'll go a long way in the Service.' She wondered, though, just how well his blue-blood family would take to their son marrying a Japanese woman, and a widow to boot. But the Baillieu name and money could always be counted upon.

'You really should give it some thought, if he's all that keen.'

'Grace-san, I don't want to hear any more.' Hiroko's voice shook. 'No more, please, no more.'

'Really, Hiroko, why not for pity's sake? You've just got to start planning ahead, and think of your future. You really couldn't get a better catch than . . .'

Hiroko's moan stopped her mid-sentence.

'Stop it! Stop it! I don't want to hear any more. No more! No more!' she cried, her voice rising on every word. She stared at Grace, white-faced, her breath coming in shuddering gasps, then she turned and ran from the room.

Hiroko stood before her bedroom mirror, still shaking, staring at her reflection. Slowly at first, then in a frenzy to rid herself of them, she tore off her flowered dress, then her petticoat, then unrolled her stockings and kicked off her high-heeled sandals. Walking to the wardrobe, she removed a kimono lying in a neat stack with the others, and quickly unfolded it, slipping it on to seek its reassurance. Reaching for an *obi*, she carefully tied it tightly around her waist, enclosing herself intact within. From a lower shelf, she took down two snowy white *tabi* and slipped her feet into them. With a tissue, she wiped away her lipstick, then pulling back her long hair which hung in a heavy fall to her shoulders, she twisted it into the traditional tight knot at the nape of her neck. She slid her fingers along the gold chain, then stopped at her cross while staring at her Japanese image in the mirror.

'Never a *Nisei* bitch! Never! Never!' she intoned.

'What on earth's name are you doing?' Grace's voice broke her reverie.

Without turning, Hiroko lifted her eyes to gaze at Grace in the mirror. 'If you don't mind, Grace-san, I'd like to be alone now.' Grace stared at her, noting the transformation, and rejecting what she saw.

'Well, really! You're such a strange little thing! I mean, what hope is there!' Grace's exasperation was barely veiled and all her initial dislike when they'd first met seemed to reassert itself.

When Hiroko didn't answer, she gave a short laugh, turned on her heel and walked out, slamming the door on a friendship that was never quite the same again.

7

A HOME OF HER OWN—HAWAII, CHRISTMAS 1930

Boy's plans lay spread out on the study floor. Hiroko looked closely at them, then picked up a detailed drawing of a house which seemed familiar. She remembered where she had first seen it. This was a more finished version of some sketches Boy had taken with him when they went to Mianoshita.

'What is this one?' she'd asked.

'It's the home I will build for you one day, my darling,' he'd answered.

'But where?' She'd gazed at it, trying to imagine from its roughly outlined facade what it would be like inside.

'Wherever you want, in heaven, on earth, wherever,' he'd replied, pulling her to him. As they'd kissed and rediscovered each other, there was no more talk of the house he would build.

Boy must have worked on the plans when she returned to Tokyo ahead of him, she thought. For they were fairly finished, and attached to the outer sketches was a more detailed drawing with measurements and specifications for the rooms within. Taking them across to the window, she studied them carefully, trying to visualise what it would look like when built. She could see the influence of the shrines and buildings he had studied in Japan were coming to fruition in this sketch of a large house with its graceful up-tilted cedar bark roof, the entrance-way's slender timber pillars left plain and undecorated rising from grey slate floors. There was a sense of symmetry and grandeur, but a restrained use of decoration lending a simplicity she felt at home with. He'd even indicated the landscaping surrounding the house with its raked pebble courtyard, stone Japanese lanterns and a garden in which he'd started to outline a water fountain, and where the trees, bamboo and flowers would be.

As Hiroko studied his drawings, a slow feeling of excitement started to build. She quickly moved to her desk and getting out some sheets of paper and a pencil, started to outline and roughly sketch how she would like certain aspects of his plans to be developed. She would find a Japanese builder, and the house would incorporate all the grace and beauty of the best architecture of her far-away homeland.

Gare had said he would transfer the title of their Waikiki home to her, to build onto, or to change as she wished. At first she'd demurred, but her sound business sense had convinced her to accept his generous gift. But dark memories of that place still haunted her.

This house of Boy's which she would build would be totally Japanese. But where? she wondered. Boy had often spoken of a favourite place in Maui. But she wanted to create something a little further away from Hattie and Gare. A place where she could escape to, and unwind. Maybe it could be in Honolulu, as it would be better there for the children with their schooling and friends. Cutting through her thoughts, a demanding voice called, Mamma, mamma, I'm hungry!'

Gerard rushed into the room and grabbed at her skirt, as if to claim all her attention. 'I'm hungry!' he repeated, pulling at her to follow him.

Firmly she pushed him back, clucking at him. 'Gerard-chan, you just be patient and wait,' she chastised.

'I want to eat my *sushi* now. Now!' he yelled, his hands on his hips, his face reddening as he stared defiantly up at her.

'Go out of this room at once, and you just wait until I'm ready.' Hiroko pushed him struggling to the door, and closed it firmly behind him, ignoring his howls of protest.

She sat down shakily, resting her head in her hands, feeling a growing frustration, her creative flow of thoughts about the house shattered.

Slowly, she walked out onto the verandah overlooking the garden and bay beyond, a welcome breeze fanning her face, cooling the anger she felt towards her son. He was really becoming almost impossible to handle, so unlike his sister Gina. But Gina was a gentle child, and far less robust than her twin. Her occasional bouts of asthma added to her fragility, and intensified Hiroko's concern for her daughter.

She strolled down into the garden, away from Gerard's protests, thinking again of her house plans, before eventually going back inside for their evening meal.

After a sound scolding, Gerard had been sent to bed early, but couldn't sleep. He listened to the soft breathing of his sister in the bed alongside his, and turned over to stare out the window at the darkening night sky. He could see the outline shapes of the Laysan ducks as they flew low across the star-bright heavens towards their wetlands. A sudden pain in his leg made him groan, and he lay back, his sense of hurt and anger consuming him. He could still feel the sting of his mother's stick on his legs as they throbbed their protest. Hiroko had pushed him from the room, shouting at him to go, and he'd looked across at Gina, glowering as he ran past her and she followed him.

'Gera! Gera!' she'd called after him.

'Go away,' he said, hot tears of pain and anger coursing down his cheeks. But she had continued behind him, a quiet little presence there for him as always.

'Don't worry, it won't hurt for long,' she promised. 'It never does.'

'What would you know, you don't know anything,' he growled at her.

'I do, I do so! Anyway, you shouldn't keep trying to make her angry,' she said, piqued.

'Shut up and go away!' he'd shouted at her.

He'd thrown himself fully clothed into bed, trying to shut out everything around him, ignoring Gina as she moved around the room, quietly preparing herself for bed. He'd make his mother sorry. She'd be really sorry for treating him like this, he fumed. Turning to look at Gina now soundly sleeping, he slipped quietly out of bed and climbed out through his window, dropping the few feet to the garden below. He crept around to the verandah and passed the dining room where he could see his mother sitting, talking to Gare as Lalana cleared the table. The light fell full on her face, and he hesitated and stared at her, his anger and hurt mounting.

He ducked and sped past the French doors opening to where she sat, and continued down to the study, then quietly eased open the door and let himself in. His eyes, now accustomed to the dark, could see the plans still spread out on the floor. He stared at them, considering. These were the things his mother had been looking at for so long and they must mean something to her. His eyes rested on the scissors on her desk. Quickly he reached over and, picking them up, took up the first papers he could see and started cutting away.

He reached for one plan after the other, cutting savagely this way and that, really starting to enjoy the mayhem he was creating. He ignored the growing sound of the scissor blades knocking against the desk as they hacked through his father's plans, his breathing loud and laboured as he warmed to his task. He didn't hear the door swing open, but a sudden shaft of light blazing into the room spun him around, and his mother's scream as she stared at what he was doing shocked, then filled him with his first real taste for revenge.

* * *

Gerard sat staring across at the white foaming wake as his grandfather's boat sped across the choppy waters of the Kaiwi Channel towards Honolulu. A sudden chill made him hunch down into his jacket, pulling its fleecy collar up around his ears. He ran his tongue over his lips, tasting the spray which glistened on his face. It tasted salty just like his tears, he thought.

Gare looked at the boy, thinking how small he was, hunched into his jacket. Now as his grandson headed towards the age of eight, it was hard to know which way he was going to go. It was now or never to try and get him back on the rails before it was too late, he thought.

'It's not completely his fault.' Hattie had stood firm when Gare told her of what happened. 'Hiroko just won't take enough interest in him. She neglects him and he's simply reacting to that.'

But the ache in her heart when she saw her Boy's plans so defaced had made even her good-will towards her grandson wilt.

Luckily, Gerard's random slashing had not completely torn through many of the plans. Already she'd had some of her girls on the plantation quietly start to repair them.

'I'm going to take him out of your hair for a day or two,' Gare proposed. 'We'll go over to the house at Waikiki, and Hiroko can join us in a day or so, and we can discuss then what she wants to do with the house. Get her mind off everything.' Not a word had passed between mother and son since the night she discovered Gerard's destructive act.

Gare wondered too, if now might not be just the time to think about visiting his brother Jack in Australia. It could do Gerard a heap of good to take him to the 'Winganna' homestead during his school holidays, to ride horses and generally rough it a bit. He could join in on all there was to do with Jack and Molly's family on their sprawling twenty thousand acre cattle station in the north of Queensland. The boy needed to get away from his mother for a while, and it was an ideal chance for him to spend time with Jack and Molly's sons, Tom and Bill. Gare thought for a moment, searching his mind for the boys' ages. Yes, young Bill would be about the same age as Gerard, and Tom a couple of years older. He had a hunch that Gerard and Bill, a bit of a tear-away at the best of times, would get on well and become mates. Yes, he'd write to Jack and organise it.

The fast approaching shores of Honolulu looming ahead interrupted his thoughts.

'Hey, Gerard, we're almost there. You get your butt over here and give me a hand now.' He looked on in appreciation as the small boy hopped to and expertly handled the ropes just as he had taught him. Quietly, he nosed the boat into the small jetty, and watched as Gerard threw the coil of rope cleanly over the pylon to hold the boat fast. Hino, his Hawaiian house-boy, took over the wheel, throttling right down as Gare and Gerard picked up their few belongings and jumped ashore.

Gare turned to Hino.

'We'll be right now. See if you can bring the boy's mother back, and Gina too if she wants to come, the day after tomorrow. OK?' He waved briefly as Hino and the boat sped away, heading back towards Maui.

Later that evening as they sat on the beach, their lines drifting in the water, waiting for the fish to bite, Gare reached across to the boy sitting hunched over his rod, and ruffled his hair.

'Hey, what are you thinking?'

There was a long silence, then 'What's Satoshi like?'

'I don't know, I've never seen him. I've never been to Tokyo, but you've seen the snaps,' Gare answered.

'Yes, but what's he really like?' Gerard persisted, remembering the browny-coloured image of a little kid with funny spiky hair standing beside his mother, and a tall man with light hair who she said was his father, Boy.

'I guess he's just a kid much like you, and getting on with things,' Gare answered, wondering at the sudden interest.

'She likes him better than me,' Gerard looked away.

'That's not so, your mother is doing things all the time for you and your sister,' Gare said, noting the gruffness in his grandson's voice.

But Gerard didn't answer.

It was just as Hattie had said, Gare thought. You had to hand it to the old girl.

'She likes him more than me,' Gerard repeated, turning to his grandfather with a look of defiance. Gare hesitated, then reaching across, he lifted Gerard's chin and looked straight into his eyes.

'Well then, you'll just have to prove yourself a whole lot better than Satoshi, eh son? A whole lot better than him.'

Gerard stared back at his grandfather in silence, then a slow smile lit up his face.

'I'll be better, Grandpa. I'll be the best,' he promised.

* * *

'Forgive me, Father, for I have sinned.'

'Sins of the flesh, or of the mind, my child?'

Hiroko hesitated.

'I have had impure thoughts, Father,' she answered.

She could feel the cold of the Confessional creep around her, a silence broken only by footsteps and occasional scraping of the benches in the pews being pushed back as people knelt in prayer.

It was Christmas Eve, and Our Lady of Peace Cathedral was starting to fill, yet no sense of festivity had as yet touched Hiroko.

She held her rosary to her breast.

'My son, Gerard, I'm always angry,' she paused. 'He's . . . it's always so difficult,' she went on.

'Go on,' the priest prompted.

'He's often so—so rough and violent. He's not . . . he's not Satoshi. I want Satoshi to be here too.'

'You must cleanse your heart of any unkind or impure thoughts towards your son, and pray for his and your guidance,' the priest intoned. 'Is anything else troubling you, my child?'

Hiroko could hear him standing and sensed his haste to be away.

She shook her head, still unsatisfied, but somehow

strengthened with the thought that if nothing else, prayer alone might answer her.

She rejoined Gina waiting for her in the family pew, ready for the evening service to begin.

They had arrived in Honolulu the day before to join Gare and Gerard, and would all go back tomorrow to Maui, to be with Hattie for Christmas Day. She still couldn't reconcile herself to calling the Waikiki house her own, although she felt at one with where it sat, high overlooking the ever-changing landscape of sky, sand and sea. Gare was keen to discuss future plans, and she went along with his ideas to please him. But memories of that awful night after Grace's party were still vivid.

She felt Gina's little hand slip into hers as the procession of priests and choir boys moved majestically down the centre aisle.

Together, they joined in the hymn of Christmas joy, and she felt her heart lift, momentarily cleansed of her worries as they receded in the resounding notes of thanksgiving for the birth of Jesus Christ.

Later that night, when they were all sleeping, a sudden wind sprang up, racing across the Diamond Head Crater and down through their garden, to sweep an oil lamp on the verandah from its ledge. Soon the hungry timbers were soaking up oil, then as quickly, a flame which sprang to life was fanning its way across the floor, devouring everything in its path.

Gerard stirred; he was in a circus, and his dream was carrying him on a horse's back, its hooves in the sawdust making a cracking sound as they circled the ring. It was hot and he could smell burning.

The fire's glow intruded on his dream, and he opened his eyes, staring in wonder at first, then alarm, at the flames sweeping across the verandah and licking into the wall of his bedroom. He jumped up and ran to Gina, shaking her awake, coughing now as the acrid smoke hit his throat. She was always slow to wake, and frantically he pulled at her.

'Gina, Gina, wake up, hurry, it's a fire, wake up.'

Unsteadily she sat up, coughing violently, and he pulled her out of bed and together they groped their way from the room and out into the garden.

'Mamma, Mamma!' she wailed.

'You wait here!' he cried, running back into the house, dodging the flames which were now racing through the hall towards his mother's and his grandfather's bedrooms at the back.

Hiroko's room was already filled with smoke, and she lay unmoving, lulled by the dense pall of smoke surrounding them. Gerard shook her, crying 'Mamma! Mamma!', the tears pouring down his face. He didn't want her to die, she mustn't die.

She stirred a little and he helped her to sit up. 'It's a fire, hurry, hurry!'

'Gerard-chan,' she murmured weakly.

He dragged at her, pulling as hard as he could, but she kept falling back. Frantically, he shouted and she gradually responded, then slowly she staggered with him out into the garden, coughing as the flames engulfed the curtains and shot towards her bed.

Gina ran to her, helping her lie down.

'Gare, where's Gare?' she cried weakly.

But Gerard was away racing around to the back of the house, now burning like a beacon, and climbed through his grandfather's bedroom window. The old man was awake, and coughing frantically as he groped his way to the door into the hall, but it was already in flames. Gerard grabbed him, pulling him back towards the window.

He tried to speak but the smoke rushed into his throat, and he just held on, pulling the old man to the window, then pushing and pulling him out through it to the clear air beyond.

They sát dazed, watching the house burn to the ground, unmindful of the people who had collected and the old fire engine which had arrived too late.

Gerard felt his grandfather's hand patting him on the back, and then a glow of recognition as others learned of his actions and praised him for his bravery.

'Am I better than Satoshi?' he quietly asked Gare. 'The very best,' his grandfather answered, winking at him.

Later next morning, as Hino steered them across the bay away from Waikiki, Hiroko looked back at the charred remains where the house had once stood, and felt a cleansing away of what it had come to represent. In that moment of new-found elation she knew what she would do. This was perfect, the only place to build the beautiful Japanese house Boy had promised her. And build it she would.

# 8

GRANDFATHER'S GIFT—JAPAN, JANUARY 1939

Arriving at the small timber house in Ebisu, Hiroko noticed that the door was decorated with a garland of bamboo interlaced with tiny golden oranges swinging wildly on their strings in the icy wind which had sprung up. A thick rope of straw, intricately plaited, hung across the doorway to guard against evil spirits, and bless those within. It was the New Year, and she had almost forgotten the Shinto festivities in her anxiety to see her ailing father and to make contact with Satoshi.

Small branches of pine had been planted in deep bowls on either side of the door, and she experienced a sense of well-being when she saw them. As purveyors of strength and happiness, she felt she would need all they had to offer to carry her through the next weeks.

She looked across the small moss-covered garden, and thought that soon these same New Year tokens would be replaced by black and white cloths draping the front walls of her house, announcing her father's death. She shivered as this reality confronted her. But she was here now, and over sixteen years had lapsed since the anguish, shame and sorrow of their last parting. They had both hoped his staying in the family home would help keep an open door for Satoshi to return, and he had refused to accompany her then or later when she wrote. She recalled how initially he had made clear his disappointment in her leaving.

'Why run from your enemy?' Yukio had asked.

'Maybe it's an honourable retreat, father,' she had pleaded. 'And I'll come back.' But who could have known that it would have taken so long?

That he had sent for her now had at least partly lifted the weight of parental disappointment in her actions, and she hoped that it was not his death alone which summoned her.

'Daughter.' The old man turned and looked at her, his face ashen, with two unnaturally high spots of colour accentuating his cheekbones.

'Father.'

Bowing low, Hiroko moved over to the pile of *futon* on which he lay. She knelt beside him, trying to hold back the tears. 'You've come, you've come.' He coughed, his frail body shaking with the effort. She reached out and touched his shoulder, willing the strength from her younger spirit into his.

Looking up at her, and struggling for breath, he whispered, 'There's much to say, and so little time. All these years lost, but we won't talk of that. You are my only child, and I've lived long enough and seen enough to know that the path we take is predestined.'

He lay back, his eyes closed, breathing in short shallow gasps as if conserving every precious breath. 'Maybe you should rest, father—we can speak later.' She touched his forehead lightly with her hand, smoothing the fine parchment-like skin. He opened his eyes, and they shone with a brightness she knew was the feverish last stage of tuberculosis. 'No, no, it must be now, there's so little time left.

'Hiroko-chan, the winds of change are upon us. I fear this war will bring terrible times for all of us.' He paused. 'You must leave here as soon as possible, after I've gone. There's much danger for you here now.'

The coughing this time was harder to stop, and she helped him to sit as he coughed up globs of veinous blood into a bowl beside him. There was a smell of sickness and death in this room, and looking around, she felt as though she had stepped back into another time and place of which she was no longer a part. It was so cramped and confined. She had grown used to a world of wider spaces and sense of freedom. She rang the small bell beside his bed, and Ume, still there as her father's housekeeper, appeared, pushing aside the *shoji* screen and kneeling at the door.

'I want you to bring me a bowl of boiling water and a towel,' she said. 'And hurry, Ume.'

She took a tiny bottle from her purse and when Ume appeared with the bowl, she dropped a few drops into the water. Together, they helped hold his face over the steaming bowl as Hiroko loosely draped the towel around his head and shoulders to trap the aromatic vapour that rose from the water. A strong smell of eucalypt filled the room. 'Breathe in, Father, this will help you.' He coughed a little and she could hear him wheezing in the steam in short, shuddering gasps.

'That's enough,' he cried weakly, and she signalled for Ume to remove the bowl. Then laying him back against the pillows, she gently wiped the steam from his face.

'You should have been a doctor,' he smiled at her.

'It's the thing I would have liked most, if I had been clever enough,' she answered, bowing her head modestly. He looked at her. Until that tragic time of her husband Boy's death, she had been such a dutiful and pleasing daughter. But then she had gone far away, and since then there had been only the letters and pictures of the two grandchildren he hardly knew. He could see their faces now, suspended in a landscape so lush and vivid, yet sadly unfamiliar. And Satoshi, his eldest grandson, so cruelly withheld from him and from Hiroko all these years by the Nakamura clan.

He closed his eyes, half-drifting into sleep. Then remembering more urgent claims to his consciousness, he forced himself to wake and sit up, beckoning his daughter to him.

when in Paris with Boy. She had never worn it. The occasion had not arisen, until now.

Earlier that day after arriving at Hattie and Gare's Waikiki house, Hattie's maid, Lalana, had helped her unpack. As Hiroko removed the dress from its cotton cover, she had gasped anew when seeing it. A slip of silk satin, the simplicity which had attracted them both when she and Boy first saw it hanging in the tiny boutique tucked away off the rue de Saint Germaine, spoke of timeless elegance. She had stroked the silken satin, its ruby sheen contrasted with her creamy skin. Boy had insisted they buy it. Maybe tonight for Grace's party she would wear it.

Turning, she looked at herself in the long mirror. Is this how the *geisha* felt before dressing for a special event? Her mind wandered to when she was fifteen and returning home with her father as dusk fell in Shibuya. A palanquin had stopped on the street alongside them. A white hand emerging from its gold brocaded kimono sleeve languidly pushed aside the screened window. Above it, glowing in the palanquin's flickering light, she'd glimpsed the girl's face, an immaculate white mask with its carefully bowed scarlet mouth, and enormous kohled eyes beneath the blue-black lacquered sheen of her coiffeured hair. Hiroko had stared fascinated at this apparition, then the tinkling laugh of the girl rang out and she suddenly realised this elaborately attired person was probably only her own age and already part of a mysterious, formal other world. This brief glimpse of the *geisha*, she recalled, had spoken of a wider shore of experience, beckoning her to step outside what would normally be in store for her.

Staring at her tiny figure reflected in the mirror, Hiroko swept up her hair into a high roll, turning her head this way and that to take in the effect. She wondered how different her life would have been if she had been born into a poorer family and sold into the highly structured world of a *geisha*. She missed much of the familiarity of her Japanese home, yet life here was so abundant seemed indifferent, and was a prickly little kid, he thought. You just had to know how to handle him.

'I've been thinking,' Gare mused. 'Hiroko needs to have a home of her own, rather than being here all the time with us. You know, a place she could get away to with the kids when she wanted, and just come and go as she pleased. There's all those plans of Boy's still packed away in the study, and there must be something amongst them. And we've got that old beach house in Honolulu we hardly ever use.' He paused. 'Maybe she could do something with that. If she could throw herself into a totally new project, it could be just the thing to get her mind off Satoshi.'

'Well maybe, honey, but I wouldn't count on it,' Hattie replied.

'She's still often homesick, you know, Hattie, and to have her own place might be just the answer.' Gare was warming to this idea. 'She could even bring her father out here, though I guess his health's not up to it.'

'The truth is, I think she wants him to stay in Tokyo in case there's any chance he could somehow get hold of Satoshi for her.' Hattie was unconvinced.

'Well, I've got a feeling that her own house here would help,' Gare concluded. 'Tomorrow I'll get all those plans of Boy's together and talk it over with her, and we'll see what we can do.'

Honolulu

Sitting on her bed in her chemise and scanties, Hiroko slowly rolled the tops of her silk stockings firmly around her garters, then slipped her tiny feet into her high-heeled satin pumps. She sat back and gazed at the two dresses hanging on the wardrobe door. Which one should she wear? she wondered. There was her crêpe de chine, its soft blues and discreet beading beckoning with a reassuring familiarity which comes with many wearings. The other, a Vionnet model, was one she had bought

'Listen carefully, Hiroko-chan. There are many things to tell you, about what has taken place over the years, but I'm too weak now.' He paused, gasping for breath. 'As my sole heir, it's important that you have all the papers I have kept for you. They will tell you much that you will need to know.' He turned from her for a few minutes, and she laid her hand gently upon his arm. Then he went on, his voice getting weaker. 'The deeds to all the property involved will be yours to keep and to later pass onto your children . . . my grandchildren, as you will. You have a good mind, Hiroko-chan, and you must act wisely as there is much wealth involved. It's our ancestral birthright and must be put in very safe keeping.'

He gasped for air, then went on. 'I do not trust the Nakamuras. They have involved the *Yakuza* in their dealings with me, and have behaved dishonourably and you must take great care, especially now.'

She looked at him, feeling a pang of indebtedness and fear. 'Maybe if I had stayed,' she murmured.

'Maybe, maybe not,' he replied, 'not after all that happened. You had to do what you thought best. It's of little matter now.'

One never pays one ten-thousandth of *giri-to-on* to one's parents, she thought with sadness and a sense of guilt.

Seeing the shadow pass over her face, he said, 'Please, carry no burden, daughter, I am well satisfied.' He reached out and touched her. She bowed deeply, feeling a little of the heavy weight of *giri* lifting. Raising her head she looked at him, her face wet with tears.

'Thank you, Father.' He nodded, and there was silence for some minutes, and then her voice shaking a little, she asked, 'Father, about Satoshi—have you heard anything of him recently. Anything at all?'

She held her breath, hoping against hope that at last he may have some news for her.

Yukio shook his head. 'Not for a long, long time. It's just as I wrote to you.' His voice shaking with anger, he continued, 'It's hard to believe that they wouldn't even allow him to see his own grandfather whenever I wished. And now the boy is grown. It's just too bad, but I did try, daughter.' There was a note of appeal in his voice.

'To do this to us,' she said, her voice low with emotion. 'They'll be sorry one day.'

He held up his hand to quieten her. 'That was then, this is now. One has to move on, and there is no time left for recriminations.'

Gathering his strength, he pointed to the corner of the room. 'I want you to take that chest and everything that is in it. Look now, so we can go through what is there.'

She went across to the large black lacquered chest which had excited her imagination as a child. Each corner was encased in brass, and the front panel was intricately inlaid with mother-of-pearl and coral, depicting scenes from the floating world of Yoshiwara. The tableau she had always liked most was that of two young lovers sheltering under a parasol, indicating that they had spent a night of love-making, and behind them a finely carved rural scene with Mount Fuji in the distance. The girl had a tentative air of shyness as she looked at her lover. She was dressed in a long floating kimono simply decorated with plum blossom, her hair swirled up to reveal the curved nape of her neck. Her lover encircled her protectively with his arm. Often, when gazing at them as a child, Hiroko had imagined herself in just such a situation, and now she thought of Boy and their day together at Hara, long ago.

As she unlocked and opened the chest, a sweet smell of sandalwood rose. From inside the smoothly fitted drawers and shelves, she drew out many documents and carefully went through them with her father. At length, she came to the bottom of the chest, and her father told her how to remove the false floor by pressing a hidden spring. There, carefully hidden, lay two long, narrow but deep boxes. There were also three very old books and a sword in its scabbard, wrapped in cloth.

'Go ahead, open the box,' he bade her, 'but carefully, now.'

Hiroko unknotted the tie around the light sandalwood box and inside, carefully rolled in further wrapping, was a silk scroll. She lifted it out and painstakingly unwrapped the long fine sheet of rice paper covering. Then spreading it out on the tatami floor mats, she gently unrolled the scroll on top of it. As she did, she drew in her breath, marvelling at the beauty of the piece.

'Sesshu?' she asked, looking up at her father in surprise. He looked at the painting, and smiled weakly at her. 'Yes.'

Sesshu, she thought in amazement, lightly touching it with her fingers. As one of Japan's most renowned artists of the fourteenth century during the time of the early Ashikaga shoguns, Sesshu was perhaps the most noted of all Japanese painters in the style favoured by the Chinese Sung dynasty. This eight-foot-long *Sansui Chokan* possessed the dreamlike quality of the *haboku* style, depicting a fishing village so skilfully worked that she felt she was looking through the window. The artist had caught the spirit of the place in an almost lyrical blend of brushwork and monochromal shades.

Hiroko knelt in silence, contemplating the work for some minutes, then crossing herself and bowing her head, gave thanks for such beauty. Looking up, she felt her father's feverish eyes upon her. 'So,' he said. 'I can see you realise its true value. The other is a continuation of this one, so best leave it as it is, as you would only have to repack them, and they are very fragile. They have been in our family for generations now, as has the sword.' He lay back, fighting for air.

'Make haste, child, and pack away the scroll. They must all go with you.'

'And the sword?' she asked.

He hesitated, then in a low voice she could barely catch, said, 'I would like to have given that to my first-born grandson myself, but . . .' He looked out of the window, and lay so still that she was frightened. Then he turned to her. 'I hope he will have enough of the blood of his honourable Sen ancestors to treat it with respect. You must do what you think best. Will you pack it all away, daughter—I must rest awhile.' He closed his eyes.

With great care, Hiroko rolled up the scroll and placed it in its box, then replaced it with the other documents. Then she neatly clicked the floor of the chest back into place so that there could be no trace of its hidden contents. She went across to where he lay, and gently stroked his forehead. Briefly, he opened his eyes and smiled faintly at her. She remained sitting with him, until Ume insisted on taking her place, while she took some much-needed sleep.

Four days later, Yukio Sen was dead. His small frame, neatly contained in a simple pine coffin, lay in state in the main reception room of his home, with his photograph gracing the lid, and incense burning at either side on the small Buddhist altar behind it. The room was crowded with people, and outside a table had been erected for visitors to leave a token payment towards funeral expenses.

Many of the guests Hiroko had not seen since she was a child. They cursorily, if politely, acknowledged her presence. She knew they did not approve of her, and perhaps that was why in a final freeing of tradition, she had earlier that morning decided to lay aside her kimono and wear Western dress. She had chosen a fitted black wool Lucien Lelong suit and deep blue hat with a dark silk veil that partly screened her face. She felt she needed to distance herself from a world to which she no longer truly belonged. The morning following the discussion with her father, she had put all the contents of the chest into safe keeping at her bank, awaiting her departure. She and Ume had then packed many of her father's books, paintings and personal belongings and the chest itself, ready to be shipped back to Hawaii. She had organised to lease the house to a local business family, and Ume would stay on with them, caring for it in her absence.

A movement at the door made her look up, and there

was a young man dressed in naval officer's uniform and accompanied by an older woman, whom Hiroko recognised as Michiko, her former sister-in-law. They bowed deep obeisance before the coffin, and moved to the other side of the room, partly obscured by the crowd of people.

Hiroko could not tear her eyes from the young man. Everything in the room fell away, and she stared at her son with all the longing of those years of missing, loving and wanting him. She was totally unaware of the people, the priest, the incantations. She stared hungrily at him, absorbing every precious detail: the small neat head sitting erect and proudly on his shoulders, the black hair cropped short, his ears and nose just like his father Noboru's. She noticed that the sadness of the occasion emphasised the fine line of the boy's mouth and the expression in his eyes. His stature was smaller than that of Gerard's, but poised and controlled, she saw with satisfaction.

He was truly her child, her first-born, her Satoshi-chan. But as Hiroko thought this, a tremor caught at her throat. She was, after all, gazing at a stranger, a young man of her flesh and blood, but not nurtured by or a reflection of her upbringing, not of her world. This child had become a man who knew nothing of her, nor she of him. She felt the tears start to flow, and was glad of the soft screening of her veil.

Suddenly, sensing the intensity of her presence, the boy turned and looked across the room at her. For an instant, their eyes met, and he politely looked away. Then as if by some ineffable instinct, she saw him look back and hold her gaze.

She made to move towards him, pushing through the people, ignoring their glances. She was within feet of him, her eyes never leaving his face, when Michiko suddenly turned and saw her, and giving her a cold hard look of dismissal, took him by the arm, and hurriedly left through a side door. Hiroko remained, her body frozen in shamed frustration, riveted by the flash of hatred and contempt she had seen on Michiko's face. Then a rising anger propelled her to the door, just in time to see them drive off in a long black limousine. She stared after them in dismay, seeing Satoshi's face in the rear window looking back at her with a searching expression that soon receded in the distance.

all. Just stay up. Use your arms.' He demonstrated the sweeping *Kobori* style of swimming. 'Like this.'

Looking up at Omura-san, and hating him, Satoshi shouted at him, his fear overcoming any form of deference. 'How dare you—my mother will make you pay for this!' He knew she would, when she came back.

Omura-san only smiled, and picking him up by his arm and leg, threw the struggling boy back into the water again.

* * *

Satoshi must have slept, for suddenly they had arrived at the Academy, and the driver was opening the door for him. He turned to his aunt Michiko, bowing and thanking her. She touched his arm, her eyes contemplative. 'You slept soundly, Satoshi-chan.' Unexpectedly, she smiled at him. 'If there's anything worrying you, write and tell me. Now, take your bag.'

'I will miss Grandfather,' he said, although he'd rarely been allowed to see the old man. She didn't answer, but there was a tightening of her mouth. 'I will go to his shrine very soon,' he said as if to himself. She motioned to the driver to go, and with an almost imperceptible nod of her head, she was away. He bowed again as she left, wondering what had so angered her.

* * *

'You will live as one who is not living,' his *sensei* at the Academy had told him. 'You have already passed into the next world. You are not of this world. Believe that you are already dead, so what happens to you then is of no consequence.'

Satoshi had closed his eyes, blotting out all around him. As he did so, the sharp *thwack* of a switch on his back jolted him back to the present. 'Open your eyes— see, but do not see, keep them open and look ahead. Let your spirit leave your body.' The *sensei*'s soft insistent voice swirled about him. 'Let your mind leave its cage and fly into the open fields, your heart cease its beating, and lie still. Your eyes see, but do not see. Your breath slows. Now you are not of this world. You are as one dead, and nothing matters, nothing matters, so you have the strength of one who is dead . . .'

Satoshi listened as the voice went on: 'You do not exist. You are a shadow, a mere nothing.' He felt lightheaded, and stood there unaware of time or being. It was a disembodied sensation, yet strangely powerful. His hands were cold and wet with perspiration, the hands of another. And he was surprised when he pressed them to his cheek just how cold and wet they felt. All awareness of self, his persona, seemed to dissolve into a tranced presence. It was so peaceful, almost dreamlike, this release into something outside himself, with the freedom of being—yet not being. Now he could float strong and free like some giant bird, touching down wherever and whenever he wanted. He was here—yet not here, invincible, removed from the hurts, ills and worries of his daily life.

For some time, he remained in this state, then with a sudden snap, he fell to his knees and started to cry in deep wrenching sobs of release. Just as abruptly, he started to shout and laugh with the sheer exhilaration of discovery. He could do anything, anything. It was intoxicating, fantastic.

His *sensei* stood quietly by. After some minutes, remembering him, Satoshi scrambled to his feet, bowing low. Master Yukan returned the bow, then placing his hand on the boy's shoulder said, 'Satoshi-san. Today you have learned the key to conquering yourself, your exams, whatever you do. You have experienced the "sweat of muga". You have gained control of yourself by losing all self. This lesson will never be forgotten—never!' Unexpectedly, the switch came down on Satoshi's back, driving its message home, deep into his psyche. The boy neither flinched, nor moved, but bowed in total acquiescence.

'Remember, "*Kaeru no Tsura ni mizu*" . . . it's like pouring water on a frog's face.'

Later that evening, walking to the house where he was billeted, Satoshi breathed in the pure air of early spring with an invigoration and awareness that he'd never experienced before. He had been given the key to a whole new existence, and one that would give him control and mastery of his own fate. He had never known this sense of purposefulness before. It lifted him to another plane. Now he could live with the strength and certainty of death. Anything seemed possible.

An early moon was rising in the evening sky, casting her tentative first light across the outer reaches of the Inland Sea and the mountains behind. It took his thoughts back to when he was a tiny child in a car on his way to Lake Ashimoko. His grandfather Yukio had pointed out the beauty of Fuji-san, glowing in the clear moonlight and rising from the landscape, detached, omnipotent. As the car sped past, he could remember reaching out with tiny arms and squealing with delight, as if to embrace the shimmering snow-capped peak, so pristine, so beautiful.

The faces in the car after all this time were shadowy. But the man with fair hair was there, laughing and looking with eyes like the sea at his mother. He had shrunk away from him, fearful of his strangeness, and nestled into his mother's lap, feeling the protective warmth of her body.

Fuji, with her towering white peak bathed in silvery moonlight and with stars twinkling brightly around her, had forever afterwards reminded him of that time and his first feelings of insecurity.

Now resting against a wall and gazing up at the moon, he had a fleeting memory of turning to his mother in the car, and the expression of anxiety on her face. With a start, he remembered that look, and realised that he'd seen the same expression on the woman at his grandfather's funeral earlier in the week. Then she must surely be his mother. The thought drained him of all emotion.

His mother? He had long thought of her as gone away and now probably dead. Aunt Michiko and the family never mentioned her any more. His memories of his Aunt Michiko's early rages, the beatings whenever he asked and her repeated shouts that his mother had gone away and left him, came rushing back. But this woman at the funeral must have been his mother.

Satoshi sat down at the side of the road, rerunning the scene through his mind, and the expression in her eyes as she had looked at him. The memory of the warmth and comfort of her arms around him as he'd sat on her lap filled him now with a bitter sadness, and he felt hot tears running down his face. How could she have abandoned him to the harshness of life with the Nakamura family, and to the trials of Aunt Michiko? How could she have not loved him—his own mother?

He got up, breathing deeply as he had been shown, trying to rise above the weakness of such sadness. With his resolve renewed, he took from his satchel a small woodblock drawing that his *sensei* had handed to him after the lesson that day. It was of a young child scooping a pitcher of water from a well, and splashing it over a large immobile frog. Satoshi gazed at it, singing the Haiku verse: '*Kaeru no Tsura ni mizu*,' repeating the line until he arrived home.

Later that night, he knelt before the small shrine in his room, with a photograph of his father, Noboru, in uniform. He prayed to the spirit of his dead father, his father's father, and now to his grandfather Yukio, to guide him on his chosen path. The sliding back of the *shoji* screen made him look around to see Miko, the daughter of his host family. She knelt at the entrance and bowed her apologies for intruding. He looked sternly at her; she was far from pretty and hardly worth noticing. Bowing even lower, she handed him a long parcel with an envelope attached.

'It was left for you this morning, Satoshi-san, by your late grandfather's servant, Ume-san,' she murmured,

9

SATOSHI'S DISCOVERY

With his aunt Michiko sitting stiff and disapproving beside him, Satoshi looked back at the small figure in her strange blue hat, staring after them from his grandfather's doorway. He'd sensed the intensity of her presence, her veiled eyes holding his, and the echo of a shadowy memory drifted into his consciousness. If only they'd spoken. Could it be . . .? But surely not, she looked so different from the memory of his mother he'd held close to him all these years. He had hoped that she would be there at her father's funeral. But his quick glance around the funeral guests had seen no-one who resembled her.

Without being told, he knew that somehow this woman was important to him. Watching her figure disappear, he felt a strange curiosity mixed with sadness.

He turned to ask his aunt who this person was, but she was staring out of the window, and he could tell by the rigid line of her body that she was angry, and that now was not the time for questioning. I will find out later, he thought, leaning back, enjoying the unaccustomed comfort of a cushioned head-rest. Camera-shutter glimpses of faces, doorways, other lives, flickered past them. A sweeping motion of power as the car shifted gears onto the highway added to Satoshi's anticipation.

In less than an hour, he'd be back at the Eta Jima Naval Academy.

His sense of well-being was abruptly cut short as their car entered the long city tunnel, its cement walls enveloping him in an oppressive grip. He felt the muscles in his stomach tighten, and with an involuntary intake of breath he tried to ward off the terrible claustrophobic fear that threatened to swallow him, as it always did in any enclosed space. His breathing became rapid and shallow as the familiar tightness gripped his throat. He tried to still his fear, leaning back, closing his eyes and breathing slowly. As he did, memories rose, piercing, distinct. He was in the cold waters of Lake Gasenji, a small figure just six years old, and he could see his *sensei* Master Omura's face leaning over the gunwhale of a small boat, as he sank again into the dark waters.

'Swim, Satoshi, swim!' Desperately, he tried holding his breath, terrified of swallowing or breathing in that soft insidious liquid. Clawing and scrambling, he fought for the buoyancy he'd seen in others. His head surfaced again, and he gasped for precious air, trying to reach out for the sturdy comfort of the boat from where Omura-san had thrown him. Was it only minutes ago?

'Use your arms, keep your head up. Swim, like this. Swim for your life, Satoshi!' Like a crab clawing its way in a sea of jelly, Satoshi flailed his arms, trying to keep on top of the water. As he went down again, tiredness and despair swept over him. Why was Omura-san doing this? What would his mother say, if she knew? For a moment, he almost relaxed at the thought of her, opening his mouth to call her name, and then he choked as the water surged into his throat. Panic made him kick hard, and he felt himself float up to the surface once more, choking and coughing. Hands reached out, and pulled him into the boat, where he lay crying and shivering with the cold. Omura-san knelt over him, rubbing his arms to get the circulation going.

'Satoshi, you almost have it. When you kicked to come up, you came up. Now you just have to stay up, that's smiling shyly. 'Please excuse me.' She backed out, sliding the screen into its place.

In the street outside, he could hear the harsh cry of the tofu man, and the occasional ringing of his bell as he peddled his wares past the wooden houses. Miko's mother had stopped the man, and he could hear her high voice chatting to him as she bought fresh blocks of bean curd. He looked at the letter with a feeling of apprehension. Removing it from its envelope, he saw that it was written on Washi paper in fine flowing *shodo* (calligraphy). A faint floral perfume, light and exotic, wafted from the page. He bent to smell it, and as he read, a stirring of memory took him back once more to the arms of his mother.

My son,
Seeing you today was like seeing the image of your esteemed father reborn before my eyes. He would be so proud of you, to know that you are at the Naval Academy at Eta Jima. You have a long and honourable family tradition behind you and much to live up to.

So, the mysterious woman was his mother. At the mention of his parents, he felt a familiar flicker of that terrible pain and emptiness he'd always known. Steeling himself, he read on.

It is with especial sadness that I write at this time, with the loss of my dear father and your grandfather, Yukio-san. Neither you nor I have seen as much of him as we should during the past years, and it often takes such a loss to make one fully realise that. He was a wise and admirable man, a scholar with much knowledge and wisdom to pass onto us. I trust you will pray for his spirit. Since leaving you and this country so long ago, my heart has remained here, and I have never stopped thinking of you and your welfare, and hoping we could meet. When I left for overseas, I tried to take you with me, but that was not to be.

The Nakamura family chose instead to raise you. There is much we should talk about, and we will, one day. But it seems that now is not the time.

We are seeing great changes here now, much of which disturbs me as they are not in the true spirit of Yamato. In the words of your esteemed grandfather to me not long before he died, our sword should be knowledge, and by following the true Bushido or our traditional warrior way of honour and fairness, we will show compassion and understanding in all that we do. Remember, 'No aru taka wa tsume o kakusu'—a wise hawk hides its claws.

With this firmly in mind, he requested that I pass on to you our family sword that has passed from first son to first son for twelve generations. It is now yours to guard carefully and to only ever use wisely and with discretion. I pray for your safety and well-being, and that one day in your journeying, you will choose to seek me out.
Your loving mother,
Hiroko.

Her address he noticed, was in a place called Hawaii, USA.

He sat still for some minutes, gathering his strength. The letter left him at first saddened, then with a rising sense of anger and resentment. Who was this woman to lecture him? And who was she to talk of honour? How could she know and understand what was really happening here, a mere woman? It was the height of impertinence for her to be telling him. She did not see clearly or understand the might and power of *Bushido*. She was just a silly, weak woman who had deserted him and her country. She was not a true mother of his.

Turning to the package, he opened it with great care. A long drawn-out sigh of appreciation fell from his lips as he withdrew the sword from its box and heavy black silk outer wrapping. The handle was of a simple satin-smooth wood with the Sen bamboo frond family *mon* (crest) carved into it.

He removed the protective leather scabbard and there was the curved blade, superbly honed silver-blue steel, seemingly invincible in its perfection. Reverently, he took the sword in both hands and felt an electric thrill of possession that was almost orgasmic.

A scrap of yellowed parchment had fallen from the scabbard. He picked it up and written in elegant Heian characters were the words: *'bushi no nasake'* . . . 'the warrior's sense of mercy and benevolence'.

And beneath it was written,

Isle of blest Japan!
Should your Yamato spirit
Strangers seek to scan
Say, scenting morn's sunlit air,
Blows the cherry, wild and fair.[4]

Carefully folding the paper, he returned it to the scabbard, then going to a chest containing his clothes, he took out a yellow gossamer silk scarf. He threw it into the air, watching it slowly float, light as thistledown, to the floor. As he watched, he thought of the golden hair of that *gaijin* (foreigner) with his mother. Then picking up his sword, he threw the scarf into the air again, and with a shout of *'Banzai!'*, he arched the blade through the air and sliced the scarf once, twice, then again and again as it fell to the floor. He didn't notice Miko watching him with shining eyes through a slit in the screen as the young man of her dreams turned into a warrior.

10

FLIGHT—TOKYO 1939

Boarding the large clipper plane at Hanada Airport that chilly February afternoon, Hiroko felt her usual sense of uneasiness. She feared flying, but her desire to leave Tokyo, hastened by the discussions with her father and anxiety to remove his precious Sesshu scrolls before anything happened to them, overcame her nervousness.

The malevolent expression on Michiko's face had forewarned her of unpleasantness if she stayed. The long anguished night after the funeral and her first unsatisfactory glimpse of her beloved Satoshi after all those years of waiting and wondering, together with the knowledge that her father was no longer there to aid and protect her, had left her feeling lost and abandoned.

Her life was no longer here in this closely structured and mannered society. However, one part of her still longed for that once easily assumed familiarity of belonging to an ordered, if patriarchal, existence. But the pull of new horizons and the life she had now made for herself and her children as part of the Baillieu family in Hawaii had long overcome the strictures and obligations of her youth.

As her father had advised, she must leave and leave quickly. His books, pictures and furniture, including the chest and the personal items she wished to keep, she had packed and left with the Canadian Pacific Line to be shipped to Honolulu later that week. She took with her only a small trunk containing a few clothes and her mother's and grandmother's jewellery which her father had given to her, along with a selection of his rare books.

She packed in a separate soft leather bag an ancient urn containing her father's ashes, the scrolls carefully packed in silk cloth and a light wooden box stamped with the family *mon*, along with the deeds of his Ebisu house, some commercial property in Kyoto and Tokyo and the summerhouse at Lake Ashimoko. This she was to carry onto the plane with her. The Arita porcelain urn, delicately decorated in sea swirls of deep blue and silver on a creamy white background, had belonged to her father's mother, and had been kept for just this occasion. It was wrapped in a heavy silk crêpe de chine *furoshiki* together with a lacquered tablet clearly inscribed with her father's Buddhist name.

After Yukio's cremation, she had requested the loyal and trusted Ume to supervise the gathering of his ashes. They were put into the urn along with the small vital bones representing different parts of her father's body, selected by Ume and including the Buddha-shaped Adam's apple, considered the most sacred of all.

'Take my ashes with you,' Yukio had requested, 'and when this coming battle is over, I wish you to return them to the shrine at Hakone overlooking the forest and lake of my boyhood, and place them in the family tomb.'

Hiroko had bowed her head in acquiescence, feeling the pain of imminent loss of this scholarly and gentle man. He had lain still a while looking out at the bright golden fruit on his favourite persimmon tree, the silence broken only by the harsh cry of passing black birds and his sudden bouts of coughing.

Then turning to her, he had said, 'I have no sons or sons-in-law and my eldest grandson has been taken away by his father's family. By their action, it is clear that the Nakamura family have not extended their rightful respect and courtesy to the house of Sen.' Looking up at her, he said, 'If, daughter, you feel that Satoshi should rightfully inherit this property in time, it is for you to decide. I have brought you up to think well in business matters,' he smiled at her, 'and in your case the old saying "a woman can have no house of her own in the Three Universes", we will have to bend a little.'

He had another severe coughing bout and lay back, panting and weak. She smoothed his forehead with a damp cloth. He felt hot and feverish. 'Father, you must rest a little.'

'No, no,' he answered, looking anxious, 'there's so much more to say and so little time. Hiroko, as a true daughter of our old and honourable *samurai* family, you have much to live up to now. As has been the custom of my father and his father before him, our sword shall be our knowledge. We will win our rightful place, not through ignorance and brutality, but through true understanding and our power shall come through using knowledge to further our great nation. Well gone are the days of *sakoku*, as more and more we look outward to the world beyond, truth and expansion.'

He paused, then went on. 'Unfortunately, before change for the better, there is often terrible conflict. The Kami-Kaze wind of the gods shall blow through our land, bringing with them enormous change. It's best for you to be away from here at this time, and return later with the productive peace that will come. *No aru taka wa tsume o kakusu,* A wise hawk hides its claws.' He smiled at her, and turning on his side, closed his eyes.

Later in the early hours of the morning, with Hiroko still beside him, he had released his last breath with a long drawn-out sigh.

The trip out to the airport had further added to her sense of alienation. The unfinished business with Satoshi and seeing her father, then gaining his blessing and forgiveness only to lose him, made her feel that this was truly the end of her life in Japan.

Speeding through the crowded streets, her taxi had been suddenly stopped by an accident only a few cars away in front of them. An armoured tank leading a convoy of trucks had veered in front of a small truck loaded with melons, hitting it head-on so that it skidded and bounced into an adjacent pole. As they came to a stop, then eventually crawled past, she remembered the dazed expression on the driver's face, still bleeding, and he in shock from the crash. He was an old man, and she could see that he was in pain and near collapse.

A strutting young army officer, with a belligerent air of assumed command, had the melon truck pushed aside as though it were of little consequence. She had seen him roughly shove the old man when he staggered to his feet in protest. With not a hint of concern or deference to the other's age and weakened state, the officer had laughed and leapt aboard the tank, motioning the convoy ahead with never a backward glance. As the trucks rolled by, she had glimpsed the other young faces, set and determined in their pursuit of war, and her heart sank. Would this be her Satoshi too? Would he have treated the old man in this same shameful way, hiding behind the protection of his uniform and rank? Was this to be the new order of the day?

She had closed her eyes to the noise of the crowds and the look in the old man's eyes. It was all so ugly. War was ugly.

Her father's words floated back. 'It will be very bad for you to stay here after I'm gone.' What was happening to her country, the country of her birth, of her ancestors, her beloved Japan? This new nationalistic hum and fervour, rather than imbuing her with pride and a sense of participation, filled her with foreboding.

'You have changed, Hiroko-san,' her friend Suzue Ueda-san had said when she came to pay her respects, not long before Hiroko left. Over tea, they had spoken a little of their schooldays and happier times so long ago. But Hiroko felt that a gulf of changing attitudes and experiences now lay between them. Gone were the happy-go-lucky days of whispered girlish confidences and, it seemed, their pact to be lifelong friends.

Her friend's politely veiled embarrassment and disapproval of her marrying a foreigner and leaving all her responsibilities behind now lay—an unspoken buffer—between them. Suzue talked a little of her son Hideyoshi-chan's training at the naval college, and of her husband General Hideyoshi Ueda who was in charge of an army battalion, with a sense of quiet pride in their chosen paths and commitment to the Emperor.

Looking at Suzue, her snowy *tabi*-covered feet carefully tucked to one side, so neat and contained in her best silk kimono, her sweet face alight and animated as she spoke of her family, Hiroko felt a rush of fondness for her friend. She thought that but for meeting Boy and their going away, she could well have been sitting there, just like Suzue, speaking and thinking much as her friend did.

With a new elation, she felt she had been released from a cage of hidebound traditions and expectations. Admittedly, she had moved into yet another world of certain customs and manners, but it was one more of her making and not so dependent on that of others.

When Suzue rose to go, Hiroko hurried to her case and extracted a small parcel. With a deep bow handed it to her friend. That once familiar smile of pleasure lit up Suzue's face, as with a gasp of delight she unwrapped and held up a string of Mikimoto pearls glowing a soft pink in the late afternoon light. Alongside them was a small red and gold brocade *omamori* with the name of the goddess Amaterasu, from whom the Emperor was descended, written on the outside.

'Why, it's the one we got the day our class went to Ise,' Suzue said.

'The day our friendship began,' added Hiroko. 'I want you to keep it for me until I return with my father's ashes. It will help protect you and your family, and keep our friendship alive, despite the distance that lies between us and whatever may happen.'

Tears rose in Suzue's eyes. 'Nothing has really changed, Hiroko-san,' she whispered, 'not in our hearts.'

She reached out, touching Hiroko's arm. 'I will keep it safely for you, until you return.'

Now, after hours of relatively smooth flying, the plane touched down at Guam. She had been unable to sleep and had watched as the island rose to greet them, its fringing coral reef a ring of opalescent blue-green set in a cobalt sea. Then they were flying low over brilliant stretches of dense jungle highlighted by towering groves of coconut palms that rushed past them, so close they seemed like a lush green carpet.

She glimpsed long white windswept beaches, lagoons fringed by outstretched curving palms and strange stick pandanus trees. As they flew in low over Apra Harbour, she could see its silvery waters stretching as far as the capital of Agana.

A heavy rain squall had followed them in from the sea as they landed, bouncing onto the tarmac and skidding to a halt. It wasn't until they reached the air terminal that she heard there was a typhoon warning, and that they would not be proceeding until the weather cleared.

Hiroko felt shaken by the landing and the sudden oppressive humidity after the chill of Tokyo. Taking her case with her, she went to a waiting room to freshen up. She saw reflected a small Japanese woman, plainly if expensively dressed in her linen slacks and light jacket, and sighed. She felt caught between two cultures and couldn't wait to get back now to the comfort and beauty of her Hawaiian home.

She sponged her face from a bottle of rose-scented water she kept for travelling, then applied a light cream. As she smoothed it well into her skin, she started to feel a sense of rejuvenation. A touch of coral lipstick, and her face took on a new vibrancy—the large white diamond earrings Boy had given to her when they married providing a magnificent flashing foil to her blue-black hair.

She sat in the small airport restaurant drinking tea. A tall man she had noticed sitting in front of her on the plane was looking across the restaurant towards her. She returned his gaze with a feeling she had seen him somewhere before.

She took another quick look. He was in earnest conversation with a young Japanese man who had also been on the flight. They were speaking in low voices and it was impossible to hear what was being said. She noticed the man who had stared at her was dressed quite casually in pants and white shirt, and looked American.

He had some of Boy's clean-cut good looks, but not the golden laughing quality of her Boy. And then she remembered—he was very like that man of the night of Grace's party, the one she had almost erased from her mind. She turned away, pushing those dark memories from her, and she thought of Boy with a pang . . . so long ago since his death, but only yesterday in her heart. There had been other men attracted to her, but always she felt as if she were still part of Boy, just waiting for the time they would be re-united in the promised spirit world of heaven.

She toyed with the ayuyu crab salad. It had a delicious coconut flavour but she was too tired to eat. The young Japanese man with his black-lacquer eyes so still and yet assessing, reminded her of Satoshi, and she wondered how he had felt when he read the letter she had sent with Ume. At least I will have made contact with my son, she thought, and given him the chance to write to me, if he wishes.

But she had written so many letters to him over the years. None was ever answered. And she wondered if this time, having seen her, he may just respond.

Later, she wandered back into the terminal, buying some aromatic banana-flavoured biscuits and a woven palm leaf basket for Lalana at a stall run by two Chamorro women. A message came through the loudspeaker announcing that the typhoon had changed direction and veered north and away from their flight path, so they could board once more.

Hiroko slept for the remaining hours of their flight, the young Japanese man's face appearing and reappearing with that of Satoshi's in her dreams.

11

GERARD—HONOLULU

Gerard swam in slow, powerful strokes in the swell just off Diamond Head. He loved the feel of the sea on his body and, like flying, the sense of weightlessness it imparted. This was his element, perhaps the place where he most felt at one with himself and the world. It was truly '*he enahu*', a merging and melting with the flow of the ocean, the air and the heavens beyond.

The sun was receding from the sky, hastening to its home beyond the horizon, leaving a trail of brilliant incandescent bursts of colour. Each wisp of cloud caught refracted light, palest spun gold to deepening pinks, sienna, magenta and fiery red against a brilliant clear turquoise backdrop.

The ever-changing opulence of the Hawaiian sky had long been a touchstone in his life. He turned over, looking at the heavenly artwork opening up above and around him. But the perfect moment had not yet arrived. Ten more minutes, when the sun finally set and evening rushed in with its deeper greys and blues and the first scattering of pin-point stars, that would be the moment.

He backstroked, feeling the muscles in his neck and shoulders tightening and relaxing as he built up pace. Then turning towards the shore, he swam steadily into the beach, catching a wave closer in to the shore.

That special moment had arrived as he walked up onto the beach, gazing at the stars twinkling into life across the heavens as the last rays of deepening green sank into the sea. The first lights from the street lamps were starting to flicker along Kalakaua Avenue, and a heady mix of plumeria frangipani, coconut oil and the smoke from cooking fires wafted down across the beach on the evening breeze.

Towelling himself dry, Gerard bent to pick up the lei that Lalana had made him earlier in the day with flowers fresh from the garden. It had been waiting for him in fragrant welcome when he arrived back from Maui. Tying his towel in a sarong around his waist, he circled the lei about his shoulders so that its perfume floated with him as he bicycled along Kalakaua Avenue past the Kuhio seawall and up the hill towards Diamond Head and the home Hiroko kept overlooking the sea.

As he rode under the timber *torii* gate and up along the driveway past the carefully raked sand garden, and saw the house with its elegant lines and graceful curve of its tilted roof, he felt the thrill of homecoming. This was truly home. Not the lush green Maui plantation, nor the endless vista of the family's 'Winganna' property in Queensland, Australia, but here.

Hiroko had had it built to her own and his father Boy's planned specifications by local Japanese craftsmen, on the exact place where Grandpa Gare and his grandmother Hattie's beach house had once stood. In a sense, despite his youth, that night and the fire had been a turning point for him, when he realised that he, Gerard, could take control when needed.

With a pang he recalled that it was not long after the fire, when they were staying at 'Winganna', that Grandpa Gare had died. But not before he had left generous provision in his will for Hiroko, and her plans for the house. It was a classical and graceful Japanese residence of free-flowing, aristocratic proportions. She had cleverly incorporated some of the best of European and Island design, so that it sat resplendent yet harmonious in its surrounds, its patrician Japanese restraint and classicism blending comfortably with the lushness of the spectacular Island backdrop and vegetation. Grandma Hattie, he remembered, had eyed it with surprise and suspicion at first, but she too had grown to love it, and spent much of her time there when she first came to Honolulu for her medical tests and treatment at the onset of her illness.

The wicks had been lit in the stone lanterns at the front door and cast their shadowy light across the terrazzo floor as he parked his bike near the entranceway.

'You're late, Master Gerard.' Lalana's broad good-natured face looked concerned as she greeted him at the door. She followed him into the outer vestibule where he removed his sandals. 'Your mother's waiting out on the lanai. She arrived back two hours ago, and was not too pleased as she thought you'd be here to greet her.'

He could never do anything right for Hiroko. He felt his stomach tighten as he walked through the steamy *ibusuki* bath house and out onto the spacious lanai, the light falling soft and diffused through the *shoji* panels.

'Mamma.' She turned to greet him, a smile lighting her face, but not her eyes, he noticed.

'Gerard-chan!' She moved over to him, embracing him, then standing back laughing. 'My goodness, you get bigger every minute—so tall now. Come, I want to talk, and then you can get changed for dinner.'

She looked tiny and fragile, he thought. She wore a yellow and white flower patterned silk kimono, the tightly fitting *obi* emphasising her birdlike frame. He was surprised to see her in Japanese dress. She hardly ever wore a kimono, favouring the colourful Hi-lo Hattie cottons cinched into her waist. It was always a spare, sleek look. No billowy *muu-muus* for her. Her oiled black hair with its deep upswept roll across her forehead was caught up with combs at the back, emphasising her long neck and delicate jawline. She was still a beauty, but one whose life spark and animation had been stilled from within.

'You've signed up then for the naval reserve, Lalana tells me,' she said.

'Yes, but it's flying I really want to get into. Bill and I flew with old Buster Morris in his tiger moth on the property next to "Winganna" last holidays. It was great,' he recalled. 'And now Bill's planning to go off to Canada to train as a pilot and I just wish I could go too.' Since receiving his cousin Bill Baillieu's letter, he thought constantly about flying. This was the thing that appealed to him most.

'Well anything's possible,' Hiroko said slowly, 'but I had hoped you would come back to Maui and help out there for a while longer.' She hesitated. 'It's going to be difficult, Gerard-chan, with the war in Europe and my being Japanese. It's not even as though I was born here.' She was still, and he sensed a longing and a conflict she could not express. Changing the subject, she went on.

'I hear you've been busy while I've been away, *ne*?' He nodded and told her what had been happening at the plantation on Maui during her absence. He spoke with an authority and understanding for one so young. She could see that already Gerard was slipping quite naturally into his place as head of the family.

As a small boy, especially since the fire, he'd been Gare's shadow, listening and watching. After his grandfather's tragic death, he continued to learn from Hattie and herself all there was to know in running the plantation. He'd quickly become friendly with the plantation managers, expanding his knowledge and familiarising himself with the working of the business side. As if to take the place of his grandfather Gare, he naturally took the lead in whatever he did. But now, what was to happen with this war moving closer to them? She would probably have two sons involved. Not for the first time, Hiroko felt a real sense of dread.

She hadn't realised until now just how much she was coming to depend on Gerard. If only Satoshi had been part of our life too, she thought, with a familiar ache. She had tried, but somehow she couldn't feel for Gerard as she did for her first-born, the one wrenched from her life.

She looked across at her second son, his face expectant, waiting for her to speak. He always seemed so tightly coiled, containing himself, waiting for the moment of release. Maybe as a *Nisei*, and with the strength of the Baillieu name and wealth to back him, he would be safe from any animosity here. But she wondered and worried. 'Your father would be proud of you,' she said suddenly, looking at him appraisingly. At the thought of Boy, a shadow passed across her face.

'Mamma, what is it?'

'Nothing, I was just thinking,' she said. 'Pour me a drink, will you, Gerard-chan? Have one too. Lalana mixed them specially for us.'

He reached for the tall crystal jug, the ice clinking against its sides as he stirred. Tiny white orchids floated on top of the frothy melange of fresh lime, mango, coconut milk and white rum. As they sat in the velvety night sipping their drinks, Gerard wondered what it was that she wanted to tell him, but did not hasten the moment by asking. He had never felt truly at ease with her. She made him only too aware of that other side of himself, the Japanese side, which as yet had not fully emerged or been encouraged, but had somehow been submerged in Hawaii and his many holidays at 'Winganna' in Australia.

'Winganna', the sprawling cattle property outside Townsville in Queensland, was owned by grandfather Gare's younger brother, Jack Baillieu, and his wife Molly. It had become a second home to him. Jack's sons Bill and Tom had been more like brothers than cousins—especially Bill. With Bill, it was almost a meeting of souls, bonded by a shared sense of rebelliousness and, lately, a passion for collecting everything they could on flying, each determined to outdo the other.

Gerard recalled how they'd race their horses downhill towards the highest holding fences near the homestead, and as they sailed over, he would experience that exhilarating sense of lift-off, a freeing that heightened his desire to conquer the vast skies above 'Winganna' and his island home. And now, he thought, this passion they shared to become airborne was fuelled by the oncoming conflict, and he couldn't wait to get into it.

His uncle Jack wasn't all that keen on their doing anything that didn't relate to work around the property, and would always get stuck into Bill. Tom never seemed to do any wrong in the eyes of his dad, but then Tom was always a bit of a suck-up-sissy anyway. He had a sudden recollection of their cousin Jill, who had come to live at 'Winganna', standing up for Tom when he and Bill had been teasing him unmercifully one day after they'd found him crying just like a girl over something or other. He could see her face now, alight with indignation as she tried to comfort Tom. As girls came, she was OK, he thought, but always hanging around them and staring at him with those big blue eyes of hers. But then he and Bill could always give her the slip whenever they chose. He smiled, remembering how easy it was.

It was Bill who'd more than filled the role of the half-brother he'd never met in Japan. Knowing Hiroko's leaning towards Satoshi, he had chosen to largely ignore the Japanese side of himself as retaliation for the ongoing sense of his mother's rejection. It was a dualism that he had never really come to terms with.

Hiroko had made sure that both he and Gina spoke the language well, but unlike his twin who embraced the whole of her background—both East and West—Gerard knew comparatively little of his Japanese inheritance. It was a shadowy, almost unknown world, and this often made him feel at a disadvantage, especially now with all this talk of war, and the death of a grandfather in Japan whom he had never really known. It seemed to be coming back to haunt him.

In the seventeen years of his life, it had taken every inch of skill for him to blend with the varied settings and situations in which he'd found himself. But he was a chameleon by instinct, with an easy charm when he wished, and good looks. For Gerard, it was a fortunate blending of the best of both worlds, as his twin sister Gina had laughingly once told him. He was surely learning the power of his presence, with everyone but his mother.

Hiroko was now leaning back gazing at the sky. She seemed more than usually reflective tonight.

'And Grandfather Yukio, how did it all go?' he asked awkwardly.

'He was very sick and exhausted towards the end,' she sighed. 'We had so little time.' Then as if to reassure herself, 'But now he's at peace with his honourable ancestors, and with our Lord,' she added, crossing herself as she spoke.

She didn't want to elaborate, he could see, and he fell silent. He'd long felt cheated of this side of the family, a side of his inheritance which he knew so little about. There had only been the few letters, and the picture on his mother's bureau of a strange old man who seemed part of another world. And now it was too late to ever get to know him. He experienced a sudden sense of loss.

He thought of Gare, and of the father he had never known. Gare had been more like a father than a grandfather, he recalled. He'd been the one person he felt he could completely trust, could really talk to. Gare would always listen, and treat him as if what he thought and said counted. Sudden memories of the events surrounding Gare's death at 'Winganna' crowded in, unbidden, and he pushed them back. Everyone of importance in my life seems to die, he thought, with that familiar hollow of loneliness.

'I saw 'Toshi,' Hiroko said suddenly. He looked at her in amazement. 'Where? How did you manage that?' She didn't answer, and when she turned to face him, to his surprise he saw that tears were trembling on her lashes. He had never before seen her cry, and she looked at him with an expression so tragic that it touched an inner chord with a bitterness he could hardly bear. This was the son she truly loved, the one she had longed for, not with any great outward show, but without ever ceasing. This was the son she had passionately missed and loved—Satoshi, not him.

He couldn't bring himself to go to her or say anything. A dull ache of disappointment held him firmly to his chair. She suddenly got up and with a small bow, said, 'Excuse me, Gerard-chan, I'll be back soon.' She left the room in a quick flutter of silk, like a bird seeking refuge, her white *tabi*-covered feet moving fleetingly across the polished boards.

Some minutes later she came back, looking pale but composed. She was carrying a large parcel, carefully wrapped in deep red paper with cream chrysanthemums scattered across its surface, and on top some neatly folded black silk.

'For you,' she smiled up at him. 'First the top one,' as he lifted it carefully and held it up. It was a fine black silk kimono with the embossed Sen family bamboo *mon* in deep blue and red. As he looked at it, he felt a strange sense of transgression—this had belonged to someone else such a short while ago, and now gone forever.

'It's very old,' she said, 'a ceremonial kimono, and I know Grandfather Yukio would have wanted you to have it. Now open the other one,' she added as he laid it aside. Carefully, so as not to tear the paper, he opened the parcel, and inside was a long slim sandalwood box tied with dark blue cotton ribbon. He touched its smooth surface.

'Go on, open it,' his mother softly chided. Untying the ribbon and lifting the lid, he was aware of a faint musky sandalwood perfume as he looked inside. In a cotton cloth was a large lacquered box, its ivory and gold inlay catching the light. He lifted it out, marvelling at the intricate patterns. He ran his fingers over the delicate shapes of flowers and butterflies along its sides, observing how in one corner of the box, from a sea of reeds bent to the wind, a graceful crane took flight. He stared at the bird as if transfixed, sensing that moment, that breathtaking leap and lift into the sky.

'It was your grandfather Yukio's,' he heard her saying, 'from Edo (Tokyo) in the last century, and so very old.'

He looked across at her, his mind a turmoil of conflicting thoughts and feelings, for the Japanese grandfather he had hardly known, and of what she had just said about seeing Satoshi, anxious to know more, but sensing this was not the time to ask.

'Look inside,' she said.

'There's more?'

'Silly boy, just look.'

Inside lay a large flat book.

'It's one of the first 200 sets printed in 1834 of Ando Hiroshige's "Fifty-three stations of the Tokaido". Fifty-five if you include the bridges of Edo and Kyoto,' said Hiroko. 'It's really quite rare and precious now.'

This book, the ancestral sword and the scrolls were probably amongst her father's most treasured possessions, she thought, as she sat back, watching him open it.

Gerard saw that the prints had been specially bound in Japanese washi, with transluscent rice paper sheets between each page to protect them.

As he turned the pages, it was like setting out on a journey into a highly stylised magical landscape, timeless in its appeal. There was a deep stirring within him, a sense of familiarity and belonging with the ever-changing seasons depicted in the fresh, free-flowing style of the artist. He was there, part of the elements, as he passed through the paddyfields and mountain passes, across rivers and lakes to the sea, all depicting the detail of daily life as the artist had experienced it on his journey along the great Tokaido Road.

He could almost feel the sunlight of the long afternoons, the bamboos bending before the driving rains on the slopes of the Suzuka river outside Sono, the warmth and camaraderie in the intimate glimpses of the inns at Akasaka. The colours and shapes of Hiroshige's landscape seemed to draw him into its heart, as he moved with the streams of pilgrims and adventurers alike, stopping to pay homage at the Buddhist temples and Shinto shrines along the way, waiting to be ferried across rivers and lakes, passing farm workers bent over their crops in the enduring peace of the countryside. And always, Fuji, the largest shrine of all, ever present to guide them along the way.

Gazing at this almost ritualistic pilgrimage, Gerard sensed a similarity in the animistic spirit that linked the two islands he had sprung from, Japan and Hawaii.

'Your father and I travelled down the Tokaido road. We were so happy then,' Hiroko mused. 'We never did the entire trip. We planned to . . . but by then it was too late.' She looked up at her son. 'You will have to complete it for us one day,' she said. She smiled at him, and he felt momentarily warmed that she'd confided in him.

'I would like to have gone with you and father, and grandfather too. I wish I had known them,' he said, feeling cheated and angry at the fates that had deprived him of this other life of which he knew so little. First a father, and now a grandfather in Japan, whom he'd never known. This book was the closest he'd ever come, and it would be all that was left.

'One day you must go,' Hiroko affirmed, as she gazed at the precious pictures. But he knew instinctively that it would be very different by then.

12

HATTIE'S DREAM—MAUI

The hollow bell-like sounds of halliards banging against steel masts in the bay below her bedroom dragged Hattie Baillieu from a heavy sleep. Awakened, she lay still, silently cursing the strong winds that had triggered those tiny alarms.

As always in that still blue time before dawn, worrying thoughts started to rush in. Willing her mind to shut them out, she turned on her side and soon started to drift, trance-like, into a light then deeper sleep.

She felt herself floating through a dense mist as though on wings. The mist grew lighter and she was looking down on a large grey shape. As she floated in closer, the mist suddenly lifted and everything was bathed in a golden light. Below, she saw a line of ships with decks stretching as far as the eye could see. Sailors strolled the decks and went about their work purposefully, yet unconcerned. Everything seemed orderly yet relaxed.

She drifted in across a becalmed ocean, glassy in its perfection. She hovered, willing herself to get in closer and be part of what was going on, to actually step onto the deck. But her dream kept her suspended aloft.

A young man looked up at her, and something in the sweetness of his gaze caught at her throat with a wrenching sadness. He laughed, throwing back his head and closing his eyes as he did. There was something in his look so familiar that it sparked a long-lost memory. She wanted more than ever now to land on the deck beside him. But some overpowering force kept her pinned in space.

In a voice that wasn't her own, but deeper and with an unfamiliar accent, she heard herself call out to him, 'Hiro. It's me, Hiro, it's me.'

He stared up, unseeing. But she could see the carefree expression on his face changing to one of wonder, then concentration, as his eyes started to scan the sky. Suddenly she was aware of a deep droning from somewhere far away. It drew closer, became louder and louder, and she was suddenly frightened.

The sky had darkened but the sun glared bright red and menacing. She tried desperately now to get to the young man, to lift him from the deck. But her arms moved as though bound in leaden bands and she was being drawn away from him. The once golden deck was bathed in a white light, the sun a red ball against the white. She was being sucked away from him in whirling turbulence that became an overwhelming roar, like the eye of a hurricane.

A shadow dark as night had enveloped the deck and the young man threw up his arms. Flashes of light and metal strafed the deck, exploding in great bursts of flame that leapt towards her. An overwhelming sadness engulfed her as she watched the flames springing up everywhere on the deck below.

Suddenly the ship sank, and there was only a dark slick of oil spreading across the sea, and bobbing on its surface, leis of plumeria encircling small white cloth-covered boxes with strange black lettering.

Dimly through her sleep, she could hear ships' bells faintly beneath the water and she awoke once more to the sound of the halliards ringing below in the bay. She was still sobbing with the terrible anguish and loss carried over from her dream.

'Gran, what's wrong, why are you crying?'

Already in her school uniform, Gina was standing at the side of the bed, a worried expression on her smooth young face.

'It was a dream, only a dream.' Hattie sat up. 'But it had such a feeling of . . . somehow it was so real.'

She drew Gina to her, seeking comfort in the familiar warmth and childish reality. There were dark rings beneath Gina's lower lashes and a pale, transluscent fragility to her skin. Hattie could hear a faint wheeze as the child inhaled shallow breaths, as if to place less stress on her lungs and hold at bay the asthma that always hovered and threatened. She had been given none of Gerard's physical resistance. Even before birth, Gerard had commandeered his twin's share of robust strength, and arrived the more dominant and demanding of the two.

'Were you dreaming about Grandpa Gare?' Gina asked.

'Dreaming yes, but no, not of Grandpa. It was like . . .' Hattie hesitated.

'Like something that's coming,' Gina interrupted, homing in intuitively. Not waiting for an answer, she slid off the bed.

'Gran, can we talk about it later? I've really got to fly now. It's my piano lesson, remember? Can you give me some money for lunch, but hurry,' she went on. Hattie looked at the clock as she reached for her purse.

'But it's only eight.'

'I know, but we're starting early. 'Bye Gran!' She gave her grandmother a quick kiss and was gone.

Gina could never wait. Everything was for the moment, to be lived and devoured in large gulps and without delay, almost as if her time was measured, and she'd let no one deter her. At the moment, all her energy was going into her music. It was a calming panacea to her bouts with asthma.

Hattie lay back. Just for five minutes more, she reassured herself, before getting up and starting the day.

Her dream still hung there, casting its shadow around her heart. A vague sadness and sense of incompleteness always seemed to be with her now that Gare was gone, like unfinished business. She willed her mind back to the details of her dream. She remembered hearing someone once say that unless one consciously recalled the dream immediately upon awaking, it was gone forever.

A sixth sense told her that this was a dream of precognition, of something linked through the past to the future, and important to remember. She had seen through a fish-eye lens, the landscape of her dream taking on a conical curve to allow her to look both backwards and forwards in time. What was the name she had used she wondered, and was it really her calling or someone else? She tried to hear the voice in her mind. It was a little like Hiroko's, but not Hiroko, she knew.

Hattie walked out onto the balcony, to a sea sun-washed to a glistening aquamarine, the white capped waves whipped up by the Kona winds throwing their spray into the air. It was going to be a clear day, despite the wind, and the sun hung low on the horizon. As she looked, she remembered the blood red orb of her dream against the dark shadow in the sky, and she shivered in apprehension.

Hattie was not one to take lightly these feelings of foreboding. Superstition was her second nature, and from childhood she had known that this intuitive sense which she shared with her fey New England grandmother was the gift of second sight. In her case, only a occasional fleeting experience, but one that made her certain that this dream was a warning, and later, as she breakfasted on coffee and fruit, she recorded it in her diary.

'Hiro.' That was the name she had called out. 'Hiro.' Such a strange name to use, she thought. Maybe that was how she'd seen him—as a hero. But no, it was his name. How Gare would have laughed at her, she thought.

At the memory of Gare, her heart sank. Would this sense of loss never leave her? Death to her was not the mysterious and frightening thing it was to most. But an unexplained death, a life and a relationship cut short and ended before it had worked out its time—that was another matter. With Gare, she had been given no warning as she had earlier for Boy, and now the two were gone. She knew that somehow Boy's death had never been quite reinforced in her mind, as she had not seen his body after death. He had been there, whole and vital to her before he left to go overseas, and then he had never come back. There were missing pieces that still had to be filled in and explained.

She recalled her grief and anger when she learned that Hiroko had arranged Boy's cremation before leaving Japan. At first, she had refused to believe that the ashes in the urn were those of her son. It was almost laughable; in fact, she had laughed—then cried, at the incongruity of the whole thing. Only Hiroko's grief-stricken face and sense of dismay at having done the wrong thing had pulled her together. She saw in that instant the young woman's love for him, and putting her arms around her, Hattie felt that this, and the twins, were Boy's parting gift to her and Gare, and that they must go on from there.

It's been eighteen years since Boy's death, she thought, followed later by his father's fatal accident in Australia. Gare, her Gare, always so strong with a vitality and light that one could never imagine being extinguished so soon. It was he who had given her strength when Boy died. Gare who had taken Hiroko and the children, almost as if they were his own, and made them an integral part of the life on the plantation in Maui. It had been Gare who had discerned Hiroko's ability to manage and assist with their numerous business interests, and Gare who, diverting the energies he had once put into Boy, taught her and showed her how to adjust to their life on the Island.

To Gerard, especially, he became a second father. The little boy had followed him everywhere like a small shadow, drawn to his expansiveness and warmth. What cruel twist of fate had pinioned Gare beneath the tractor that day while throwing the boy well clear? How were these choices made—that one life should be spared and another taken, as if by some whim of chance? When Gare's brother Jack had cabled with the terrible news, she had left Hawaii almost immediately, telling him that everything must wait, the funeral, everything, till she got there.

She couldn't and wouldn't believe that he had gone. She had to see the body for herself.

Hattie remembered her surprise when Jack's wife Molly had tentatively suggested she could lend her a black dress for the funeral. It was only then that the full realisation had dawned. 'A black widow, me?' She had laughed and laughed, her laughter ending in hysterical tears. 'Are you crazy?' she'd cried. 'There'll be no widow's weeds for me. Nothing will ever make me wear black, not ever.'

She had insisted that Gerard take her to exactly where the accident had happened.

'Let Jack show you,' Molly had offered.

'No, Gerard will take me,' she had demanded, her voice rising. Molly had given her a searching look, she remembered, then said quietly, 'Gerard loved Gare too, Hattie. Be easy on him. It has been hard for him, too. He hasn't even cried or . . .'

'Well maybe it hasn't been as hard as you think. After all, Gare was my husband and he's only a child.'

'That's exactly what I mean,' said Molly. 'Gare was like a father to him.'

But Hattie wasn't to be dissuaded. She resented the taking of the one, and leaving of the other, that he had survived and not her Gare. She should punish him for that.

Molly went on. 'He has bottled it all up, and the shock of seeing his grandfather like that. He even tried to push the tractor off him, can you imagine?'

But Hattie said nothing. Her mind was made up. Gerard would take her to where it had happened.

It wasn't far from the homestead, in one of the lower paddocks, and it had only taken them twenty minutes or so to walk there. They had hardly spoken; she felt too angry and upset. How could Gare have left her like this, especially now with Boy gone, and Hiroko and the children to care for?

Gerard seemed to sense her feelings. He mostly stared at the ground, his head bent forward and shoulders hunched, his hands in his pockets, she recalled, hurrying slightly ahead of her, scuffing his shoes against the hummocks of grass as he went.

How could Jack have ever settled in this god-awful place? she thought. It was so dry, and unending in its harshness. There was none of the lush and more contained beauty of her beloved Hawaiian island. The sun here had a probing intensity that wouldn't let up. The heat was almost tangible.

Eventually, they arrived where it had happened. The tractor had been removed and there was nothing left to mark the event. Gerard didn't say anything, but stopped walking. 'It was here?' Hattie asked. He nodded, still looking at the ground, at anywhere but at her.

What a god-awful place to end your days, she thought again. Somehow she had never really imagined what it would be like when death came, or where it would happen. Simply that it would be when they were together, of that she'd felt sure. So much for my sixth sense, she thought now.

'Take care of yourself, hon!' She could hear Gare's voice as he'd left that morning before flying out to Australia. He'd laughed and winked at her and she recalled how she had called, 'Wait Gare, wait.' She had run to him and had given him a last hug and kiss, as if to prolong their parting.

Maybe she had sensed something even then. But that was how it had always been between them, she thought now, the small sense of sadness, a death-like winding down at every leave-taking.

'Can't I go back now?' A small voice cut across her thoughts. Gerard was staring at her with a brooding expression.

'Of course not. Don't be silly, you stay right here till I'm ready.' The boy said nothing. She knew she shouldn't have been so abrupt. There were shades of Hiroko in her dealings with him, but she couldn't help herself. A light wind had sprung up and the air was full of black ash from the seasonal burning of cane on the coast. She sat heavily on a tree stump, staring around, looking for some indication of the event.

'Come here and sit down,' she called to Gerard, who had wandered off, and was staring moodily into the distance. He acted as if he hadn't heard.

'Gerard!' she called louder. 'Do you hear me? Come and sit down at once!' He came a little closer and sat staring at the ground.

He could be a perverse creature she thought. She just couldn't feel for him as she did for Gina. Aware of Hiroko's indifference to him, she had tried to get closer but it was always as if he wanted to push her away. Molly's voice intruded on her thoughts. 'Don't be hard on him.'

Stupid bitch, what does she know, she thought angrily. She remained, taking in everything that was there, trying to will some last message, some link with Gare from this desolate spot. But nothing came.

Gerard tried not to look at his grandmother. Silly old ding-bat. Sitting there like a parrot in all those colours. Why come here anyway? It was all over now, he thought. He felt hungry and wished he hadn't traded Bill the last of his humbugs, as he could have been eating them now.

He stared down at the ground feeling angry and very tired. He just wished he could go home. But where was home now that Gare had gone? No one really wanted him, here or on the island. Even Gina had changed and was always caught up now with her silly piano. Maybe it was his fault that it had all happened, anyway. If he hadn't pointed out that hawk hovering above them, Gare may not have looked up when he did and turned over into that ditch. Yes, it was his fault. That's why Gare was dead. It was his fault. He, Gerard, had caused it all.

Despite the heat, he started to shiver uncontrollably, his teeth chattering. 'Grandpa, Grandpa!' His voice seemed to resound in his head. 'Grandpa don't leave me, don't die, don't die.' And he was pushing and pushing that big ugly thing, but it wouldn't move.

His grandfather's head and shoulders only were showing from beneath the upturned tractor, his face white, and in a voice that didn't sound like his, he was gasping. 'Hattie! Hattie!' Just two words and then silence, with only the occasional far-off sound of crows calling to one another, as if nothing had happened, and his own breathing and grunts breaking the silence as he strained to push that thing away.

And then he was running, running back to the homestead, as fast as he could. Maybe they could still save Grandpa.

Should he tell her? he thought. Why not, it wasn't that important. 'Hattie,' he said.

'What did you say?' She looked at the boy.

'He said your name.'

'Who?'

'Gare, before he died,' Gerard said.

'What else, what else did he say?'

'Just your name. He said it twice, "Hattie, Hattie",' the boy said looking away from her.

So they had been together after all in that last moment. She leaned back and felt all the breath leave her body in a deep, drawn-out sigh, and the tears started to flow, washing down her cheeks, to cleanse away all her feelings of frustration.

'Come,' she said, her voice gentler, reaching out to take his hand. 'We'll go back now.'

* * *

Now as she looked out across the bay, she started to write her dream of the night before in her clear, round hand. She wrote, with a deepening feeling of premonition and that there was a message somewhere that she should be able to fathom.

When she had finished writing, she reached for her small, well-thumbed copy of *Of the Imitation of Christ*,[5] a book she always kept with her. It had been her guide through the long months after Boy's death, then Gare's. It replenished her spirit and was a comfort she hugged to herself. She flicked through the pages, then picking up her pen, underneath her dream copied out:

> *. . . . write, read, chant, mourn, keep silent, pray, endure crosses manfully; life everlasting is worth all these battles, and greater than these. Peace shall come in one day which is known unto the Lord, and there shall be not day nor night (that is, of this present time), but unceasing light, infinite brightness, steadfast peace, and secure rest. Then thou shalt not say, 'Who shall deliver from the body of this death?' nor cry, 'Woe is me, that my sojourning is prolonged!' for death shall be cast down headlong, and there shall be salvation which can never fail, no more anxiety, blessed joy, companionship sweet and noble.*

PART TWO

13

JILL—SYDNEY, AUSTRALIA, 1939

'You bring the money?'

Jill said nothing, just stared at the fat man in his shabby white gown, standing at the door. He held it half-closed behind him, so she couldn't see inside.

'Did y' bring the money?' he repeated.

She nodded, still without speaking.

'Show me,' he said.

She didn't have to search her bag; it was sitting on the top, in a long white envelope, unsealed.

She handed it to him, looking at his fat fingers with their nicotine-stained nails as he took the envelope, then quickly counted out the notes. He had pink, pouchy hands and she wondered if they were the ones that were going to work on her body. She shuddered, feeling sickened and now quite frightened.

'Well, come in then,' he said impatiently. She followed him inside, her legs leaden and cold.

'Wait just a minute,' she said, the firmness in her voice surprising even her. He turned and stared at her. 'Yes?'

'I'd like to speak to my anaesthetist,' she said summoning all the dignity she could.

'Y' what? Look, what's going on? Do y' want it or don't you?' he demanded. She stared him straight in the eye, hating him. 'I haven't decided, and I'll have you know that I'm a doctor's daughter,' she lied, 'and if anything untoward happens, you'll pay for it.' Her voice high, yet authoritative, seemed to belong to someone else.

'A doctor's daughter eh?' He gave her an assessing look. She was glad she'd worn her new Jaeger skirt and cashmere twinset. She'd dressed carefully to impress, including her best shell-pink swami camisole and scanties, as though a veneer of sophistication would cloak her body from what she was about to do. She'd been unable to do up the top hook of her skirt, her tummy already swelling, and had felt a further hardening in her resolve to go through with it.

'Well, you wait in here till you make up your mind what you want to do,' he said, leading her into a small waiting room, then left taking the money with him.

She looked around the dimly lit room with its ugly chintz curtains and pea green walls. The 'Laughing Cavalier' smirked at her from his gilt frame. Sitting straight on the chair, she looked down at her carefully enamelled nails. She had painted them last night and thought now how good they looked against the dark navy of her skirt. It was a wonderful red and they shone like polished rubies against her tanned skin. Looking down at her shoes, she felt a glow of satisfaction. They were navy and white toe-peepers Gina had sent to her from Hawaii. She loved wearing American shoes. Somehow they set one apart, gave a reassuring elitist feel.

Lifting her leg, she circled her ankle, looking at it admiringly. What if her ankles swelled up? Without warning, she was crying. Damn, damn, her mascara would run and she wanted to look terrific in this sordid place. What the hell was she doing here anyway, she wondered, looking around her.

'I'll come with you,' her friend Maria had said.

'No, I'll be fine. Just stay at home in case I need you when I get back.' It hadn't been easy to persuade Aunt Molly to let her come down to Sydney a week earlier.

'But school doesn't go back till next Thursday. Why do you need to go down now?' Molly had asked, worried by Jill's pale face. 'Well, there are things to get and do, and I just want to spend some time with Maria, go to the cinema—you know. And they're happy for me to stay. Please, Aunt Molly, don't fuss.'

The long train ride from Townsville down to Sydney was exciting at first, the heady feeling of just getting away from 'Winganna' on her own. She felt so grown up and independent, especially as she was a real woman now and streets ahead of the other girls. Her bravado was short-lived when she thought of what lay ahead. 'But you can't be preggers, how can you be?' Maria had said when she first told her of her fears.

'I'm four weeks late and I just know. I can feel it. And look at my boosies, they're enormous and all veined and funny.' She whipped open her blouse to reveal two full breasts spilling over her bra.

'Well, maybe you've been eating too much,' the more pragmatic Maria had said.

'Honestly Maria, don't be silly.' Jill was always stick-slim and could eat like a horse and not gain an ounce. 'I just feel it, all heavy and headachy. And yesterday I brought up my breakfast.'

'We've got to find someone to help, but I can't ask Dad, he'd think it was me.' Maria's father was the doctor, a specialist physician.

Jill wondered now what her own father and mother would have thought, and wished they were there to help her.

Sometimes in her dreams, she still had visions of lying on a hard dirt road on that breathless summer's day all those years ago. It was hot, so hot, and she was looking at a body lying alongside her. The woman's dress had big orange and yellow iceland poppies painted on it, and as a light breeze sprang up, the fine silky material ruffled and fluttered so that the poppies looked almost real, bobbing their heads and swaying in the wind. As she reached out to pick them, suddenly everything was blown away in a frightening willy-willy of dust. She'd wake up crying after this dream, and the anguish of it would hang around her for hours afterwards.

Eventually, between them and Maria's mother's daily help, they had found the name of a doctor who would perform an abortion at his clinic at Bondi. For sixty-five pounds. Feeling nervous, yet angry at having to be there, she'd sat opposite the dark little man with his oiled hair, his expression watchful behind steel-rimmed spectacles.

'Do you have to examine me?' she'd asked. 'I've told you all the details, and I'm obviously pregnant.'

'Did you really think I wouldn't examine you to verify it. Just what kind of doctor do you think I am?' he'd asked, defensively.

'A dirty little abortionist,' she'd felt like shouting, 'and there's no way I'd be here if there was any alternative.'

She'd suffered his hand exploring deep into her vagina, holding herself tense, angry with him. He'd prodded around too long, she thought, hating everything that was happening.

How could she ever have done it, let herself get into this situation in the first place? It had happened so quickly, she could barely remember it now. She had been with Billy Carr in the back of his father's old Daimler after the party. They'd just kissed at first and she rather liked it. Then he was pulling at her skirt and suspenders. She'd tried to push him away but, with the effects of the party punch and the heat of the moment, nothing seemed to really matter. And why not go all the way? He was the best looking boy around. He wasn't Gerard Baillieu, but then Gerard was so far away in Hawaii. She would practise for him, become the perfect lover for Gerard. She was sick of just reading about it anyway, she reasoned. Now she would know what it was really like. Then it had been all over so quickly. One minute, Billy's strangely soft penis growing hard in her hands, then thrusting into her and out so fast, leaving that wet sticky stuff all over her legs and dress. She could hardly bear to look at him, feeling so inexperienced and a total failure.

She was only too aware of the incongruity of Benny Goodman's 'In the Mood', scratchily playing through the car radio. She had giggled suddenly. Billy looked at her anxiously, his face so young, untouched.

'I'm sorry,' he said. 'Usually I can go for hours. It's this damn car.' She'd said nothing, scrubbing away at her dress with a tiny lace hanky that was totally useless. Then as if to reassert his masculinity, he'd added, 'It was your first time, wasn't it?'

'Don't be silly,' she'd answered. 'I just felt tired, that's all. Really, you can be such a bore, Billy.' She'd turned her back to him, staring out the window and wishing him miles away so that she could be home, and close out the whole hideous night and have a good cry.

She became aware that Dr Veitch had been speaking and was looking hard at her. 'So you'll be at my clinic at nine on Monday morning, and bring sixty-five pounds cash with you, in an envelope,' he added.

'Oh my God, where will I get that without Aunt Molly asking why?' she'd said later to Maria. But she managed. Her beautiful baroque pearls that had been her mother's were hocked in a dark little shop in Castlereagh Street. 'I'll get them back later,' she said confidently to Maria. 'I'll simply ask Gerard to pay for them.'

'Will he?' Maria's sweet honest eyes had stared at her in surprise.

'Of course, he's mere putty in my hands,' Jill had boasted, thinking, if only it were true.

The fat horrid man in his frayed gown was back, but without the envelope.

'Well?' he said.

'Very well, let's get it over.' She stood up steeling herself and followed him, past two young girls sitting pale and frightened on a bench outside in the hall. God, they looked about twelve. She smiled at them, feeling quite worldly at seventeen.

'In there,' he said motioning to a cubicle. 'Get everything off, everything, and put on the gown that's there, with the opening at the front.'

She had wanted Dr Veitch to see her resplendent in her new clothes, not some seedy old gown. But what the hell, she just wanted to get on with it, and quickly now. Carefully, she folded her things as she undressed, and put on the long white cotton gown, opening all the way down the front. A narrow fly-speckled mirror reflected her in the voluminous garment. But at least she looked good in white.

Should she take her things with her? They might disappear in this ghastly place. She decided to bring them all as the fat man appeared saying, 'Come on, we haven't got all day.' She followed him, out into the hall and through another door.

'Good Lord, have you come for a week?' A tall raw-boned woman with the reddest hair Jill had ever seen called out to her as she came into the room. A tiny white token nurse's cap sat perched on the back of her luxuriant hair. So unhygienic, Jill thought, ignoring her comment.

Dr Veitch, looking quite at home in his small domain, was laughing along with a large man, who turned as she entered.

'I believe you wanted to meet your anaesthetist,' he said, the veil of sarcasm not lost on her.

'And are you?' she said ignoring Veitch and looking straight at the man's shiny red face. The skin was so smooth and shiny, it was eerie.

'You could call me that,' he said with a smirk. Suddenly she felt quite frightened, looking at the white operating table with its big round light shining down mercilessly upon it.

'Come on, up you go!' She couldn't feel her legs move, but somehow she was climbing up onto the table. It was so high and she clutched the gown around her. The nurse was laughing loudly with Dr Veitch, but all she could see was the large mask in the anaesthetist's hands.

'What are you going to do?'

'Just slip this on, smooth as cream, and you can start breathing in deep and counting,' he said. She felt it go over her face. 'I can feel my heart beating,' she cried out in surprise.

'Well thank God for that!' the nurse said and their burst of laughter was the last thing she remembered before the smell of chloroform and darkness enveloped her.

The sound of a cheerful voice on the radio, announcing the time, and then she was vomiting, her head over the side of the bed and someone holding a dish beneath it. A woman's voice was saying, 'A good strong cuppa, and you'll be right.'

Her head felt dreadful, so large and full of bees. She was aware of a dull dragging ache in the pit of her stomach and a thick pad between her legs. But it was over, and she was alive. It was Allan Toohey's voice on the radio, so she must be.

All she wanted to do was sleep. She heared the clink of a cup and a woman's voice, 'Come on dear, come on, get up, you can't stay here. Have this nice cup of tea and you'll be right as rain.' She felt the woman hauling her into a sitting position. Her stomach hurt dreadfully, and she groaned.

'Now come on, you can't stay here, you've got to sit up and have this tea.' The good-natured briskness in the woman's voice gave way to a steelier note. She propped cushions behind her. 'Thank you,' Jill said weakly. 'My clothes?'

'They're on the chair there, so have your tea, then get dressed.' Jill drank the tea, hot and sweet. It was good, and she was really thirsty. There were two hard ginger nut biscuits on the side. She hadn't eaten and maybe this would help her feel stronger. She dunked them, letting the soft biscuity mush slide down her throat between sips of tea.

The woman was back. 'Good girl, I'll help you dress.'

'Will you please order me a cab?' Jill was starting to feel really sick again. She struggled into her clothes, wishing she'd just brought old loose pants and a shirt. There were so many things to put on. The pain was getting worse. How could she ever get back to Maria's house?

But then the door was closed firmly behind her and she was walking unaided down the front steps to the cab, only forty minutes after a full anaesthetic and by now bleeding freely.

She could hardly believe the amount of blood on the seat of the cab when she got out. It was running into the creases of the leather seat in a dark red pool. How could there be so much? Thrusting a pound into the driver's hand, and anxious to get out before he discovered the mess on the back seat, she staggered to the front door.

'You all right there?' he called out. She didn't hear him; she was desperately pulling on the door bell, and fainted into Maria's father's arms when he opened the door.

* * *

'You should have told me.'

'Daddy, I didn't know what was best to do.'

'She's lucky to be alive. It still could be touch and go. Bloody butcher!' Maria's father added, more to himself.

'Has the bleeding stopped?' Maria asked.

'For the time being. It's a good thing that she's as strong as she is, and so young and resilient.' He looked out the hospital window, with a sense of futility.

'Doctor?' a sister beckoned to him.

'You go and sit with her for a while. I'll look in later. Go on,' he added gently, seeing Maria's stricken face. 'You can always come to me, you know, Maria.' She hugged him. 'I love you Daddy. It's hard for her; she misses her real parents.'

'I know,' he said. As he turned to go, he suddenly stopped. 'How did she pay for it?'

Maria hesitated.

'We took her mother's pearls to a pawn shop in Castlereagh Street and hocked them.' He looked at her with an expression at once sad, yet exasperated. 'Run along now,' he said, 'but don't tire her with too much talking.'

Jill was propped up in the bed with a saline drip, her eyes closed and her skin so pale, her fair hair in two thick plaits stretched across the pillow. She looked fragile and quite beautiful, Maria thought.

At the sound of someone entering the room, Jill's eyes flew open. She didn't say anything at first, just gazed at the large bunch of deep red carnations in her friend's arms.

'What a heavenly colour. They're quite beautiful, thank you darling. Did you bring my things?' she asked anxiously. Maria nodded.

'Thank God, I can't bear wearing these ghastly shrouds.' Jill gave a little giggle.

'I've got something else for you, look.' Maria waved a large overseas airmail envelope under her nose. Jill reached out for it.

'It's from Gina, Aunt Molly's re-addressed it. How divine, how positively divine! Be a darling and open it and read it for me, will you? I feel just too exhausted,' she said. 'Hurry, I can't wait.'

A faint scent of gardenia rose from the air-letter sheets as Maria unfolded them and a creamy gardenia, pressed flat by the pages, fell into her lap. She handed it to Jill who, cupping her hands around the flower, inhaled the perfume.

'God, it's as if I were there,' she said. 'Go on, what does Gina say?'

'Honolulu, October 16,' Maria read. *'Darling Jilly, you'll never guess. I'm home from college already, hooray!*

'My study trip to Europe this year was cut short. I'd only just got started at the Sorbonne, then such goings on as you wouldn't believe. I got out of France just in time it seems, in the tiniest ship, the "Costa

Esmerelda" filled with people leaving Europe, and lots of excitement, though sad to be going, too.

'One old lady, Mrs Rubenstein, never stopped crying, can you imagine, till one day they asked her to play the piano for a concert. You should have seen her face, and she played like a dream. She helped me with my playing too. Such a darling.

'We even had two birthday parties on board with party hats, bon-bons, balloons, the full thing. The food was awful though, but lots of lovely French champagne, not to mention boys!

'My music studies at the Sorbonne never really got off the ground, and it got really scary there at times. One day, a group of German soldiers marched into the quad and their C.O. demanded the names of all the Jewish students. Luckily my friend there, Anna-Louise Levy, had gone back to her parents the weekend before, and she hadn't returned, so they missed her. I just hope she gets away too, as we hear awful stories of what might happen to them if they are caught. Anna gave me a tiny bottle of Chanel No. 5 perfume before she left, so she must have known that she wasn't coming back to college. I hope this war is over soon and I can go back and see her again.

'Now about the holidays . . . you've just got to get over here, somehow, Jilly. Ask Jack to make a booking for you to leave as soon as you finish your exams, the very minute, do you hear? I've got so much organised for Christmas and parties galore! And just hope I don't get sick again. I have a new doctor treating me and he says as long as I stay calm, that's the secret. Fat chance!!! Gerard is being a real bore, as usual. And just so full of himself. Mamma and he are always arguing. But he's away a lot, as he's training as a pilot now. He does look good in his uniform though. And as for his friends!

'Mamma has given me my own suite of rooms now. I can't wait for you to see them. I had them painted in deep coral with lots of white and chartreuse—it *looks so exotic. Gerard has told her that she has to provide the same for him too. He always wants everything I have, and more. But, why not? I was also given a beautiful white Bechstein baby grand for my birthday. It's wonderful as the sound carries right across the bay. Feels as though I'm on a giant stage like a concert pianist. In fact, that's where I'm heading. My teacher said she thinks I have what it takes. I'll just have to practise like mad, at least for six hours a day. Can you imagine? But for the moment it's wonderful just to swim, play tennis and party at night, where I show off with my boogie-woogie! It's the kind of jazz I love.'*

Maria looked up from her reading. Jill was asleep. She folded the letter and placed it on the table near her bed. She then carefully arranged the flowers in a glass vase near the window, and with one last look at her friend, quietly left the room.

Later that night when Jill awoke, she read through the letter again, dwelling on thoughts of seeing Gerard. It was six months since she'd seen him, and she couldn't wait.

She recalled their last meeting. He'd come to 'Winganna' to catch up with Bill before going back to Honolulu, where he was based as a naval cadet, training to be a pilot.

'I'll go and pick him up,' Jill had offered.

Molly looked up from her ironing, a worried frown creasing her good-natured face. 'But darling, you've only just got your licence, and it's a fair drive to the Garbutt air base. Are you sure?'

'It's nothing, I've driven into town dozens of times,' Jill said, overstating the issue to get what she wanted. 'And anyway you're far too busy to go now.' She gave her aunt a little hug. 'Please, please let me go.'

'Well, all right then.' Molly smiled at her. She never could resist Jill's persuasiveness.

I've loved him forever, Jill thought as she saw Gerard

come out from the air base swinging his duffle bag and squinting into the harsh Northern Queensland light. She ran to him, throwing her arms around him, pressing herself to him, her eyes alight. He drew back, frowning at her.

'Hey cut it out Jilly,' he said, startled by the naked look of adoration on her face.

She drew back, momentarily abashed, then lifting her chin. 'Really Gerard, don't take yourself so seriously.' He grinned at her, fully taking in her appearance for the first time.

'Hey, what have you done—you look sort of different.'

'Oh nothing really. How's Gina?' she said, feigning indifference, but pleased he'd noticed. She'd gone to some trouble to dispel his thinking that she was still just a kid. She'd cinched in her waist to accent her breasts and slim hips around which swirled a full skirt over her long tanned legs. She was having trouble balancing on her high heels, and hoped he hadn't noticed.

Her plaits had given way to a pony tail, her long blonde fringe sweeping low over one eye. She'd practised her Veronica Lake 'come hither' look and turned it full on him.

'And Hiroko-san, how is it all going?' she asked, remembering their long talks as children during his holidays at 'Winganna' when he'd vented some of his rage and disappointment at his mother's indifference.

But he seemed far removed from their shared confidences now. 'Mamma's just fine. She saw Satoshi in Tokyo,' he added casually.

'Satoshi? She didn't!' Jill couldn't hide her surprise. So this hated half-brother from his mother's past was a reality. She could never understand how or why Hiroko could possibly favour anyone over Gerard. And wondered about her.

'How, where, tell me, tell me?' she questioned, hardly waiting to hear.

'Nothing to tell, really,' he answered shortly.

She pulled back. How many times in the past she had

coaxed him back from his sense of sadness and resentment! Her feelings for Hiroko had been coloured by his pain of rejection, but her practicalities asserted themselves. 'How long are you staying?'

'Just a few days. Then the guys and I are planning to somehow fenangle a flight to see some of the action in Europe.

'Oh, no, Gerard,' she said, any thoughts of Satoshi quickly dispelled. "But the war . . . it's dangerous now and . . .'

She didn't want him to go. He just grinned at her and shrugged. 'Where's the car Jilly? . . . Come on, let's get going.'

That was Gerard, always dodging and weaving, always on the move, Jill thought now, nestling into the hospital pillows. She looked at Gina's letter again, dwelling on its postscript.

> *P.S. I've got so many of Grandma Hattie's things that I want you to help me go through. She even left me her house on Maui with the studio and everything. But I miss her terribly and can't bear to go there alone any more, so will wait till you come and we'll go together.*
>
> *I want you to help me sort things out, as there's just so much there, and you're always good at getting things in order. I know she would have liked you to have some of her things too.*
>
> *So hurry, hurry and come soon. Hugs and kisses, Gina.*

As she put Gina's letter back on the table, she noticed a small parcel lying alongside it. Wondering who had left it, she carefully unwrapped it, and there was the soft chamois bag, and inside, her mother's pearls glowing in the night light. She looked at them in wonder for some minutes. Then with a sense of joy, she quickly opened the note that accompanied them. It was from Maria's father.

'Dear Jilly', it read, 'I'm sure she would have wanted you to keep them, especially now. Remember, we're always here if you need us'.

She felt tears of gratitude and relief. So her darling mother must still be watching over her. 'Thank you, Mummy,' she whispered, 'thank you.'

14

CEMETERY—SYDNEY, 1940

The wind blew steadily, washing the rain against the windscreen in large spreading pools of water. Jill flicked the wipers to a higher speed, trying to clear the visibility as the blades arced their way across the glass. Leaning forward, she peered through the windscreeen.

A high wall with two tall stucco gate-posts appeared at the end of the road, grotesquely ornate with what appeared to be vultures perched on either side. As she drove closer the vultures became angels, somewhat the worse for wear, crouched in uneasy supplication on either side of a large open entranceway marked '10 MPH'.

She drove through, and suddenly acres of headstones appeared, spread out like some crazy patchwork before her. How will I ever find her, she wondered. She pulled over onto the side of the road, closing her eyes and trying to remember her mother's face. It was so long ago, and only fleeting expressions remained. Try as she might, she couldn't even clearly recall Freida's voice. I should be able to sense telepathically where she is, she thought. 'Mummy, lead me to where you are,' she prayed. 'Please dear God, help me to find her.' A tapping on the window and a muffled 'You OK?' startled her. She opened her eyes to see a face staring in through the glass. It had the vacant fixed stare of a simpleton. She drew back.

'Yes, I'm fine, thank you,' she said, and drove on.

After a while the more imposing headstones gave way to simpler, smaller stones laid low to the ground. Row upon row of them lined up amongst assorted shrubs. There was no flamboyant show here, no tombs or giant engraved headstones, no pyramids or sphinx, she smiled to herself. And yet it had been a life as important as any. The once vital woman and this uninspired uniformity were completely at odds, she thought. Surely Molly could have done better for her only sister Freida than this. But Molly had often resented her younger sister's vivacity and freer lifestyle, and maybe this sombre shrine was her only way to add a final note of conservative restraint and disapproval.

As for her father, he'd just cut himself off from everything to do with the funeral, Jill remembered. The love he'd had for his wife did not follow her into death. The funeral arrangements and the ensuing wake Stan had left to Molly. It seemed that grief made him want to distance himself from everything that reminded him of her, including their only daughter. But that was Daddy, Jill reminded herself. He'd only ever really been there for her mother. It was almost as if she were a mere afterthought, and when they were together she'd often felt an outsider, an intruder to their intimacy. But when he was away, her mother more than made up for it, lavishing her with love. And now she too was gone.

After organising for Jill to stay with her Aunt Molly and her family at 'Winganna', Stan Ferris had headed back to his numerous business interests overseas, his fatherly love now relegated to occasional gifts and visits from abroad, and a generous allowance for her upkeep and schooling.

Parking her car, Jill got out and started looking from one plaque to another. With each inscription, tiny threads of a past life seemed to reach out to her. She wondered as she read each one, and looked at the fresh or faded flowers left there in an odd assortment of jars, vases and the occasional can. Who were these people? Where and how had they lived and died? And where were the signs signifying the essence of that vibrant woman, her mother, whose life had been snuffed out prematurely on that country road all those years ago.

She ached to know more about her, to feel her arms around her in a warm and loving mother's embrace.

How deflating to think that all the intricacies of a lifetime ended here in this dismal place. Is this all there was in store for us? she thought.

Reincarnation seemed an attractive alternative at that moment. She stood up. She was being silly and maudlin, she chastised herself. The past was the past. There was no bringing her mother back from those faded shores. She had learnt to adjust to being without her, but her heart ached and she felt close to tears. We never get over such a loss, she thought, never.

After wandering around dozens of headstones, Jill saw a gardener working on one of the beds.

'Can you tell me where I'd find Mrs Freida Ferris's grave?' she asked.

'Protestant or Catholic?' he asked abruptly.

Jill thought a minute. 'Well, Protestant, I suppose. C of E,' she added. Her mother had been a deeply religious woman, but not in the formal sense of churches, communions and the warming sanctity of sermons followed by the Sunday roast.

'You're in the right area then, but what year did she die?' he asked.

She thought in vain. Numbers, dates, anything numerical seemed to evade her. Always when she most needed it.

'I think 1933,' she answered vaguely, thinking: why did everything always come back to numbers? She hated them. Then she recalled she was eleven when they had the accident, so it must have been 1933.

'That's in the older part, beds number eleven and twelve M, behind those big pepper trees right over near the stone fence,' he said, pointing.

Jill got back into the car and drove over to the grove of trees he'd indicated. She got out and walked past them to a bed of tired-looking rose bushes. It looked so bare and uncared for. She sensed no warming kindred spirit from another world. No sixth sense of recognition. Just nothing. Well so much for my spirit guide, she thought.

She started to look at the different inscriptions, some of them so worn, she could barely read them. Then there it was.

Her heart gave a jump as she looked at it, the small chipped block of sandstone with its bronze plaque now covered in verdigris. With difficulty, she read, *'In loving memory of Freida May Ferris, who died tragically, May 14, 1933. May she rest in peace.'*

That was it, there was no more.

Gently she laid the two large fronds of frangipani and hibiscus beside the plaque. They looked strangely out of place, like some exotic tropical bird that had flown into a desert wasteland and landed on the wrong tree.

A feeling of final parting and loss washed over her, and she thought, well, I've seen it now and I'll never come back. Closing her eyes, she prayed, 'Darling Mummy, I love you, love you.' She hesitated then went on. 'Why did you die before we ever really spoke? There's so much we had to say, so much I wanted to know, all the things I didn't know. And you weren't there. Why did you have to leave me?'

She felt tears of self-pity welling up and running down her cheeks, and a dull sense of deprivation.

Feeling stiff and drained, she got up and turned to leave. As she did, the sun appeared from behind a dark swirl of clouds, and as it shone through the misty rain, a rainbow seemed to spring to life from the ground not far from her, arching its way up and across the sky and out to sea.

She caught her breath with a sudden surge of elation and hope. It was a sign, a pointer. Her place was over the sea with Gerard, they would be lovers and, war or no war, she'd go to him.

She looked down at the ugly grave. 'Your spirit

doesn't belong here either,' she said softly. 'I'll take you with me, to where Gare is buried.'

Hattie would not have minded, she thought. My life is there now.

15

HATTIE—OAHU, JUNE 1940

Arriving at her grandmother's small house, Gina smiled in greeting to Lalana who had stayed on to look after the property after Hattie had died, until Hiroko decided what best to do with it.

'Miss Gina, it's good to see you. The days are so long now with Madam gone.'

'I know, I miss her too, but at least she's at rest and out of all that pain.'

Hattie had decided to buy this house after the fire destroyed the Waikiki beach house both she and Gare had given to Hiroko, and Hiroko had built her new home there. It was her base whenever she came over to Oahu from Maui, during the last few years as her health deteriorated.

Sitting in the large, sunlit studio that had been her grandmother's favourite room, Gina leaned back in the old bentwood Windsor rocker sipping a coffee. She remembered how often when she visited her grandmother, Hattie would be sitting in this same chair and gazing out over the bay, sometimes talking aloud to herself in imaginary conversations with Gare. They had spent so many times together sailing those emerald seas that filled this extinct volcanic crater and she still felt he was there for her.

Gina wondered now where she would start.

'I want you to go through and list everything in the house,' Hiroko had said. 'It will really help me, Gina-chan, there's just so much sorting out to do.'

'But Mama, Grandma left the house to me. Doesn't that include everything in it?'

'Most probably, but we still have to know what is there.'

Looking around at her grandmother's big exotic paintings, the old easel and her wooden carry case of precious oils, brushes and turpentine, Gina felt her closeness. She would probably keep this room just as it was, she thought, and when she wasn't practising the piano, she would continue to paint there as her grandmother had first encouraged her to.

She well remembered lying on the comfy old velvet chaise longue, watching Hattie work vivid colours onto canvas in the vibrant shapes of Island life.

'Here, you get going too,' she would say, giving Gina big creamy sheets of shelf paper and pencils and paints.

They'd work away in companionable silence, sometimes breaking it with a swim, or Hattie would say suddenly, 'Let's do the cards. I've got a feeling that something's brewing,' or 'Something's about to happen,' or 'Something's not quite right,' choosing the phrase that best suited her mood of the moment.

Sitting out on the spacious deep-eaved verandah, overlooking the graceful curve of Hanauma Bay with her golden retriever, Kit, lying at her feet, Hattie would carefully, almost reverently, spread the black baize cloth, then taking her cards from the silk scarf in which she kept them, would get Gina to shuffle and cut the cards. Hattie would say, 'Think of what is most important to you at this time. Empty your mind and think only of that.' Then she would start to lay down the beautifully engraved Persian Tarot cards, teaching her as she went.

'You have a feeling for it, you'll be good,' she told Gina. 'Just remember that it's what you bring to the cards that counts. It's a meeting of your mind, body and spirit with the cards as a touchstone. The major arcana is symbolic of our state of being while the minor arcana symbolises the movement and change taking place around us,' she explained. 'You just look, feel and interpret what you see. You're the catalyst in bringing forth an understanding, a clarity of vision from our ambivalence. The cards are the intuitively chosen beacons to light the way.'

As Gina watched, Hattie continued, 'As I see it, there's nothing really mystifying in the Tarot imagery; it's a crystallising of myth with reality. We are fixing change at a point of time, purely to reconnect us to the realities we know deep within. It transcends all outer manifestations, fashion, cultural change and the current ways of looking at things. Patterns emerge as it puts us in touch with our psyche, and through that we can relate to the outward happenings we are experiencing. It's simply a matter of striking that hidden chord.'

Then laughing, 'Don't look so serious child, these will be your cards one day, and I want you to use them wisely and well.'

Gradually, she took Gina through the seventy-eight cards, teaching her their different configurations.

'We'll do the Celtic Cross spread today, it's right for you now,' she'd say, and Gina, fascinated, would watch the pictures take shape. She came to recognise them, giving her own interpretation, knowing that Hattie's reading would far surpass hers. Looking at her grandmother's all-seeing blue eyes, she never doubted for an instant that her instincts were anything but right.

With her silvery blond hair tied up in a coil high on her head, her gold bracelets jingling their accompaniment, Hattie would lay the cards out with the seriousness of a seer about to foretell all. Gina loved it. They were some of the happiest moments, she remembered, those long sun-filled holidays home from school, with Hattie in the studio. But since Gare's death, much of her grandmother's vitality had drained, and each year she seemed to fade a little more, leaving most of the decision making to Hiroko and her lawyer. And now cancer had worked its final destructive break-down.

Her very last reading had been only a month before she died. She had come out of the hospital, thin and frail like an exotic bird with its brilliant plumage clipped, her wasted body lost in her swirling vibrant *muu-muus*, determined to get home to the surroundings she loved.

She did not visit the Maui plantation any more, and depended heavily upon Hiroko and the manager to keep everything running smoothly.

There had been no rain for weeks, Gina remembered, and the Kona winds blew in relentlessly off the bay, ruffling the usual calm.

'We'll sit inside today darling,' Hattie had said, 'and for God's sake, pour me a whisky!' She laughed.

Propped up against her Tapa cushions and with shaking hands, Hattie had started to prepare the table. Handing the cards to Gina, she said as always, 'Think only about what you want an answer to, and transfer your energy to the cards.'

'Let me do yours today, Gran,' Gina had offered.

Hattie looked at her with a little smile and answered, 'Let's not waste time darling. It's what's in store for you we need to know about.'

Gina had looked down to hide the quick tears that filled her eyes at the thought of her grandmother dying. Please don't let it happen for ages, dear God, she prayed. Then trying not to think of Hattie and stilling herself, she thought, What will happen to me now? Will I meet someone? Yes, will someone come into my life to love me, someone wonderful? With her eyes closed and concentrating on that thought, she felt the satiny coolness of the cards slipping smoothly through her fingers as she slowly shuffled them. She then cut them into three and handed them to Hattie, who fanned them out face-down in an arc on the cloth, and asked her to select ten cards. She liked to select quickly so that it was an instinctive rather than a premeditated action, and choosing the ten cards, she handed them to Hattie who then pushed the others aside, then laid the cards face up in the shape of a Celtic cross.

They both gazed at the carefully worked picture of divination glowing in its certainty. Gina gave a long drawn-out sigh, then looked up at her grandmother and said. 'It's incredible, isn't it?'

'Not at all,' answered Hattie. 'It's all there darling, it's all there. Now, where to begin?' She looked up at Gina, smiling. 'Well you've got your wish as you can see,' looking at the Knight of Cups. She frowned as she saw the Hermit card with its shrouded figure carrying his lamp and scythe.

'But it's not going to be easy with this young man.' She paused. 'You will have to give up something, something that is very important to you. There's a love there, a big love, but . . .'

'But what Gran?' Gina broke in anxiously.

'Well what do you think?' Hattie asked.

Gina looked silently at the cards. It was hard to be objective with one's own reading. She looked across at Hattie, disquietened by the troubled expression in her eyes. 'I see many things, but I'm not getting an intuitive feeling, it's too close to me. I'd rather you did the whole thing,' she replied quickly.

'You'll fall in love,' Hattie hesitated, searching for the right words. 'Maybe Gina, things aren't always as they seem, you know. You must be true to yourself and take care and don't be too hasty.' She paused, looking at the Three of Cups. 'I see a birth, a baby.'

'What, so soon?' Gina laughed. Hattie picked up the card of the Devil. 'You'll be coming to terms with something that's not easy, and something that will be very big for you. It will come right out of the blue,' looking at The Tower struck by lightning. Her fingers rested on the Knight of Cups again. 'He's a very beautiful young man, sensitive and clever, but there's something there, it's almost as if . . .' she hesitated.

I wish I could be with her to help her through it when it happens, Hattie thought, but knowing she wouldn't.

First love, that wonderfully heady and romantic passion, when everything is totally centred on that one person and all else fades. It had been like that for her and Gare. And the strength of their love had lifted them from the wealthy but confining New England background to the promise of a fresh, freer start here in Hawaii. Anyway, they'd made it here, and in a big way. What evil fate had cut it short—first with the cruel loss of her son, Boy, then with her beloved Gare? If only he was here to help me now.

'And the Four of Wands?' Gina voice cut across her thoughts.

'Your music, you must keep going and working hard, as it will bring you great joy and will open many doors. It won't be easy but every effort will be worthwhile in the long run.'

She looked back at the Tower again. 'There's something quite beyond your control that you'll have to deal with. Things will change for you very suddenly.'

'And not always for the best?' Gina asked, worried now.

'Well, it's what comes out of that, what finally emerges that counts,' Hattie said. 'Things have to change for growth and new awareness. We can't be hidebound by false illusions,' she laughed. 'Not for too long, anyway.'

Her eyes travelled to the Devil's card. 'We have to look at the downside of most things as well as the good, including things within our own makeup, so it's never easy.'

'And the Fool has turned up as he always seems to,' said Gina.

'So it's time for the big leap of faith,' laughed Hattie.

Her smile faded as she looked at the Fool in relation to the other cards. Then she looked up at Gina. 'But of course you must always look before you leap, darling. And look long and hard this time.'

'Oh Gran, don't make me feel so nervous about the whole thing.'

As she looked at the Three of Swords card showing the body of the dead King Agamemnon floating in his bath with Aegisthus and Clytemnestra his wife both piercing his heart with a sword while a third sword stood upright from his body, Hattie thought: how often we pay for the joy or real union with our soul-mate later with tears of separation and loss.

'Pour me another little nip, will you, Gina?'

She leaned back, closing her eyes. A sudden sharp stab of pain pierced her chest. She held her breath, trying to ward off its severity.

'Gran, your drink.' Gina's anxious face hovered above her. 'Are you all right?'

'I'm fine, it's nothing this won't help,' Hattie said, taking a long drink. She looked across at Gina. 'There will be a marriage and a child,' she said, touching the Three of Cups card with its floating figures of Eros and his bride Psyche. She looked away from the cards and out across the bay, at the sea now reflecting the opalescent pinks and blues of the sky, the white foam capped waves whipped up by the wind. The sea horses were up and away today, as always with the Kona, she thought.

She sat silently looking at the sea, then said quite suddenly, 'You will have a daughter.'

'How can you tell?' Gina broke in.

'It's a feeling, I just know it will be a little girl,' said Hattie. 'But there's one thing I would like you to do,' she added. 'If you would call her Sophie for me,' she smiled at Gina.

'Oh Gran,' Gina moved over and gave her a hug. 'You'll be here and you can tell her all these wonderful stories you used to tell me and Gerard,' she said, knowing that she wouldn't.

'Well darling,' Hattie went on, looking at the Two of Pentacles with Daedalus in his workshop surrounded by the fruits of his labours, and the vines heavy with grapes and the rolling green hills behind him, 'there will be plenty of money and property. But you must learn how to make it work for you. Hiroko will help you there, she has a great head for business and you will too, one day. Or maybe your child, but . . . there's so much conflict ahead for all of us. This Island paradise of ours can't remain remote from it all forever.' She was quiet for a moment.

'When you marry, keep your financial affairs quite separate. Hal, my accountant, will be there to advise you. And remember darling, Gare always said you can't do better than invest in good property, and this war will bring prices down, so there will be many opportunities coming up. Just be aware of what's going on around you.'

Looking at the card showing two young men astride a rearing horse, Gina said, 'Somehow, the Knight of Swords always makes me think of Gerard and me, probably because they're twins like us.'

'But not like you,' added Hattie. 'You know, I think this young man of yours is going to come from another country, but in some ways it will be a sense of deja vu. Almost a pre-ordained happening from another place, but not so different.' The two-edged sword, she mused. Ebb and flow, black and white, night and day. 'Things will never be quite the same again for you. But that's good. Just remember there are two sides to everything.'

'And a star to top it all,' said Gina looking at Pandora seated before her open box from which a dark ominous cloud of insects was flying. Above hovered a shining star in which stood a luminous female figure in white robes.

'And when Pandora shut her box, all that was left inside was Hope,' said Hattie. 'And that's the most precious gift of all to get us through anything.' She reached out and took Gina's hand. 'So whatever happens darling, always carry your faith close to you, because that is your strength.' She lay back on the cushions and closed her eyes.

'Why not rest a while, Gran, I'll take Kit for a swim.'

'Yes, you do that, we'll chat further later.'

And that had been the last reading. Gina got up and walked across to the chest where the cards were kept. They were still there, waiting. She touched the scarf, and suddenly tears that had been held back in the past month flowed freely.

She buried her face in the scarf, crying for that vital woman who had been like a mother and guiding spirit to her for as long as she could remember.

'Miss Gina?' She looked up at Lalana's worried face and smiled through her tears.

'As you can see, I'm getting a hell of a lot done,' she said. Kit's bark downstairs reminded her. 'I'll take Kit for a run and a swim and then we'll have lunch and I'll get on with things afterwards,' she said, giving Lalana a hug before skipping down the stairs.

Once in the water with Kit running up and down along the beach, Gina experienced that glorious sense of being at one with the elements. She swam lazily, feeling the water slip past her skin in swishing rivulets, the sun warming her back, contrasting with the fresh coolness of the sea.

A dark young man running along the beach made her think of Hattie's Tarot reading. Was it only two months ago? So much had happened since. I wonder who he'll be, she thought, then Hattie's worries clouded her sense of anticipation.

Her thoughts travelled to the war in Europe and to her friend, Anna-Louise Levy. Only this morning, the papers had carried a picture of a German soldier goose-stepping under the Arc de Triomphe. It was terrible, terrible and all happening so fast. She lay on her back, floating with the current. There had been no word from Anna-Louise in answer to her letters for so long now. She felt a pang of worry, but as she looked up at the cloudless shimmering sky, that whole war-torn scene seemed unreal and remote on this perfect Hawaiian day.

16

JILL'S TALISMAN—HONOLULU, JANUARY 1941

The smooth, flawless face stared back with cool appraisal. Jill moved the lamp so that the light was cast onto her face. Not a shadow to conceal or soften. No half-truths. This was her outer shell, the mask she presented to the world, and tonight it was to be perfect.

She looked closely, assessing her fine skin delicately tanned by the sun. Her mouth, which she'd always felt was too wide, she controlled and contained with a few deft strokes of a lip brush.

Candid eyes, pools of blue ringed by long lashes, looked out with veiled invitation. To add depth, she lightly outlined them with a little Kohl. As a final touch, with quick sure movements she applied a light cream to her hair, accenting its golden sheen and fragrance.

Toiletries over, she sighed and stood up, smoothing the new dress over her hips. It clung in just the right places, accenting the shape and movement of her small rounded breasts and bottom in a discreet display of understated sexuality. She felt good in her clothes, confident in the effect they always had.

Now, jewels . . . which ones? The other women would be over-loaded, no doubt, so why not just be totally free of any decoration for once as a foil to the others? But then, maybe something very plain and simple.

She went to a wall safe and opened it, pulling out her jewel case and appraising the jewellery stored in its velvet-lined drawers. Lying almost hidden by a fold of velvet, she saw a brooch that had belonged to her mother Freida.

She brought it across to the light and the beauty of the Art Deco piece made her draw in her breath, and her heart quicken with the excitement of possession.

It's the most perfect thing she thought. It was a finely worked golden figure of a nymph, poised as if in flight. In the raised palm of the nymph's hand rested a sun, its golden rays studded with diamonds which flashed with reflected light, while around her flowing hair was a circlet of white sapphires. She had a sudden sense that it had lain in wait for just this moment, to be rediscovered, like a talisman from her mother.

As she gazed at it, memories of Freida and that last morning they had spent together came rushing back. She remembered her mother sitting at the breakfast table, in the early morning light of their kitchen. She could still see the colour of her eyes. Even without make-up, they had a startling intensity, the whites so white against the blue.

'You'll be late darling, I'll drive you to school,' her mother said and smiled in almost conspiratorial exchange. They were always late, a shared thing. And rather than handling it with anger or impatience, there was an unspoken tryst that one would help the other.

Their Sydney home was an assortment of Freida's favourite pieces, the booty of many trips abroad. It was a grand house, Jill recalled, no obvious show of wealth, yet wealth there was. From her earliest childhood, Jill had been aware of cushioned elitism and security, but this carried its own price, as she was soon to discover.

Her mother was cutting her toast in that funny way she had. First, a straight finger wedge cut an inch from the crust, then at right angles she quickly cut three more fingers right to the other crust, so that the slice formed an almost perfect geometrical pattern of four neat fingers.

She then carefully spread each one thickly with her favourite coarse-cut Scottish marmalade, and sat eating dreamily between long sips of steaming Darjeeling tea. Jill could never imagine her mother's breakfast ritual in any other way. It seemed far more in keeping with the wife of a derby-hatted English civil servant than the big boisterous maverick of a man Freida had married.

'It's all right, Mummy, I'm going with the Andersons.'

'Well, I'll pick you up after school and we'll drive out to the airport and meet Daddy. He's flying in late this afternoon and says he wants to take us out to dinner.'

Freida sipped her tea. 'Evidently his trip to Japan didn't go so well this time. He says things are changing there and he's worried.' Her face brightened. 'But he's bringing some lovely things back for us, including a special piece of jewellery for me.'

'What do you think it is?' Jill had asked.

'He wouldn't say, we'll just have to wait.' Freida had leaned back in her chair, pushing up her long fair hair, then twisting it into a chignon which she secured with a comb. It was a familiar gesture which Jill now automatically did herself in almost the same way. She remembered how her mother had then said, 'And I have a special surprise to tell you both later.'

'Tell me now, Mummy, go on, I can't wait all day.' Jill sat down staring at her mother expectantly. 'I won't move till you do.'

'Well, maybe I had better tell you now then,' Freida laughed as she reached out and took her daughter's hand.

'Actually, I only found out yesterday. It's why I've been so unwell.'

'What's wrong?' Jill looked alarmed.

'Nothing's wrong, in fact quite the opposite. You see, we're going to have a new baby in the house.'

'Whose baby?' Jill asked.

'Why, ours of course, silly.'

'Ours?' And then it suddenly became clear.

'Oh, my God, how will you cope,' Jill said, already

assuming a responsible air for one who had only just turned eleven.

'We'll get a nanny, and you can help.'

'I just hope it's a boy then,' said Jill. 'I'd like that. We've got enough girls.'

'What, there's only you and me.'

'That's quite enough for one family,' Jill answered gravely. Her mother had laughed. 'Maybe you're right.'

'Anyway, now you know. Not a word to Daddy, though . . . I'll tell him later,' she said. 'So remember, I'll pick you up after school and we'll drive out to get him.'

Jill had given her a kiss and left the room, then came running back.

'When is it due?' she asked.

'It could well be another Christmas baby like you, so isn't that lovely,' her mother had answered.

A little brother at Christmas. All day she had hugged the thought to herself. It was a secret that made her feel special and apart from everyone else that day. They would call him Christopher, that would be right for a Christmas baby, she had decided.

As always, her mother was late in picking her up from the small exclusive school. She drove onto the highway, the sleek Riley sports car that Stan had given her for her last birthday leaping ahead faster than she realised.

Jill and Freida chatted happily, mostly about the baby as they drove away from the urban sprawl and into the open countryside, still nine miles away from the airport . . .

How could things be so perfect, so happy one minute, and so changed the next? Changed forever, Jill thought now, resting her elbows on the dressing table, her chin cupped in her hands, staring straight into the mirror.

She saw not her own reflection, but that of her mother, lying on the dirt road, motionless, the wind catching the brightly coloured poppies of her dress. Jill had lain there, dazed. It was hot and the dust blew around them in small eddies from a passing willy-willy, as if gently urging them to get up.

Why was she here? This really wasn't the best place to lie like this. Her school uniform would get all dusty. What would Daddy say when he saw her like this? She heard the harsh cry of a crow passing low overhead, its black body filling the sky above her and shadowing the sun that shone hot on her face. Her head ached so. She tried to lift and turn it a little, and as she did, she saw the car upside down, its wheels still spinning.

What a place for it to be . . . Mummy's beautiful new car, she'll be so angry if she sees it like that . . .

Thoughts like fragments of bright glass slipped across her mind in a moving kaleidoscope, positioning and repositioning as she turned it around, looking at each different pattern.

She remembered a car stopping and the sound of running feet and voices coming towards them, then being lifted as she drifted into unconsciousness.

She had awakened to a room that was strangely bare. Where was everyone? Why was she here? She felt so tired, and as she tried to move her arms and legs, it was as if they belonged to someone else in a strange disconnected way. Like the wooden German doll on strings Daddy had brought back for her.

A sudden wave of desolation made her cry out.

'Mummy! Mummy!' She could see her mother floating near the door, smiling at her. Why didn't her feet touch the ground, and why didn't she come any closer?

She could see the outline of the door behind her mother, showing through her body and as it opened and a nurse came in, the shadowy figure disappeared.

Now everything was coming back fast, clearly etched memories crowding in on her. They were turning over and over and she could feel herself flying through the air, then a sudden hard bang that made all the breath leave her body in a rush. Was it screaming she heard? Yes, it was her mother screaming out her name. 'Mummy,' she shrieked, 'where are you?'

A man in white, she didn't know who he was, was bending over her and injecting something into her arm, and then it was as if she were floating in a warm sea of jelly, just floating, then drifting into a wonderful sleep.

'Who's Christopher darling?' It was Aunt Molly sitting by the bed holding her hand. 'Jilly, who's Christopher?'

'He's my baby brother,' she had answered dopily, still half drugged.

'There, there, everything's going to be fine, just rest,' her aunt said, stroking her forehead lightly with her fingers, just as her mother so often did, to coax her to sleep. And she had drifted off again.

That night when she awoke, a small night lamp was alight by her bedside, and a nurse sat dozing in the corner. But it wasn't the nurse to whom she looked, but the shadowy figure of her mother who sat in the chair right by her bed. Freida smiled at her, reaching across as if to touch her.

'Mummy, it's you,' she whispered. Her mother's lips moved and she could hear the voice inside her head.

'I have to go, my darling.'

'But Christopher?' Jill had whispered.

'Don't worry, he is with me,' her mother had answered. 'Safe and well. I want you to be happy Jilly. You'll have to grow up very fast now that I'm not here with you.'

'Yes, Mummy,' she answered. 'I'll miss you.' She felt the hot tears trickle across her cheeks and onto the pillow.

'There's no need. I'll always be with you in spirit. Just think of that. No one can see me but you, and I'll be with you and love you always. Just hold on to that. And Jilly, I want you to be as good at everything as you can be. I'll be there watching out for you.' She had leaned over as if to kiss her. 'Goodbye my darling.'

'Mummy!' she had called as the figure disappeared.

And that was the last time she had seen her. But from then on, Jill remembered, she had somehow been able to cope with the loss. Even better than Daddy. Everyone had said so.

As she sat staring into the mirror and back to those strange disembodied days that followed the accident, she recalled that no-one had needed to tell her her mother was dead. She already knew. It had been her mother who had come to her in the room, to soften the loss, and it was from then that she knew there was life after death . . .

She pinned the brooch to the shoulder of her dress. Against the midnight blue, it shone out like a small beacon.

It's just right, she thought, this precious jewel her father had brought back for her mother on that fateful day. Its discovery today had a special significance, Jill thought, as with a growing feeling of anticipation she picked up her purse, and with one quick backward glance at her reflection, left the room.

17

AMATERASU—1941

'You should have rung me, Jill, I'd have called for you.' Gerard looked so good in his naval uniform, she thought. He was well on top of things, with only a faint shadow about his eyes which made her wonder.

'Maybe a lift home then,' she answered.

He contemplated her in a long steady gaze. 'Sure, why not.'

She was quite beautiful now, he thought. Still self-contained with that air of detachment, a trait he found attractive, so different from Iman. He watched Jill as she circled the room, graceful and at ease, chatting with the assorted guests. She had blossomed since they had last met at Christmas eighteen months ago, when she came out to holiday with Gina and his mother. Looking across at him, she caught his eye and smiled, as if in question.

There was something really fine about her, he thought, and somehow comforting—she belonged to all he knew that was familiar. She was a golden girl, all sunshine and light, no hidden recesses. She was not Iman.

Iman. Across his consciousness came visions of her eyes, like liquid amber you could sink into and be lost forever. As quickly as the memories arose, he pushed them away.

He took a whisky from a passing tray and drank

quickly, then took another to assuage those thoughts that came to knot his gut. He moved around the room talking, laughing, but hardly noticing or taking any of it in, his eyes only drawn back to the one ray of light that seemed to offer him some kind of reprieve.

'Gerard darling?'

It was Gina, looking anxious.

'Let's get out of here, soon. Jilly wants to go, it's just too boring. All the same old faces. No one exciting or new and I've got a big day tomorrow. Would you think we can politely disappear?' She looked at him appealingly. 'Give it ten minutes,' he said.

'Do you really want to call it a day?' he asked Jill later after dropping off Gina.

She looked at him, surprised. 'Why it's only just beginning,' she said as if she meant it.

He laughed. 'I'm starving,' he said. 'Let's get something to eat.'

As they were seated in the restaurant, he looked at her, long and appraisingly, then reaching across the table, touched her brooch.

'Amaterasu O-Mikami,' he said, smiling.

'Who?' she asked.

'Amaterasu. How right for you,' he added.

'Amaterasu?' she said, looking down at the nymph, its diamonds sparkling in the table's candle light.

'She is the sun goddess and *kami* of the high plain of heaven, the most august of all the Japanese *kami*, and quite a girl.' Gerard laughed.

'Is?' she queried.

'Very much so, alive and well,' he answered.

'Do you feel a part of all that?' she asked.

'East is east, and West is west,' he smiled. And she could tell he wasn't to be drawn. To change the subject, she talked about the brooch.

'It was my mother's,' she said. 'Daddy brought it back for her, but she never wore it.' Not wanting to dwell on those days, she then said, 'Tell me more about this Amaterasu?'

'She is the great sky-lightening deity, from which our present Emperor of Japan is descended.'

Looking at him, Jill mused at the interesting blend of East and West he presented. It seemed that both cultures had decided to be kind to him in bountifully bestowing their gifts, but there was an uneasy merge, almost as if something had been missed in the final makeup. Gerard was an enigma, a riddle to be solved, with a mystique which drew her to him.

'Really?' she said.

He ignored the slight scepticism, and went on.

'Her brother Susa-no-o-mo-mikoto, the earth *kami*, misbehaved so badly, she became angry and hid away in a celestial cave.'

'And then what?' Jill asked.

'She took all the light with her and the earth and sky were thrown into a terrible darkness. Her tears of sorrow fell to earth and formed the sea that the islands of Japan sprang from,' he said, examining his cutlery. 'So to entice her out of her refuge, all the *kami* gathered and made merry with singing and dancing and all kinds of heavenly entertainment.' He smiled at her. 'So curiosity got the better of her, and she was lured from her cave, bringing the warmth and light back to the world. After this, Ninigi-no-Mikoto, her grandson, was told by the *kami* to descend to the Great Eight Islands, as Japan was then called, and to rule there. As a symbol of his authority, Amaterasu gave him three divine treasures, a mirror, a sword and a string of jewels. These became the three regalia of Japan's imperial throne, while his great grandson, Emperor Jimmu, became the first human ruler.' He paused, as if far away at that moment.

'And her brother?' Jill asked.

'Oh him,' he smiled, 'she got the better of him too. He turned over a new leaf and returned to favour.'

'C'est la vie, c'est Gerard,' she laughed, reaching over and touching his arm. 'So who knows, maybe you too are descended from the gods.'

'A part of me is,' he answered, quite serious.

He gazed at her radiant face as she laughed and chatted, and as the evening progressed, his recent loss of Iman was gradually pushed aside by the warmth of Jill's presence. They spoke of the past, the times spent together with Tom and Bill at 'Winganna'. Of the mishaps, and the fun and all the shared moments that had bonded them in a layer of mutual background memories, which now made things seem so easy and relaxed.

It was in this nostalgic mood that he reached for her when they went back to his apartment, and in that vein that he made love to her for the first time. It was all so uncomplicated, somehow so familiar. None of the great highs or lows that came with the intense passion of truly loving. This was more a balm to the spirit, a sexual feeding of the body while keeping the soul intact.

The next morning as Jill lay in his bed looking at him, deep in sleep, she thought, Oh my God, why did I come back here? Now that we've made love, his interest will die. Her head ached, as did her body from muscles little used. Quietly she got out of bed and went into the adjoining bathroom and turned on the shower, stepping under it and feeling an intense relief as the water hit her skin.

Why had she come back here with him? She should have strung the whole thing out longer, kept him waiting, hungering for her, building on it. If only she hadn't had so much to drink.

The evening had passed in a sort of diffused glow, she thought. Then he was kissing her. In her anxiety to retain his interest, yet feeling that she would be compared with that girl Gina had mentioned, the one he'd met while he was away, she had gone along with him. More as if to replace the other one in his life, she rationalised now.

She loved Gerard, but he wasn't hers, yet. And nothing less would suffice. But now, she had probably wrecked the chance of anything ever happening between them. Since the abortion, apart from occasional petting, she had turned her back on sex. Her emotions had frozen over, and last night had done nothing to change that.

He had come in a great burst, like a pent-up wave that had been slowly building, only to be too quickly released in one giant wash into and over her. She reached down, feeling herself still swollen from their love-making. She hadn't climaxed, had never come, she thought. She hadn't even acted out her part. The whole thing had been a disaster.

Closing her eyes, Jill put her face and hair under the full force of the shower, feeling the water stinging her skin, washing away her despair. She didn't hear him enter the bathroom till she felt his mouth kissing her breast, then down her stomach and between her legs, his mouth and tongue reaching deep into her. She tried to push him away, but her arms were mere feeble flutterings.

'Gerard, stop it, stop it,' she cried. But he seemed oblivious to all else but his intent.

He carried her, dripping, to the bed and, lying back, he grasped the nape of her neck and brought her unwilling mouth down to his erect penis. She thought she heard him whisper 'Iman', and in that moment, she hated him. But she felt his need for her and this time she acted out the part expected, as she felt his excitement build.

He roughly pulled her up to him, his mouth on hers, and guiding her hands, built his passion to a high point of arousal. With a shuddering groan he came, and there was silence. Tentatively she kissed him as his fingers cursorily stroked her back. There were no words of love, and she drew away from him.

A sudden ray of sun streamed in through the windows across their wet bodies, as it rose to meet the early morning sky.

'Amaterasu,' she whispered. Her eyes, momentarily despairing, met his.

'Amaterasu,' he repeated, stroking her damp hair.

18

HIROKO'S PRESENTIMENT—HONOLULU, FEBRUARY 1941

Hiroko sat gazing at the evening sky, drifting with that slow merging of day into night. It was a time that often made her feel as though she were caught in a no-man's land, where nothing was what it appeared to be. It was a reflection of everything that was happening. Europe at war. Japan now in the thick of it, and America experiencing an uneasy peace, possibly on the brink of battle. She wondered how long until her adopted country too was in the conflict. And if America and Japan were on opposing sides, what then? She worried not only for herself as a Japanese-born citizen and her children with their Japanese connections, although American by birth, but also for her many Japanese and *Nisei* workers on the Baillieu Maui plantation.

In her early days on the plantation, with her understanding of their social and economic needs, she had helped Gare build a strong working force. Like her, the Japanese workers had responded to the natural beauty and bounty of their adopted island home, quickly adapting to their new lives while retaining many of their traditions and much of the culture of the old. They had helped her transition, and had overcome her sense of homesickness through the mutual familiarity of language and food. They were more like family now and she had established a great working team under the two Hawaiian managers who had been there since before Gare died.

Gerard's participation in the plantation had always been encouraged by his grandfather Gare, she recalled, and he'd responded well, showing a natural resourcefulness in taking charge. But since joining the navy and his time away overseas, he'd pulled right back, and sometimes sensing the conflict within him, she felt he was not sure now where his allegiances lay.

What would be the general attitude if America and Japan were to fight each other? What of their loyalties then? Since returning to Japan for her father's death and funeral, her feelings of displacement and her brief sighting of Satoshi and the hateful Michiko—she knew now where loyalties lay. But what of others?

Her sense of foreboding was highlighted by the thought that as a pilot in the American naval air reserve, Gerard could soon be in the thick of it, fighting along with the others. His whole life had prepared him for it, she thought wryly. Since a young boy he was always spoiling for a fight. His inner conflict had made him increasingly self-centred and since his flight to Europe, he'd become often reclusive. But his sense of inner unease, and the antagonism she often felt flowing from him towards her, or to anyone who opposed him, she did not take personally.

Despite what Hattie had said to her at different times over the years, Hiroko felt she had done all she could for Gerard. Any sense of not fulfilling her role in his life she pushed aside as thoughts of Satoshi surfaced. Where in the world was he now? Her brief glimpse of him at her father's funeral all those years ago remained clear and intact. But never a word from him in answer to her letters. She had even written to Michiko but those letters too remained unanswered.

Her old school friend Suzue had not replied to her enquiries either. Then one day a short note arrived. It stated politely that it would be better if Hiroko did not ask her to try and contact Satoshi any more as it was proving difficult, and that her husband did not want her to be in contact at all from now on. She was apologetic, but Hiroko knew that with the increasing hostilities and Suzue's son Hideyoshi and her husband in the Japanese armed forces, Suzue would never dare to step out of line.

The phone rang and Hiroko hurried inside to answer it.

'Hi, Mamma!'

At the sound of Gina's voice, her spirits lifted.

'What time will you be here, darling?'

'I'm sorry Mamma, but there's a party tonight at the Takeuchis and I promised Mardi Cottington I would be there. I'm going to wear that yellow dress you gave me,' Gina reassured her.

'But you weren't feeling so well earlier; are you sure? You don't want to risk having another attack, Gina-chan.' Hiroko could hear in the breathless voice the ever-present reminder that her daughter's asthma was not far away. Despite being urged to stay calm, Gina always pushed herself—and maybe one day too far.

'I was hoping to see you tonight, but if you . . .' Hiroko hesitated.

'I feel just fine, truly Mamma, and anyway we can always catch up tomorrow.' Then, detecting her mother's melancholy, 'You don't mind if I go, do you?'

Hiroko heard the note of guilt in her daughter's question and her next suggestion confirmed it.

'I mean, if you're feeling low why not get Gerard to come over? I think he's free tonight. Unless he's seeing Jill again.'

'Don't worry Gina-chan, I'll see. Now enjoy the party and take care. We'll talk tomorrow.'

Hiroko replaced the receiver, feeling drained. Going to the kitchen she unearthed a bottle of whisky and poured herself a long measure, adding ice. Taking the bottle and ice bucket with her, she went back out to the lanai, settling into her chaise longue. As the whisky spread its warmth, she sensed that she'd entered a phase in her life where everything around her was gaining momentum while she remained dormant, unable to effect change while change was happening all around her.

She thought of Grace's daughter Mardi. Tall and vivid like her mother, but without Grace's inquisitive and judgemental nature. Now that the Cottington family had moved back to Hawaii from the mainland, Mardi and Gina often saw each other. But she had seen less of Grace. Although Grace still acted out her godmother role with gifts for the twins on their birthdays and at Christmas, a polite coolness had replaced the warmth that the two women had formerly shared.

Dark reminders still intruded of that night after Grace's birthday party all those years ago. Often she would awake from a dream that the man was on top of her again, pummeling her into the bed, and she couldn't breathe. Michiko's face would appear scornfully smiling, and sometimes her face would change into that of the young Japanese man she had seen at Guam, his still eyes watching as if assessing her. She'd wake, her heart pounding, and lie fearful of the night sounds outside, thinking her attacker would suddenly reappear. Since the rape, the sexual side of Hiroko's life simply did not exist, and she had shunned any romantic overtures or attachments. After Hattie's death, she had slipped quite naturally into the role of the Baillieu family matriarch. Baillieu was a name to be reckoned with on the island, she reminded herself with renewed confidence, and surely that alone would stand her and the family in good stead. She refilled her glass and drank slowly, savouring the sense of letting go, and drifted into sleep.

19

GINA—HONOLULU, OCTOBER 1941

'Katsura, what is it? I had a message to ring you, urgently. Is everything all right?'

'I can't talk now. I wanted to see you first but it's not possible.'

'What do you mean?'

'I have to leave.'

'Leave where?'

'Leave here, leave Honolulu.' He sounded terse.

'How, when? I'll get packed and we can go together.'

'No, Gina-san. Listen to me, you must be calm, it's only for a short while, but I have to go today.'

She sensed in his voice the anxiety underlying the firmness.

'But Katsura, you can't go, the baby's due soon, I need you. You can't go, I won't allow it,' she added, panic overcoming any restraint.

'I will send for you and the baby. Goodbye, my Gina-san.'

There was a click at the other end. For a second, she couldn't believe that he had actually hung up on her. She clicked the phone again and again. 'Hello, Katsura! Katsura!' Feverishly she repeatedly dialled his number, but each time it was engaged.

Was he serious? What did he mean by going away?

After the tenderness of their love-making the previous night, it wasn't possible that he could even think of leaving her. But he'd said, 'I'll send for you and the baby.' That meant two months away, so why was he going for so long and to where?

She sat on the edge of the bed, her heart beating so loudly she thought it could be heard in the next room. I've got to remain calm, she said to herself. It won't be good for the baby if I get upset. I'll try and see him and stop him before he leaves. I'll go to the Takeuchis, she thought, maybe that's where he called from. They'll know what's happening. Her sense of relief was short-lived when she tried ringing them and their line was also constantly engaged. Somebody must be there, she thought, I'll drive out and see what's happening.

She threw on a light jacket and within minutes was speeding along Kalakaua Avenue and into Kapiolani Boulevard and up into the hills.

She pulled up at the wide iron gates, but they were locked, so leaving the car, she went in through a small side gate and started to walk up the long, darkened driveway to the big house nestled into the hill. A sharp pain in her side made her stop and rest under a spreading African tulip tree.

Looking up the driveway, she suddenly noticed that things weren't as they usually were. Most of the brazier flares along the drive were unlit; usually, they were a blaze of welcoming light. Tonight only a few stray lamps flickered forlornly. The house, too, was mostly shrouded in darkness, an odd light here and there pinpointing where it stood. A bashful moon peeped out, then hid again behind large puffs of darkened cumulus. An evening breeze had sprung up and all the perfumes of the garden wafted around her, sparking memories of her first visit here—the night she and Katsura had met. She closed her eyes and pent-up tears suddenly streaked down her face, releasing the many uncertainties of the past few months.

Was it only February when she had been brought up

this driveway? She remembered her first glimpse of the mansion on top of the rise, and Japanese paper lanterns like brilliant fireflies fluttering across the spacious verandahs. The velvety sounds of Glen Miller's 'String of Pearls' wafted down to greet her, mixed with snatches of laughter and conversation. There were shadowy figures dancing on the verandah, the myriad colours of the woman's dresses glowing warm and bright in the lantern light, offsetting the flashes of white and khaki of the men's service uniforms.

Gina had leaned forward and asked her driver to slow down so she could take it all in and hold the beauty of the moment a little longer. The night was clear and balmy with stars strung across the sky, unleashed in diamond brilliance. Inexplicably, she felt a shiver of apprehension and she drew Hiroko's chinchilla cape closely around her.

'Drive on,' she said, after glancing at her compact. Her face glowed unnaturally white in the moonlight, in sharp contrast to her long thick hair, more auburn than black. She had swept it up in combs and pulled down a few curling tendrils to soften the effect. She blotted her lipstick a little to restrain the fullness of her mouth and the voluptuousness it gave to her delicate face. She had always been conscious of her full mouth and, with a growing awareness, the effect it had upon men. Their eyes, after first meeting hers, invariably went straight to her mouth and the luscious promise of those soft lips, almost childlike in their perfection.

'You are lucky, Gina,' Hiroko had said on Gina's return from Europe, surveying her daughter with sharp eyes, taking in her ingénue grace, an air that came with a confidence more innate than acquired. 'You're a real child-woman.'

Gina had smiled, more irritated than pleased by her mother's perceptiveness. 'And a lot more woman than child,' she'd retorted and laughed with the heady sense of all that lay before her.

It had been only a few days after their conversation that she had visited Hattie and had the Tarot cards reading. And it was not long after that that things had begun to happen, starting that night in February when she went to the Takeuchi party.

She had swept in through the wide front doors, pleased with the effect her arrival always had. She'd discarded her wrap, revealing a pale yellow georgette dress that gave off a sheen in the lantern light. Backless, with its slim skirt slit high, it revealed enticing glimpses of her shapely legs and body. Within minutes she was surrounded by men, moths drawn to a vibrant new flame.

The band had swung into 'That Old Feeling' when she felt a hand on her arm. Turning she saw Mardi Cottington, Aunt Grace's daughter, saying, 'Darling, I'd like you to meet Katsura Kurosawa.'

She looked up and was aware of dark eyes, warm and amused as if privy to some secret joke. They had danced, their bodies moving in a sort of perfect harmony, she remembered, and it seemed to her that she had been with him from not only that moment, but forever . . .

'But you're only starting to meet men, so why this one?' Hiroko had objected later. 'Gina, you've only just begun.'

'So, I've begun, and this is it,' Gina had answered coolly.

And when Hiroko had again protested, she had replied, 'Well it was the same for you, Mamma, you often said so,' knowing her mother couldn't deny that. 'But it's different now,' Hiroko protested. 'It was another world then. It's not the same, nothing ever is, especially now with the war in Europe and things changing so fast. You have to be flexible. You can't be fixed on just this one person you hardly even know, and a Japanese man too. It won't bring you happiness,' she had added.

'Mamma, you're Japanese, I'm half Japanese.'

'All the more so because of that,' her mother had answered. 'You're not truly Japanese and you could never adjust to the life of being a Japanese wife, or be accepted there. It's too restrictive. You've just no comprehension of what it would be like. You've not been trained for it, Gina.'

Gina had said nothing. What was the point? She'd felt sure that Katsura was a free spirit like herself. Her mother just didn't understand.

That first night together had been so delicious. They had danced and talked, surrounded by others, yet closeted in their own world of mutual discovery. No-one else existed. The Takeuchis had been in Hawaii for only two years, but already Haruo Takeuchi, a wealthy importer, had set up valuable trade links in many areas, mostly in photographic and medical equipment. Katsura was their new house guest, on a year's training assignment with Mr Takeuchi.

Miyako Takeuchi, the softly spoken, diminutive wife from Kyoto, with a passion for English chamber music, had soon established herself as a generous hostess, and they often entertained the upper echelons of Hawaiian society on quite a lavish scale. She played viola, and organised many musical soirées at her home. Once Gina had been invited to play at an afternoon of Mozart. She had not altogether been surprised when Mrs Takeuchi approached her to play for the guests later that evening, suddenly jolting her back to the reality of the party.

'Why yes, I'd be delighted, if you really think so,' she had replied, hesitating. 'I would like to hear you play very much,' Katsura remarked with a smile. So, in the room she laughingly called 'le petit Versailles', with its mirrored walls and enormous Bohemian glass chandeliers bouncing facets of light all around the room, Gina, outwardly calm, seated herself at the magnificent concert grand piano. She waited for a hush to descend, then looking only at Katsura, she slowly made love to him with her music.

At first she had played a short sparkling Chopin Mazurka, then moved into the quieter more reflective mood of Debussy's 'Claire de Lune'. Finally, she had played the haunting melody of 'Night and Day', the notes a reflection of her feelings . . .

Sitting now in front of the deserted house, a sudden beam of car headlights coming down the driveway drew her back to the present. It was Taiio, the Takeuchi's Hawaiian chauffeur.

'Why, Miss Gina,' he said, surprised. 'What are you doing here?' Then before she could answer, 'They've all gone away,' he added looking rather uncomfortable. 'I've been paid off.'

'What do you mean, all gone. Mr and Mrs Takeuchi, too?'

He nodded. 'I took them to the airport with Mr Katsura two hours ago, and they've gone.'

'Where to?' she asked, feeling faint.

'I'm not sure, maybe back to Japan,' he answered.

'All of them?' He nodded.

She couldn't believe it. It just didn't make sense. 'I've got to go and see if he left a message or something.'

'I'll take you then, and let you in,' he said, concerned at her state, 'it's all locked up now.'

He unlocked the front door, and she walked in disbelievingly. Despite the furniture still there, some of it covered in loose cotton dust covers, the house had a newly deserted air, as if hurriedly abandoned. Even the kitchen showed signs of a sudden exodus, a packet of open rice crackers, some tofu and pickles, a still half-filled teapot and cups, mute reminders of a hurried snack. As she wandered from room to room, she saw that many small personal items had been swept away and others left behind, some spilling out of partially packed suitcases.

Moving into Katsura's former room and study, she saw that his books and papers had gone, with only a few stray items of clothing left littering the floor. She bent down and picked up a photo of herself and Katsura taken in a happier moment at the Banyan Bar overlooking the beach in the courtyard of the Moana Hotel. It was propped against the empty pigeonholes of his desk top. Turning it over, she saw a small umbrella had been recently scrawled on its back with all its romantic significance, and under it both his and her initials written in Japanese characters.

She looked up to see Taiio at the doorway.

'Yes, they've all gone,' was all she said.

'I'll take you to your car, Miss Gina.' She followed him down the wide curving stairway, but stopped in the hall looking into the mirrored drawing room. She called to Taiio, 'You go ahead, I'll join you in a minute.'

Walking over to the piano, she pushed aside the dust cover and lifted its lid. Sitting down, she looked across to the chair where Katsura had sat that night and started to play 'Night and Day', her emptiness drowned in the wash of notes that spilled into every corner of the house.

* * *

'Jill, can you join me?' Gina sounded fraught, and Jill could hear her rapid breathing.

'Where are you, is Katsura with you?'

'I'd rather not talk now. I'm at the Moana in the courtyard . . .'

'I just couldn't bear to go home,' she said when Jill arrived fifteen minutes later, in response to the urgency in Gina's voice.

Gina was waiting, wan and frail, her pregnancy barely concealed by her long jacket. She had ordered coffee and was already on her second brandy, while Jill listened to what had happened.

'I can't believe it,' Jill commented. 'He's mad about you, he wouldn't go off just like that.' To herself she thought, but maybe he would. There was something very private about Katsura that had always given her the feeling that he only lent himself to the occasion, was never truly part of it.

'And so the Takeuchis have taken off too,' Jill said thoughtfully. 'You know, Gina, I feel as if something's brewing. It's like the calm before a storm. I mean, the news from home's just dreadful. Everyone's joined up and rationing has begun. As soon as I've finished training at the hospital, I'm thinking of joining the WAAF. I'll wait till your baby comes, though,' she added, seeing

Gina's alarmed expression. 'Don't worry, I'll be here for you, and Hiroko, too.' She clasped Gina's hand.

Even if that bastard isn't, Jill thought.

They sat quietly for a while looking across at the old banyan, its lustrous dark green leaves and massive twining trunk lit up by the lights from the hotel. A sprinkling of white dinner jackets, evening dresses and jewels, the gleam and clink of crystal and occasional pop of champagne corks lent the evening a festive air.

It's hard to believe that in other parts of the world, people are starving and falling in battle, Jill reflected. She didn't feel right here any more, enjoying the bounty of the islands while others suffered, especially since Gerard had left for Canada. Nothing had really been resolved there either, except a promise to write and meet when he next came back on leave.

She knew what Gina was experiencing. That first dreadful sense of abandonment when a lover has gone. Loving too much gives an incredible licence to the one who's loved, Jill thought, the cool detachment on Gerard's face the morning before he left some weeks ago still cutting deep. A kind of perversity takes hold so that the loved one becomes disdainful, even totally resistant. This love is theirs to do with what they wish. He or she can ride the heady course of either scorning or returning the love that's so freely given. It wasn't fair, but there it was.

'It becomes a delicious, capricious game,' she said aloud.

'What does?' Gina asked.

'Oh loving, being loved, not loving, the whole bloody thing,' Jill said.

And in a way I've been the loser all along, she mused. Maybe I should change the rules of the game. But how?

'What am I going to say to Hiroko?' Gina asked suddenly. 'I mean she has always been so against this whole thing, anyway.'

'Just tell it as it is—what else can you do?' Jill answered gently.

20

WEDDING—HONOLULU, MARCH 1941

Gina lay listening to the steady tick of her bedside clock, its gentle rhythm comforting in its familiarity. For a while she floated in a warm, half-awakened state. A sudden sharp movement of the baby brought her back to her chilly reality. Katsura was gone. His 'I'll come back for you and the baby' had meant nothing.

In that grey span of the hours before dawn she lay, feeling leaden and depressed, wondering what she should do next. Should she have trusted him? It had been her decision to go ahead with the pregnancy. He had let her decide, saying he'd be happy either way. And what did that amount to when you thought about it?

Looking back on the events of the past months, she saw a pattern taking shape that until now had not occurred to her. It had really begun that first night they met at the Takeuchis. He had let her plot the course of their relationship, going along with her as if it was the most natural thing to do. But was it? She sat up wide awake now. Even their wedding plans he'd gone along with, she remembered.

'When will you marry me?' she had asked as if there could never be the slightest doubt that he would.

'Do you want to just yet? You're so very young still, Gina-san,' he'd answered, smiling at her.

'But there's the baby,' she'd said. For some reason she didn't feel threatened or anxious about her pregnancy, it seemed the most natural thing in the world, a proper culmination to their weeks of love-making. She felt complacent, drifting in a euphoric state as time rolled ahead of them in an unending vista. It was only when she informed Hiroko that the first real doubts started to intrude.

'It's crazy, you just can't go ahead with it, you're too young, you're little more than a child yourself,' her mother had said. 'How can you look after a baby, and where? In Japan?' Hiroko continued agitatedly, 'We could be at war, don't forget, and things will get much worse before they get better. And we know nothing of his family. They've no doubt arranged a marriage for him in Japan. And how can he support you?'

'We love each other and I want this baby,' was all Gina could think to reply.

Despite Hiroko's strong opposition, Katsura and Gina were married, in the small St Stephen's Church in the Nuuanu Valley. It was the one she had sometimes visited as a child with Grandma Hattie when they drove to the HanaiaKamalama, Queen Emma Summer Palace.

She had always been drawn to the exquisite Mary, Mother of Christ statue, gazing at its calm beautiful expression, and the *lei* of fragrant frangipani strung casually across her shoulders, making Mary a part of the island and a reality in Gina's own life.

'I will marry here one day,' she had told her grandmother.

'Oh don't be silly, darling. You'll have a big white wedding at Our Lady of Peace cathedral. I absolutely insist!' Hattie had laughed.

Later that day at the Summer Palace with Hattie, they had taken tea from the enormous hamper which Lalana had brought along. Hattie had put up her easel, sketching through the long afternoon, with Kit lying peacefully at her feet, while Gina swam and played at the edge of the stream with its legendary stone monoliths, the Canoe of the Dragon stone and others with their strange ancient carvings including the stone ghost dog Kaupe. 'He would come into the valley and howl at the moon,' Lalana had told her, her large brown eyes rolling as she spoke of him. 'It was very unlucky if you saw him, as children who had seen Kaupe have been known to disappear.'

Lying amongst the lush soft ginger plants with the light filtering through the palms and umbrella trees and listening to the rush of water from the Kapena Falls, Gina had listened as Lalana regaled her with many of the tales of ancient Hawaii.

She could almost see the young woman who, fearing the gods would take her husband in sacrifice, had bewitched him into becoming part of the great breadfruit tree on the very banks on which she now lay, a tree which later became a revered and powerful influence in the lives of the people until the time of Kamehameha the First. Lalana also told her of the fierce battles between the hero Kawelo and the strong men of Kauai, where they had fought with torn-up trees as giant clubs. She spoke of how the mighty wauka tree, used for making Kapa, had first sprung up from the sacred site deep in the Nuuanu Valley at Pu-iwa where Maikoha had been buried by his daughters at the side of the stream, and from where the wauka trees had spread throughout the Hawaiian islands.

These childhood visits had brought Gina in touch with the true beauty of the island and its people, their ancient beliefs and history giving her a sense of belonging.

She had taken Katsura there before their marriage and he too had been delighted with the beauty of the place and her stories. Afterwards, when taking him to the Kyoto Gardens, with their three-tiered replica of the Sanji Pagoda in Nara, he had been quiet and reflective, and she knew he was thinking of his home. He had started to tell her a little of his life in the outskirts of Nagasaki. How his father was descended from seven generations of a rice-growing and *sake*-brewing family.

'I am his second son, so the pressure has not been so great for me to go into the family business,' Katsura had said, 'but I chose to get involved anyway, even as a young boy.'

'So, why are you here?'

'Things are changing. I needed overseas trading experience, and the chance came with Mr Takeuchi, my father's friend. It is best I remain here for the time being.'

His answer had not satisfied her. But they had travelled across the Pali Highway into the Pauoa Valley to the Honolulu Sake Brewery and Ice Co. While Katsura spoke with the manager, Gina sauntered through the old factory buildings steeped in the pungent odour of the sweet rice wine, chatting with the workers who still practised their traditional hand labour methods. Later, from the Nuuanu Pali lookout, standing braced against the wind, Katsura had taken many shots of the golden valley that fell away to the sea on the distant horizon.

Two weeks later, they were married in the small church at Nuuanu, Gina exuberant in a cerise silk dress, a circlet of fragrant pikake and lehua blossom in her dark hair. Gerard had given her away, with Jill and Hiroko, the Takeuchis, and a few close friends as the only other guests.

'I'd wanted a big splendid wedding for you, Gina-chan,' Hiroko said wistfully at the small reception she had given afterwards in the pink forecourt of the Royal Hawaiian. Gina thought of Grandma Hattie with a sudden pang.

The chiming of her clock brought Gina back to the present. It was uncomfortable lying on her back, yet it seemed to be the only way she could, now that her stomach was growing bigger. The first rosy pink rays of dawn were reaching into the morning sky, promising a golden day ahead. Her hair felt hot and heavy and she coiled it up on top of her head, but the combs wouldn't hold and it fell about her neck. She walked over to her dressing table, turning on the tiny mirror lights, and looked at her face—so pale, lost in the mass of hair surrounding it.

Reaching into her drawer, she pulled out some scissors

and carefully started cutting the long tresses. Feather-cutting as she had often seen the women doing at the beauty salon, she continued until her hair sat close into her head with a longer duck's tail at the back. Going to the bathroom, she washed her hair under the hand spray. It was so much quicker than before. Then, towelling it dry, she combed it in seconds, flicking it with her fingers, then snipping any longer bits that suddenly appeared.

Returning to the mirror, she angled it so she could see the sides and back. It felt wonderful. Her face had taken on a new vitality, the small straight nose, high cheekbones and long neck dramatically revealed. Her eyes seemed larger, and her generous mouth sat well with this new gamine look. She felt a charge of renewed confidence, and smiled at her reflection. Whatever happened now, whether Katsura came back to her or not, and she felt sure that he would, she would still have his child, and that was something no-one could take away from her. And she had her family, her friends and her piano. Yes, she would go on working towards her concert performance, and everything would be fine. With all the unbounded optimism of youth, she slipped into her bed, and within minutes was in a deep and untroubled sleep.

21

NEW ARRIVAL—HONOLULU, DECEMBER 1941

The night had an atmosphere of expectancy. Was it the approaching Christmas festivities and the coming birth of her baby? Gina rested on the couch, gazing out across the garden to the velvety sky. There was something in the air, a kind of closing in, and despite the heat she shivered. A lone towering cloud brought back visions of the Haleakala crater, and its ghostly shapes that whirled in the mists of her childhood memories.

Gina had returned there not long after Katsura had left, and remembered ascending in the small bus for what seemed like hours, driving past dark volcanic rocks glinting silvery black in the early morning light. Suddenly, there she was at the rim of the crater, looking down into miles of purple-shaded moonscape, a vast area of old cinder cones and lava flows, dormant and desolate, yet with the possibility that it could erupt into life again. It was clearly etched in her memory from years before when she first saw it, and there it was again, just the same, a place where time never seemed to move. That was its strength, its comforting certainty that she looked for now.

A strong smell of sulphur, biting in its pungency, assailed her and she sneezed violently, her eyes watering in an instant protective wash. She retreated a little, pulling her jacket around her shoulders. Never would she forget the compelling wonder of this spiritual house of the sun. She felt at once clear-headed and decisive, with the ability to see things as they were. If she did not hear from Katsura soon, she would go to Japan and look for him there. She would find and confront him. Try as she might, she did not feel ready to step into the cold lone landscape of life without him—especially with their baby arriving. Somehow she would try to trace him. She remembered the heady sense of relief as her spirits lifted with her decision.

Gina had turned and made her way back from the crater's edge, passing an elderly Japanese couple along the way. Taking in their orderly appearance and sense of unity as a further sanction of her decision, she nodded to them, greeting them easily in her mother tongue, and noting their faint look of surprise, as though trying to match her obviously Western demeanour with her fluent Japanese.

How strange it was. She felt comfortable with the many threads of nationality woven within her, whereas with Gerard . . . She thought of her twin brother. During those early years before Hiroko had sent him away to school, he had seldom been calm. She felt a closeness to her twin, but it was always coupled with the feeling that he sought to push her away from him.

Her first real experience of this had been years ago, when she was lying in her attic bedroom, its white wall covered with Hattie's and her own paintings, and pictures of her favourite film stars. A full-length mirror, later to reflect many anguished adolescent hours, was tilted so that she could see whoever came up the stairs. Still weakened from an exhausting bout of asthma and a night of coughing and fighting for her breath, she was propped up with pillows and staring listlessly out the casement window at the tops of the gently swaying bamboo fronds, partly veiling her view of the sky. She always liked that fresh clear green against the blue, but wished she could see more of the sky. She loved looking at the sky, and longed to be able to fly into its endless reaches.

She could hear her mother admonishing Gerard in the kitchen below. He was shouting back and there were the sounds of a scuffle as he ran off. She turned to face the door, and a tiny kitten nestling in the warmth of her legs on the quilt awakened yawning, staring at her with the still blue eyes of a baby. It was the most precious thing she'd ever had. The first living thing. Gina reached down, softly running her fingers through its silky fur, feeling the tiny frail bones within. It stretched luxuriously as she stroked it, and then curled into a ball and was asleep again. She smiled at this little friend, a companion to help her through the long dreary hours spent alone, sick in this room. There were more shouts and she could hear her mother calling after Gerard, and the thumping on the stairs as he ran up to her room.

She turned and looked at the mirror and his reflection as he approached, his face contorted and red with anger. She drew back, pretending to be asleep as he burst into her room.

'Wake up, wake up!' he shouted, venting his frustration.

'Go away, Gerard,' she murmured, still with her eyes closed. 'I feel sick—I just want to sleep.'

'You're always sick, always sleeping. I have to do all your jobs, it's not fair. She spoils you. You just do what you like.'

'Go away,' Gina repeated. She could hear her mother now calling from the bottom of the stairs.

'Leave her alone, Gerard. You come down here at once, you come down, do you hear?'

Gina lay still with her eyes closed, willing him to leave the room.

'Spoilt baby, baby!' he shouted at her, pushing her hard against the wall. She kept her eyes closed, hoping he'd lose interest and move away, but her lack of reaction seemed only to infuriate him further.

'This'll wake you up then!' he cried, and picking the

kitten up by its back legs, he whirled it around and then hurled it with all his strength high against the wall.

She heard the yowl of pain and the sickening thud as it hit the ceiling then bounced onto the wall, and was out of bed and picking up the tiny inert body as her brother raced from the room. Her own scream was a sound and feeling that she'd never forgotten, and the deep sense of injustice and loss had never left her. Nor had a wariness of Gerard, which remained to this day.

He had opposed her decision to go to Japan and find Katsura when she first proposed the idea. 'You rush headlong into everything. There's no point in chasing him now, it's a dangerous time to go anyway. And what would you achieve? If he wanted you, he'd be here with you,' he added coldly.

Lying on the couch now, Gina's heart sank at the thought of those words, and suddenly the baby kicked. She felt so heavy and unwieldy. As she rose to go to the bathroom, she felt a slow trickle of fluid start down her legs. With a stab of fear, she realised it was her waters breaking. A deep intense pain began moving up her legs and into the base of her spine, so intense she held her breath as if willing it away. Staggering back to the couch, she lay there gasping. It was too soon, the baby wasn't due for three more weeks. And no one was here. Panic set in with that realisation. Hiroko was in Maui, Jill not due to arrive until next week, Gerard was away flying overseas somewhere, and her darling Hattie gone forever. She started to sob in unrestrained bursts of anguish.

'Katsura, Katsura!' she cried. She felt her chest tightening in that frightening way before an asthma attack set in. It was a year since her last bad attack. Not now, not now, please, she silently begged. She tried to calm down, and dragging herself to the phone, rang downstairs to Lalana, but there was no answer.

The ride into the hospital set high in the hills seemed the prelude to a night's endless journey into hell. The contractions came hard and heavy, yet with little or no movement from the baby, its head well positioned, but her body loath to let it go. The intermittent screams of pain that rose from her lips seemed to come from some other disembodied being. Faces came and went, some concerned, others long hardened by such suffering. At one stage, her breathing seemed to stop and they administered oxygen in a desperate attempt to give her some relief.

'Mamma! Katsura!' Vainly she called for someone to lift her away from this place of pain. Eventually, she saw Lalana's smooth good-natured face, now creased with anxiety, hovering above her.

'Hush, Miss Gina. you'll be all right. Hush now, you hear.' She sat there, never leaving Gina's side, stroking her forehead, gently coaxing her to be calm.

'Where's mamma?'

'She's coming, she'll be here soon. Everything's fine now, you hear. You just pop out that big beautiful baby, come on now.'

She coaxed and wheedled Gina into a calmer state, sometimes singing to her, the songs from the Nuuanu Valley days, in her deep husky voice. At other times when the contractions worsened, she held tightly to both of Gina's hands, urging her to be calm and breathe deeply. But nothing happened.

She seemed to cling to the baby as though it was her last link to life itself.

As dawn broke, she grew more accustomed to the pain, and became aware of her surroundings. The faintest pale pink light danced across the rim of the sky, lighting the way to a squadron of planes roaring their way across wide open spaces. Small, seemingly harmless specks, yet harbingers of horror.

Lalana sponged Gina's face, speaking reassuringly and urging her to drink a little. The earlier asthma attack had subsided, but the tightness in her chest was a reminder that it was only a temporary reprieve.

'Your mother's arriving first thing this morning, and she'll want to see that baby when she gets here,' Lalana softly chided, but a cold feeling of apprehension was starting to close around her heart. Gina smiled weakly up at her, and immediately the contractions started up with renewed intensity.

Her doctor was back, the occasional blur of his masked face looming closely, then receding in a circle of unknown faces. She had been wheeled into another theatre, and the harsh pool of the theatre light shone down in relentless scrutiny.

Gina felt no longer captain of this frail craft, her body. It now belonged to someone else to toy with and play out its deadly game. Her spirit seemed to have deserted her, there had been no half-time, no rest from this struggle on her field of pain.

'Mamma! Mamma! Take me away, I can't bear it any longer,' she cried out at one stage, sweat beading her forehead. Then 'I'm only a baby, too,' she whispered, repeating her mother's words.

'Push down, now. Come on, push. Push!' the sister was urging her.

With her legs suspended high in their straps, she felt like an animal trapped in a world suffused with red. Was it an inferno? Had she died?

She could feel the doctor's hands reaching up deep into her stretched birth canal. She became desperate to rid herself of the enormous thing within her, and bore down hard as if forcing it away. There was the cold slap of metal forceps sliding within her, a sharp needle prick and a cutting through her flesh as she screamed out in this last unbelievable assault and shock of pain. Then with a sudden rush, she felt the body that had lain within her slide away, as if it had been wilfully waiting for just the moment that best suited its arrival.

Gina didn't see the rosy, perfectly formed baby girl who opened her lungs at 7.50 on the morning of 7 December. Sophie Harriette Kurosawa announced her arrival to the world, only five minutes before Commander Mitsuo Fuchida guided his 183 bombers, dive bombers and zero fighters towards the static of Hawaiian music from their radios on that perfect Sunday morning. Then like charmed messengers of the gods, dropping without warning and unhindered into the heart of Oahu . . . Fuchida's joyful 'Tora! Tora! Tora!' resounded onto the pages of World War Two history, almost drowning out the cries of a newborn child.

Gina was in shock, fighting for breath and for her life.

22

HIROKO'S LOSS—1941

The throb of the ship's engine rose and fell in harmony with the sigh and moan of the early morning Kona wind as it whipped across the waves, bringing with it all the old familiar scents from the islands.

As soon as she'd received the call from Lalana at the hospital, Hiroko had summoned Malo, her long-time house boy and chauffeur, to ready the big cruiser for departure. She had slept fitfully in its comfortable cabin, with its touches of Hattie and Gare, and their happy days together fishing the teeming waters around their beloved Maui. The strong currents carried them through the Molekai and Maui channels, across the shimmering aquamarine reaches towards Oahu.

The sun had risen early and played out its sparkling symphony with water and sky. Hiroko barely noticed this, her thoughts with her daughter and what she would now be going through. The imminent arrival of a grandchild made her aware of the passing years, and her own vulnerability. Where had the years gone? It was difficult to believe that she was going on forty-two and that Gina was about to be a mother at the tender age of nineteen. If only she had waited. That whole business with Katsura had turned out so badly. Hiroko had never taken to him, or trusted him. And Gina? The girl's youthful vitality rode a fine line with the ever-present shadow of her illness. Her asthma attacks, though not as frequent, were often severe, and she prayed that Gina was staying calm and able to cope at this time.

Hiroko thought of Boy and the love they had shared. What did she really have now? Her beloved Boy was long gone, also Hattie and Gare. Gerard was away and getting on with his life, and Satoshi would never be a son to her, not now with all that had passed. And now Gina was about to be involved with a child of her own.

And so, who do I have close to me? she thought, shivering as a cool breeze swept along the deck. *We really are alone in this world, small islands unto ourselves.*

Feeling aware of all the losses in her life, her mind lingered on Satoshi. She thought of the day he'd come into this world, a freezing mid-winter's afternoon, and she had stayed to give birth at her in-laws' home in Ebisu. She would have preferred to be with her father, but with no mother or other womenfolk there in attendance, there didn't seem much point. And Noboru had wanted her to stay where she was.

Even then, his sister Michiko had exerted her influence. 'You must be here with us—I have spoken to Noboru and he agrees,' she said with that irritating proprietorial air she always adopted with Hiroko.

She recalled Noboru's amused rejoinder whenever she'd mentioned the unreasonable treatment she'd experienced at the hands of his sister. 'Well, she's a fire horse remember, so what do you expect?'

That was true, she thought. Women born at that time were reputed to be man-eaters and too strong for their own good. Often baby girls born at such an unpropitious time as the year of the Fire Horse were quietly smothered at birth. Mothers, fearing such an event, did all they could to avoid a pregnancy in the year of the Fire Horse, in case they had a daughter.

But Michiko had escaped such a fate, and had more than compensated for her lack of beauty and sweetness of nature with a commanding presence and sharp tongue that she'd exerted from an early age—without fear of contradiction. If anything, her family seemed to aid and abet her. It was Michiko, not her mother-in-law, who had supervised all the preparations for Satoshi's birth. Michiko had brought in the midwife, and advised Hiroko on her diet, ordering that no spicy foods were to be served to her. Michiko had insisted that she wear the Iwata-obi binding cloth around her burgeoning stomach from the fifth month, and had accompanied her to the shrine to pray for the safe delivery of a son. And it was Michiko who had unearthed the old family bed with its strong supporting back to assist Hiroko in her final squatting position to deliver the baby. She also insisted that the umbilical cord be cut with the old carved bamboo knife that had been used for just this purpose in the Nakamura family for generations.

Michiko had brought in the wet-nurse when Hiroko was unable to provide enough breast milk for her strong lusty boy. It had been Michiko who had helped dress him in his beautiful kimono-shaped gown thirty-two days after his birth when they took him on his first visit to the Shinto shrine, where the priest briefly bestowed the rites of purification and blessing. Often she even carried Satoshi strapped to her own back—to give Hiroko some respite, as she explained—but in effect to bond him closer to herself.

'It will only be a matter of time before she takes him from our bed,' Hiroko complained to Noboru. The tiny child still slept with them at night. But her husband had shrugged it off as women's talk, and after she had seen him with Michiko in the bath house and suspected their involvement, she wondered how long it would be until Michiko removed her from Noboru's bed. Then Noboru had been away so often with his regiment, and with his death it had largely fallen to Hiroko to try and keep some control of her situation within the Nakamura household. However, when it came to family matters, Michiko's word was law, and for Hiroko, it soon became a losing battle.

Like a bird released from its cage, she had flown into the wider world of Boy and his family. But the price she'd paid had been a heavy one: Boy's sudden death and her being forced to leave her small son behind. The driver of the car that had hit Boy had never been found, and once more she felt the dark presence of Michiko and her threats move across her mind. To shake it off, Hiroko hurried out of the cabin, and up towards the bridge, bringing coffee and brioche with her.

They were only twenty minutes out of Honolulu harbour, cutting through the blue-green waters of the Kaiwi Channel, when away on the horizon to the north-west, they saw a dark cloudlike shape moving towards them with a growing hum as it came closer.

'What the hell is that?' Malo, now at the helm, leaned forward, peering into the distance.

'Whatever it is, it's coming this way,' Hiroko answered.

Sipping their coffee and staring into the distance, they were silenced by the strangeness of the sight. The dark distant cloud fanned out as the planes flew steadily closer, and the roar of their engines preceded them as if in triumphal fanfare.

'Looks as if the whole air fleet's out exercising,' said Malo, without taking his eyes off the on-coming squadron. He turned to Hiroko, perplexed. 'Maybe it's those B–17s they say are coming in from the West Coast.'

Hiroko shrugged, her thoughts back with Gina. 'But would there be so many of them? Anyway, it's not long until we arrive now, Malo, so I'll go below and get ready, as I want to leave as soon as we dock. Will you radio through and have a car waiting?'

He nodded, his eyes still on the ominous sky.

She took one last look at the approaching mass of planes darkening the sky. There was something frightening in the way they moved relentlessly, without deflection, as though on a predestined course, threatening to overwhelm with their noise and presence the usual serenity of this island paradise.

Malo nosed the cruiser into the still sleeping Honolulu harbour at 7.45 a.m., just as the first high-level bombers crossed Oahu's shore line at 10 000 feet. They rose to 15 000 feet, then breaking into two groups, one headed for Wheeler Field in Central Oahu, and the other made for Hickham Field and Ford Island. The dive bombers turned seaward in a wide turn that would bring them back into Pearl Harbor from the south, with Zero fighters flying in escort. Below them, the whole Pacific fleet, Battleship Row, lay tranquilly side by side, basking in the still life of an undisturbed Sunday morning.

As Hiroko's cruiser berthed, the sounds of violent explosions and a shout from Malo brought her hurrying up on deck.

'My God, they're attacking us—they're attacking us!' Malo shouted in amazement, as if doubting his own words. Her stomach lurched in fear, her thoughts for Gina and the baby.

'Where? What's happening?' she cried, as she raced up in time to see a cloud of dense black smoke rising to the sky from the direction of Pearl, while billowing smoke and deafening explosions arose from the centre of the island.

'Those bastards, they're attacking us,' Malo leaned over, switching on the radio.

'What? Who?' Hiroko repeated. But he looked away from her, and then she heard the familiar voice of announcer Web Edwards from 'Hawaii Calls' tensely repeating: 'This is no drill. Pearl Harbor is under attack. This is no drill. This is the real McCoy.'

She started to shake uncontrollably. 'I'm going to Gina—you stay with the boat,' she told Malo. 'I'll ring you from the hospital.'

'I'd better come with you,' he said, his big face anxious.

'No, no, I'll be fine, and I might need you to get us back to Maui in a hurry.'

Her driver was waiting, and they sped along the Kapiolani Drive, deserted as usual on a Sunday morning. No-one had yet comprehended what was happening. Only a few people wandered on the streets.

Hiroko urged the driver to hurry, and as they headed down town towards the hospital, a plane roared low overhead, and as she looked fearfully from the window, she saw the two red suns emblazoned on its side.

'Heavenly Father!' She crossed herself and lay back, her heart beating wildly. It was a Japanese attack. Her own countrymen were attacking Hawaii, so what would happen now? If they have declared war, what then? Her thoughts raced and she quickly donned her dark glasses, and tied her hair back in a scarf, thankful for her tailored pants and jacket that gave no hint of her Japanese origin. The sound of more distant explosions and smell of smoke further alerted her to act quickly now to protect Gina, the baby and herself.

I wonder under which name she is registered, Hiroko thought, starting to panic, remembering the red sun symbols on the attacking planes.

As they drove in through the hospital gates, they were forced to the side of the road by a fleet of ambulances speeding out past them, their strident sirens heightening her fears. But minutes later, as she arrived, all thoughts of the chaos outside disappeared, with her only concern now for her daughter.

'I'm Mrs Baillieu, Gina's mother,' she said to the sister in charge.

The woman looked at her impersonally, then with a brief 'Come with me', led her to a waiting room.

'I'll get Dr McCauley for you,' she said, turning to go.

'No,' Hiroko said firmly, 'I will speak with him later. I want to see my daughter now. Where is she?'

The sister, her eyes flinty, gazed at Hiroko.

'She's had a disturbed night and is very ill. It's best that you speak with him first.'

'I demand to see her now,' said Hiroko, her tone

precluding any argument. She caught sight of Lalana emerging from a room down the corridor and ran to her.

'Lalana, what's going on? Where's Gina?'

'Oh, madam, thank God you're here.' Lalana's face, grey with tiredness, crumpled and tears flowed as she reached out towards her.

Without a word, her heart stilled, Hiroko brushed past her and into the room. She could see at a glance that Gina was experiencing an extreme asthma attack. The doctor was leaning over her, giving her an injection while a nurse administered oxygen.

'Gina, Gina!' She moved quickly to her side and clasped her daughter's cold hands, willing her to breathe.

Wan and spent, Gina lay fighting for her every breath in short rapid pants. Hiroko looked up at the doctor, her eyes questioning.

'She's had a pretty rough time, we'll have to watch her,' he said.

'Can I stay?' Hiroko whispered. He nodded. Then her voice faltered. 'And the baby?'

He smiled at her. 'A beautiful little girl.' Closing her eyes, Hiroko crossed herself, her silent prayer of thanks now a plea of mercy for her daughter's life. There was a sudden commotion at the door, and a sister looked in.

'It's an emergency, doctor. Come quickly!' She looked flustered, Hiroko noted, now aware of hurrying feet and raised voices in the corridor outside. Lalana looked up. 'What's happening out there?'

As if she hadn't heard, her eyes still on her daughter, Hiroko said, 'I want to hear about Gina now. Tell me everything, from the moment you arrived.

'It's been very bad for Miss Gina,' Lalana answered, her face softening as she recounted the night's events. When she'd finished, Hiroko was silent for some time, focused on her daughter, then turning to Lalana asked, 'Did you register her name last night?'

'Why sure, Madam, they asked me to fill out the form as soon as we got here,' she answered.

'And what name did you use?'

'Why, Miss Gina Baillieu,' Lalana answered. 'I wasn't going to use that no-good's name,' she added darkly. Hiroko let out a long sigh of relief, then leaned back closing her eyes.

'Now you just sit tight,' Lalana said, getting up and moving to the door. 'I'll go and see what's going on out there, and bring you back a nice hot coffee while I'm at it,' she said briskly, bringing a note of normality to the sense of foreboding that was threatening to engulf them. Hiroko gave her a wan smile, then leaned forward to smooth back the damp hair from her sleeping daughter's flushed face.

Swansong

Gina's lapse into a fitful sleep was but a brief reprieve. Later, as she again fought for her breath in quick shallow bursts, she felt a needle prick in her arm, and the doctor's face swam before her. She tried to breathe in through the mask as they urged her, and was now aware of other voices, and a familiar one. Was that her mother standing there beside her? She felt a surge of relief. 'Mamma, you're here.' Had she spoken or did she imagine it?

'Gina-chan, Gina-chan.' She could feel Hiroko's cool hands clasping hers, then lightly smoothing her hair back from her forehead. She moaned as a sharp shooting pain in her chest intensified, then quickly subsided. She thought she heard the sound of explosions somewhere distant, then as the morphine took effect she could feel herself floating, suspended on a warm cloud of dreaming. She could hear a voice speaking to her in Japanese. 'I felt as if I knew him as well as myself, yet we had never spoken.' She realised it was herself saying these words from somewhere else. Her voice continued, recounting an event to convey some long-lost message, but to whom she couldn't tell. Her voice continued, 'The first time we met was at Ise, purely by chance in the autumn of 1956 at the Jingu shrine. I saw him standing there, in contemplation, looking into the distance at I know not what.'

The mists of her dream lifted and she could see it all clearly. As she walked across a courtyard, the crunch of gravel beneath her feet made him turn, and he looked straight across at her and into her eyes. The silent message that passed between them was unmistakable. It was at once a look of suffering to be replaced by one of warning as if urging her from this place. She looked back with a searching intensity, then gave a barely perceptible inclination of her head as if to say 'I understand'. She drew her long white wrap closely around her and hurried on. He had turned from her, and sneaking another look at his bowed head and shoulders as she passed by, Gina felt a rush of compassion and a longing to stay with him, as if wishing to lift his mantle of suffering and spare him any further torment.

Waking to another sharp chest pain, Gina opened her eyes to see Hiroko bending over her. 'Mamma, the baby, my baby?' she cried.

'She's fine, just fine, you must rest now Gina-chan,' Hiroko answered.

'No, no, there's no time.' Gina paused, fighting for her breath. The pain in her chest was increasing, threatening to swallow her up. 'Mamma, call her Sophie for me,' she whispered. 'Hattie wanted Sophie. She's to be named Sophie.'

Her mother's face was receding and something clicked within her head and she lay quite still. Then at the end of a long, long tunnel she could see herself, a tiny child running towards a towering figure with golden hair.

'Daddy! Daddy!' With arms outstretched and a sense of glorious homecoming she felt him scoop her up, whirling her around, and she was laughing and laughing with delight, safe and secure in his arms. A brilliant golden light flooded across the sky and she felt herself moving towards it in weightless wonderful flight. She was so happy now and nothing else mattered.

As Hiroko felt Gina's hand go limp and still within

hers, she knew her daughter had gone. She sat without moving in a limbo of timelessness. It was Lalana's cry of alarm when she returned to the room that jolted her to action.

23

TO LOVE AND HONOUR
HONOLULU, DECEMBER 1941

The voices of the Andrew Sisters floated out from a parked car as Jill walked briskly along the tree-lined avenue, then into an office building, and stood waiting for an elevator.

As it arrived, a tall dark-haired man stepped out. She turned for a quick second glimpse at the now retreating figure as the door slid shut. It wasn't him. But something in his bearing brought Gerard back to her as powerfully as if they had just met. Jill leaned against the wall of the elevator feeling herself fall a thousand flights into the well of memory, and the unresolved business of her last meeting with Gerard before he left for Canada.

'It's great news, Jilly,' he had said, his face alight with anticipation. 'It seems Bill and I will be doing the same flying course. We'll both be training at the same place.'

'And then what?' she had asked, an ache in her chest. He'd looked at her.

'Who knows? If America comes into the war, then it will be on for young and old. Bill will be flying with the RAAF and could be seconded anywhere. As for me, well it all depends whether Uncle Sam goes into it or not,' he had said.

She could still feel his warmth, the urgency of his need for her, his body curved into hers as they danced at the officer's club the night before he left. It had been at once exhilarating and frightening. He would be gone within hours, maybe forever. She had felt her heart hovering within the circle of his light, which at any time could be plunged into darkness. To stave off the hour she had drunk quite a lot, they all had, and the air was electric with impending change.

'What if you end up fighting the Japanese? I mean how will you feel with Hiroko and everything . . .' she'd asked him later as she lay in his arms, gazing into those dark Eurasian eyes.

He stiffened as he thought of Satoshi and his years of resentment, hating him and his mother's obsession with her missing son. And now with Katsura's disappearance, Gina's unhappiness, he felt the familiar rising anger. Revenge for all those past hurts would be very sweet. 'We'll destroy whoever the enemy is,' he said, and came into her with a fierceness Jill had never before experienced. But it was a response she felt belonged to something quite outside herself, and it left her feeling even more isolated and cut off from him.

He had left early the next morning. In the two months since then, she had drifted in a sea of discontent. She had tried to use the time in getting closer to Hiroko, thinking that this would be a way to win Gerard over by bridging the differences, largely unspoken, which still lay between mother and son. Gerard had shrugged it off whenever she had questioned him. But she'd pursued it, wanting to get to the bones of what was hidden from her.

'Has she ever really spoken to you about Boy or Satoshi? I mean have you ever sort of had a heart-to-heart about how she felt about all that happened?' she went on, warming to the idea, gazing up at him, her eyes searching his.

'Jilly, don't keep harking back to the past. There's nothing to talk about.' His face darkening, Gerard moved away.

'Well there's something bugging you, what the hell is it?' she exclaimed, unable to restrain herself. 'Is there someone else?' she went on when he didn't answer, pushing into a territory she knew would do her no good.

'Just take it easy now, Jilly. I'll see you,' he said, turning from her, slamming the door as he left. She heard him drive away, gunning the motor as he went.

'Damn! Damn! Damn!' she fumed, hating him in that moment, knowing she was not the one in control.

With Hiroko, try as she might there was never any real exchange of confidences. It was as if the woman had a wall around her with a 'keep out' sign. Always the smile though and the politeness, but never a letting down of her reserve or a getting in close with 'girl talk'.

'You're always asking questions, Jill-san,' Hiroko said one day, irritated. 'Just like Grace.'

And now's not the time to pursue that one, Jill thought, noting Hiroko's reaction, but never one to hold back, she said, 'Aunt Grace? Really?' Her question hung but went unanswered.

'Damn her,' Jill thought, but she smiled as she hid her inner fear that she'd never be brought into Hiroko's confidence.

* * *

It was Gina's pregnancy and need for her after Katsura's sudden disappearance that had decided Jill to stay on longer.

'Jilly, do you think Katsura will come back to me?' Gina had asked again and again.

'Of course he will, don't be silly, it's only a matter of time. Everything's upside down now with the war and all that's happening,' Jill had answered, feeling far from sure herself.

'Tell you what. I'm going away next weekend to the Big Island to stay with Mardi Cottington and everyone will be there, and she wants you to come too, so why don't you? You could do with a break. We'll just lie around, swim and relax, and try and forget everything,' Jill went on, mirroring her own desires.

'I can't,' Gina had said. 'Katsura may just ring or try to be in touch at any time. I daren't leave, not now,' she'd added.

Jill had returned to Honolulu on the Monday after a Sunday when they had all sat around the radio, stunned by the news of the attack on Pearl Harbour and fearful of another. She was thankful that Gerard had been away and not one of the many victims. Again and again she had tried to ring Gina, but there was no answer. She rang Hiroko in Maui, only to learn from one of the servants that Miss Gina was in labour and that Mrs Baillieu had left for the hospital to be with her.

Her first thoughts were that maybe the shock of the bombing had brought on Gina's labour early, or that she had been hurt. A feeling of guilt that she hadn't been with her hung heavy, only to be compounded when she was finally able to get to the hospital late Monday afternoon to learn that it was all over, and she was too late.

She felt stunned, beyond tears, but with an overwhelming regret: she should never have gone away when the birth was so close and with Gina in such a state. She should have been with her. Maybe it would have been different then, she mused as all the old associations with her mother's death came rushing back to haunt her.

It wasn't until she saw Hiroko in the hospital, standing so small and defenceless, holding Gina's baby, that the full sense of loss swept over her. She put her arms around them both and wept.

'I'm going back to Maui in the morning,' Hiroko told her later. 'Things are not good for us here now,' she added. 'The baby is staying on in the hospital for a few more days. Lalana will stay here with her, and . . .' she paused, looking hopefully to Jill, who nodded and said, 'I'll be here, don't worry, I will stay with her.'

Hiroko's face was like a mask, as though she could only just bring herself to force the next words out. 'I'm arranging for the funeral. It's to be quiet and private, and of course her,' she paused, her voice breaking, 'my Gina-chan's ashes will come back with me to Maui. I'm arranging it all,' she repeated more to reassure herself.

Jill had taken the tiny baby from Hiroko. She was sleeping peacefully, so calm in the midst of chaos. Her eyelashes fluttered against creamy skin, and she was just so perfect with her tiny snub nose and a beautifully formed mouth, like her mother's. A feeling of such tenderness swept over Jill as she held the child. 'Sophie,' she whispered, 'Sophie.'

'There's almost no one left now,' Hiroko murmured. 'Only Gerard.'

'And there's Sophie,' said Jill, looking across at her.

'Yes, the baby,' Hiroko agreed, glancing absently at the small bundle in Jill's arms.

'Does Gerard know? Has he been told anything yet?' Jill asked.

Hiroko shook her head slowly. 'As soon as he hears about the bombing he will come back,' she said simply. Then she moaned suddenly as the thought hit her for the first time. Her two sons in the armed forces of opposing nations, were now about to fight each other. She held herself very still as the realisation washed over her, then looking across at the baby in Jill's arms she started to move away as if to distance herself from the child whose birth had helped her only daughter die.

'Let me tell him then,' Jill asked anxiously, only too aware of Hiroko's withdrawal. A verse from a hymn she had often sung in chapel at school floated into her mind, and she could hear the girlish voices singing in full-throated unison, words only half realised that had always sent prickles up her spine.

God moves in a mysterious way,
His wonders to perform.
He plants his footsteps in the sea,
And rides upon the storm.

As she gazed down at Sophie's sweet face, Jill knew with an absolute clarity what she must do. The child would become hers and Gerard's. Gina would have wanted that, she thought. And maybe this would be the way he would finally come to her.

'Hiroko, let me care for Sophie, she can stay with me and Lalana will help,' she added.

'But aren't you going back to Australia'? asked Hiroko. 'What about your job and . . .'

Jill cut in. 'A physio can work anywhere, especially now, and you know money's no problem.' She paused. 'You have to go on running the plantation and I will stay on here. I don't really want to return to Australia now, anyway.' As the idea took shape she went on excitedly, 'We could move into Hattie's old house. Gina was fixing it up to live there, and Gerard will be there.'

'Gerard?' Hiroko looked surprised.

'Yes, we will live together,' Jill went on boldly. 'I love him, and we're going to marry anyway,' she continued, fairly running with the ball now.

Hiroko gazed at the girl's flushed face and said nothing at first, then simply, 'It won't be easy for you, Jill-chan.'

'But I want to do it,' Jill replied, and to add a final emotive seal of approval, she added, 'And Gina would have wanted it this way, too.'

And so it was arranged.

It was with Sophie in her arms that she met Gerard twelve days later when he arrived back from Canada, a week and two days after his sister Gina's funeral.

He saw them both, and he knew.

They were married quietly the following week in the tiny St Gabriel's church on Maui's beautiful Hana coast, only two hours before Gerard flew out to the Philippines to fight as an American, now at war with his mother's and his ancestors' countrymen.

PART THREE

24

TO KURE—JAPAN, 1945

Daihachi Isawa was on the train to Kure. He had taken an earlier train, as he had heard that there may be another raid of B-29s and it seemed safer to leave now.

How strange it is, he thought, this pre-occupation with time. We are so geared to time. It's as though our lives are structured within some vast clock ticking away in steady syncopation. Inwardly, he hummed a childhood melody to the beat of the wheels as they passed over the wooden sleepers. It helped to give a sense of rhythm, a continuity that comforted him.

He was on his way to see his young grandson, Matsuhiro, who had been ill. There was so little food now and the boy at twelve was still so thin and needed building up. He had brought with him some precious sweet potatoes for the boy and a little dried kelp and fish, tied carefully in an old *furoshiki* which had belonged to his wife. Everything was so much harder now, he mused. His wife was gone, buried in a raid earlier that year. The expression on her face would stay with him forever. He saw it clearly still, a white mask smiling to him despite the agony he knew she must be feeling as she lay, pinioned by the masonry that had once been their home and facing certain death in a sheet of flame that had already started to engulf the ruins.

Like an ant pushing futilely at a rock, he had tried to move the beam that held her fast.

'Go, dearest, go!' she cried out at length. 'Let me die in peace. Help me to die in peace,' she had wept. 'Go to our daughter and grandson, he is the future now, please go!'

It had been as if her Buddhist faith had given her the strength to accept with equanimity the unthinkable, death by immolation, he thought, as helplessly he had watched the flames devour and extinguish her frail being.

He had been overcome with a fury, shouting and screaming like a madman, scrambling through the wreckage and out into the laneway, oblivious to all around him.

It was madness, all madness and still not finished, he thought. Sitting now in the comparative peace of the carriage as it rattled its way across the countryside on that sunlit morning, he suddenly felt so old and useless, twice his sixty-odd years. He hardly noticed the train stop as they pulled into Hiroshima. As they moved away, gathering speed and leaving the town behind them, he took out his old heavy pocket watch. It was 8.03 a.m.; they were making good time. Chewing on a salted plum, his spirits started to lift a little. Soon this war would be over and they would resume a normal life, victorious. His three sons Akira, Atsuo and Hiroshi would be back from across the ocean and life would return to the old ways.

As they thundered across the wooden bridge over the Ota river, a glint of silver high in the sky caught his eye, and behind it a white contrail slashing the deep blue of a clear summer's day. He tensed. It was a 'B-chan' bomber, heading for where, he wondered, and on what mission of destruction. Maybe it was a reconnaissance craft, or about to drop more leaflets. They had been falling from the sky for weeks, urging people to surrender.

Idly, his eyes followed the aircraft and then it seemed to disappear in a flash of white light. He stared in amazement at the distant sky above where they had just been. It was lit with a brilliance he had never seen before.

He watched, transfixed, as it gradually changed to a fiery glow. There was an excited buzz of voices in the carriage as everyone looked out at this extraordinary phenomenon. Whatever had happened in Hiroshima was unlike anything they had ever seen.

A strange purplish cloud now hung in the sky and they felt a sudden dull thud against the side of the train as the first shock waves reached them, and with them came a rush of wind as the sky started to darken as if it was night. He was filled with a growing sense of panic. He must get to his daughter-in-law and Matsuhiro quickly; there was so little time, and he had plans for the boy.

25

MATSUHIRO—JAPAN, 1948

Like a burning reminder of many summers before, the stifling heat of July had arrived suddenly. But Matsuhiro thrived on heat. It gave him the energy to move at times when others wilted by the wayside or dozed fitfully, waiting for the cooling rains or the first stirrings of a passing breeze. He particularly liked the stillness of the tropic midday with the heat striking the ground, then bouncing back to meet him.

The sun spelled energy and power and was his god, if god he needed. But how did one harness the energy of the sun? It was the difference between life and death, those two old friends, the black and white, ebb and flow of one's existence.

Matsuhiro had mastered the skill of preserving vital energy or *ki* and working with, not against, it. His young mind and body were now tuned to a fitness that only long hours of toughening and honing with a single-minded discipline could produce. His strength was that he took his limits and then expanded them. They became reserves of power which, through practice, he could call upon at will. He had marshalled his *izen*, his spirit centred in the lower abdomen for effortless control, giving him tranquillity.

Like his father Akira, he would make his life control,

not comfort-oriented. The baubles he would leave to others.

In an earlier age, Matsuhiro thought, his father might have lived the life of a highly born *Samurai*, but today he took the discipline of *bushido* into the boardroom and corporate networking as he rebuilt his financial empire from the chaos of a country recovering from war.

The finality of *seppuku* Akira translated into a ritual disembowelment that could be practised on a mental level with a similarly effective finality. And so would he. Unlike his father, he rejected his role in the accepted network of mutual indebtedness, seeing it as something quite apart from his way of operating. *Giri*, or loyalty to his parents, particularly to his father Akira and grandfather Daihachi, was strong, but the sense of *giri*, or obligation and duty to others, had long been a more nebulous force in his own life, to be sidestepped at will. He saw it only as a duty to impose on others in their obligation to him. *Ninjo,* the more human or emotional feeling of indebtedness, was purely a tool to be used in the manipulative process of others.

His early *sensei*, Iwatsu-san, a master of *kenjutsu,* had noted these manipulative tendencies in the young Matsuhiro and saw them as a weakness to be expunged. Realising his mistake, Matsuhiro had learnt to hide his real thoughts and do purely what was expected of him and to do it well. He gave the appearance of being part of the group while remaining apart from it. Perfection for its own sake was anathema to him. The ultimate goal lay in making all those so-called perfect elements dovetail to the pattern he required.

Matsuhiro well remembered the day over three years ago when his grandfather Daihachi had arrived by train in a state of great anxiety, talking of the white flash in the sky over Hiroshima, and his fear of what was to come. It was from that day that Matsuhiro's whole life had changed. His grandfather had come to live with them, and taken charge of him.

A master of *akido* and *karate,* Daihachi had started to

train Matsuhiro in the martial arts, teaching him to fight without emotion.

'Anger and fear, they will always defeat you,' he said. 'You must clear your mind of all such feelings. The mind must be relaxed, yet ever watchful as it sees all in that instant. One must aim to achieve a state of *mushin on shin*,' the old man said. 'It's a state of selflessness where one's instincts are sharpened to their fullest, to deal effectively with whatever faces them.'

The state of *suki* was to be purged. 'It only invites trouble and attack,' he told the boy.

An apt pupil, Matsuhiro had blossomed under his grandfather's tuition and that of other selected *sensei*. His hands became his eyes in hand-to-hand combat, moving with a fluidity and flowing grace, and showing equal skill when practising *kendo* and *kenjutsu*.

With the advent of the American occupation, and his father's return from a war spent mostly in Indo-China, his life had moved to the next phase. Akira, a former highly placed banking official, saw the need to turn defeat to his advantage by ostensibly working with his victors. His thwarted spirit of nationalism was now diverted into consolidating his wealth and creating a massive *yakuza* power-base for Matsuhiro, his only son.

Adding to Daihachi's teachings, Akira pointed out that their country was now going through a time of transition, and that, he taught his young son, is the most valuable time of all. That is when you can move with all the different streams and take all they have to offer, he said. Then as they merge to become a fast moving river, new opportunities will arise and increase as each stream flows one into the other.

The thing is to remain strong within oneself and go with the flow, he told Matsuhiro. Not merely carried in it as an ant among thousands, but above it, looking down, knowing when to change direction and where to move to next, always taking what you need from the one you are leaving.

Control was the lesson Akira passed on to the young

Matsuhiro. And true control often meant giving the appearance of being the underdog. Taking a secondary stance can be a position of great advantage, he pointed out. For it is there, he said, that you can learn from the mistakes of those who appear to be on top. Their weakness can become your strength. Look, listen and capitalise on what you learn—no matter how or where, he urged his son.

Now, reflecting on his time with Akira, Matsuhiro remembered a day like this one when you could almost feel the heat waves rising from the ground. He was just thirteen, he recalled, and his father had summoned him from school. 'I thought this might be of interest to you.' His father's seemingly casual invitation, Matsuhiro had learned, was invariably a precursor to something important.

They had left for a bath house that Akira usually attended, just outside town. On arrival, they were led into a small room behind the bath house and Akira bade him sit in a corner and be still. As was the case wherever they went, his father was treated with great respect and courtesy, he noted. They were then ushered into an adjoining room and served tea. As they finished, a wizened man entered the room and, bowing deeply to Akira, asked him if he was ready. Akira nodded and a young girl, probably not much older than himself, Matsuhiro thought, helped his father remove his clothes and don a *fundoshi*.

The room itself was like stepping into a small gallery. Around the walls were pictures of designs of every description worked onto all parts of the body. It was then that Matsuhiro noticed a table covered with an array of needles and bottles of different-coloured dyes. The girl was deftly massaging a cream over Akira's strong back with light firm movements, while the old man busied himself preparing the needles.

Across his father's back and chest was a swirling dragon tattooed in brilliant greens and red. Matsuhiro had never seen it before, as his father was always clothed in his presence. But now he looked at it in wonderment. It was beautifully drawn and from it emanated a movement and strength. The dragon's mouth breathed fiery orange and yellow flames, and beneath it lay a fallen warrior.

Akira was seated on a low wooden stool, and turned so that he sat side-on to the boy.

'Look closely, I want you to watch all that happens,' he commanded.

'Hai!' With a quick nod, Matsuhiro did as his father bade and sat cross-legged nearby.

As the needle began its succession of quick painful jabs, and he watched it piercing his father's flesh, it was as if it pierced his own slender body. He felt every needle sting magnified by his imagination, and watching the blood flow, felt his head begin to spin as if he would faint.

Akiro never took his eyes from his son's face as if willing him to rise above what was happening. Matsuhiro sat still, remembering his *sensei*'s words, 'mind, but no mind', and breathing deeply, gradually gained control of himself. 'Today you must do the sky,' Akira told the artist. 'I want the sun very bright and strong and to be riding high in the heavens,' he commanded.

Matsuhiro watched as the old man picked up a curved bone, the head of which contained a succession of tiny razor-sharp needles, and inwardly recoiled at the thought of it piercing his own skin. But his father gave no sign of pain, not even in his eyes that were stilled like darkened pools, without a ripple of emotion.

For over an hour, he sat and watched his father endure the torture of the needles with never a flinch or murmur. Matsuhiro observed that a glassy sheen of perspiration, from the heat of the day rather than the pain he must be experiencing, gathered and started to run down his father's cheeks. The young girl gently patted his face dry with a towel, but was quickly pushed aside.

At one stage, she brought in small cups of green tea which Akira waved away, but motioned for his son to accept. But the boy, raising his chin, also declined. He would travel this journey without sustenance, as did his father. Bowing deeply, she left them.

Later as they took their leave, he saw a group of American soldiers had arrived at the bath house. They were jostling each other, laughing and making much noise. It surprised Matsuhiro just how open and boisterous they could be, almost like children, he thought disparagingly. Silently, they slipped past them to where the car was parked with their driver waiting for them. His father's face was now a tightened mask, and he wondered if the pain was very great. Looking up at him, and as if to prove his worth, he said quietly, 'Father, I too will get tattooed one day when it pleases you.'

Akira turned to his son, his face softening. 'You will,' he said, 'but not until you have grown to be a man.'

But privately Matsuhiro knew that he would never subject himself to such a torment.

26

ATSUO'S PLEDGE—JAPAN, 1952

When he was well enough to listen, Atsuo's father Daihachi had told him that, as the human cherry blossoms fell from the sky in that icy winter of 1944–1945, the island of Hokkaido was rocked by severe earthquakes.

'The *kami* were angry as they could see what was happening,' Daihachi said, thinking of his lost youngest son, Hiroshi. 'The *kachi guri* turned sour in our mouths and there was no glory, only bitterness and defeat.' The young pilots had drunk their last drops of the ceremonial *sake* before taking off to their appointment with death. It had further bound them to their obligation '*sonju*' to the Emperor, but would it have tasted any the sweeter for that? Atsuo wondered. Looking at his father, he whispered the words of the Emperor Meiji.

The young men depart for the garden of battle.
In our fields,
Old men alone.

He had a sudden flash of memory from his school days when the whole school had risen as the director stood before them in full dress uniform, the gilt braid on his jacket shining in the morning sun that streamed through the large open windows. The sound of the *Kimigayo* rose as they had sung their sacred hymn to their beloved Emperor on his birthday. As their '*Sazareishi*' resounded through the hall, the school Director had unveiled the portrait of the Emperor and Empress, bowing his deep obeisance as he did.

Atsuo had sung with all his heart, caught up in the fervour and intensity of his feelings and the purity of that moment. It was a total commitment to their Emperor, a god-like being, a force outside the mundaneness of their lives. It was given freely and with a strong sense of dedication. It carried him well beyond the coldness of that day and the hunger in his belly. It was a glorious and complete act of giving that transcended all others. It imbued him with a sense of power. Anything was possible with that kind of commitment.

It was this same kind of purpose that had armed him for those months of double-dealing in Hawaii, and then taken him through his war in the Philippines and Malaya. It had helped sustain him through his injuries and his country's subsequent humiliating defeat.

The months of painful surgery to heal the radiation burns and scars inflicted by the bomb at Hiroshima had only inflamed Atsuo's patriotism and renewed his desire for retribution.

The weeks of nausea, of drifting in and out of consciousness, his burns festering, were only part of the 'atomic disease' which spread itself throughout his body. His leg, which had been exposed to the first flash of the blast, was so severely burned that the contracting scar tissue had locked it almost at right angles, and he was forced to hobble painfully about with a stick.

His older brother, Akira, through his power as *oyabun*, was able to organise reconstructive surgery from one of Japan's best surgeons. But the hospital, still poorly equipped and stocked, became his private torture chamber. He was held down by straps and nursing staff as the surgeon, without anaesthetic and its releasing balm of sleep, cut through tendons and muscle tissue, then completed his operation by slicing and transferring strips of skin from Atsuo's good leg to sew over the massive wound. In vain, he had tried to stifle his screams and overcome that long dark journey into his agonising hell. But his leg had healed, and now with the aid of his stick and only a limp to show for it, he could walk again.

The memory of that time had left its mark. Atsuo's face after surgery was that of another man. The good-looking Atsuo of his youth was replaced by a grim, scar-faced man who looked years older than he was. The shock and pain had turned his hair prematurely white, while his eyes, weakened by the blast, had retained their sight but were so sensitive to light he now wore dark glasses even at night.

'If only my Hiroshi was still here,' Daihachi kept saying.

'But father, Akira and I are here for you now and things will change; we will see to it,' he said, trying to win over his still grieving father.

'Nothing will bring back my Hiroshi,' was all his father had answered.

Atsuo was silent. His suffering had amounted to little more than a fleeting sigh from his father. Any of Daihachi's spare energies aside from mourning his wife and Hiroshi were directed to Akira's son, Matsuhiro. It was as if he, Atsuo, simply did not exist.

But at least Akira understood. There had always been a bond with his older brother. As Akira surrounded himself with a growing web of power, he had drawn Atsuo into it.

'You must fully understand all that is going on,' he told his brother. 'You will help lead Matsuhiro from behind and be there to guide him when his time comes to be *oyabun*. Your physical strength may have suffered, but not your insight and understanding, Atsuo. They will be there for him.'

One afternoon in the early autumn, he had summoned Atsuo to his home. Atsuo arrived with a sense of foreboding, hardly noticing the small grove of persimmon trees now heavy with their plump golden fruit, the sight of which usually gladdened his heart. He had not seen Akira for some weeks, and now when he greeted his brother he was startled by the change in him. Akira had become so thin and lines of suffering cut deep into his face.

At first, they discussed business matters at some length. Ordering the maid to bring them *sake*, Akira then turned to his brother. 'It's about Matsuhiro. We have discussed it before, but I want your full understanding that from now on you will act as adviser to my son. Do I have your word on that?'

Atsuo bowed low, giving full acquiescence to the request, then glanced at his brother in concern. Akira at forty-two was only a few years older than himself, and his request puzzled him.

'I don't understand,' he said. 'Surely you are the one to best advise and guide him. Why should I take your place?'

Akira didn't reply at first, and Atsuo could see that his brother was having difficulty in controlling his emotions. He looked away, so as not to embarrass him. After some minutes Akira, now composed, began.

'You have your wounds Atsuo, and now, it seems, I have mine.' He hesitated, then, his voice growing stronger. 'It's cancer, and I don't know how long I've got. Maybe months, maybe only weeks. Either way, the end will come quickly.' He paused, then added with a faint smile, 'But it will come more peacefully, knowing that you are behind my son.' As he spoke, he reached out and gripped his brother by the arm, looking deeply into his eyes, with the urgency of a dying man.

Akira gestured to his maid. Kneeling before them, from a lacquered tray she carefully poured warmed *sake* into two cups. As *oyabun* and the older brother, Akira had his cup filled six-tenths full, while that of Atsuo's was filled only four-tenths of the way. As in his first initiation into the *oyabun-kobun* relationship of the *yakuza*, symbolising the blood ties both within the family and the *gumi*, Atsuo sealed his pledge with the exchange of *sake* cups before the small Shinto shrine.

'No one else must know of this,' Akira said. 'There are too many out there just waiting to take over from me. Once they sense a weakness, they'll move in fast.'

The brothers looked at each other with cold deliberation. Atsuo didn't need to be told that Akira as *oyabun* and leader of one of the most powerful *yakuza* clans in the country, had enemies from rival gangs. They would gather like vultures at the news of his illness and impending death, anxious to wrest control of his brother's vast racketeering network. Akira had survived many an attempted coup before, and now was the time to close ranks and call on the loyalty of his hundreds of *kobun* or *yakuza* followers. The Isawa-*gumi* was not about to be defeated.

Furthermore, the brothers were only too well aware of what was at stake. Their joint participation in the war in the Pacific had not been inconsiderable, and Akira had emerged with an international network of contacts that now stretched into China, Taiwan, Korea, the Philippines and America. Before the war, as *oyabun* and a highly placed banking official and part of the *zaibatsu,* Akira had forged firm links with the ultra-nationalistic Right in the Japanese political spectrum. The Right had targeted the Pacific Basin in its destructive plan of territorial expansion.

It was Akira who had organised Atsuo's surveillance mission in Hawaii, creating his Katsura Kurosawa persona and fictitious family background, and it was Akira who had implemented Atsuo's speedy departure before the planned surprise attack on Pearl Harbor.

During the five years of conflict, Akira had fed his own considerable fortune by supplying his country, hungry for natural resources, with iron, radium, copper and tungsten from China and Manchuria to keep its war machine going. Following Japan's humiliating defeat and the advent of the American occupation, both brothers had managed to escape being interned at Sugamo prison by the occupational forces in the post-war purge on war criminals.

With his network of high-level contacts, Akira had unofficially become a key adviser to top US personnel, and a link man in rebuilding a city from the wasteland of war. But behind the scenes he had worked to actively foil MacArthur's bid to break up and eliminate the *Zaibatsu*, Japan's still powerful financial combines.

To ingratiate himself, Akira sought to weaken the Communist Left by unearthing high-standing members of Japan's growing Communist factions. At the same time, he was establishing an invaluable network of contacts to add to the strength of his pre-war *gumi*. With his growing band of committed and loyal youths drawn from the ranks of demobilised young men, hungry for jobs, a purpose and a place in the 'new Japan', Akira was there at its inception, helping to lay the groundwork and so scoop the spoils. Now entering its vital reconstruction period, Japan was emerging like Phoenix arising from the ashes of its military defeat. 'Wealth alone is not enough, it's only the beginning,' he told Atsuo. 'We need to be right where the power decisions are made, and so help shape them. It's not just a matter of being in on the ground floor, but actually creating it, moulding it as we want.'

To this end, Akira had fed the American intelligence network, providing them with ready access to information, services and raw materials. More importantly, through his *kobun*, ready to promote the political Right, he provided an arm to fight the feared growing Communist influence, sending in his men as strike breakers to protect powerful Japanese industrialists from the labour problems of emerging trade union and Leftist leaders.

Rapid changes had started to take place as Japan began to regain its industrial base and be influenced by Western industrialised democracies. Unburdened by equipping and maintaining a large defence budget, Japan could now channel its energies into rebuilding its economic strength. The conservative Liberal government of the immediate post-war years, with funds from much of the plundered wealth of the *yakuza* bosses, merged with the Democrat party to form the Liberal Democratic Party (LDP). Akira and Atsuo had by then established an influential pipeline to the top political hierarchy, providing muscle and money where needed.

Money they had earlier siphoned from the black market in necessities in the first hungry years after Japan's defeat was now coined from cornering a luxury market and catering to all the realms of pleasure, as the country began to grow and prosper. Gambling, drugs and prostitution were still the mainstay of Akira's fortune. He also maintained control of *Mizu Shobai* in bars and restaurants across the country, wherever lucrative kickbacks could be enforced. His passion for Sumo wrestling had long bought him a stake and control in that popular national pastime.

Catering to a nation dispirited after its defeat, Akira and his clan had found a ready market for one of the most lucrative of their money-earners, amphetamines or Speed, the panacea to depression.

Later it was claimed that even the *Kamikaze* pilots, as they fell, used the chemically induced high of Speed to intensify the finality of their flight. Had Hiroshi his brother also scored a hit to spur him in his glorious last act? Atsuo later wondered.

With his increasing wealth and influence, Akira had now become a *Kuromaku*, the unseen string-puller, a key figure in behind-the-scenes power brokering in Japanese politics and industry. He was a prime money-mover, a bestower and receiver of *giri*. Now he was branching into real estate and the transport industry.

'We have to expand internationally,' he told Atsuo. 'It's essential that we look to getting a stake and, ultimately, control in key international industry. If it has potential and we can get it, we'll take it,' he laughed. And with trips to the Pacific and the United States, Akira established influential foreign contacts that would work to his political and personal advantage.

Unlike his older brother, to whom power was purely for the pursuit of power, Atsuo clung more to his nationalistic ideal. He saw their political ascendancy essentially in terms of managing and regaining the power and position his country had lost in its shameful defeat by their enemy. And the enemy they would remain. Japan would rise again. Atsuo would do everything to play his small part in helping to restore it to its former glory. The taint of foreign influence was useful only as a stepping stone to regain what was rightfully theirs. *Kokusaika* was to be used purely to gain control from without rather than breaking down their own unique identity.

The operation of the *yakuza* had only ever been upheld by Atsuo as long as some part of the traditional custom of *ninjo* still existed. To his mind, the strong-arm tactics of extortion and violence, even murder, were acceptable only so long as they were cloaked in the softer guise of *ninjo*. Honour among thieves had a reality that brooked no argument.

It was this, Atsuo thought, that he must still impress on his nephew Matsuhiro. Maintaining the powerful *oyabun-kobun* tie was its strength, and there must be no dissension within the ranks, especially now with Akira's illness and imminent death. He would see to it that the traditional line of authority would prevail through the *oyabun*, and everything worked to an overall purpose and plan that would lead to the nation's rise.

In keeping with his purist theories, Atsuo led the life of comparative austerity, rejecting any sense of ostentation or grandeur that his fortune entitled. Rather, he clung to the concept of *wabi* and his peaceful home surroundings were uncluttered by unnecessary ornamentation. Later that evening when he returned to his home he changed from his dark Western suit into a cotton *yukata*. He felt upset by all that had transpired that afternoon, and still found it hard to reconcile himself to a life without Akira. The responsibility that his brother had transferred to him hung heavy, as did the realisation that it would not be easy to get young Matsuhiro, a person very much of his own mind, to follow his path.

After cleansing his mouth and hands, he went into the large bare room that overlooked his raked pebble garden and stood before the simple Shinto shrine. It comprised a high wooden shelf on which stood a finely worked replica of the Grand Shrine of Ise. On either side was a small mirror and a frond of the sacred sasaki tree. Below were some talismans to the kami, an offering his wife had placed there earlier of uncooked rice and some small winter pears, freshly picked from their garden.

Atsuo looked at the mirrors and thought of how they symbolised the spirit of Amaterasu, the sun goddess. Catching a glimpse of his reflection, so tense and sad, he remembered the words of the '*Jinnoh Shotoki*'.

The mirror hides nothing. It shines without a selfish mind. Everything good and bad, right and wrong, is reflected without fail. The mirror is the source of honesty because it has the virtue of responding according to the shape of objects. It points out the fairness and impartiality of the divine will.[6]

He knelt on the *tatami* before the shrine, then with a small bow followed by two deep bows, he prayed for his brother, as the image of Akira's ravaged face floated across his mind. With his hands held at chest level, he gave two loud claps, then bowed once, followed by a deeper prolonged bow.

Later, at the evening meal with his wife and young son and daughter, Atsuo once more clapped twice as a mark of gratitude to the kami, as he and his family ate the offerings with their meal.

Very soon, Atsuo thought, he would take Matsuhiro to the Grand Shrine of Ise to pray for his father.

27

DEATH OF AN OYABUN—JAPAN, DECEMBER 1953

Matsuhiro gazed at his father and felt the cold fingers of despair curl around his heart. The older man lay thin and spent, his once robust frame now faded almost to a shadow that merged with the dark blue *futon* on which he lay, his head cradled on the wooden *hako-makura*.

Quietly, Matsuhiro knelt at his side, looking at the face he loved etched in suffering as the cancer laid waste to what had once been a vital force. Sensing someone's presence, Akira's eyes opened, alert and watchful. So, the spirit was still strong, his son thought. He leaned forward in obeisance, holding back his tears, then faltering slightly, he repeated a *waka* verse his *sensei* had taught him long ago.

Yume samete
Futto kanashimu
Wa ga nemuri
Mukashi no gotoku
Yasukaranu Kana.
Ito kireshi
Tako no gotoku ni
Wakaki hi no
Kokoro karoku mo
Tobisarishi kana.[7]

> Awaking from a dream
> I grieve.
> My sleep no more is so peaceful
> As in the olden days.
> Like a kite
> Cut from the string,
> Lightly the soul of my youth
> Has taken flight.

Akira gave a weak smile, then motioning his son to move closer, in a faint voice replied, '*Hi e yamu*', 'I am sick with the sun'. The subtlety of his *waka* was not lost on Matsuhiro. Akira was silent a moment.

'There's so little time left for me now, and many things to discuss. You have done much as I hoped you would my son, but . . .' he paused, then went on with great effort. 'You still have a lot to learn, so until you have reached the age of twenty-five I have nominated that your Uncle Atsuo will act as caretaker *oyabun*. He will teach you all that you do not know as yet about the funding of the organisation I have created.' He paused, drawing in enough vital breath to keep going. 'He will then step aside for you.'

'And what if he doesn't want to step down then?' Matsuhiro asked.

'He will,' was all his father said.

He closed his eyes, exhausted, and Matsuhiro sat motionless, feeling overcome with a growing sense of inadequacy. Maybe his father doubted his abilities to replace him, even in three years' time, a span that seemed to stretch forever. He felt a sense of deep shame that he hadn't been able to earn his father's full confidence and to assume the position of *oyabun* now. This man, who had become his mentor, he loved with a single-minded intensity.

On a low wooden table beside Akira's bedside lay the short *kotachi* sword, used in hand-to-hand combat or the ritual disembowelment of *seppuku*. Its blade shone silvery-blue in the afternoon light.

Matsuhiro looked at it, taking in the beauty of its workmanship, and made a quick decision. Laying his left hand on the table, he picked up the sword and as he did, his father's eyes flew open in time to see Matsuhiro bend his full weight onto the hand in a sudden jerking action and as his finger joint snapped he sliced through his little finger, removing the top joint. He didn't falter as an agonising pain shot up his arm. Without expression, he took a fine white cloth from his jacket, then wrapping the severed joint in the cloth, he bowed in deep obeisance as he presented it to his father.

Inclining his head to his son, Akira accepted the bloodied package and placed it against his heart, holding it close. Slow tears welled and spilled onto his cheeks.

'Farewell, my son,' he murmured, 'you are truly the *oyabun*.'

A sob welled up from deep inside Matsuhiro, and he threw his arms around his father, calling out his name, hoping to will his life force back.

His mother rushed in, and together they sat for the remaining forty minutes it took for his father's spirit to finally leave his body.

* * *

It wasn't until after Akira's death that Matsuhiro fully realised the importance in which his father was held went way beyond their town. As *oyabun*, he had followers throughout the country and abroad. The mourners who came to their large home, now draped in black and white bunting, to pay their final respects seemed never-ending.

Not for his father had there been the crass flamboyance often associated with other *yakuza* leaders, but rather, a pared-back way of life that nonetheless carried the weight and assurance of real money. Akira had enjoyed the best life had to offer; he had shared none of his brother Atsuo's monastic leanings.

'We will lead from behind,' he had often told his son. 'True power does not need to surround itself with all the trappings of success, but rather control the trappings of others and feed their desires and need for them. As my heir apparent, you will occupy the place of chief mourner at my funeral, and beside you will sit your Uncle Atsuo, so that everyone will know that you are my chosen successor.'

Akira had requested a simple ceremony for family and friends, but on the day of his funeral, hundreds of mourners started to arrive and pour through the small Buddhist temple near their home. Flowers and wreaths were in profusion, and Matsuhiro noted many of the prominent businessmen and politicians, and some top American servicemen he had met through his father, had come to pay their respects. A line of cars, many luxury imported limousines, Cadillacs and Lincolns, formed a slow-moving procession past their home, and the police were called in to keep control. The news was out, which was not at all what his father would have wanted.

Matsuhiro's last meeting with his uncle had disturbed him. They had visited the Grand Shrine at Ise to pray for his father. He had sensed his Uncle's disapproval, never quite manifested, but there like a shadow between them. This tense and brooding man, who lacked the geniality and warmth of his father, had always disconcerted him.

He decided that, when the time came to take over from Atsuo, he would keep him on as titular head of the organisation, and so have a greater freedom to do what he liked, while leaving Atsuo up-front to face any flak. He would respect his father's wishes and learn all that he could from his uncle, but he would make sure that it was he, Matsuhiro, who pulled the strings and not Uncle Atsuo.

As he and his uncle had walked towards the shrine, the wide path beneath its towering pine trees was almost deserted. He took heart from the crunch of gravel beneath his feet, and remembered his *sensei* telling him that listening to that familiar sound was a form of meditation, preparing one for a clarity of mind and vision needed to fully pay homage to this sacred place.

His uncle, walking a little ahead of him, was talking about the Emperor Hirohito, and how as a young man, his first duty as Emperor and high priest of Shintoism had been to make a lone pilgrimage to the Shrine at Ise where the relics of the sun goddess Amaterasu were kept; and how only the Emperor could go beyond the white curtain to commune with the spirits of his ancestors.

Uncle Atsuo had spoken at length of the harshness of the Emperor's boyhood, preparing him for the task ahead. 'For hours he would be made to sit straight and still by the Grand Master of the Household, staring only at the horizon so as to strengthen his weakened eyes and learn the importance of will.'

Matsuhiro listened, knowing that Uncle Atsuo was attempting, in his long-winded way, to draw a parallel to what lay ahead for him. He smiled to himself. How ridiculous his uncle was, living in the past the way he did. The war had been lost after all and his revered Emperor had had many of his powers stripped away. So where was the greatness in that? His two most vivid memories of the Emperor were when, as a young child in the arms of his mother, he had looked above the thousands of red suns floating on a sea of waving white flags, and seen high above them on a balustrade, a small rather lonely figure almost lost in a long army cape, astride a magnificent white Arab horse. His stillness was in strange contrast to the frenzied movement and sounds from the people below. Matsuhiro recalled how the swish of the flags and resounding shouts of '*Banzai! Banzai!*' had swelled around them, almost deafening him, and he had clung to his mother, wishing they could leave.

The next occasion when he had seen Emperor Hirohito had been in Tokyo just after the war had ended. The Emperor's long black Rolls Royce had driven slowly past him, towards the *Dai Ichi Seimei* building. He recalled how many of the people around him had thrown themselves down onto their knees, touching their bowed heads almost to the rubble which they had been busy clearing away from the city's bombed-out streets. From beneath his bowed head he had stared at this person in his dark suit and high shiny black hat, whom they had revered as their living god. The Emperor had looked neither left nor right, he remembered, but straight ahead, and again sat so still. The car had passed on and Matsuhiro had felt a distancing of himself from someone who was part of something he wished to forget. Then everyone had gone on with their work of clearing away the shattered buildings. All he could think of was his ever-present hunger, and the sweet potato his grandfather had promised when he got home.

Now as they walked towards the shrine, Matsuhiro dutifully listened to his uncle, silently disagreeing with most of his theorising. It was an out-of-date imperialism he saw as having nothing to do with his country now. But he still had much to learn from Atsuo about the inside running of his father's organisation, and if it humoured his uncle to pretend that he shared the same vision, he'd go along with it. Until he knew everything Uncle Atsuo had to pass on, he was useful. And after that? Well, he'd see what could be arranged.

To Matsuhiro, the pursuit of power was very much a secretive and personal thing. Once acquired, what he did with it was his own affair.

28

ATSUO'S PEACE DANCE

What did the younger generation know of sacrifice or of true reverence and respect, Atsuo thought bitterly as he regarded his nephew Matsuhiro's unreceptive expression gazing at the Grand Shrine. But hadn't it always been so, he mused, those who suffered the humiliations and hardships, and those who benefited from them?

His thoughts drifted back to an evening in 1947, just two years after the dropping of the bomb at Hiroshima, and the song that had haunted him ever since.

Pika to Hikkatta
Genshi e no tama ni
Yoi-yaga!
Tonde agatte Heiwa
No hato yo . . .[8]
The atomic ball
loosened like sharpest
lightning
then fly upwards,
the doves of peace . . .

As the words of the Peace song crackled forth on the loud speakers, he recalled how crowds of young girls in elaborate kimono and with flowers in their hair emerged from the Shintenchi Quarter, dancing the new *Heiwa-Odori* or Peace Dance.

He had walked along the road that led to the Cemetery for the Unknown Dead, high on the rise of Hijiyama. It was a relief to get away from the commercial hubbub of the 'great peace sales', the screeching gramophones, the drinking and jostling as crowds of people joined in the dances and processions. Their almost frenzied display of self-conscious celebration was in direct contrast to the simple, more dignified beauty of the memorial the year before, when thousands of glowing white candle-lit lanterns, each one bearing the name of a dead or missing loved one, had floated down the Ota river and out to sea.

At last, reaching a small shrine, he had placed on it a sprig of the sacred Sakaki tree and some rice cakes that he'd brought with him. He then knelt and with one small then two deeper bows, he quietly prayed, asking for his brother Hiroshi's forgiveness and guidance. As always, he felt a sense of shame that it should be he who was kneeling here and not his young heroic brother Hiroshi. It was he, Atsuo, who had not been able to fight to the end and meet an honourable death; his wounds had seen to that. A sudden chill wind swept across the hill, and with it came the sighs of a thousand spirits.

Only that morning at eight-fifteen, to commemorate the very moment the bomb had dropped from the heavens, hundreds of white 'peace doves' had been released. They rose to the sky in a rush of wings and flash of white feathers, taking his heart with them, soaring aloft in a surge of elation and hope. But that had been the only high point of the day, he recalled.

Was it only eight years since that terrible day when he had staggered painfully out onto the hot asphalt of a street still molten from the fires that had sprung up everywhere after that blinding flash in the sky?

One minute, he had been lying on the *tatami* beside a brick furnace, dozing fitfully after a night sleepless with the pain from a shrapnel wound in his thigh. He'd heard the high drone of an aircraft, then a sudden flash of light had filled every corner of the room as if walls did not exist. Then, he remembered, came a rush of wind and a wave of intense heat that had hit him in a deafening roar as everything collapsed around him.

Freeing himself from the fallen timber and bricks, he had staggered from the house, dazed, and to his surprise when he looked down, he was completely naked. All his clothes, apart from the torn remnants of a light vest, had disappeared from his body, and one side of his chest was lacerated and bleeding. It was like moving through a nightmare in slow motion, without any point of reference from which to begin. There were no familiar shapes and sights left to mark out where a home had stood only minutes before, but which now seemed like a lifetime ago. There were no fond-remembered landmarks to gladden and comfort, just nothing but steaming ash and rubble in a flattened landscape.

Who were these people staggering around him with their shocking burns, their bloated faces and bodies? They were alive, but only to face the unrelenting vomiting and diarrhoea which lasted for days, culminating in a slow painful death. They crept past him, looking for water, for succour, for relief, for the hospital, for their children. Disfigured families clung together in a limbo of pain and disbelief.

His first terrible fear had been replaced by a nagging sense of guilt, then shame, that he had survived, burnt and in pain, yet still spared to move helpless among the shattered limping creatures, more like blackened scarecrows from another world than the orderly neighbours he had known. He remembered he had reached out to steady an old woman, and as he grabbed her arm, her skin had slipped like a silken glove from her frail body, leaving just a soft pulpy mass of dark flesh. Like a peeled satsuma plum he'd thought, as he recoiled in horror.

Atsuo recalled how, when on that peaceful hill of Hijiyama just two years after the bombing, the lights from Hiroshima below shone like a beacon to renewed life and hope. As he walked back towards the lights, he'd pondered: where were the signs of a spiritual re-awakening, a purity of thought and action that went with building something sound from the ruins? Instead, all around, a kind of corruptive commercialism was even more rampant than before.

This cashing in on the souls of the dead was like vultures feeding on the agony of the departed. But wasn't that how life sprang from death, Atsuo reflected. It's as if we're caught between two fires, the spiritual and survival. Just as he had moved into the growing black market and Akira's *koban*. At first he'd reasoned it was based purely on survival, then with a growing awareness that it provided a way for him to manipulate and profit from the despised American Occupation machine, and lift his family into the prosperous 'New Yen' class.

This machine had still to be handled carefully. He recalled that the next day after his visit to Hiroshima's peace ceremony, word had reached him through the Isawa *gumi* that an American officer had been making enquiries as to the whereabouts of a Katsura Kurosawa.

'Who was this person asking these questions?' he had enquired, and been informed that it was a Major Gerard Baillieu. 'And what was he told?' Atsuo continued coolly, without moving a muscle or betraying his cold inward shiver of fear.

'Why, that we had no idea of such a person, Atsuo-san,' his informant had replied with a bow. He'd thanked him, knowing in that instant that he'd notched up yet another favour, in a long list of obligations to be worked through and called upon at some time in the future.

Fourteen years since his short sojourn in Hawaii, Atsuo thought, as he left Ise's Grand Shrine with Matsuhiro. With all that had happened, it seemed more like fourteen hundred and far removed from the war he'd suffered in the Philippines and later at home in Japan.

And that girl who had so briefly been his. What was her name? He searched his mind. Even her face seemed nebulous, replaced by so many others. He had not thought of that part of his life for a long time, but now recalling the name Baillieu, it was back to haunt him.

Gina, ah yes that was it, Gina Baillieu. She had wanted so much, he remembered. Too much, she was spoiled and wilful, but had a certain charm, he reflected. She had served her purpose at the time, as had his guise as Katsura Kurosawa. What of the child? he suddenly thought, as memories came crowding back of the girl's pregnancy and those last hectic days on the Island, when he and the Takeuchis had taken flight before the discovery of their part in the siphoning out of information that had helped set up the bombing of Pearl Harbor. No doubt the child would have been well and truly cared for in that family with all their money. But with its American grandfather and *Nisei* mother, it was not truly Japanese, so of little concern to him now.

A slow anger burned as he thought of all that he'd been through, and what they'd all suffered here at the hands of those *gaijin*. And then the final insult with Gerard Baillieu in Japan and causing trouble with his enquiries. But he had soon put a stop to that. There'd be no way Gerard would ever catch up with him . . . then or ever.

29

BILL—HOMEWARD BOUND, 1946

Rounding a corner, Bill Baillieu caught sight of a grove of peppercorn trees, and behind and below them the brilliant blue of the Mediterranean harbour of Ville Franche. He walked over to the trees with the delight of discovery in their associations with home. Their leaves shimmered in a delicate silver lacery, and as he walked under their boughs, the smell of summer shot him right back to 'Winganna'. He reached up, picked a frond of the pale pink peppercorns, crushed them in his hand then, burying his face deep in his cupped palms, inhaled their peppery fragrance.

Then sitting on a small wooden bench, thoughtfully provided for just such a moment, Bill felt totally at one with all around him. Trees had souls, he thought. And like people, the spirits that dwelt within them were good or bad. His thoughts went back to the 'Bad Banksia Men' in the May Gibbs stories he'd so loved as a child. In a sense, they had been spouting a Shinto belief, he reflected and smiled. Shintoism as he'd seen it and the characters of the Australian bush seemed worlds apart. But were they?

He'd never been given to reflection, especially anything that smacked of religion, but his experiences in the past three years had forced him to become more of a philosopher. So much had happened, life and death forces had turned his mind inward, searching for some kind of answer. After demobilisation and this short sojourn in Europe, he was on his way home.

There had been a strange regret in leaving that Nagasaki farm he'd grown to know so well. Working through the changing seasons, the harshness and beauty of its landscape were now firmly stamped upon his soul. Bloody hell! He needed a drink, a thousand drinks. And he needed Maria. But how would things go with her now, he wondered, after all this time?

Bill leaned back, gazing up at the sunlight riffling through the leaves. This tree was a young spirit, a nymph, he decided, tossing her long silvery blonde hair so that it swirled around her shoulders as she danced. He could almost see the rise and fall of her breasts, her long slim legs barely touching the ground as she moved gracefully across his mind. God, he was really going troppo! He smiled to himself. A few weeks at 'Winganna' and his mother Molly's tucker would soon have him back on track.

Resting his head against the trunk, he stared out to sea. It was just like a postcard . . . a million miles from the post-war Japan he had just left. Visions of the place kept floating in and out of his mind. His thoughts returned to that first sighting of Hiroshima the evening he had driven in with an American convoy. It was 6 August 1946, one year to the day of the dropping of the bomb.

The evening light had receded, and the sky deepening to a gun-metal grey gave contrast to hundreds of flickering kerosene lamps. He had stared, disbelieving, across the miles of tangled timber and masonry where once a city had stood. The vast flat emptiness of the surrounding landscape had made him feel conspicuous, like some foreign totem rising triumphant from a fallen field. He felt at once a trespasser, yet uncomfortably vulnerable, as if he should somehow crouch down and merge with this flattened city.

A steady rhythmic beat of drums filled the emptiness with its slow monotonous sound. Clapping hands, rising and falling in a staccato rhythm, picked up the beat, and in counter-point, high wailing voices singing to the souls of the dead rose to accompany them on their way to the next world. Bill watched as the men and women of Hiroshima formed a circle, moving around and around as if in a trance to the hypnotic beat of the drums. The women sang as they went, and he felt a sudden urge to join them. Paddy would have been right in there singing his lungs out, calling to him to join in.

Paddy! Suddenly the blue Mediterranean day didn't seem so bright any more. Bill looked down at the shelaleagh stick he always kept with him. Picking it up, he read the names of their captors, painstakingly engraved in the wood. He ran his fingers along its gnarled surface, now worn smooth with age.

The sense of rage he always felt when he thought of Paddy and that bastard Hitachi gripped his gut. He should have finished that bastard off when he had the chance. But they had disappeared, the lot of them, taken off in those twilight days after the dropping of the bomb. Bill and the other prisoners had been swept up with the occupation forces and put to work in the clean-up before his discharge. He'd given the names of their captors to the American commanding officer, to go on trial, he hoped. He grimaced. He could well imagine those Nips' names getting lost in the logistics as the Eighth Army swung into action in General Douglas MacArthur's bid to rebuild a defeated Japan, beginning with the demobilisation of the Japanese forces.

He had seen MacArthur's triumphant arrival from Okinawa in an entourage of cars on 8 September 1945, only six days after the signing of the Japanese surrender aboard the USS *Missouri* in Tokyo Bay. With the raising of the American flag above the Embassy, star-spangled banners had become the order of the day, along with daily directives flowing from MacArthur's offices in the *Dai Ichi Seimei* building.

The arrest and trial of Japanese war criminals had begun in earnest, but apart from giving a few details and names, he hadn't been called upon to play much part. All he wanted to do now was to get home, away from the smell of war, and to pick up his life at 'Winganna' again. There was plenty of time to catch up with his tormentors later, Bill reassured himself. He at least owed that to Paddy and the others.

Memories of his grandmother's sharp eyes staring at him over the steel rims of her glasses, her 'Now, William, you should do unto others as you would have them do unto you' came to mind. He snorted.

'Well, Granny, I've got a surprise for you. If I'd been half the mongrel to them that they were to us, I'd have them hung, drawn and quartered many times over, and still come out ahead. So how does that grab you, eh? You mealy-mouthed old bat!' he shouted, his words floating over the sea below.

The doughty old lady had always been moralising about something. As kids, they had let her words slip away unheard, treating her with scant deference while getting on with the real business of doing what they wanted. But surprisingly, it was often one of her many phrases that had come back to confront him during the long years of his internment.

Granny May, Bill thought. Her life had seemed to function purely as a back-up to her daughter Molly and her family. She was always there, but like the wallpaper, hardly noticed except when she berated them for one thing or another. She really didn't relate to any of us. Her life, he remembered, took place within a set of moralistic values and attitudes that acted as a buffer between her world and what was really going on.

Granny May's two daughters were so unlike her. Molly, his mother, warm and loving and always there for them. And Aunt Freida, the colourful tear-away, flying around the country and overseas with her wealthy husband, Uncle Stan Ferris. He was a big powerful man who exuded *bonhomie* and the fruity scent of Havanas, and

255

who was always bringing them back large, lumpy presents from far-away places. Strange-looking things that smelt foreign and had little relevance to their life on the farm. Bongo drums from Brazil, carved masks from the Trobriands, an enormous bird-shaped jar from the Sepik, clogs from Holland, a box of Wayung puppets from Indonesia, and so on. Fascinating at first, but soon to find their way to the back of the toy cupboard. Later, he had given them all to Jill. It seemed the right thing to do at the time.

His Aunt Freida's sudden death had done little to ruffle his grandmother's stoic acceptance. 'She's safe in the hands of our Lord now,' she had informed them all, as if that alone could take care of everything, even a mother's grief.

Then Jill had come to stay with them, as Uncle Stan was always away and couldn't look after her. She'd arrived at 'Winganna' in his uncle's big flashy American car, piled high with her trunks. She was only eleven, two years younger than himself, and she looked so clean and neat. That was his first impression of his cousin, and one that stayed with him. He and Tom, until they went away to school, always had the seat out of their pants and a wild, unkempt appearance that suited their life on the farm. But Jill had the air of a hothouse flower, even then.

Jill had thrown herself into the life at 'Winganna' while at the same time holding herself apart a little, as if always poised to take flight. It must have been hard for her, he reflected. He'd never really wondered as to what she must have felt before. Tom had been closer to her, then Gerard when he visited. And she had become Gran's pet. She was the only one who bothered to listen to the old lady. Not that any of it seemed to impinge as she chatted away and helped Gran with her interminable crocheting.

He well remembered the evening Jill, her face aglow, had come down to dinner carrying a small camphor-wood chest of drawers. She was fourteen, and it was the first time he had noticed that she was becoming quite beautiful. With blonde head held high, she had walked triumphantly into the room and said, 'Guess what, everyone? Gran has given me all her jewellery.'

'All of it?' Molly had looked startled.

'Yes, every single piece. Isn't it wonderful?' Jill had smiled at her.

'Well, really Jill, I thought . . .'

'You don't mind, do you?' Jill had turned her radiant face to his mother, her blue eyes candid and wide.

Molly had hesitated, then had gone over to the girl, giving her a hug.

'No pet, of course not, if it makes you happy,' was all she had said.

But he remembered how quiet his mother had been at the table that night. Her eyes had dwelt on the different pieces with a look of regret as Jill had taken out each one, trying them on for all to see.

'Gran thought it much better to give them all to me now, while she was still alive so she could see the enjoyment they gave,' Jill had said as if to dispel any doubts. He recalled how his grandmother had come in during the parade of jewels, smiling at Jill and saying, 'A pearl for a pearl,' with a significant look at Tom and himself.

To his young eyes, they had seemed like buccaneers' booty. There were silver linked chains of amethyst and pearl necklaces, tiny seed-pearl chokers, a string of opera length baroque pearls his grandfather had brought from the 'Far East'. As well, there were gold bracelets with garnets, warm, browny stones the colour of the eyes of his mother's dog, Chloe. There was even a graceful silver coronet of tiny diamonds and blue-green aquamarines that his grandmother had worn when she was presented at court, before coming to her new life in Australia. He remembered how fine it had looked sitting on Jill's fair hair, her eyes taking on the sparkling light of the stones.

Looking back now, Bill could remember the collection quite well because of the stories Jill had told about each piece as she opened the small drawers to reveal yet another assortment of rings, earrings, brooches, bracelets and necklaces. There was an ivory elephant necklace, he remembered, with a glinting diamond eye, that Uncle Stan had brought back for Gran from one of his trips to Africa. That was the piece he'd liked most. He could remember reaching across and holding it up to the light so that the eye flashed different colours.

'It's made from real elephant's tusks,' Jill had said. 'And the white diamond's from the mines in Johannesburg. It's a collector's piece.' Then, matter-of-factly, 'Of course I will add this collection to my mother's jewels when Daddy gives them to me.'

But, he recalled, apart from the few precious pieces she had brought with her when she first arrived, her mother's jewels were mostly dispersed amongst an assortment of women who came and went in Stan's life following Frieda's death.

In one of the drawers was a collection of shell jewellery from the Pacific islands . . . thick clusters of pale pink and creamy white shells, some threaded as leis. Afterwards, Jill had often worn them on the farm with her bare sun-dresses. They were so different from anything anyone else she had, and they made her seem even more exotic.

Bill remembered there had been a large emerald and diamond ring set in white gold with diamonds sitting either side of the flashing green stone. It was like looking into the dam at the bottom of the property on days when the algae turned the water to a clear green. It was cool and mysterious. He'd looked up and had seen a sadness in his mother's eyes, and he'd blurted out, 'Mum should have that one.'

A sudden quiet descended at the table, and Jill looked up, startled, then over to his mother. She slipped the ring onto her finger, looking down at it as if trying to decide something. Even now he could recall Jill's expression. It was one of apprehension as if everything was about to be suddenly swept away from her.

'It is beautiful,' his mother had said, adding, 'on your young hands.' She had given a little laugh. 'It wouldn't look half so good on these rough old things,' she said looking down at her hands, careworn and reflecting the work they did.

For the first time he'd really looked at them. Till then, they'd just been Mum's hands, always around them, doing things, helping them, making and finding things, feeding them, patting her dog, or hugging him. He noticed now how freckled they were from the unrelenting sun, and the tracery of fine lines crinkling the backs of her fingers. But he loved them.

'They're better than yours,' he'd asserted defiantly to Jill. But she had ignored him, and feeling on safer ground, was saying. 'Are you sure Aunt Molly? I wouldn't like to take what's yours.'

'Don't be silly, pet,' his mother had answered. 'We'll have no more of that.' She had paused, looking fondly across to Bill. 'But maybe you had better put them away now, and we'll get on with our meal.'

Now leaning back and looking up to the shimmering canopy of peppercorn leaves, he thought of home. It would be like stepping back into a world he'd moved so many lifetimes away from, and he wondered if he could make that transition. Apart from Molly and his girlfriend Maria, they had all moved on and away from 'Winganna' to play out their part in the assorted theatres of war . . . his father Jack to New Guinea, Tom to Singapore. Jill had gone back to Hawaii, and Gerard?

Since early in the war, he'd had no word from Gerard, and during his long captivity on the Japanese farm, he'd often wondered just how Gerard must have felt fighting the countrymen from which he was descended. His mind went to Hiroko, and the largely unspoken pain he knew Gerard had experienced at the hands of his mother's seeming indifference. A sense of shared resentment rose as he thought of the cause of it, Gerard's Japanese half-brother, Satoshi.

With a bit of luck that bastard would have been wiped

out along with all those others he thought, picking up the shelaleagh at his side and slicing it through the air in a single sweep of the *Samurai* sword's ritual beheading.

# 30

BILL'S HOMECOMING
QUEENSLAND, AUSTRALIA, 1947

Settling back into the couch, Bill turned to Maria and smiled. Then as if staring at something far off, went on, 'We had to bail out. We'd been hit midships, probably incendiaries. They'd knocked a hole in the aircraft and suddenly the instrument panel was gone, shrivelled up before our eyes. The elevator control must have jammed and we went into a steep dive. We were falling—it seemed like five hundred miles an hour. I could hear the rear gunner screaming.' He paused. 'Poor bugger.'

She nestled in closer, feeling his warmth, seeing the pictures take shape vividly as she filled in the unspoken detail in the spaces left by his terse descriptions.

'We must have fallen around thirteen thousand feet,' he went on. 'I had my feet up against what was left of the dashboard trying to pull her out, but I couldn't do it on my own. I yelled out to Jim who'd been in the bomb bay. He suddenly appeared; then we pulled like crazy and used the trim. We got her out at around fifteen hundred feet. She was too far gone though, so me, Harry my flight engineer, Jim and the gunner . . . what was left of him . . .' he laughed, a short bitter sound. 'Well, bloody old Jim tied a harness to him, just in case. We put on 'chutes and jumped out, but I hit my head against the door, a real rabbit killer. Felt as though my bloody neck was broken.'

She timidly stroked the back of his neck. From far away, he went on, 'And there we were, falling out of the sky. It was a clear night. Just a few puffs of cumulus. The stars were all around us, too many and too bright— we bloody well cursed them. They were all lit up like flaming flares! As I fell through the clouds, there was a sudden up-current dragging at the parachute. It kept buffeting me. I could see a big pale cloud coming up below and I braced myself for another whack of air.'

His body tensed.

'I remember pulling up my legs and stiffened, waiting for the wrench. Then I'd hit ground. It was covered with white sand.'

She laughed. 'Some cloud!'

Hardly hearing her, Bill relived the moment. 'I must have gone out to it for a bit. I remember picking myself up and starting to walk along this bloody long beach. Everything told me to keep moving.'

Maria's arms around him were going to sleep under the weight of his body, and she disentangled herself quietly, pulling away and curling up at the other end of the couch. She reached for her cigarettes, lighting one and silently handing it to him, then another for herself as he went on. He needed to talk, and she was willing to listen.

'I was looking out for Jim, and the others. I could hear a swishing noise like truck tyres in the sand behind me. I looked back, was frightened it was the Nips, but I couldn't see any lights—nothing.'

He drummed his fingers on the couch arm, staring at nothing. 'But there was still that noise, swishing, just like tyres. My head was starting to clear because after a while I looked down and suddenly realised I was still dragging the bloody 'chute behind me.' He grinned at her.

'What happened then?'

He drew long and hard on his cigarette. 'Well, they got me.' Then he laughed. 'But I'm here to tell the tale.'

She turned to him, sensing he'd reached a cut-off point.

'No, tell me about it Bill, that's if you want to. Jill told me that after the crash in Malaya you were taken to Singapore, then shipped out to Japan, then to Nagasaki. But apart from that, we know nothing.' He didn't answer, so she added gently, 'You know sometimes it's better to talk these things out.'

'Well, if nothing else,' Bill said with a smile, 'we escaped the hell of the Burma railway.'

'To go to another hell?' she asked, her voice softening.

'Come on, Maria! What's there to tell?' He looked away. How could he describe to her, to anyone, the beatings, the endless treks, the voyage in that hell-hole of a ship. There was the hunger, always the hunger and the hopeless sense of rage he felt when he looked back at that time, a huge chunk out of his life, lost and gone forever. What was the point in rehashing it all now? He answered simply, 'We worked the coal mines in Nagasaki. One day after the other, down we'd go and just dig in that bloody black hole. What's there to say about it?' He subsided into silence. Suddenly he hit out. 'I'll get that mongrel, though.'

'Who?' Maria asked.

It was as if he hadn't heard her and was in another world. She sighed and got up.

'I'll go and get us something to eat,' she said. 'You rest a while and we'll talk later.'

He hardly noticed her going. He was back in that make-shift room, now operating as a surgery. He could smell the pungent ether even now as he remembered coming through the surgery door, trying to stay on his feet. His legs were still shaking, badly ulcerated and weakened after weeks of surviving on one bowl of mush a day, and aggravated by a bad bout of dysentery.

'What's up with you?'

The little man sitting at the desk stared at him,

unblinking eyes behind round steel-rimmed glasses. The eyes were opaque, Bill noticed, like black licorice, absorbing all light, giving off nothing.

The doctor's face was blotched with dark red patches, 'grog blossoms', Bill thought, noticing how the man's hands shook as he made a cursory examination with his grimy stethoscope. An almost overpowering smell of stale sweat, even stronger than the stench from the camp, rose from the man's flaccid body, as always covered in a wash of oily sweat. Doctor Bloody Death, they called him. His reputation in the camp for his cruelty and callous indifference to his countrymen was already legendary. It was just their luck to get a drunken quack like this one, he thought.

'I need something for the dysentery and my legs,' Bill said.

The doctor had pushed him back onto a bench. 'You know, it's buggers like you that's making it harder for the rest of us. Malingering, that's all it is, just sheer bloody-minded malingering. There's nothing wrong with you.'

Bill made as if to get up and punch him, but the doctor pulled back and hissed, 'Touch me and you're dead meat!' He called to the guard. 'Take him away,' and turned his back on him.

It was anger that kept him going that day, Bill remembered. The sharp pains in his feet and belly, at times so excruciating he felt he'd pass out, only served to fuel his anger and visions of sweet revenge. After the war, I'll get that bastard, he promised himself.

The day had passed, as with so many others, in a state of detachment and half-conscious blur. They were working deep into the mine now, the suffocating heat at times almost unbearable. Every instinct within them waited for that moment when, like men returning from the grave, they came up to the surface and took in deep gulps of precious air.

Working beside Bill was another kid from the bush, Roo Delaney, just eighteen and at first full of tall tales from the vast cattle station of his youth that he'd left earlier in the year to join up. Roo described in lurid detail the torturous experiences, all larger than life, that had eventually brought him as a prisoner to this Nagasaki mine. Months of starvation had now reduced Roo to the same skeletal proportions as the rest of them. Bill noticed with alarm that he also had a progressively worsening case of dysentery. Roo was shaking and feverish when they came up out of the mine that night for *tenko*, the interminable check parade and head count that took place every night and following morning. Bill stayed close to the boy, occasionally supporting him while talking quietly, trying to keep his spirits up, at least until they'd lined up for the grey liquid mush that passed for their evening meal. If lucky, it would be hot. It went down a little more easily then.

That night, for some unknown reason, there had been a sense of desperate optimism in the air with more talk, jokes and laughter than usual, he recalled. Suddenly an old truck with high sides and a drop-down back drove fast into the compound, scattering prisoners as it went. With shouts and the butts of their rifles to aid them, the guards started pulling men out from the food line and herding them into the truck. All was silent now, the laughter and talk giving way to a wave of apprehension that rolled over them with only the occasional shouts and groans as men were hit.

With Roo clinging to his arm, Bill felt himself pushed and pummelled into the truck along with the others, until packed in like cattle with barely room to move, they took off.

At first they travelled through the blacked-out city of Nagasaki, its taller buildings rising like silent guardians of a ghost town. Leaving the city, they sped past row upon row of tiny timber houses which soon melted away to the more open space of the surrounding countryside. At the edge of the city they were stopped at a checkpoint, the guards falling back with gutteral cries and looks of disgust, motioning the truck to pass on out of sight and smell with its fouled cargo.

At first, the men talked volubly. Death was an ever-present but never quite spelt-out fear. Rather, their apprehension gave way to wild surmising as to where they were going, with florid allusions to exotic holiday destinations where food, booze and girls abounded, with each sexual fantasy out to top the other. After an hour of bumping and jolting there was no more talk and a silence descended with only the odd curse and groan welding them like travellers on a voyage to purgatory, standing now in a wash of vomit and excreta. After a while they hardly noticed the stench.

They sped on through the night. In the early hours of the morning, after what seemed like a lifetime, the truck turned into a large yard surrounded by a cluster of low-eaved farm houses and pulled up.

They were unloaded and herded towards a smaller hut at the back of the others. Like dying men they fell upon the troughs of water at the side of the hut, pushing their heads and faces deep into the water and slaking their thirst in deep spluttering gulps, hardly aware of the guards' shouts, sharp kicks and rifle butts.

Bill helped carry Roo, now barely conscious, to the trough. His own feet and legs were raw with large weeping sores, but he hardly noticed. A searing desire to drink long and deep replaced any other thought. Turning from the trough, he splashed Roo's face and lips with the water, and as he partly came to, the boy groaned and in a growing state of delirium, started calling for his mother. Bill carried him into the hut and laid him on its earthen floor.

A small woman, her face the yellow-brown colour of the earth, came into the room with two guards. She was dressed so that she was almost totally covered in the dark blue and grey loose cotton garments of the farm worker. A white cotton scarf almost entirely hid her hair and was swathed to cover her nose and mouth, and her hands were encased in small white cotton gloves. Her reactions, he noticed, were very controlled. She made no response to the smell or appearance of the prisoners, the deep folds of her scarf giving off a wonderfully clear white reflection in the light of the oil lanterns.

Her cleanliness and her grace, each movement beautifully controlled and precise, her eyes downcast and never actually looking at them—yet he felt sure, aware of everything that went on—overwhelmed him with a sudden longing for the comfort of home. At the same time he knew a deep sense of shame and degradation at their own filthy state.

Loss of face knows no boundaries.

The woman was carrying a large earthenware pot of hot soup. As they lined up, she ladled it into bowls. He remembered that first taste of a slightly sweet and grainy pumpkin soup. He'd hated pumpkin as a child, but that night it was the most wonderful thing he'd ever eaten. It was a taste that at once calmed yet rejuvenated his spirit; a simple joy he'd never forgotten.

Bill polished it off, then tried to force some soup between Roo's lips, but his eyes had rolled back and were now staring at some distant vista of the mind. The two guards looked on with amused contempt. One came over and kicked the boy hard in his side. Roo didn't move or cry out but gave a low groan and continued to murmur for his mother.

Bill knelt and cradled Roo's head in his arms, looking hard at the nuggety little guard who smirked back at him. The other men had fallen back at the attack, a dark resentment fuelling their desire to lash back at their captors. Their sense of survival just as swiftly smothered it. The guard called out and two more came in. Then roughly pushing Bill back against a wall, they hauled the boy away.

Minutes later they heard a sickening scream that hung and reverberated in the air for what seemed like hours, a sound he'd carry with him forever. Then one shot, followed by a babble of talk and laughter from their captors.

Roo's violent death marked the beginning of their captivity on the Nagasaki farm. The hard labour and beatings were still a haven compared to the harshness and brutality of the mine.

They were kept alive on pumpkin and sometimes corn soup. Their sores and weeping flesh soon gave way to callouses and rotting feet from working long hours in the waterlogged rice paddies. Their skin at first burned, then toughened and tanned in the sun and winds. Dysentery came and went, leaving weakened rag-like men desperate to get on their feet and keep going.

Despite their lack of freedom, Bill felt at one with this strange land and slowly a feeling of respect grew for the farmers who worked it.

With their men away at war, it was mostly the women of the house who were running the farm, and an uncle and grandfather, too old to fight.

Each day had its own rhythm that soon became almost second nature to Bill and the men. Arriving mid-winter, their first thoughts were to survive the cold, and they were issued with old padded cotton jackets, flimsy protection against the biting winds. But as they strengthened with their physical labour, they increased their ability to withstand the whims of the weather.

Their one luxury was the makeshift bath house they'd constructed, attached to their hut. Its large timber barrel was filled and fuelled every day to provide hot water. At night, sitting on rough benches alongside it, they had a preliminary wash-down, pouring a bamboo pitcher of water over themselves and scrubbing off the dirt with bags of rice bran. Soap was merely a memory. Then they would slosh themselves down with hot water, shouting and laughing like children, occasionally flicking each other with the long damp *tenugui* cotton cloths they used to dry themselves. Often after cleaning themselves, they'd take turns to sit in what was left of the steaming water and luxuriate for a few precious minutes in its warmth.

At first, the back-breaking work of planting the rice

seedlings in those frosty sunlit fields seemed the hardest thing he'd ever had to do. But gradually his stiffness gave way to a new strength and suppleness as he followed the farmers, his work developing a certainty and speed, often to the accompaniment of one of the children's flutes.

Bill could still picture the sharp green of young rice plants as they gradually rose and eventually lay like a spreading jade carpet above the water-covered fields. At night, exhausted, he'd fall into a deep sleep to the strangely comforting sounds of croaking frogs. A sudden glimpse of Paddy O'Brien's sharp quixotic face intruded, laughing at Bill's first clumsy attempts to control the oxen and work an old wooden plough. Paddy had taken over from him with a charm and flourish that typified this tough little Irishman from County Armagh.

Like Bill, Paddy had also come to Japan in a contingent of prisoners captured in Singapore, shipped across in the stinking hold of a Japanese merchant vessel. He'd even survived its sinking off the coast of Yokohama, with only a gammy leg to show for it. His leg, which had healed without the use of splints, was now permanently bent and shortened.

Not long after arriving at the farm, Paddy had fashioned a stick from a dead branch of persimmon tree. It was a broad rounded cudgel, complete with curved handle, worn smooth by his constant polishings. Down one side were notches and tiny scratched names of their Japanese captors.

'My special shelaleagh,' he called it. 'When the day of reckoning comes, they're all here,' he told Bill, proudly running his hand along the grooves, 'every man jack of them.'

Paddy's dare-devil ways and irreverent humour earned him many beatings. 'I've looked old Father Death in the face too many times to fear him now, laddie,' he told Bill. 'We're sort of mates, you know,' he laughed. And true to his word, Paddy lived life on the razor's edge, knowing just how far he could push a situation, and often, just for the hell of pushing it that little bit further.

The chief target of his barbs was a stocky, shaven-headed guard, Hitachi, or 'Shitachi' as they called him. Paddy's silver tongue waxed lyrical, coating insults with over-sugared metaphors, bowing low as he delivered his horrible homilies, to the amusement of the other men. Hitachi seemed fair game to Paddy's glibness, his perplexity as to the full meaning of Paddy's remarks giving way to laughter and swagger or an instant lashing out with his rifle butt if he felt things weren't quite as they appeared.

Hitachi's growing resentment seemed to feed Paddy's almost predestined desire to further taunt and tempt death, in a cat and mouse game of playing with time. Bill's warnings to lay off Hitachi were met with either a laugh, an oath or Paddy simply bursting into song.

Often when out working in the fields, Paddy's clear tenor voice would rise in glorious sound, mostly singing the sentimental ballads of his homeland. And in that instant, the beauty of those pure notes and the changing seasons as reflected in their landscape, bonded them . . . both captives and captors. Bill recalled how one of the older daughters, Chio-san, would become quite still, standing up from her planting or harvesting and listening with a rapt expression, before being chided back to work by the other women.

One morning quite early, while working in the fields, they heard the faint hum of a bomber. They looked up and saw the distant sky over Nagasaki city suddenly light up in a brilliant flash of white that spread like contained sheet lightning. The surrounding sky shone with a strange bluish-green light, then as if from deep inside the earth there shot an enormous pillar of purple fire, racing with great speed high into the heavens. They stared in amazement, transfixed and silenced by the scene. A giant mushroom of billowing cloud rose into the sky then slowly descended. Minutes later there was a hollow roar and four muffled thuds resounded in the distance. Then a shock wave rocked the ground beneath their feet.

As if at some unseen signal, the birds had stopped singing, and all sound ceased while every living thing hung suspended in a vacuum. Then the guards started shouting and talking excitedly among themselves, and some had run back to the huts.

'Holy mother of God, Holy mother of God,' Paddy kept repeating as he stared at the horizon, which was now assuming a surreal shape before their eyes.

'It's the end,' he told Bill, crossing himself. 'This is it, laddie, the Apocalypse is upon them.'

They huddled together, talking excitedly, new hope uniting them. Paddy jumped to his feet, and in a high, strong voice that had so often carried them through their long days and nights, started singing a rousing 'Land of Hope and Glory'. In a white fury, Hitachi appeared, shouting and swinging the butt of his rifle against the side of Paddy's head. The crack of wood on bone rang out in sickening reverberation, silencing those golden notes, the ghost of which still hung around them as Paddy fell to the ground. Before they could move, Hitachi aimed his gun and shot Paddy in the face. Then without a word he turned, and strode back to the huts.

By now, a roaring blast of hot wind had swooped in across the fields, as if to scoop up and carry the soul of the little Irishman with it.

The suddenness of Paddy's death and the maelstrom now roaring around them had left him in limbo, without any feeling at all, Bill recalled.

'He was gone, and I . . .' his voice broke as he looked across at Maria coming back into the room with a tray of drinks. At last he could feel those long repressed tears coursing down his face and he didn't try to stop them. She reached out and took his hand, holding it tight. He put his head back and let the tears flow, easing the memories of that dreadful day.

He hadn't cried then, he remembered, nor felt anything. Just a cold emptiness and terrible fatigue. He picked up the bloodied body of Paddy, surprised by its lightness, and carried him across the green and gold fields to where they had buried Roo and two other prisoners the year before—on the side of a small hill rising from the rice paddies. He recalled how the Japanese farm workers had disappeared, and for the first time, this motley bunch of six Australians and two Englishmen had the land to themselves.

They hardly spoke, their earlier sense of optimism now dashed by the reality of Paddy's death. As they dug his grave, Bill was aware that Chio-san and her younger sister had come out from the farm house and were walking towards them. She carried a folded cloth in front of her and her sister a deep bowl and towels. Reaching them, she suddenly and unexpectedly bowed low, as did her sister, then kneeling beside the limp body of Paddy proceeded with the ancient rite of *Yukan*.

They were dressed, he noticed, not in their usual work clothes, but in old, worn kimono and each girl wore a belt of straw. Removing Paddy's tattered clothes and the rags that had bound his feet, they washed the blood from his body, first with water, then dabbing on alcohol and wiping it dry with a small white cloth. Gently Chio-san bathed then combed his fair hair. The bullet had left little evidence of its lethal trajectory, just a scorching of the skin and hair around a small hole slowly seeping dark red blood.

Taking a small cloth *zuda-bukura* from her belt, she pared his nails, then those of her sister and herself, carefully placing the parings in the bag. She then slipped some coins into it to pay the ferryman on Paddy's voyage into the next world, and tied it around his neck.

Without pausing, Chio-san eased Paddy's feet into white *tabi* that had had their soles removed, and over them fitted straw sandals, tying them firmly with long white cords. Then in final tribute to the voice which had given them so many hours of pleasure, she dipped a shiny leaf from the *Shikibi* plant into a bowl of fresh water and drew it gently across Paddy's mouth, moistening his lips, still amazingly intact after the blast that had stilled his voice forever. She then wrapped his body in a fine white cotton cloth. Never once did she look up as she expertly and gently shrouded his body in the precious stuff.

Her sister lit incense at the head of his grave, and placing scarves over their heads, they knelt beside it, clasping their hands in supplication, and softly chanting a Sutra as Bill and the other men lowered Paddy's body into it.

Leaning forward, Chio-san gently laid a knife across Paddy's chest to ward off evil spirits and bad luck. It was then that Bill noticed she had brought with her Paddy's shelaleagh, his stick of retribution. As she started to place it beside the body, Bill stepped forward and gently but firmly took it from her, looking deep into her eyes as he did. She said nothing, but her saddened expression gently pleaded with him: let there be no more anger, no more deaths.

She motioned that the body should be in a sitting position as they covered it with earth, but Bill decided that they would leave it as it lay, and the sisters resumed their chanting as it was swallowed up by the soil of the land they had all worked during those long and gruelling months.

Later that evening, when they had returned to the hut, there was a meal of rice with a little dried fish and slices of dried persimmon and damson plums, a meal unlike any they had been treated to in the months of their captivity. For each man, there was also a tiny china cup of warmed *sake* wine. Not quite an Irish wake, but the memory as clearly etched as if it was yesterday . . . unlike the following weeks of American occupation and their demobilisation which had mostly faded into oblivion.

'Cheers, darling!' As Maria handed him a whisky, she raised her glass.

'To us.' Bill smiled at her, trying to still his sense of dissatisfaction. He was home, but what now?

She leaned across and kissed him gently on the mouth. 'Things will pick up, darling, you'll see. We'll make a good life here.'

'Yes,' he answered, looking out across the paddocks that seemed to stretch forever. 'But it won't be in farming.'

31

BILL AND JACK—'WINGANNA', QUEENSLAND, 1947

'Dad, I've been meaning to talk to you.' Bill paused.

Jack regarded his son, still gaunt, though a heap better than when he'd first clapped eyes on him on his return from France six months before.

Bill continued, looking straight at his father. 'You've got to get a full-time manager in, and . . .'

'What the hell are you saying?' Jack broke in.

'I'm saying I just don't want to do any more farming,' Bill answered. 'Look, Dad, my heart's never really been in it. I just want to fly, get a civvy job in flying,' he went on.

'Well, thanks very much. That's a heap of help to me. And where the hell do you think the money's coming from to pay a full-time manager? Just where's the money coming from, eh? It doesn't grow on trees, you know.' Jack turned on his son. 'You're a dead loss. You know that? For Christ's sake, just who the hell do you think you are!'

Bill could see the colour rising in his father's face as he got up out of his winged chair and started pacing. He looked so old, and Bill's heart went out to him. Gone forever was the towering figure that had put the fear of God into him as a kid.

'Have you spoken about this to your mother?'

'I don't have to,' Bill answered, 'she knows.'

Jack said nothing. Suddenly he felt exhausted, and he sat, his head thrown back against his chair. That whole bloody war, he thought, it had changed everything.

'Well Dad?'

'Well, what's there to say? It seems you've made up your mind.'

God, what a washout, Jack thought. Part of the joy of 'Winganna' was in seeing his sons take over, and building on what had been achieved. Tom, who'd loved the land, was now gone; his body, or what was left of it, rotting in some God-forsaken jungle. He felt tears rise, and turned his head so Bill wouldn't see. His beloved Tom, gone. Wasn't it always the way? Those you loved most were the ones you usually lost.

'We'll speak again later, Dad,' Bill said. It would be useless to continue now, he knew, not when his father was in one of these moods. Better to leave it with him to mull over.

Jack hardly noticed Bill leaving, and continued to stare out across the paddocks. Already a heat haze was gathering, and the golden summer grasses were shimmering with the midday intensity he so loved. The drumming of cicadas rose, a deafening crescendo of insect percussion, then died away as if by some magic signal, only to start up again minutes later.

He loved this place. It was a tangible almost physical love, a feeling which had carried him through that long march on the treacherous Kokoda trail. It had kept him upright when others fell beside him, and given him purpose when everything around him looked hopeless. Those little Nip bastards hadn't got the better of him. Not Jack Baillieu. And this wasn't the end to it. No way. He could feel his anger rise again. God, they were animals, he thought, trying to push away the ugly scenes as they rose before him. Animals!

He rose to his feet, walking across to the cabinet and pouring himself a whisky, barely passing the water over it. He tossed it back, then poured another. That was better. He felt his spirits rise and a sense of calm return as the liquor spread its warmth.

'Why didn't you tell me?' Jack said accusingly to Molly later.

'Tell you what, dear?' Without missing a beat, Molly continued brushing her long hair, looking with calm indifference at her reflection in the dressing table mirror, a heavy old cedar piece which had been her mother's. In the days long ago when such things mattered, she had placed the mirror where the light from the French windows was at its most flattering, a soft diffused light that fell onto the mirror, rather than her face so that any lines and unsightly folds almost melted away in the kindlier light, and made more bearable the passing of the years.

Out here, she well knew the havoc wrought by relentless Australian sun and temperatures, where a woman's face was exposed to the whims of weather at its harshest, and where the bloom of youth was soon dissipated.

Molly sighed, looking at her hair. The pepper and salt shadings of oncoming grey did nothing for the yellowing of her skin. If only it would go completely white. At least then the contrast would give her skin a lift. Images of Mary Williams' feathery white hair picking up every stray light that passed, and creating an almost halo-like aura around her otherwise nondescript face, came to mind, and she sighed again.

'You should have warned me,' Jack said again.

'About what?' She looked at his reflection staring accusingly at her.

'That Bill's doing a bunk.'

Molly turned, and said softly, 'What did you expect? After all he's been through,' she added.

'And what about me?' he fumed. 'What about what I've been through . . . doesn't that count for anything? When I think of it, God Almighty!' he breathed out heavily, lost for words.

'I thought at least you'd understand, Moll,' he went on when she didn't reply. He sat heavily on the end of their bed. She felt an irritable urge to tell him not to sit there, as she thought of the creases in her freshly ironed cotton cover. Then seeing the expression on his face, held her tongue.

'I know, love.' She thought of Tommy, and an ache rose inside her, as it always did when images of his merry face came to mind. But Bill, she sighed, had always been the tear-away, even as a small boy, taking off on his bike, his horse, then later in his car and planes, whatever moved him fastest from place to place, as if just the act of getting there was in itself the answer.

'Bill's had a rough time of it too, Jack,' she added. He said nothing, then in a quiet voice, 'We all have to pay our dues, Moll, and his are here now, when I need him. I won't forget this.' He got up and walked out of the room.

Molly turned back to the mirror, playing with her hair again. What did it matter? What did any of it matter any more? Soon, they'd all be gone. She felt so tired, a dragging tiredness which was with her from the moment she awoke each morning. She moved through the day as though wading through treacle. Everything was an effort now. No joy, no bright lights or heights, but more a vast wasteland of greys and browns to get through.

She wished she was with Tommy, secure in the other world she often pictured to herself. A golden place of deliverance, where one lived in the divine light of the Lord's presence.

'Dear Lord, please help me,' she said, bowing her head and crossing herself as she murmured the litany. It was an oft-repeated plea that made almost bearable the nebulous twilight world of memories and regrets she floated through day after day. Prayer had become her panacea.

32

MOLLY—'WINGANNA', QUEENSLAND, 1952

'And who did you say went with you to the Harrisons?' Molly asked.

'No one, love. I've already told you.'

'Oh yes.' Molly looked out at the rain belting down against a large galvanised iron shed near the side gate. She laughed a little, to soften the situation and make light of her forgetfulness.

'I'm worried about Bill,' she said suddenly. 'He's been away over there far too long. I'll try and get a food parcel to him.'

Jack looked at her and said nothing. His deep uneasiness at Molly's state, as he now called it to himself, surfaced and he tried to push it away. After all, she looked OK, was eating well, everything seemed fine. Except she just didn't seem to remember things, and it was getting worse. Maybe Doc Sloane should come out and take a look at her later today. He knew she wouldn't go herself.

'What, just because I forget little things?' she laughed when he first suggested it. 'Don't be silly, Jack. I'm OK. I'm fine,' she added. 'Just a little tired. You know how it is.'

He'd laughed with her. She was right, he must be imagining things.

But that was before the wandering started. Two months ago when he'd come home she wasn't there. No message, or anything. He hadn't worried until darkness fell, and there was still no word from her. That wasn't like Molly.

An embarrassed call came from Ted, his station hand, at around nine that night saying he'd just picked her up. She'd been sitting on the parapet wall of the lower dam down near the roadway.

'Said she couldn't find her way home, or some such thing,' Ted told him, then laughed. 'After thirty years of living here!'

His clear hazel eyes had looked questioningly at Jack when he called round to pick her up fifteen minutes later.

'Moll's had a lot on her mind,' Jack answered shortly. He'd declined a beer, discussed the weather and left with her soon after.

He looked across at her now, as she knitted. Her long silvered hair was tied in two thin plaits and twined around her head. She was still a fine looking woman, if not the striking beauty of their first meeting. He'd read somewhere that we don't notice changes in those around us, because time allows us to become conditioned to them gradually.

He remembered how, on returning from the war six years ago, he first saw her and noticed the new careworn expression and fine tracery of lines that had sprung up, veiling the bloom and the impression of youth he'd always carried with him. Work and worry had whittled her away and wrought their cruel changes. His years of absence from the farm and Tom's death as well as Bill's internment hadn't helped either. Now Bill and Maria, after their marriage, had moved into town where Bill worked as a flying instructor.

The thought of this made Jack forget Molly. A cold anger and disappointment squeezed his heart. He got up abruptly from the table, knocking over the milk jug as he did. Molly regarded it and said nothing, but reached down and patted Chloe, her border collie. The dog, disturbed by the crash, was sitting on her haunches looking up expectantly at her mistress and then down to the dripping milk. Molly motioned to her to lick it off the floor, then looked away, staring absently out the window.

Her reaction returned Jack to worrying about his wife again. A couple of years ago she would have given him curry for such awkwardness. Now, she hardly noticed. It was almost as if the house could fall about their ears without Molly turning a hair, he thought, gazing around him.

She had always kept it so beautifully before, a shining, welcoming place aglow with polish and the smell of bees wax, and large bunches of fresh gum shoots in vases when flowers in their garden were scarce. And now, if it wasn't for Mrs Jamieson, their housekeeper, coming in for a few hours each day to keep things going, God knows what it would be like.

The whole weight of the situation pressed down on him and he sighed.

She looked up. 'What's wrong, love?'

'Nothing to worry about.' He bent down and kissed her lightly on the top of her head. 'You'll be in around five?' he asked casually.

'Yes, I'll be here all day,' she said. 'Maria's bringing over little Tommy.' She smiled at the thought of her grandson. 'If you get back early, you'll catch them.' She hummed to herself as she knitted away, the big tortoise-shell needles clicking an accompaniment.

It was a sound he'd long associated with their life on the farm. The needles were hardly ever out of her hands. During some of his darkest moments in New Guinea when on that interminable march, these were the thoughts that had come back to comfort him. Molly had been the definitive homemaker, her baking, her jams and preserves the pride of numerous local country shows, and along with her handicrafts, taking off prize after prize.

He looked at her lined hands with their thickening knuckles, still nimbly knitting up ball after ball of wool, but not the intricate stitching and patterns of before, just interminably long wide blocks of stocking stitch. 'They're for rugs, or scarves,' she'd said when he asked her what she was making. After they'd reached a certain length, she'd cast them off and toss them aside. The cupboard was full of them. He'd stopped asking, thinking that maybe they were a form of comfort—they called it 'therapy' now. He recalled the wards of young shell-shocked boys weaving and knitting their way back to sanity.

'And who went with you to the Harrisons?' Molly asked again. He didn't answer, what was the point?

'I'll see you later, love. Tell young Tommy if I don't catch him today, I will on the weekend,' he added, knowing it was a useless request; she would never remember, but at least it bridged his going, and not having to answer her question yet again.

After he'd gone, Molly sat for some time, concentrating on her fingers as they whirled amongst the needles and wool. The ringing of the phone broke her reverie. She got up and walked slowly towards it, Chloe at her heels. It was an effort to do anything really, she thought. The ringing persisted, but where was the phone? She felt upset and angry with herself. This was crazy. The phone? She must know where it was after all this time. As the sound drew her towards it, it stopped. She looked around wildly, feeling agitated now. She couldn't hear it ringing, and still hadn't found it. She felt a deep well of resentment brim up, then overflow in tears of frustration and fear.

She leaned against the wall, closing her eyes as if to blot out the room and its contents. What was happening to her? She was only fifty-four and that wasn't old. She felt well, if a bit slowed down, but that was to be expected, after all she'd been through. She had seen Jack looking at her this morning with that expression of deep exasperation which she saw so often on his face now. A stab of fear shot through her. What if he went off and left her? No, he wouldn't do that, not her Jack, not her husband. But a lot did, she thought, particularly since they'd come back, and some so changed. Take Marge, she thought. Her Jim had come back randy as a coot. He couldn't get enough of it. And if Marge didn't oblige, he'd find anyone who would. And he still had his looks, so it wasn't hard.

Molly's thoughts drifted back to the phone again. Maybe it was Jill calling. She thought of Jill and Gerard. Jack had cut off all contact with her since she went to Hawaii to join Gerard.

'She's Jap happy,' he'd said bitterly. 'I for one am not going along with it, do you hear? Don't you ask me to, either,' he'd whirled on her when she had protested. 'She's a traitor, and I'm not saying any more, that's my final word on it.'

But of course it wasn't. 'And after all we've done for her,' he'd added later. 'She's not even ours yet we brought her up as if she was. And it was for you I did it,' he turned accusingly to her. 'For your dead sister's child. And now look at what she's done. Where's the thanks, the gratitude in that?'

'But you love Gerard too, Jack,' Molly reminded him. 'He's your own brother's grandson after all, and . . .'

'And Gare would turn in his grave if he knew what was going on, and what we've been through with those Jap bastards,' Jack broke in. 'Do you think he was ever really happy with Boy marrying one of them? I ask you, do you think he was?'

She said nothing. What was the point when he was in one of his moods?

He went on. 'I tell you, Hiroko might have been a pretty, bright little thing, but I'm sure Gare really regretted that Boy didn't marry Grace.'

'But he loved Hiroko,' Molly said, adding, 'and so did Hattie, in time.'

'Love, love—what does that amount to when they turn out to be the traitorous bastards they really are! You weren't out there in the jungle with them, Molly. You just don't know the half of it, and you never will.' He sat silent a moment, then went on.

'If you'd seen what they did to the women and kids, maybe then you wouldn't be so mealy mouthed, so God-damned sanctimonious,' he said grimly. 'But you just wait, it'll all come out in time, and then we'll see if you change your tune.'

Molly sighed. It all didn't bear thinking about. Walking over to a day-bed, she lay down and almost immediately fell into a deep sleep.

'How are you feeling, Mater?' Maria's anxious voice awakened her. She sat up. Why had Maria always insisted on this 'Mater' business, Molly wondered, smiling at her daughter-in-law. She had requested so often in the beginning, 'Just call me Mum.'

'But I can't,' Maria had answered gently, wondering how best to say it. 'You're not my mother, I mean.' She added quickly when she saw the hurt in Molly's eyes, 'You're as good as, but it's just not the same. My own mother's Mum to me, and you're, well, you're Bill's mum.'

So somehow 'Mater' had slipped in, Maria's halfway acknowledgement to her wishes, but for Molly, a strange Latin term locked well away in school, and a poor substitute to gaining a daughter.

'Mater?' Maria repeated.

'What dear?'

'How are you feeling?'

'Just fine and dandy, why wouldn't I be?' Molly answered defensively. 'I just took a short kip, that's all.' But when she saw the time on the oak grandfather clock that Jack had brought over from the States before they were married, she said, 'Is it really that late?' Then smiling at Maria, 'Well it's time for tea,' she went on. She looked across to Tommy, who had suddenly run into the room, his small arms outstretched.

'Gran! Gran!' She picked him up, this dark-haired version of her beloved sandy-haired Tom, whirling him around and around. She hugged him to her, kissing him on both cheeks.

'Yuk! Don't kiss me so much, Gran, it's sissy.'

Reluctantly she let him go, and he ran off with Chloe following, barking after him.

'It's Jack's birthday next week, and I'd like to have a surprise party with all the family here,' Molly said later over tea.

'Do you think you should?' Maria asked, looking over her cup, apprehensive at the thought.

'Why not? Just something small. A special tea. Say at around six when he gets in.' She warmed to the thought, thinking about the days of baking and the wonderful teas they'd enjoyed before the boys went away to war. They were really something!

She recalled the big table laid out under the crimson flowering poinciana tree, the white damask cloth shining with her silver, her Royal Doulton china and Waterford crystal. And the food. It had been a real spread! Fresh chicken sandwiches, steaming cornish pasties and sausage rolls. The boys had always loved them with the spicy tomato sauce she made herself. There was meat loaf, salads and her own mayonnaise. Her big cut-glass bowl was filled with a sherry trifle, and an angel's food flummery lay in her special silver bowl frosted with a fine patina of ice crystals. Sometimes, depending who was there, she added a fresh cream-filled Swiss roll, and occasionally when she felt like spoiling them, there was a devil's food chocolate cake, and always her favourite boiled fruit cake. But the *pièce de résistance*, as Jack always called them, were her rolled paper-thin cucumber sandwiches. Their lightness almost defied description. She smiled at the thought. No one in the district could match them. White bread as finely sliced as tissue paper, just holding together the luscious pale green slivers of cucumber in light-as-air rolls. They literally melted in the mouth, and she could never make enough of them.

'So we'll have a birthday tea,' Molly said decisively.

'Well, if you say so, Mater.' Maria thought of Bill and his father and the open animosity that was now only too evident whenever they met, and her chest tightened. But Molly needed something to look forward to, she thought.

'I could come over early and help you,' she smiled across at the older woman.

'No, no, I want to do it all myself. It will be my present to Jack,' Molly answered.

33

MOLLY—WALKABOUT

Molly had awakened with a sense that there was something she had to do that day. It hung around her like a refrain of some forgotten melody, her mind seeking, searching it out, but still it eluded her.

Jack had gone off early in the ute, and she moved around the homestead, her eyes always drawn to what lay outside beyond the windows and screened doors as she passed them. The house seemed so quiet and dark, and she could see that outside there was already a shimmering golden haze. It's going to be a real stinker, she thought. It'll be a hundred degrees scorcher, I'll bet. There was something in Jack's expression as he left that morning. A look of regret, as if he was holding something back. But then he'd gone off whistling, and she had been left wondering how to fill her day.

She drifted back to her bedroom, to the wardrobe. It was a heavy mahogany piece that ran the full length of her dressing room. It had belonged to her sister Frieda, and when she had died they had moved much of her furniture and possessions into 'Winganna'. It was here in safekeeping for Jill. But so far Jill hadn't sent for it.

She thought of the tiny wan girl who had come to live with them as their own, when Freida had died. Jill shouldn't have married Gerard. Jack was probably right.

You'd be looking into those black eyes, she reflected, and have no idea of what was really going on behind them.

She recalled the long holidays he'd spent here at the homestead as a boy, with Tom and Bill, riding all over the property, and Jill always tagging on behind them. Even then she had worshipped him, she remembered. Worshipped him. The words revolved in her mind, like the cranking up of an old rusty engine. She just couldn't think what it was that was worrying her today.

What was it? There was something there, but she couldn't place it. Molly sighed. Her mind was as sharp as a tack for past events. But for things of the moment, it was like struggling through a darkened tunnel, with no shafts of light to show the way. Things dropped out and away, gone forever. The immediate past just didn't exist.

Mrs Jamieson, her daily housekeeper, put her head in the door.

'You all right, dear? I'll make us a cuppa before I get started.'

Molly nodded. Mrs Jamieson was regarding her strangely. 'Do you want a hand dear?'

Molly looked down and realised she hadn't finished dressing, and was still in her satin slip. 'No,' she said quickly, 'I'll be right.'

'Okay, well I'll get on with it then. I'll give you a hoy when the kettle boils.'

Molly pulled the large wardrobe doors wide open and ran her hand along the dresses, hanging neatly in a row. Most of them she had made herself, and so much of her energy had gone into each one, she could never bear to part with any of them. She riffled her hand across the linens and crêpe de chine, some taffetas, a couple of Thai silks, but mostly cottons. Fine light things that were coolest on days like this.

She looked at them fondly as she ran her hand backwards and forwards, feeling the soft fabrics float against her skin as if caressing her, whispering their reassurance. Every one could tell a story, she thought.

Molly reached up for a red and white check and held it against her, staring critically into the full-length mirror. Not bad, she thought, but too bright for today. She had first seen it in the 'Women's Weekly', and copied it right down to the same big white buttons that opened all the way to the hem. She had been tanned and plumper then, and it had looked good. Jack had always liked that dress.

Throwing it onto the bed, she took out another, a navy cotton with a white Peter Pan collar and cuffs. It was too stark and made her look yellow. She had made it specially for Gare's funeral. The service had been held in the big Sacred Heart cathedral, and Hattie had arrived in her brightest muu-muu, all reds and pinks and yellows and a bright floral lei around her neck. The local guests had been shocked, but Hattie couldn't have cared less what they or anyone else thought.

From the moment Hattie had arrived, there'd been trouble, Molly remembered. Hattie hadn't lifted a finger except to give orders. And she had left all the catering for the tea and the cleaning away afterwards to Molly, leaving the very next day, taking Gare's body back with her on the plane to Hawaii.

Jill had gone with her then to spend her school holidays. And that was the beginning of Jill's moving away from them. She recalled the asparagus rolls, left over from the tea, which she'd packed for Jill to eat on the way. She'd always loved my asparagus rolls, Molly smiled.

The thought of them sparked a faint flare of memory, which died as quickly as it had come.

Next Molly took out a flowered green and yellow shirtmaker. She had worn it to Tom's final speech day at high school with her wide panama straw hat. A spasm of pain clutched at her heart as she thought of Tom . . . Now where was that hat? Frantically, one by one she started to pull out the dresses, throwing them onto the bed till she found it tucked into a hat box on a shelf behind them. She put it on, then turned to the remaining dresses that were still left hanging. There was her old friend, the navy and tan gingham. It was a Madras cotton that seemed to get softer with every wearing. She had managed to buy that piece of fabric, she remembered, for only two shillings and sixpence a yard. Heavens, what a bargain, and she had worn and worn it.

During the long Christmas school holidays she had taught Jill to sew on the big treadle Singer sewing machine. Together they drafted the pattern, then cut it out. Jill was never one for tacking anything though. It had to be made fast and worn that night. Molly smiled, remembering how Jill had a way with clothes, a real flair. She could put on a tablecloth and it would look wonderful. She ran her hand over the growing pile of dresses on her bed. Ah, there was the pale yellow hailstone spotted muslin she'd worn for the shower tea she had given for Mary Pritchard, out on the big verandah. It was early May in '42, she recalled and they had been chatting away when they'd heard a tremendous roar which got closer and closer until suddenly the sky was filled with brown and green camouflaged bombers, flying from the Garbutt Air Base and heading north.

'There goes our strike force, so that proves it, the Japs are coming,' said Jenny Henderson, looking around for anyone who'd dare oppose her.

'And you know what that means,' she added, 'wholesale butchery and rape.' The last word spun off her tongue with relish, and she looked at Molly as she said it, with a tilt of her head.

'They're just doing a rekky,' Molly had answered lightly.

'Not on your life,' said Jenny, not to be outdone. 'There'll be hordes of Japs coming down through New Guinea and into Queensland, and with the men away . . .' she had paused for full effect, 'we'll be sitting ducks.'

Molly recalled that Mary had burst into tears, and the whole tea had been ruined . . .

She glimpsed a dress which hung on a special crocheted hanger in a cloth bag to protect it. Opening the bag she saw that the dry-cleaning tags were still pinned to the dress's back. She carefully removed them; they had left little rust marks in the yellow cotton. The iceland poppies splashed across it were just as bright as the day her sister had last worn it in that accident. When the police had handed over Freida's things to her after Stan refused to take them, somehow she couldn't bear to part with this dress. Apart from a little dust from the road, it hadn't been damaged, she remembered, holding it close and picturing Frieda's face. Carefully she placed it back in its bag in the back of the wardrobe along with Freida's other dresses, which Stan had given her.

Returning to her own clothes, she took them all out, dress after dress, reliving the special moments attached to each one. She pulled out a soft blue chiffon. It had a deep boat-shaped neckline and a matching satin ribbon around the waist to which was attached a tiny spray of white silk daisies. She had loved that dress and worn it to so many of the big do's. Its full skirt was cut on the bias and it had taken her ages to sew its tiny rolled hem. The satin ribbon she had carefully sewn onto buckram to make it firmer so she could cinch it in and accentuate her tiny waist.

Molly heard Mrs Jamieson's voice floating up from the kitchen, and called back that she'd be down soon. She thought of the night of the Henderson party. She had been bending over to ladle out the punch for Jim Henderson and felt his eyes caressing the swell of her breasts rising above the low-cut neckline. Conscious of his gaze, she had leaned forward a little further so that he could see the deep pink of her nipples through her lacy bra.

She remembered his desire for her had come across the table in an almost palpable wave, and afterwards they had danced and she could feel the heat of his body as it pressed against hers. She had wanted him so much in that moment. If he'd asked, she might even have gone outside with him into the velvety night to play out their passion.

It was a night for love, she recalled, balmy, somnolent. But instead, she had gone home to her big lonely bed and, taking off her dress, had lain longing to feel his arms around her, a hot tongue licking at her breasts, her legs, her thighs, and up deep inside her. She had thought then of Jenny Henderson, and hated her, wondering if at that very moment they were making love. If they were, she reassured herself, it would be of her he'd be thinking, of her breasts, her body. She caressed herself as she imagined all the things his hands, his mouth, his cock would be doing to her, the sweat of her growing desire glistening on her skin. In a moment of arousal she had eventually climaxed, then lay feeling even more alone and deserted. She had thought of Bill and of Tom away with his battalion, and Jack now in New Guinea, and groaned. She couldn't bear to be without a man in her bed. How would she survive the long nights?

'You didn't hear me, so I brought it up to you, dear.' Mrs Jamieson's voice cut into Molly's reverie. 'Goodness, what a mess!'

Molly looked up surprised. Who was this woman? 'Oh good, tea,' she said brightly, looking at the tray Mrs Jamieson was holding. 'Just put it down anywhere.'

'Do you want a hand, dear?'

'No thank you.' Molly looked at the pile of dresses, thinking, why have I got them all out? What were they doing there on her bed? She was still holding the blue chiffon in her arms.

'I want you to put them all in a box,' she said suddenly.

'All of them?' Mrs Jamieson looked dubious.

'Yes, I'll just keep a few things and the rest can all go. That will be easier,' she said.

'Well, you have your tea and get dressed, and we'll see,' said Mrs Jamieson. She would have to talk to Mr Baillieu, this was all getting too much for her. The woman was potty, and getting worse. She needed a nurse, not a housekeeper. They really should put her away, she thought, as with a loud sigh she left the room.

Slowly and deliberately, Molly put on her blue chiffon dress. It was over ten years since she'd worn it, and it swam on her. The low neckline that she had once filled so generously now hung in folds over her breasts, showing her slip. She pulled the dress down at the back so that the neckline rose a little and hid the satin slip. There, that was better. She belted it tightly, slipping the crushed flowers into its loop. She stood back looking at herself in the mirror. She saw a small woman with long silvery hair in a dress that belonged to another time. She swirled around and around, watching the skirt billow out around her like a sea of soft blue waves, rising and falling as she danced around the room. In a high clear voice, she started to sing Jimminy Cricket's song of wishing upon a star, and its promise of dreams coming true.

As she swayed, she knocked the tray crashing to the floor. Mrs Jamieson appeared, the accusing look on her face reminiscent of Jenny Henderson's that night at the party. Molly turned on her.

'I'm not a slut,' she said hotly. 'How dare you call me that. I'm not a slut,' she repeated.

'There, there dear.' Mrs Jamieson moved towards her, but Molly pushed her away and, grabbing her panama hat, ran from the room and down the wide stairs and out into the sunshine, the heat crackling her hair with its intensity. She put on the big hat and thought, I'll go down to the dam, it will be nice and cool there. She could hear Mrs Jamieson calling out to her, but took no notice, hurrying away from the sound of that voice, with Chloe at her heels.

Passing the big iron shed, she looked in and saw her old bike. Yes, she would ride her bike, that would be best. She pushed it out onto the dirt road that wound away from the house, and rather unsteadily at first rode off to the first fence surrounding the homestead.

Arriving at the gate, she struggled with the heavy iron catch. It had always been a bugger to open, but they couldn't just rely on a cattle grid here. She opened it just far enough for the bike to get through, then pushed it shut again, hauling the cumbersome catch down to hold it.

Molly pedalled off along the road heading for the dam

two miles away near the lower end of the property. Chloe kept pace with her, her head held high, sniffing at the breeze as they went.

It was getting hotter, the sun sitting high in the sky. She should have brought a flask of something to drink, Molly thought. Still she could cool herself off at the dam.

She hadn't gone far when she pulled off the road and leaned her bike against the trunk of a poinciana tree. Its heavy foliage provided a welcome shade and she decided to sit a while.

Maybe, it would be quicker to leave the bike here and cut across the paddocks to the dam, she thought. Her dress was hot and stuck to her and she wished she hadn't worn it. She looked around. There was no-one in sight. Maybe if she took it off for a while. Yes, that's what she'd do. Unbuckling her belt, she pulled the dress over her head, leaving only her slip. That was better—she would start wearing just her slips now, that's all you needed in this weather. She leaned back against the tree, fanning herself with her hat, looking out across the endless paddocks. They only grazed a few cattle now around the homestead, and Jack was mostly away all day, busy in their canefields nearer to Ingham. He was always away.

She could see the glint of the rail line, the Great Northern Line that cut through their property away in the lower paddock. When the boys were little, she would take them down there to watch the mighty 'Inlander' steam engine thunder past on its way to Mount Isa. They'd wave at the faces peering out at them from the carriage windows, and sometimes kindly passengers would throw out their newspapers and magazines, even sweets for the boys, and once at Christmas, a whole hamper filled with goodies.

A currawong flew onto a branch above her, and with its head cocked to one side observed her with molasses eyes, then broke into mellifluous warblings. She smiled up at the bird. That sound always made her think of home, and rain. They mostly sang when the rains were coming.

Feeling weary, she lay back resting her head on Chloe's silky body, and drifted into a light sleep. A sting from an ant woke her and she sat up feeling hot and confused. It must be past midday now. The sun still high in the heavens was starting its descent. She could see the heat waves shimmering on the surface of the sun-baked grasses. Down towards the bottom of the hill through the haze she saw two figures walking towards her. She leaned forward, shading her eyes, peering at them. Chloe, disturbed, looked towards where she was staring, then up at her expectantly. Molly stood up. Maybe it was Jack back early. Putting on her hat, she started to walk towards them.

As they came closer, she could see that they were in uniform, the khaki garb of the AIF, and that one of the figures was leaning on the other as they walked along the rail track. That was strange, but maybe they were lost, she thought, and simply using the track to guide them.

She started quickening her pace, moving towards them, with Chloe running at her side, turning every minute or so to look up at her. The heat haze was really thick now, and it was difficult to see them. My God, they were in for a big storm later tonight, she thought.

As she got nearer to the track, she could see they were young men and the one leaning against the other was somehow familiar. She started to move faster, something urging her to get there quickly. She could feel her heart beating; it was so long since she'd run, she really wasn't fit any more. The figures had stopped and were looking towards her. The heat haze seemed to clear a little and her heart gave a lurch. It was Tom, it was Tom! She knew he'd come back. She'd always known he wasn't dead. Not her Tom. Calling out and waving frantically, she broke into a run, with Chloe barking at her side.

So he'd come back to her after all. It was Tom. Her heart seemed to be booming, pounding in her ears, but she felt as if her feet had wings as she flew across the paddock towards him, calling out his name, tears of joy streaming down her cheeks. Scrambling through the wire fence, she jumped up onto the track and ran towards the limping figure which somehow seemed to be ever receding now, her arms outstretched, calling 'Tom, Tom!'

She didn't hear the train's warning whistle as it rounded the bend, or feel the weight of the 'Inlander's' mighty engine and the intermittent swish of its eight carriages as they passed over her like the blades of *Masamune*[9] through silk. She was safe in the arms of Tom, her beloved son Tom, now home from the wars—achieving the cherished bushi-no-nasake, the warrior's way of mercy and benevolence.

Only Chloe bore witness, her frantic howls sole testimony to the endless sky. A small boy, peering through the rear window of his mother's car as it wound its way up the road towards 'Winganna' homestead and his grandfather's surprise birthday tea, spied a distant running figure in a big hat, and the smoke from an approaching engine.

'Granny, Granny!' he called.

Maria smiled at him in her rear vision mirror.

'Yes, we'll soon be there, Tommy darling.'

34

TOM'S LETTER—'WINGANNA', 1955

Now was as good a time as any, Jack thought, to get stuck into some sorting out and going though all the paraphernalia he had collected in his desk over the years. It was a stately oak roll-top he'd brought with him to 'Winganna' from America, and now with Molly gone, he went to it only to store his papers. The scrubbed pine kitchen table had become the place where he wrote out his cheques, orders, letters, anything that was needed day-to-day.

Molly had always kept an eye on those things for him, tidying and sorting out. She liked everything well ordered, he remembered. But since her death, he hadn't bothered with anything that took him away from the main business of keeping the property going. Things that weren't essential piled up for later. From the back of one of the small shelves, he took out a much creased air mail envelope. 'Raffles Hotel, Orchard Road, Singapore' on the front of it stopped him. He smiled to himself. Tom's little joke. His billeting had been a world away from that particular watering hole. Tom's letter had got out just before the fall of Singapore, he recalled. He went over to his big leather easy chair, now cracking where the sun beat in, without Molly's thoughtful hands there to pull down the blinds.

Leaning back into his chair's accommodating softness, he propped his feet on an old velvet pouffe and took out the letter. It was dated 30 January 1942.

Well Dad,
There's a lot I could say but not actually spell out, if you get my message, and I'm hoping this gets away with Mrs Searle when she leaves here with her kids on what they say could well be one of the last ships out.

Who'd ever have imagined that I'd be writing to you from here? Nothing is ever as it appears to be, least of all this place, and Dad, I really fear for what could happen now. The so called 'impregnable fortress' is more like a house of straw. The fleas are coming in fast and furious, if you know what I mean, and biting where least expected. They're coming down in droves overland, and there seems to be no stopping them. Not that we're not fighting our guts out trying, even in hand to hand combat. My old 303 never had it so good!

I was remembering that game we used to play as kids, you know, the treasure hunt where you and Mum would hide all the clues, but you always made us look in the least likely spots, which were often the most logical. Well, it's a pity those rules haven't been applied here.

It's not a matter of whingeing, I guess, just a bloody shame.

Without mentioning where, can you believe that we'd meet the nips head on, not in a convoy of armoured tanks but coming in on bicycles, hundreds of them riding their bloody bikes straight towards us?

As we lay waiting, it sounded like a giant picnic of kids, all chattering and laughing as they came nearer and nearer, then rounding the bend onto the bridge. I don't know which of us got the bigger surprise!

Well, we put a stop to that lot, but it's only the beginning. If the reinforcements we've been promised don't come soon, we'll really be up the creek. The stories we hear aren't too pretty, and somehow we've just got to stop those bastards from coming any further south.

I often think of Gerard. It's hard to believe he's linked to that lot. And Aunt Hiroko-san . . . it just doesn't make sense. I mean we virtually grew up together. I wonder how he feels now. He's with us in person, but what about in spirit? It's crazy that any of us should be fighting at all.

The thing that really gets to me though, is the women and kids who are still here, and now so many more of them coming down from Malaya. They missed the chance to get out earlier. I think of Mum, and everyone at home, and worry that it could happen there.

It's like living in a perpetual steam bath here, but us North Queenslanders seem to be able to deal with the heat better, though they've been doling out the old salt tablets which helps. We've been getting pretty vigorous training and plenty of action with our C.O. Lieutenant General Gordon Bennett. He's a stickler for discipline and a great bloke. He keeps the pressure up, so tell Mum not to worry.

I could take on anything the jungle or anyone else likes to dish out now. We've just returned from the Straits, and one of the sights and sounds I'll never forget is that of the 2nd Argyll and Sutherland Highlanders, or what remained of them, proudly marching to their bagpipes and drums across that bloody causeway before we blew it up and the sea came rushing in. God, what giants of men!

Jack put the letter aside and heaving himself from his chair, went over to the drinks cabinet and poured himself a more than generous Scotch, filling the glass with ice. Raising his glass in a small toast, he took a long drink, swishing the warming liquid around his mouth and crunching on the ice, then went back to his chair and continued reading.

> *This will be my last chance to get a message to you for some time, that is if the censors don't get their hands on it first.*
>
> *Hope this finds you all well. I miss you all and the old homestead. Now, no crying, Mum, chin up! What news of Bill??*
> *Your loving son, Tom XXXX*
>
> *P.S. How do you like my letterhead? I actually had a couple of brief forays there when first arriving. It's all that Maugham described and more. Life goes on much as usual there, all partying, gin slings and stengahs (a kind of brandy, creme de menthe and ice cocktail), though give me a decent Aussie beer any day! They still serve up curry tiffin (tea) on Sundays, even the usual Tuesday dinner dance with Don Hopkins' orchestra. There's no reality left. From hand to hand fighting, to this! They tell me the verandah at the Swimming Club is a great place to watch the raids and aerial dog-fights!!*
>
> *PPS. One bright spot. I've got a young Indian boy assigned to me as batman, and it makes life a lot sweeter. Maybe that's what I need at home. T.*

That was it. It was the word 'sweeter' that had stuck in his gullet before, Jack remembered now. He'd pushed it away then with the grief of Tom's death still in his heart. But now, he remembered, as if it was yesterday.

It had happened years ago. He'd come across Tom and another boy—who was it now? Ah yes, Jim Henderson's boy. He'd been going into the barn to get the harness for the horses, and heard a scuffling and giggling in the loft. He'd called out, and there'd been no answer. Those little buggers, they should have been out helping Molly, he remembered. So he'd climbed the wooden ladder that led up to the loft, and raising the trapdoor had looked in.

At first he couldn't see much except the cattle feed

and tools that were stored there. Then in the far corner he had seen the four bare legs and as his eyes moved up, Tom, his son thrusting his dick in and out of the Henderson boy's bum. But it wasn't the dick gyrating its way into the other boy that had so offended him, it was the expression on Tom's face—as if all his Christmases had come at once. An expression of total joy as he came close to climax, then reached it in a shuddering groan of pleasure.

Quietly he'd closed the door and gone outside, feeling sickened and angry. He'd leaned against the barn door, looking out to the distant paddocks, feeling as if he'd been dealt a stomach blow. God, his son, his eldest son, he couldn't be, a queer, a fairy, his Tom? Surely not, of course not, he reasoned, he's just getting it where he can. That's part of growing up, he thought. It's experimenting, that's all. At least he was not making some girl pregnant. Tom likes girls, he loves girls, his mind reassured him. This is just high jinks, goofing off. There's nothing to worry about. After all they're only fourteen-year-old kids, and kids get up to anything. But he'd felt a slow anger rising within him, and suddenly bellowed out 'Tom! Tom! Where the hell are you?'

He heard footsteps in the loft, then saw Tom's face appear, flushed and guilty.

'I'm here Dad, what do you want?'

'What are you doing?' Jack demanded.

'Oh nothing,' Tom said, then quickly, 'I just came to get some things for Mum. Ted's giving me a hand.'

'What things?' Jack persisted.

Tom hesitated, while catching his breath. 'Oh, some more bran for the chooks,' he said.

'Well hurry up and get the hell out of there,' was all Jack had said and he'd walked away.

But the vision had stayed with him, though he'd never mentioned it to Molly. Like most things he didn't want to face, he tended to push them aside till they either went away or became too pressing to ignore.

Tom had returned to boarding school, and the incident

had faded from his memory with time. Till those words in that letter. Come to think of it, Tom had never had any girlfriends, he thought now. There was always plenty of girls around, laughing, having fun and chatting, but no real girl or romance in his life. Then Tom had joined up.

He thought now of the young fair boy Tom had brought home with him during that Christmas break. They'd been very close, just mates, he'd thought, and Molly had fussed around them. He was a slender, blue-eyed boy, the kind that frizzled up in the sun. He remembered Molly at breakfast that morning after their Christmas party, saying jokingly, 'Have you ever seen such long lashes and beautiful skin? Why, Mark, you really should have been a girl.' And the boy flushing, then the look that had flashed between him and Tom. Then later they'd had that big row, and the boy had gone off in a huff to Brisbane. But before he'd gone, Jack had caught part of it. Not an ordinary all-out fight and fisticuffs between mates, but more a bitter screaming match, he recalled.

Good God, he thought, he hadn't picked up on it even then. It was there all the time, and he'd never noticed. His eldest son was homosexual, a queer!

He got up a little unsteadily, pouring himself another drink which he downed with a sense of rage and helplessness, but gradually it started to blunt the edge of his anger. He'd loved Tom, but now he felt sickened and depressed. Where had he gone wrong, he wondered. He'd given him the best schooling, and plenty of healthy outdoor life here at 'Winganna'. Molly had always mothered and spoiled him. Too much so, he thought. She'd had a thing about it, and after that bad bout of scarlet fever he'd had as a kid, all her energies seemed to have gone into Tom. If anything, she'd been over-protective.

He pulled himself up. What did it matter now, any of it? They were both gone. But what was the point to it all, he thought bitterly, staring out at the darkening landscape. Night came in quickly here. None of the gently darkening interlude of twilight to prepare one for those black empty spaces of the long night ahead. He wished he'd never read that bloody letter. He sat back in his chair and, resting his head against its comforting wing, drifted into a light sleep, the letter still in his hand.

He dreamt he was standing on the edge of a long, empty causeway, looking across to where it met a distant shore. It was evening and the waters lapped close to his feet. They were ink blue with flashes of white phosphorus and he was watching the flying fish as they leapt from the water, skimming its surface. The air was still, and a wet heat clung around him as in a sauna.

The sounds of cannon fire and explosions from the other shore were getting closer and closer. Suddenly he could see hundreds of soldiers pouring onto the causeway, running towards him, many with faces he had known as friends of Tom and Bill. They brushed past him in a never-ending stream as if he wasn't there. He had to cling to a pole so that he wasn't carried with them.

'Where's Tom, Captain Tom Baillieu?' he called out, but no one seemed to hear, or if they did, they looked briefly at him, then kept going.

Then all was silent, and all he could hear was a scuffle and giggling like the day he had caught the two boys in the loft. Then Tom's friend Mark appeared, running unashamedly naked over the causeway, laughing as he ran, his all-too pretty face sneering at him as he passed by. 'Where's Tom?' Jack called out to him, feeling sickened again and wanting to hit out at him. But he just kept running as if Jack didn't exist. He felt a dragging sense of shame. Had they been having sex again?

The explosions and shelling had started up again, and the distant shore was lit up as if with fireworks. From out of the flames and smoke, he saw a band of Highlanders come marching onto the causeway. The drum major leading them twirled his baton and the pipers played stirring ballads, more at home in the misty highlands of Scotland than this God-forsaken place. He felt a sense of elation and patriotism, his spirit carried aloft with the rising wail of the pipes and pounding drums.

As they came closer, he saw that one of the soldiers marching with them was carrying the body of Tom in his arms.

'Tom!' he called out. 'Tom, it's me, Dad,' but his voice was drowned out in the swell of the pipes as they swung past him in a swirl of blue and green kilts, their silver badges, buckles and swords shining in the last rays of the setting sun. Suddenly there was an explosion nearby and the sea crashed in across the blown-up causeway and roared towards him as he tried desperately to follow after them, calling 'Tom! Tom!'

A slamming of one of the doors outside woke him with a start, the vision of the Highlanders and the sounds of their bagpipes still fresh in his mind. Those brave bloody men, he thought, as he got up to see to the door. And his Tom had been up there with them. His boy, out there laying his life on the line along with the others. And he'd more than paid his dues, first at Changi then on that hellish Railway of Death in Thailand. Yes, he'd paid the ultimate price, so what did the other business really amount to, when you thought of it.

No matter what anyone said, Tom was there when his country needed him, a real man and up there with the best of them. Yes, Jack reassured himself, when the chips were down, his Tom had been there and that's what counted. But the bitterness of it all lingered.

35

FREIDA'S GIFT—'WINGANNA', 1956

Jill stared out at the tropical rain beating in gusts against the glass. She had been talking and catching up with Maria half the afternoon. Hearing Maria's worries and frustrations with Bill and Jack and all there was to do since Molly's death had a comforting, almost blanketing effect on her own problems.

'I'm sorry I wasn't here to help you with Molly's funeral and everything,' she said, 'it just wasn't possible for me to fly down then.' It had been, but she just couldn't have faced it.

Maria said nothing; she knew the real reason. Jill only did what suited her, always had. 'So, why are you here now?' she asked.

As usual, Maria didn't beat about the bush, Jill thought. 'I'm here to pick up the remaining things of mother's and decide what best to do with Stan's land and beach house down south. He will never come back now that he has remarried and settled in the States. He's asked me to organise everything. If I sell or not, it's up to me,' she added, her sense of satisfaction slightly exaggerating the facts.

'Jack's thinking of selling "Winganna",' Maria said, 'but he keeps changing his mind. He's just so eaten up with bitterness these days, and Bill isn't interested in ever taking over. His life is flying now. Everything is changing,' she added wistfully.

'But isn't that what life's all about?' Jill asked. She felt light years ahead of Maria, their school-girl closeness well and truly a thing of the past. There had been too many changes in her life, in herself.

'But there's Tommy,' Maria went on. 'He loves it here. He could make a life at "Winganna" later on, but nobody thinks of that.'

'Why be so bloody passive about things?' Jill suddenly turned on her. 'You care, so you do something. Speak to Jack, tell him to let go of all that bigoted nonsense . . . the war's over or hasn't he heard. And while you're at it, put a bloody bomb under Bill and get something going yourself, and stop whingeing.'

Maria said nothing, just looked at her friend, then started to weep.

Regretting the frankness of her words, Jill put an arm around her. 'I'm sorry, Maria. I just hate to see you like this. You've just got to start shaping things for yourself, and stop taking whatever's handed out.'

'It's OK for you. These days Bill just floats along and sees an opportunity as it passes him by, while Gerard's a shark, he scents the moment, noses it out, then goes in for the kill.'

Jill sighed. 'I'd kill for a drink,' she said pacing back over to the window, and hating the wet greyness of the day. Maria smiled weakly, wiping her tears. 'You don't have to go to quite those lengths. Come on, let's see what's here.'

They sat at the big kitchen's pine table, its smooth surface bleached to a pale honey by Molly's constant scrubbings.

'I can't get used to having to do everything for myself down here again,' Jill said, getting out glasses and ice.

'That's just it, you can't imagine how hard it has been just keeping things going. It's exhausting, the life here never lets up. Molly loved it, when she was well, so it was different for her.' She watched Jill choose glasses from the cabinet, flicking the dust away. 'But I suppose coming from the city, I've always felt rather like a fish out of water, and even being in the town now, I've never really adjusted. With Bill away flying most of the time, and all there is to do each day, at our cottage, and this place. It's bloody hard work, and lonely,' Maria added, her hazel eyes morose.

'Well you're always welcome to holiday with us,' Jill said, hoping Maria wouldn't take her up on it too soon. 'A G and T for you?'

Maria nodded. 'That takes me back,' she said, smiling at last. 'Remember that time at our final class formal, and we got tipsy on G and T's? And you wore that red strapless dress that kept slipping down, and Julie what's-her-name's boyfriend kept cutting in to dance with you and . . .'

'It had the desired effect,' Jill said, and they both laughed.

Later, as Jill waved to the receding car, she felt the air clear as though Maria's departure took all her own uncertainties with her. Pouring herself another drink, she started to sort through Freida's things that Molly had assiduously kept stacked away in cupboards for just such a day. Everything was stored or folded neatly inside zippered cloth bags, many of them reeking of mothballs. Moving to Molly's wardrobe, she carefully went through Freida's dresses with a sense of detachment, as if looking at someone else's collection from another lifetime, rather than that of her own mother. It was all so remote, so long ago. The fabrics were beautiful, some of them *haute couture* models from Paris. She decided she would keep them all; Sophie could well be interested in them.

If I ever have a daughter of my own, maybe she'll want to see some of her grandmother's things. They'd be well and truly antique if and when that day ever comes, she thought ruefully. She decided that all the clothes and books, the silver and most of the knick-knacks she would pack and send back to Hawaii. The furniture she would give to Maria.

At the back of the cupboard was one more bag. Jill unzipped it and as she pulled out a dress, the warm floral scent of Worth's *Je Reviens* wafted out, assailing her memories. It was her mother's perfume and the poppy dress she had worn that terrible day. She sank onto the bed, shaking as she held the dress to her.

Memories of that day clicked in and out of her mind like a fast-moving film, replaying scenes she'd long forgotten. Blinking away tears, she carefully refolded the dress and put it back in its bag. As she did, she noticed a large brown paper envelope neatly tied with red ribbon lying at the back of the cupboard where the dress had been. She opened it. Inside were letters from her father to her mother and numerous postcards from his different destinations. Her breath caught slightly as her eyes skimmed the familiar handwriting.

One card caught her attention. It was a hand-tinted photograph of Mt Fuji reflected in Lake Hakone, and was post-marked Tokyo, 10 September 1935, and read:

My darling Freida, I'm in another world here and all it needs is you. We will both come next time, that's a promise. I've established some important links which offer tremendous possibilities for future trading. The Nakamura family amongst others have been most helpful. But I feel there's something strange going on here. A nationalistic build up quite out of the ordinary. I can't put my finger on it, but somehow feel uneasy re the whole situation. Well, only time will tell.

Here's a big hug and kiss for my Jilly, and all my love to you my darling. Only weeks to go now, so keep the bed warm.

Forever yours, Stan.

Such prophetic words. And Nakamura? Wasn't that Hiroko-san's previous married name? Could it be the same family? The coincidence would be just too fantastic, she thought. It was after this trip of her father's that they had gone out to the airport to meet him, and had never arrived. Feeling she had had enough of memory lane for one day, Jill decided to postpone going through the remaining letters till she got back to Hawaii.

As she put them back into the envelope, a yellowed form slipped out onto the floor. She picked it up and opened it. It was a title deed of property. As she read through it with growing interest and surprise, she thought, well no wonder Jack had been stalling about selling 'Winganna'. She would certainly have to sort this one out before she left in two days' time. She would talk to him tonight.

36

TITLE DEED—'WINGANNA'

'When are you going back?' Jack settled himself deep into a Planter's chair, pushing out the extended arm rests to prop up his legs.

'Tomorrow evening, I fly to Sydney, then to Hawaii the day after,' Jill replied. 'I've organised all the things that are to go by sea—some I'll take with me, and the rest I'll leave with Maria.'

They were sitting on the wide verandah, sipping their coffee after a light meal and listening to the intermittent chorus of frogs from the dam below. The rain had given way to a velvety night sky, starlit and still. She had never seen the Milky Way quite so brilliant, like a luminous pathway with its one hundred million star galaxies, arcing its way across the southern heavens. Her eyes moved along its path looking for the Southern Cross, and there were the Pointer stars, leading to this compass of the southern sky.

She thought of Gina's daughter Sophie and the cloud games she played at home. She should come here one day and experience the wild beauty of this place. Hattie had hated it, but that was only to be expected with Gare dying here. Maybe Sophie would feel something for it. She missed Gerard, and wished he was with her as she wasn't sure how to handle this whole thing with Jack. But she would just have to play it by ear.

To Jill, he had always been Uncle Jack, Molly's husband, the big gruff man who worked the farm, the provider and rock they'd all leaned on. He'd let Molly rule the roost at 'Winganna', while he provided a strong, almost silent back-up to their life there.

She looked across at him puffing on his old pipe. He was still a fine-looking man, if weathered, his face more drawn now, the lines of bitterness deep. As boys, he and his brother Gare had looked like peas in a pod, she recalled from the pictures on Hattie's dressing table. But even then Gare had come across as the carefree, more ebullient personality.

She wondered what Gare's son, Boy, had been like. She had seen Hattie's and Hiroko-san's photos: creased snaps of a laughing, handsome young man, as fair as his son Gerard was dark. One day when she and Gina had been at the big house on Maui alone, they had gone through some old letters, giggling and feeling guilty, still fascinated by anything that was unexplained or unknown to them. Gina had always been drawn to the mysterious, she recalled. Poor Gina, she still missed her, but Sophie had slipped into the place vacated by her mother. She was the child who'd brought a stability to her own tenuous marriage with Gerard.

Jill lifted her chin. Well here goes, she thought. Looking directly at the old man she asked, 'Jack, what are you going to do now?'

'What do you mean?'

'About "Winganna",' she said.

He didn't answer for a minute, just inhaled deeply on his pipe in a quick succession of short puffs.

'Are you still thinking of selling?'

'I don't know.' He seemed loath to discuss it.

'Maria says Bill's not interested in ever running it now, what with his flying and everything.'

With that, Jack got up and walked over to the railing. She could see he was upset. He knocked the ash from his pipe hard against the wooden post. 'I think I'll turn in and call it a day,' he said, clearly not wanting to take it any further.

'Jack, before you go, we've got some things to discuss. Let's do it now as there won't be much time tomorrow.' She took the title deed from her pocket and held it out to him.

'I never realised until I saw this that mother had a half share in "Winganna",' she said. He didn't answer, so she want on. 'Look, I'll have to discuss it with Gerard first, but what say we get a valuation and I buy out your share of the property?'

'And then what?'

'I'd like it to stay in the family, with the young ones coming on and everything.' She paused, determined not to wilt under his gaze. 'After all, this was my home too for a long time, and I have happy memories—Gerard too.'

'I don't want him to come into it,' he snapped. 'Not Gerard! Why the hell did you ever have to marry him in the first place?'

Jill was stunned. She had never realised the extent of Jack's antagonism towards Gerard. 'I thought with all the holidays he spent here with us, that you liked . . .' she started to say.

'That was before this whole bloody war,' he cut in. 'Gerard's one of them!'

'What do you mean?'

He didn't answer, but stared moodily into the night.

'What do you mean by that Jack,' she pushed, determined not to let him off. He turned suddenly, his hands at either side of his head pulling his skin back tight, turning his eyes into slanted slits.

'These bastards!' he snarled.

She recoiled at his open enmity. It seemed like some ghastly caricature that propelled her back to her anger at Katsura's duplicity and his hasty departure just before the shock and horror of that terrible Sunday morning attack in Pearl Harbor . . . and then Gina dying. But hanging on to such enmity as Jack's had nothing to do with the sadness on Hiroko's face when she'd first seen her with Sophie after Gina's death, or with her love for Gerard and Sophie and the sense of family she shared with the Japanese workers on the plantations in Maui, all of which had now become an integral part of her life and experience. She stared at Jack slumped in his chair. Compassion welled and she sighed, recalling Maria saying earlier how his wounds from the war were still as raw, his hatred for the Japanese unabated. 'He'll always hold them responsible for Tom's death. It's a hate he just feeds on, and he won't let go. We've tried to talk to him, but he just clams up and won't discuss anything,' she had said.

But to attack Gerard like that? Jill felt her anger rising. 'You've got to let go of all that crap, Jack. It's over,' she said, 'and just not fair on them or us, and as for the . . .'

'I don't trust them, and I don't trust him!' Jack cut in. He gripped the sides of the chair, his voice thickening. 'You'll see, in time I'll be proved right. The whole lot of you Jap-happy mob will get it right in the gut one day. They'll turn on us again, it's just a matter of time.'

Jill saw that there was nothing to be gained by defending Gerard or the situation now. But she was determined not to let Jack off the hook so easily. To recover ground, she said 'Look, Jack, despite your racial hang-ups, whatever I do here is with my own money and it will be my concern. I'm thinking of Sophie and Tommy, and . . .' She hesitated, her heart contracting as she dwelt on the longed-for pregnancy, which in twelve years of marriage had eluded her '. . . and for my own children down the track,' she went on, determined to be positive. 'There's a lot of outstanding debts on the property now, and . . .'

'How do you know? What do you know about any of it?' he shouted.

She was determined to maintain the high ground.

'Look, what I suggest is this. I'll buy out your share of "Winganna", and together with Mother's half, the property will be transferred to me. You will have the money from the sale to do what you want with, and I'll take over all outstanding debts and pay you to manage the property, if you choose to do so. We'll also put on others to help,' she added. 'I want to do something really worthwhile here, Jack.'

Trying not to heed his expression she pressed on, telling him about some of her ideas and plans.

Jack methodically refilled his pipe. Miss High and Mighty, he thought. She'd always had an eye to the main chance, so why be surprised? It's as if my part in the creation of this place counts for almost nothing, he thought, angrily. He should have stitched up that business with that bloody deed years ago. He could have paid Freida off then for her half-share in the place when things were going well, and he'd be in a different situation today. He never should have listened to Molly. She was always for preserving the status quo, never wanting to offend anyone. And now this. The whole shebang he'd worked so bloody hard for all these years about to pass into the hands of some slip of a girl who had the cash to pay for it. And that bastard Gerard.

That's all that mattered any more, he thought grimly, those who had the ready cash and those who didn't. What rewards had there been for any of them who'd slogged their guts out, got wounded, and paid with their lives in that bloody awful war? Where had it got him? One son dead, and another away with the pixies, flying when he should have been right here. And Jap-happy to boot, he thought, his anger rising.

And Tom. His heart sank when he thought of him. He'd have had a go at anything, always plenty of pluck. Tom would have stood by him. He ached for him, and for Molly. He felt bone-tired, with an emptiness that wouldn't go away. How does one fill the void? he wondered. He'd tried to do it with work, and look where that had got him. Maybe if he accepted Jill's offer, things might just work out. If there was enough money in it. He could always up the ante a bit anyway if she was so keen to buy, and perhaps he'd stay on and manage the work on the old place while he decided what to do. Could be it was time for a change, but he didn't have the heart any more to strike out and create new challenges. For what?

'Well, what do you think, Jack? Jack?' Jill was looking at him, her face flushed and expectant.

'About what?' he answered.

'Oh Jack, about everything I've been talking about,' she answered, deflated.

'Look, I'm tired,' he said. 'I just want to think about things. We'll talk in the morning. Goodnight, Jill,' he said curtly, and with that he heaved himself out of the chair and went inside without a backward glance.

Damn! Jill thought. With Jack's stubbornness and resentment it's not going to be easy, but she knew it was only a matter of time till he went along with it. She would organise a valuation tomorrow and get her solicitor to set the whole thing up when she got back to Hawaii. She hadn't mentioned that Freida's title deed showed an adjacent coastal strip of property with two miles of rural ocean front further north. She wondered if Jack was aware of it. They had never worked it or done anything with it to her knowledge.

She could build a wonderful place, she reflected, right there on the Reef.

37

GERARD'S DREAMS OF THE BOSPHORUS—HONOLULU, 1958

At the sound of the wind chimes playing out their melody on the lanai, Gerard's spirits kindled. Those bell-like notes and the scent of roses in the garden beyond made him think of that night so long ago, when he and Iman had first lain together in the darkened cabin on her brother Omar's yacht as it set sail from Istanbul.

It was a secret assignation, with the added spice of this being their first time away alone together. He could hardly believe that it had happened at all and so swiftly. But with youth and dreams anything was possible, and they'd made it happen. He could still smell the tuberose in her hair, and sense the sounds and movement of the yacht and harbour outside and the keenness of his elation as they embarked on those precious few days. As so often before, these shadowy images now passed in and out of his consciousness, coupled with a longing for that time together tugging at his heart and removing him from this reality.

In his mind's eye he replayed the langurous movement of her arms as Iman slipped back her black Chador, shaking her lustrous hair free. Again he felt his excitement as she let it fall away to reveal the shimmer of her silky under-clothes and she moved towards him with that look he could never resist or forget. Even now it brought a shiver of erotic pleasure and he ached to see that face, those eyes and lips and feel the coolness of her skin against his. 'Iman,' he murmured.

His inner being reached out as Iman's shadowy image hovered over him, so light yet almost tangible, her thighs enclosing his, her arms now held high behind her head. He sensed the slow seductive sway of her hips as his hands moved up the moist shadowy planes of her body, stroking the full curve of her breasts, feeling a growing arousal as her nipples sprang to life at his touch.

Her hands were now lightly all about him, undoing his shirt, his belt and his pants, running the edge of her nails against his skin as she did. By now his cock was so erect it was a struggle to get his shorts off. Laughing and still astride him, she had pulled them part-way down his thighs, then leaning forward and licking his face then chest with hot darting bursts of her tongue, she teased her way lower and lower down his torso, till with a little laugh she sat up.

He could see the dreamy expression on her face, her eyes half closed as her hands slipped around his cock, delicately stroking it to new life, her fingers caressing its tip to an ecstasy he'd never experienced before or since. Then without removing her scanties, she drew them to one side and slipped him deep into that hot wet place, and in a slow rocking motion she had ridden him in an unrestrained delight of little cries and moans, stopping just as he thought he'd explode into a thousand fragments, then easing him back and slowly building his desire again and again as if to draw every essence of pleasure from him.

He remembered how, without once stopping the rhythm or control of his body, she had pulled off her chemise and her full breasts burst forth, their nipples jutting hard and erect close to his face as she placed first one, then the other in his waiting mouth. Then her mouth and tongue came down to meet his in a mutual ecstasy of exploration. Long afterwards, she had lain across him, wet with their lovemaking, yet so light on his body that he was hardly aware of her. Then with a brief kiss on each of his closed eyelids, she had slid off in one quick movement, disappearing into the bathroom.

Now it seemed all part of that oft revisited mirage of the mind, yet it wasn't until later when the dream had moved on that he wondered about her abandonment, the ease and expertise in someone so young, especially one from the closed world in which she lived.

For three days they sailed the seas of Marmara and the Bosphorus, clear, surreal days merging with starlit nights, on a sea as warm as milk. Iman was the other half of him, his soul-mate, the unfulfilled love he'd longed for. His body surged with the power of self-discovery.

The outer edges of a war, which would suck them all into the maelstrom of its deadly eye, lapped at their lives and slipped past as if unnoticed. They were caught up with feeding each and every sense, until at last they were replete. It was the only time that had ever existed for him, and one that gathered up the furthermost reaches of his heart and mind in an all-consuming embrace. Had he ever truly existed before or since? he wondered later. It was to remain within him as the complete oasis he constantly returned to, feeding upon it to sustain him in a later, lesser life without her.

From the time they met, it had been for Gerard like a journey into another world, and like the traveller searching for his roots, a place where he could at last feel at one with himself. While for Iman, he now felt sure, it was a reliving through him of certain moments in her past, in order to forget what lay ahead.

As she talked to him of one such time, in his mind's eye then as now, the scenes from her childhood grew clearer, and like pieces of coloured glass fell into place in the mosaic of his memories of her. He clearly recalled one such instance and her telling of a tall, dark-skinned man standing with his back to her. 'He was dressed in a short white cotton *futa*, tightly belted with a black canvas belt studded with bullets that glinted in the sun.' Gerard could still see Iman's lips as they moved, describing how the man's head was swathed in a brilliantly coloured *karbush* that hung halfway down his back, and how he carried a rifle slung easily across one shoulder. How even from a distance, she could perceive the strength of his tall body held taut against the tightly swathed cotton, his muscled bottom and strong legs clearly defined by the clinging fabric. He stood alone, almost motionless, holding aloft a thickly gloved hand.

Like scenes from a desert print, Gerard pictured two camels nearby as they stood in timeless waiting stance, their necks outstretched, their faces sleepily surveying some distant horizon. The sky above them shimmered an intense blue, skimming the sands and dark desert brush that stretched way into the distance, where a mauve haze hung suspended at the desert's edge.

A peregrine flew onto the falconer's glove, alighting with one graceful sweep of its large outstretched wings. It was a young bird from Persia, and very beautiful, as yet unspoiled by years of conditioning.

Iman had clapped her hands with delight, and felt a movement beneath her as her camel swayed restlessly beneath his saddle and richly embroidered saddle cloth.

'I was just thirteen, but already more woman than child,' she said looking deep into Gerard's eyes, reflecting someone very much at home in this world of hers. She'd clapped again, she said, and the sudden movement made the bird fly off, startled, and circle them. Then hardly moving its wings, it hovered on the warm air currents. The falconer swore and turned to her. She saw the black anger in his face and felt a stab of fear and apprehension.

With cruel dark eyes he gazed intently at her, but she lifted her chin as she stared right back at him. With a sudden derisive movement he turned away, and making hoarse sounds from deep within his throat, coaxed the bird back from the sky. It flew towards them, hesitating a moment, before alighting in effortless grace. Swiftly, the falconer placed a hood over its head, then without pause, pulled a long dagger from his belt and like steel through jelly, pierced the bird's heart with cold, clear precision. Then tossing the lifeless feathers aside on the desert sands, he turned to her in triumph.

She hadn't cried out or moved, she told Gerard. 'But the knife that pierced the bird had entered my own heart.' She could still see it floating freely above her only minutes before, its proud head bent forward expectantly. Now the peregrine's abrupt stillness gave death a reality it had never held before. Willing herself to a state of containment, she remained staring coldly at and beyond the falconer, as if he no longer existed. She ordered her servant to collect the limp body of the bird and bring it with them, then turning her camel, she rode away.

Of one thing, Iman was certain. The falconer would never do such a thing again. He would not live to do so. She would see to that.

She would have the bird embalmed and placed within a special tomb. To her it represented the passion, the fragility and freedom of youth. Its death marked her step into a more structured world which now seemed to be closing in on her.

The day had passed so quickly with fleeting insights as if it was a distillation of her life to come, she told him. That evening at her request, her brother Omar had come to visit her in her rooms. Since their mother's illness, they had grown closer and more dependent upon each other. He looked to her for the receptive ear and advice his mother had once offered, and she to his support and growing power in their male-dominated world.

Their father, a wealthy and powerful sheikh, was a kindly if distant figure. He was mostly abroad, supervising his assorted businesses in other parts of the world. Moreover, he was surprisingly lenient for one steeped in the traditions of Islam. 'I was often left to cope alone with all the intrigues of our large household, and with whatever came along,' she told Gerard.

Omar, when told of the incident with the falconer, had agreed he posed a danger and that they must protect themselves in the only sure way there was. His eyes had darkened with decision, then softened as he looked at her. 'It will be attended to, don't give it another thought,' he'd said.

As Iman told him of her life, Gerard lay back lost in her presence, reliving her every moment. Their days on the boat were behind them, and now landfall had brought its own realities.

'And was it taken care of?' he asked, reaching for her. She smiled distantly, moving away from him across to the intricately carved window overlooking the mud buildings and distant white mosque, washed a soft golden pink by the last rays of the sun.

The sky had become a lake of golden blue with dark island puffs of cloud building up around its shores. A sirocco earlier in the day had died, only to be replaced by a heavy stillness, bringing a somnolent sense of breathless expectation and impending change. A steamy mist moved in to veil the sun, as it always did after the unwelcome intrusion of a sirocco. Date palms in the courtyard below threw long dark shadows against the ground, their outstretched fronds barely moving, while the scarlet of pomegranate trees in full fruit reflected the dying brilliance of the day.

Iman had loved this time, the crossover from day to night, Gerard recalled.

'You will always be mine?' he'd asked, small doubts intruding.

'Of course, for a lifetime of lifetimes,' she had answered, gazing out the window to the bay below. She stood motionless, and he wondered what she was thinking. Later that evening, after going out to the market, he had returned to the apartment and she had gone. The room was cold and there was no sense of her spirit left. It was then he knew, even before he read her letter, that their parting was forever.

My darling,
Our little lifetime is over. It was wonderful, no?
   It is best I go now while all is so bright and good between us. Do not follow. In a few days I will be married, as arranged by my father. It is what I want, as I belong to another world, and you to yours. Just keep a place for me in your heart.
'Are you less than a piece of earth?
When a piece of earth finds a friend, that is, the spring,
It gains a hundred thousand flowers.'[10]
Iman.

38

GERARD'S RISING SUN

A gust of wind set the chimes ringing again as Gerard walked out onto the wide lanai, lighting a cigar as he went. He inhaled deeply, to assuage all thoughts of Iman, and that one oasis in his past.

His mind switched to thinking about the proposal Hiro Miyaji-san had extended to him only that day. It seemed Hiro's Japanese backers wanted Gerard as their link man in their plans to expand, but he was not sure yet if it suited him. There was a lot more he needed to know about the organisation, who was really running the show and the deal-making in Japan, and this, their latest game plan. But he'd find out. Till then he wouldn't touch it.

That he could be valuable to them, in gaining access to the Hawaiian and American mainland, he was only too well aware. His contacts were impeccable, a solid network he'd built, starting even before his war years spent flying within the Pacific rim and Europe. Later in Japan's post-war mop-up, he worked as an adviser to General MacArthur. His fluent Japanese had given him entrée to the inner sanctums of power.

After Pearl Harbor, the well-entrenched Baillieu name had ensured that the backlash meted out to other Japanese Hawaiians and *Nisei* population did not rebound on them. His mother, Hiroko, had cleverly adapted to and long established herself as part of the all-American and Island way. Her Japanese side was for family and close friends alone.

Gina's untimely death had erased any link in people's minds with Katsura Kurosawa. But he, Gerard, hadn't forgotten, and the seeking out of Katsura had become a top priority when he first arrived in Tokyo at war's end. He had hunted for him in the rubble of that burnt-out city, then just before he left Japan, he'd followed a lead that took him to Hiroshima. But there the trail had ended. War records abounded, but were still in chaos and would take years to sift through. But track him down he would.

'Will you be in for dinner, Gera?'

It was Sophie, with her pet name for him which she'd used since a tiny child. He turned to her. She was an enchanting girl, if a little too solemn, and he felt as protective of her as if she were his own.

There was no hint of Gina in her face, except maybe her mouth. It appeared she was her father's child, he thought grimly. It was almost as if she were a smaller female replica. He well remembered Katsura's sleek head and the way he would look up from under his brows. It was a mannerism Sophie did quite naturally, and it gave her a beguiling air. Her dark eyes, free of the constricting Japanese fold, were larger, with a directness and clarity that was part of her nature.

'Gera, did you hear me?'

'Yes, honey, but I won't be here as I've a meeting elsewhere,' he answered.

'You're hardly ever here,' she pouted, echoing Jill's often-used reproach.

'Well, someone has to get out there and earn the dollars,' he said, smiling at her.

'But I was hoping we could have a talk.'

'What about?'

'Oh,' she glanced down, 'a lot of things I guess.'

'Surely Jilly could help.'

'No, they are things probably only you know, about

my father,' Sophie said quickly. 'I've never really been told.'

He thought: well, now it's coming, the moment he had been hoping to avoid. He knew it would some day, but surely not quite as soon as this? At seventeen, in many ways she was still little more than a child.

'Well then, let's talk tomorrow, I must go now.'

'Fine. Is that a promise?'

'Absolutely,' he answered, bending and giving her a light kiss on the top of her head. 'But not too early. What say I take you out to lunch?'

'Would you?' She gave him a little hug.

'You choose the place,' he answered.

After he'd gone, Sophie sat perched on the rail overlooking the bay and watching the early evening clouds massing, tinged golden pink, reflecting the sun's swan song. They would be the *opua-mele-mele*, the golden clouds. No, she thought as she watched, they were becoming the darker evening or *ao-opua-ahiahi* clouds.

As a tiny child, moving between her home with Gerard and Jill in Honolulu and the sprawling homestead on the plantation at Maui, she had formed an almost mystical alliance with the Hawaiian sky. It was her friend, her confidant. Sometimes she would lie for hours, staring into the towering space above her, imagining herself as queen of the sky with an endless realm over which she ruled. She would select a magnificent chariot from a stable of stars, and in it ride to wherever she wished.

The clouds were the lands, lakes and seas she retreated to, and where her new adventures awaited. And there were the spirit clouds. As she grew her imagined world enlarged to take on whatever was her fancy at the time. At twelve, it was horses; so horses, mostly black or white Arabs, featured in her dreams. Sometimes she rode bareback like the beautiful maiden *pa'u* riders of old Hawaii who, shunning the side-saddle, galloped astride their steeds along the beach with leis of sweet smelling grasses, *mokihana* berries and glowing plumeria strung around their horses' heads and necks. They would ride like the wind, sometimes blowing their conch shell horns to entice handsome young men to join them.

After Gina's death, Lalana had helped Jill care for her, and it was Lalana who filled her life with the Hawaiian legends, just as she had done with her mother Gina.

Sophie's favourite was the story of *Ke-ao-mele-mele*, the maiden of the Golden Cloud. It was when she first heard it that her love of the skies awakened. Clouds became mythical places and people, her newfound family of brothers and sisters, so that she was not alone any more. She would ask Lalana to repeat the names of all the different ones, so she could remember them.

Ke-ao-mele-mele was born out of the head of her mother, *Hina,* and was very beautiful, Lalana told her. She was taken at birth by *Mo-o-inanea* to live high in the heavens in a house of clouds and fogs called *ke-alohi-lani* or Shining Land, with a running spring for her bath and the magic flowers *Kanikawi* and *Kanikawa*. All the clouds were appointed as caretakers to watch over the girl. As she listened, Sophie imagined that they were there to care for her also.

There were the narrow, pointed clouds, the *ao-apu*, her special guards, and the *ku-ke-ao-loa*, the Long Cloud of *Ku* who guarded the door of the house of clouds and had great magic powers.

Ka-maka-o-ka-lani, the clouds in the eye of the sun, could see all things happening far and wide and could also use their special magic. Sophie would call them when she awoke, to give her commands. She also called to the *ao-opua-kakahiaka* morning clouds and the *opua-hele* morning flower clouds, and the *ka-pae-opua* clouds that skimmed the surface of the sea where the horizon merged with the sky. Some days she would send her spirit soaring with the distant *ka-ela-lau-opua* clouds that rode highest in the sky.

The spirit world was very real to Sophie. She felt it all around her, in the trees, the flowers and birds as well as the sky. She only had to imagine, and they were there with her wherever she went.

Sophie was, of course, being brought up in the Roman Catholic faith, which Hiroko had embraced early in her relationship with Boy's family. The more animistic Shinto or Buddhist beliefs of her Japanese heritage were unknown to Sophie, yet already they'd assumed an unconscious significance.

Still blaming Katsura and Sophie's difficult birth for the loss of her daughter Gina, Hiroko had distanced herself from this child, leaving her upbringing largely in the hands of Jill and Gerard. To Sophie, this rather formal lady was *Oba-san*, the name Gerard in a quirky moment had suggested, and it had stuck. As she grew older, as with any closed door, her grandmother's Japanese world held a fascination. It was something she simply had to open and step through to learn more about herself.

'Oba-san, tell me all about where you came from,' Sophie had often asked. Hiroko was not to be drawn, however, and gave only vague answers, deeply unsatisfying to the little girl. So it was Gerard to whom she turned; Gerard who from her early years had often spoken to her in Japanese, and helped her learn the language. His Japanese identity had increasingly become a world he used to slip into—to exclude Jill.

He was pleased that the language came easily to Sophie.

'I want to be really fluent,' she told him, and he organised tutors, much against Jill's will, as she saw this as something they shared that she couldn't.

To compensate for Jill's longing and despair at never falling pregnant, despite Gerard's indifference, along had come two babies to bless her. Her first-born when she was thirty-two, William arrived right on time on 11 November 1955, as did his sister, Louise, just one year later. With them came new life into their home, and cousins for Sophie to help care for.

'Sophie, Sophie, what are you dreaming about?' It was Jill. 'Well?'

'Well, what?' Sophie said.

'Will he be here for dinner?'

'Who?'

'Darling, you know who. Gerard. You were going to ask him for me.'

Sophie smiled at her. 'Sorry, Jilly, I meant to come in and tell you, but I forgot.'

'As always,' Jill laughed. 'So, what did he say?'

'No—he can't be here, there's a meeting or something. He didn't see you on the way out?'

'Obviously not. I was busy with the babies.' What would she do with this girl? Jill thought. Always daydreaming and so impractical. But she loved her, and for years she had been the child she could never have.

'Oh, by the way, Gerard's taking me to lunch tomorrow,' Sophie said.

'Lucky you, how come? Am I invited?' Jill teased.

'Well, I . . .' Sophie looked disconcerted. 'It's just that I have something important I wanted to ask and well, he suggested it,' hoping Jill wouldn't throw a dampener on the whole thing, which she often did with anything involving her with Gerard. 'But if you want to come,' she offered.

'No, darling, don't be silly. It would be nice for you two to have a chat, and anyway we're going to a party in the evening, so I'll be busy with Will and Louise. Where are you lunching?' she asked.

'I'm not sure. He said I could choose.'

'Well,' said Jill, eyeing her speculatively, 'is it going to be a serious conversation or something a little more light-hearted?'

'Oh serious, definitely quite serious,' Sophie answered quickly.

'Well, then, you should go somewhere absolutely light, bright and beautiful, so that things don't get too grey around the edges,' Jill advised. 'I tell you what, why not the Moana? You haven't been there yet, and it's quite lovely. Gerard likes it, and the tables are well spaced for a serious conversation, so no one can eavesdrop,' she added with the hint of a smile.

It was just like Jilly, Sophie thought. Always organising

everyone. She sighed. 'Maybe, I'm not sure. I'll have to think about it.'

'Okay darling, but if you want any help, I'm here.' She took Sophie's arm. 'Come on, let's get something to eat.'

Jill thought, it's sure to be about Gina and Katsura, and she wondered how Gerard would handle it. She would have to speak to him tonight.

39

SOPHIE AND GERARD

It was strange that she should have chosen the Moana Banyan Court for their meeting, Gerard thought. He'd arrived a little early, and sat in the bar waiting for Sophie to arrive from her tennis coaching. This had been one of Gina's favourite places, he remembered, and it was here that she had first lunched with Katsura, after their fateful meeting at the party given by the Takeuchis. God, it seemed so long ago. A thousand lifetimes since Gina had arranged for them to dine and meet Katsura that day. He felt older than his thirty-six years.

He looked up the minute Sophie appeared and felt a stab of surprise. It was as if a more petite and prettier version of Katsura had entered the room. She was radiant after her morning's tennis in the sun, yet the shy little smile she threw him when she saw him sitting there was her mother's. He decided in that moment, that whatever she wanted to know, he would tell her. It was her right to know.

She came across swiftly, giving him a kiss, and looking worried, asked him, 'Is this place okay?'

'It's one of my favourites,' he answered. 'And I don't know why I've left it so long to come back.' She smiled, reassured.

'Good.' She looked around to see who was there.

'A drink?' he asked.

'Oh yes, I'm dying of thirst. A tomato juice and ice please.'

'Your mother used to add a dash of vodka,' he said, as if opening the way.

'Do you think I should?' she asked tentatively.

'Why not? Just a dash,' he said with a nod to the waiter.

'Am I like Gina at all?' Sophie asked, taking his cue.

'In many ways,' he said. 'Though maybe you're more imaginative and, I think, a lot more anxious to know about things. Your mother was more content to float with things as they happened. But you seem to want to know why.'

She seemed pleased with that. 'You know, Gera, it's really only in the last few months that I've really wanted to know all about her as a person and—' she added anxiously, '—things about my father too. It's all been sort of not talked about. It's not that I haven't been happy with you and Jilly.'

'I know,' he said. 'And I'll help you where I can, so fire away.'

'Why did my father really leave her?' she asked.

The truth or sugar-coating? He decided on the former. 'We're not absolutely certain, but it appears he was working for his government and had to leave suddenly before the attack here.'

'Was he a spy then?'

'It looks that way,' Gerard answered. 'He'd been checking out a lot of things around the islands, and was obviously tipped off that something big was about to happen, so he left—along with quite a few others,' he added. 'And no doubt, the information he passed on was a help in the surprise they sprang on us at Pearl.'

She was silent a minute, then, her voice rising, she said, 'But he knew about me, that Gina . . . that Mummy was pregnant, surely.'

'Well, of course he did,' he said, thinking, the bastard.

Tears rose in her eyes. 'Why wouldn't he have ever

wanted to come back to see me? How could he just go off like that and never want to know anything about me, or Mummy, or anything?' She sniffed, wiping her eyes with the back of her hand.

Oh God, he thought. We never get over these hurts. We just don't ever recover from our early expectations. It's as if we react and suffer from them and even try to escape from them forever, but they're always there . . . these ghosts of our childhood, ready to step in and take over when we least expect it.

He felt his old anger, the deep-seated resentment of Satoshi, Katsura and Gina's shortened life, and now here was Sophie's anguished face looking to him for an answer.

'You just can't tell her all these things,' Jill had said the night before.

'I will,' he'd answered. 'She has to know.'

'Sophie,' he said now, 'I want to tell you something that nobody knows, and it will be our secret,' he said. She looked at him, dabbing her eyes, expectant. 'I know what it's like to feel this sense of rejection by a parent.'

'You?' She looked surprised.

'Yes. As you know, before I was born my mother had a son, Satoshi, in Japan with her first husband, and because of pressure by his father's family, she had to leave him behind in Japan.'

'Oba-san has told me a little about him,' Sophie said. 'But it makes her sad and she doesn't seem to want to talk about it.'

'But what she hasn't told you,' Gerard continued, 'is that she has never really got over having to leave him. He is the only son she has ever really missed and loved.' He paused, frowning. 'So you see, I had to grow up knowing that and resenting it like hell.' He gave her a wry smile. 'So I know just how you are feeling.'

'I never knew,' Sophie said, realising now that her grandmother had never been very affectionate towards Gerard, but she'd thought it was just her way, as she always seemed to hold herself a little apart from everyone.

'I'm so sorry, Gera.'

He smiled at her. 'You've got a soft heart, so watch it! I tried to find Katsura when I was in Japan, just after the war, but with no luck. No one here knows that, not even Jill, so it's just between us.'

She nodded eagerly. 'I will find him for you, and that's a promise,' he added, 'and then you can ask him all these questions yourself.'

'Oh Gera, will you?' she said, pleased.

'You can count on it.'

'But maybe he's dead,' Sophie said as if it had only just occurred to her.

'No, I'm sure he isn't,' Gerard answered, thinking to himself, but he'll wish he was when I catch up with him.

'Come on,' he added, getting up. 'Our table's ready, we can chat about all the other things you want to know while we eat.'

Over lunch, without revealing his vengeful feelings towards Katsura, Gerard told his niece about how Katsura had deserted Gina and most probably sold them all out by being part of the lead-up to the Pearl Harbor bombing. Over dessert, he explained what he knew of her parents' relationship beforehand.

'She didn't know him very long, then,' Sophie reflected, not liking this. 'Maybe she should have waited and not married so soon.'

'Well, that was your mother. She was always impetuous and had to have whatever she wanted, straight away. Sounds rather like someone else I know.' Gerard could never resist a dig.

Sophie didn't notice, her thoughts on her parents. 'She must have really loved him.'

'I think she did,' he answered.

It appeared that Lalana and Jill had told her about the day Gina died. She wanted to know more, however, about Gina as a girl, and about Katsura's feelings towards her mother.

'I don't really know who I am,' Sophie said at last.

'Do any of us?' Gerard asked, with a half-laugh.

'I mean I just love it here, but at the same time a lot of my feelings, of me, must be Japanese. I have a longing to know more about that part of me.'

'When you've finished college, you can go there.'

'That's ages away; I want to go now.'

'Well maybe sooner, we'll see.'

'Don't you ever want to meet Satoshi?'

'No,' he said with finality.

'Is he still alive?' she persisted.

'I believe so; you should ask your grandmother.'

'I did, but she didn't tell me.'

Gerard signalled for the bill. 'I'll be going to Tokyo on business in the next month, and I'll see what I can find out about Katsura then.'

'You promise?'

'Cross my heart.'

40

JILL AND GERARD

'I think one of the greatest motivating forces in our life is based in the loss of what might have been and wasn't.' Jill was combing her hair. 'It's the thing that drives us along, till it either makes us or destroys us.'

What might have been, and wasn't, Gerard thought, his mind returning to Iman. He could still see the look in her eyes that last day. She was my 'might have been', he thought. He sat back, closing his eyes, shutting out the pleasant glow of their bedroom. Jill's voice faded, and he let himself luxuriate in the memory of Iman's body close to his. The memory was so real that he thought he could reach out and touch her. She was there, with him, in his blood, his every sinew, forever. The smell of mimosa was in the air, the sun clear and bright. His thoughts were fixed in the beauty of that place and time together.

Jill's voice came in sharp and questioning.

'Well, do you agree?'

'About what?' he asked.

'You never listen. Really Gerard, it's all like water off a duck's back.' She gazed at him, the shadow of long disappointment hanging between them.

I was Jill's might have been, Gerard thought suddenly.

She sighed, and went on. 'I was saying that it's as if

we develop these emotional habits from way back, I mean when you think about it, most of our behaviour is patterned on childhood influences, no matter how subtle.'

'So that's why you've always had to be Queen Bee,' he rejoined.

'What do you mean?' she asked, perplexed.

'Because you've been waited on and spoilt by almost everyone from day one.'

She came across and put her arms around him. 'Everyone?'

'Are you asking or telling me?' he said turning towards her. Jill smiled back at him, the question left hanging. He caught their reflection in the large mirror. They made a handsome couple. Jill tall and tanned in a brief slip of a black dress, its chic simplicity achieved at some cost. Her short fair hair was brushed sleekly to show off the pretty shape of her head and neck. Her appearance was pared down and fairly glistened with expensive polish. He was not much taller than she, with a vitality and veiled expression which women found attractive.

Jill had once told him, 'You've got those sleepy bedroom eyes. You know, the heavy lidded sort that immediately makes you think of bed and . . .' she glanced up at him for full effect, 'sex, slow delicious sex.'

What he never told her was that it was sex with another he dreamt of.

Jill had made a play of organising their life to a pattern acceptable to her. Gerard went along with it, strategically meeting her requirements, so that the myth of their making remained intact. It was a perfect arrangement on the surface. He moved with her changing currents, yet striking out alone whenever it suited him. Her surface brightness, which at first he'd found diverting, had become a lacquered veneer, a brittle shell into which she slipped almost continuously.

The loss of what might have been and wasn't. Jill's words rose again, evoking those last precious days in Istanbul with Iman. He pictured her lying in a hammock, her long white kaftan open to expose her creamy nakedness and full breasts to his gaze while, only too aware of his eyes on her, she languidly pushed the hammock backwards then forwards towards him. He'd watched, aware of his rising ache and need, delaying the moment till he'd fallen hot and hard upon her . . . sinking into those wet parted lips, lost in her mouth, her essence, drinking greedily as she opened to him and they'd devoured and merged with one another. Behind them a bougainvillea spilled over in splashes of blood red, the backdrop to a war into which they'd both soon be drawn. And forever after, whenever Iman surfaced in his mind's eye, this was the image and time to which he returned.

'So Sophie enjoyed your lunch?' Jill's voice cut across his thoughts.

'Yes,' he answered, his mind's eye caressing the last of Iman.

'Well?'

'Well what?'

'How did it all go?' She began straightening his tie.

'I told her what I know,' he said, moving away.

'And?' Really, Gerard could be quite perverse. 'Do I have to pump it all out of you?' Jill asked, impatient now.

He smiled. 'Not quite. I suggested that she should go to Japan when she finishes college.'

'Do you think that's wise?'

'Why not? She has to go sometime, then or maybe sooner.'

Jill perceived that he was reluctant to discuss it further, and she would get nowhere if she persisted now. She felt tired and wished they weren't going out.

'It's only natural, I guess,' she commented, pretending a conversational ease that she wasn't feeling.

'What is?'

'That she should be wanting to know all about Gina and Katsura now, at this stage when she's really just starting seriously to take notice of boys.' She waited. 'We have to have a complete picture of ourselves, before we can fully relate to someone else.'

'Is that so?' Gerard said absently.

'Well, our roots are buried deep within us, they're something we take almost for granted. That's your problem,' she said with a hint of malice.

'What is?'

'You have never been able to take this for granted.'

'I take nothing for granted,' Gerard answered.

'But our allegiances are something we need to feel are complete in ourselves and really centred,' she said, warming to the thought. 'They are our touchstone.'

'Are you suggesting that my allegiances are wanting?' he asked.

'No, just that they seem to be in a constant state of flux.' She smiled sweetly at him, hoping that he would respond. He said nothing, but she could tell he was annoyed.

'We'd better get going,' he said, 'we'll be late.'

'Sure, you go down, I'll follow in a minute.' She inserted pearl earrings, and critically examined the effect.

'By the way, it looks as if I'll have to fly to Tokyo next week.'

'What, again?'

'Yes, there are some people to see and things I have to tie up after that meeting last night.'

She knew better than to ask him what they were.

'Maybe I could join you,' she suggested.

'No, it will be a pretty rushed trip, probably only a few days. Perhaps next time,' he added. Jill thought that those next times never seemed to eventuate.

'Gerard, you do love me?'

He heard the familiar note in her voice. 'Jilly, don't be crazy,' he said, starting to rise.

'No, I have to know,' she gazed at him, appealing.

The weight of forced love, he thought, and answered automatically.

'You know I do; come on, let's go.'

Jill was right, he thought irritably in the car. You never quite recover from not knowing where you truly belong. It was as if he had spent his lifetime sitting on opposing fences—American and Japanese. And in the end, he thought, it merely compounded a sense of aloneness, the non-allegiance of an outsider to anyone but himself.

But maybe that's more a strength than a weakness, he reflected, his spirits rising. To play them both.

* * *

'Gerard, what have you been telling Sophie-chan?' Hiroko's voice sounded brittle. Without waiting for his answer, she continued, 'She's been saying she's going to Tokyo soon, and will see Satoshi for me.' She paused, and he could hear the quick intake of her breath.

Enjoying her dismay, he decided to string it out a little longer. 'Is there a problem, Mamma?'

'What do you mean, you know the problem only too well.' He hated hearing his mother's anguish, knowing it was for neither Sophie nor for himself.

'Surely you're not still worried about all those threats from so long ago,' he said, knowing full well the answer. 'She's just jumping the gun, her trip won't be for some time yet.'

Hiroko trembled as she replaced the phone. Gerard would never give her a straight answer. It was as if he was paying her back forever for her love for Satoshi. It was the cross she had to bear, but one she would never relinquish. Since he'd returned from the war, Gerard had become even more elusive. The early promise he'd shown in managing Hattie and Gare's plantations had flowered. The Baillieus were now a major producer of the Island's pineapple and sugar cane. But in so doing, he'd gradually eased Hiroko from the position of relative power she'd enjoyed after Gare's death, so that she now mostly deferred to him in any decisions relating to the business. She resented this, but bided her time.

She thought of her call from Sophie earlier in the day. The girl was always anxious to please, but Hiroko could not feel close to her. Gina's bringing her into the world and her subsequent death were always there as a reminder. Was it a fear of losing Sophie, too, she wondered suddenly. A fear she had cloaked under the guise of rejecting her as Katsura's daughter? But the girl was close to Gerard, and she needed a family friend. And if anyone could make contact with Satoshi in time . . . she mused. Her father Yukio had urged her to always keep the doors to discourse open. Maybe now was the time to pave the way and start building bridges.

41

THE ROAR OF A THOUSAND GOLDEN TIGERS—HONOLULU, 1959

The ride in from Honolulu airport to the Royal Hawaiian took only fifteen minutes. Atsuo spread himself comfortably in the back of the stretch limousine. It was symptomatic of Hiro Miyaji's subtlety that he would give his old friend time to collect himself, and to acquire the feel of the Island again before their meeting.

A warm aromatic smell of burning coconut oil came wafting in on the tropic night air. Atsuo lay back and closed his eyes, taking in the occasional snatches of American and Island voices, floating across from the street stalls and intersections whenever the car slowed. The Island had a beauty of its own, he thought, a skilful intermarriage of moneyed sophistication and the natural, almost primeval, seductiveness of the South Pacific.

When Hiro had first wired Atsuo a week ago, his message have been cryptic, but its import was clear. It was his closing phrase, 'the roar of a thousand golden tigers', that had Atsuo wiring back immediately with the time of his arrival, as Hiro knew it would.

'The roar of a thousand golden tigers'—he smiled, recalling the two occasions he'd previously used the phrase with his old wartime comrade. He remembered how the dawn had been about to break as they lay in a ditch in the mist-bound hills alongside the road out of

Lingayen Bay, Manila. It was April 1942, and Atsuo could recall the cold dull pain when the night air hit his lungs. They'd been waiting almost three hours, and the chill was now well settled into their aching bones.

Suddenly Hiro motioned with his rifle towards the winding road on the hill below them. There it was, the sleek outline of the Mercedes Tourer, flanked by its two outriders. Like an eel darting and slithering down the rocks, Hiro was away, reaching out for something on a tree nearby. He flashed across the road, and Atsuo could see him fixing the wire, tightening it in a thin shining line to a pole on the other side. Then they waited.

The roar of the bikes became louder, masking the high even whir of the Mercedes. They sped towards Atsuo and Hiro, now well hidden behind rocks at the side of the road. In postillion formation, they curved around the corner, racing towards their hiding place. Atsuo felt his muscles tighten; with no change in throttle sound, the wire had knifed through the leading rider's neck, leaving a grotesque sack-like shape astride the gleaming bike, while his companion somersaulted, doll-like in graceful circular movements, through the early morning light, landing with a thud in the bushes to the side of the road.

There was no pulse, Atsuo quickly ascertained, hardly surprising, when he saw the gaping wound across the man's chest baring the torn bloodied organ that had once been his heart. As he stifled an urge to vomit, a burst of submachine gun fire spun him around in time to see Hiro charging after the Mercedes that was now swerving crazily across the road. It came to a shattering stop, skidding headlong into a tree, catapulting the driver from his seat. Hiro shot him on the wing, like some errant bird, then ran to the car and wrenched open the door.

Inside the car lay a Filipino general, his face flattened in a bloody death mask, his teeth bared as if in a ghostly smile of greeting and a last attempt to maintain face.

'You got him.' It was more a statement that a pat on the back. Atsuo leaned further inside the plushly appointed car. 'Hello, what's this? The General's little lap dog?'

A tiny creature with the largest dark eyes Atsuo had ever seen lay shivering across a leather trunk on the seat at the dead man's side. It was in a state of shock. He felt its tiny heart fluttering in spasmodic bumps against its flimsy rib cage. A feeling of pity, almost tenderness, overcame him as he felt the warmth from the tiny creature spread across his hand. It lay there, barely covering his large outstretched palm.

'Get rid of it!' Hiro's words jerked him back. Without acknowledging him, Atsuo gently placed the dog inside his jacket against the warmth of his body. He turned to Hiro. 'Let's see what's in the case, eh? I'll check out the lock while you disengage the wire.'

Hiro was back in an instant, stuffing wirecutters into his pocket.

'Didn't need them. The bastard's neck snapped it for me,' he said looking back down the road. 'We'd better hurry, there could be a follow-up contingent any time.'

They found keys in the dead general's pocket. In seconds, they were struggling with the lock, then pushing back the lid.

'*A to! A to!*' Hiro's voice hit a note of reverence, strange even to Atsuo. Lying neatly stacked in splendid symmetry lay dozens of small gold ingots. The tapped radio report had mentioned a large money transhipment, but this!

'Now we'll have the roar of a thousand golden tigers,' Hiro said ruminatively, running his hand across the shining booty. Speedily, they divided the ingots into two strong sacks then, like elusive *Ninja*, merged into the countryside and back to their unit, just as rosy dawn reached out across the sky, illuminating the bay.

'The roar of a thousand golden tigers,' Atsuo mused. It was a phrase he remembered as a promise of gifts from the gods, and a call to arms from his friend, even if it was almost twenty years later from another part of the world, and to a place he thought he'd never see again.

Honolulu had changed since he was last here, he mused. There was a cosmopolitan bustle and a smell of commercialism that hadn't been there before. Waikiki with its burgeoning hotels and shops was hardly recognisable.

He still found it a bitter pill to swallow that Japan's initial glorious victory at Pearl Harbor, so well planned and carried out, should have ended so shamefully in their eventual defeat. Even Roosevelt, the American President, had called their attack 'a brilliant feat of deception, perfectly timed and executed with great skill'. Who would have thought that four years later, the imperial Japanese nation would be lying in ruins?

But things were changing, Atsuo reminded himself with a faint smile, looking through the car's darkened windows. The fast expanding market here, as in other places, was all grist to his country's race to rebuild and expand. Hiro, as one of the loyal *kobun* in the Isawa-gumi, had been sent earlier to channel *yakuza* money here. They had billions of yen waiting to be laundered and re-invested and, taking a long-range view as he did in every venture, Atsuo could see that investing in Hawaii offered a legitimate step into the American mainland.

Hiro had set up three top level meetings for him. Atsuo was amused that the list included, of all people, Gerard Baillieu. Hiro, of course, was unaware of his past associations with that family, and that's how it would have to remain, he thought. It was better that no-one knew; one couldn't be too careful, there was too much at stake.

Meeting up again with Gerard Baillieu did not worry him. Quite the reverse. There was no way he would be recognised, not now. And being one up on that bastard was something he looked forward to.

As the car paused at an intersection, some Island children ran past with butterfly nets slung across their shoulders, laughing and joking as they went. He looked at their nets and a dream he'd once had came back vividly to him. In the dream, he was running through fields of waist-high grass. He could almost feel the soft stalks bending before him and brushing against his bare legs. The day was clear and filled with sun, which shone with an unusual intensity, imparting a golden shimmer to the grass as it swayed endlessly before him.

He was with Akira, running with their nets outstretched in pursuit of a fine swallowtail butterfly. Its yellow wings were brilliant with flashes of blue, green and red, while its black bulbous eyes reflected the gold of the fields. Every now and then it would alight, quivering tantalisingly on a stalk nearby, then taking off just as they reached it.

Suddenly just ahead of them, he spied a young man in glasses running after their butterfly. To his astonishment, he saw that it was the Crown Prince Akihito, and he fell back, as did Akira, both bowing low to make way for this great personage, the son of heaven.

As Atsuo stood, he saw to his horror that the butterfly had turned into a fearful bat-like creature and that the Crown Prince, seemingly unaware, was still in fast pursuit. In vain he had run after him, calling out a warning, but the Crown Prince had disappeared, and he was alone in the field with only the sound of the wind riffling through the grass. He had awakened from the dream with a sense of anguish and despair that he, Atsuo, had been unable to save the royal Prince.

Pulling up at the sprawling pink hotel, Atsuo stepped out under the canopied entranceway, a solitary figure, somewhat stooped now and leaning heavily on his stick. Unlike other high-ranking *yakuza*, Atsuo always chose to travel alone. He had informed Matsuhiro that with his previous knowledge of the Hawaiian islands, it was only right that he came at this time. Matsuhiro had agreed, knowing that Hiro could be relied upon to quietly fill him in on any extra details he needed to know, later.

PART FOUR

42

CASTING ADRIFT—HONOLULU, 1963

Her life was like a long, long necklace of carved glass beads strung out at varying intervals by a silver chain, along which she skated, or waited for the next bead to come into her sphere. The silver spaces of waiting or skating were far greater than the precious shining beads. The beads, while colourful and enticing, were often slippery and hard to hold on to. Some were a matching shape or colour, but were often different when you looked into them. While others, which appeared different, were suddenly quite surprisingly the same. Sometimes, time spent with them seemed fleeting compared to the long silvery spaces in between. At other times it dragged.

'You should always be able to shut the door on things,' Jill was saying.

'I can't. I've tried but it's just so hard. I've never been one to let go.' Sophie paused. 'Well not easily. Not without some kind of fight.'

Jill looked at her and sighed. Withdrawal's a cold hard lesson, she thought. 'Well at least you should get in first. Before he finally casts you adrift. I mean, it's all in appearances, feelings have little to do with it. What one really thinks and feels is best kept under wraps. Just remember, it's a game darling, this thing with men and women.'

She laughed at the look on Sophie's face.

'You just have to appear to be the one who's giving him up, before he finally gives you the push,' she suggested briskly.

Sophie said nothing, looking at the woman who had played mother to her all these years. Jill can be a bitch, she thought, but is often right. But where were the lights and shades, all the nuances of a relationship? She hated herself for not being more decisive, for her own lack of resilience.

'Just remember the hammer and the nail, the hammer and the nail,' Jill repeated for good measure. 'Which one are you?'

Sophie took a long sip of her wine. She reflected for a moment. 'Sometimes one, sometimes the other,' she answered. 'These truisms, Jilly, really, it just doesn't work that way.'

'It does, you know,' Jill said.

'It wouldn't take a genius to decide which one you thought you were,' reminded Sophie with an arch look. They sat, relaxed, enjoying their wine while listening to the shrill drumming of cicadas crackling the outside air as the afternoon temperature red-alerted their response. It was a curiously comforting sound that said summer is here, and all is well.

'I mean what does he do for you?'

Sophie rested her head against the deeply cushioned couch, closing her eyes and thinking of David's dark expressive eyes that gazed at her with a beloved directness and intensity. Memories of his early passion for her enclosed her like a cosy blanket. Her initial guarded reaction and surprise had given way to an equal response in her. The long heady days and nights of seizing every precious if fleeting moment to be together. Then the longer days, nights and months of realisation that it was not progressing to any real commitment. A realisation that their relationship was to remain in a semi-detached state.

She had decided on a separation, and left him, spending her days drifting in hollow floating inactivity, always with the wistful expectation that his occasional phone call evoked. David always declared his love, but offered her nothing to build upon.

Intermittently, she worked, her freelance articles mostly being published, but she was simply marking time. Then the almost chronic state of suspension where she would just drift along from one non-event or person to another had abruptly disappeared, when after almost a year of not seeing each other they met.

'But I love you,' he said over and over, as if more to convince himself than her. Sophie had taken it at face value and believed him, needing his words. They were married, hurriedly, almost furtively. She recalled Gerard's purposefully remote expression in the church, and thought of her mother. *So am I like Gina, marrying in haste, but hopefully not repenting at leisure?*

Someone told her afterwards, 'Didn't you know, passing passions were always David's specialty. He's a great one for that.'

She had almost come to terms with the pain of loss to other women, the dull humiliating ache and anger. Tears didn't come as readily or so often now, but mostly unexpectedly—when a song, a glance, a fleeting memory returned with its sudden reminder of a shared moment. She knew now the meaning of to die of a broken heart. Some large hand was squeezing that vital place within her, squeezing until only a dry kernel was left. After only two years of marriage, pain and loneliness had become familiar bed-fellows.

From far away, Sophie heard herself answering Jill. 'At least we got married, if that counts for anything, I guess. I mean what else does one do in desperation when trying to hold on?'

'Steer another course,' Jill answered. 'Actually, it's the best way of losing someone. Holding on, I mean. You need to give them plenty of rope, a long, loose rein.'

Sophie felt like rejoining, 'What, so they can hang you?' but didn't. Anyway, who was Jill to talk?

Later, she lay baking in the mid-afternoon sun, until the heat reached a point that was no longer comfortable. Diving into the pool, swimming languidly till she cooled down, Sophie floated on her back, looking up at the sky with its occasional wisps of cloud breaking the endless blue. She thought of her spirit cloud friends from childhood, and wished they had the same power to comfort her now. Their charm had receded with age.

I need to change the rules of the game with David and me, she thought, but how? It was such an effort to step out of the passive, reflective role she'd played.

For as long as she could remember, there had been a small voice somewhere in the recesses of her memory urging her onto something. Yet it was as if there was a sound barrier it couldn't penetrate. She had always been aware that something was missing from her life, in spite of being over-compensated for the loss of her parents by growing up in the well-endowed world of Jill, Gerard and her grandmother.

Power-broking, the throwing of the dice, she had left to others. Hers was a world of feeling, of reaction rather than action. But always, there was that missing link to the voice within her.

Sophie's dream

She could feel the ground shake beneath her feet, a fearful shaking, as if at any moment chasms would open beneath her and she'd fall into an abyss. But this time there was no parting of the earth, no falling and falling into darkness, just a flash of light so brilliant it ate into everything with an intensity that offered no refuge. With it came a wall of heat that hit her in a searing, suffocating wave. Then in her dream she felt herself floating above inert human shapes lying in a heap of rubble that was once her home. She hovered above dispassionately observing a scene of which she was no longer a part. She saw a young child pulling herself up from the rubble and with surprise realised it was herself, but long ago in different clothes, and a setting that was foreign yet somehow familiar.

Floating nearer, she could see that the child was crying bitterly as she picked up a charred doll. An intense pang of sadness overcame her as she looked at the doll, trying spirit-fashion to take hold of it herself but unable to will her body any closer. The sound of crackling made her suddenly aware of fires bursting into life around the child and other figures lying unconscious and semi-naked nearby. Desperately she called out a warning, but no sound came. She tried to reach out for the child but a strong hot wind began to tear her away. Terrified, she felt herself flying through the air, the wind howling around her as if with a million anguished voices, then just as quickly she was dumped into the deep swirling water of a river below.

The river flowed dark and oily through a sheet of flame. She was being carried faster and faster in a sea of bodies, many browned and burnt, strange roasted creatures from another world. Hundreds of others huddled together on the banks as they swept by. 'Kio-chan! Kio-chan!' In a voice not her own, she was crying out again and again in growing desperation to the small head of a child she could barely see being carried away from her in the fast-moving current. Fires were all around them now. The sky above them was the purple dark of night. Distant thunder rolled across the heavens, then heavy drops of rain fell on her upturned face. She was so thirsty. She opened her mouth to the sky, drinking in the rain in noisy gulps. It tasted bitter. She felt something brush against her arm. It was a child. She reached out to cradle the child in her arms, and looked down at Kio-chan's sleeping face and the heap of charred rags dragging behind her. Then in horror, she realised that the rags clothed nothing. Only the head and chest remained. On the forehead was a round red sign of the sun, and in the growing light she saw that it wasn't Kio-chan but the forlorn remains of some other child. Then she knew, her

Kio-chan was gone, and she moaned with a terrible sense of loss.

Laying the child gently on the river bank, she looked up and saw a rainbow arc of light right above her. She was being lifted towards it, higher and higher, till looking down to where once there were bodies, all she could see was a sea of paper lanterns and the glow of a million candles as bright as the flames that had once engulfed her. They were floating out to meet the distant dark stretch of ocean. She wept and wept, as if carrying the sadness of the world in her heart.

Raising himself on his elbow, David peered at the sleeping Sophie. The golden light of a Hawaiian dawn filtered softly through the white cambric curtains, billowing and parting in the early morning breeze. He'd been awakened by her moaning and now he could see tears glistening on her lashes, her lids still closed as she cried bitterly in her sleep.

Reaching across, he shook her gently. Her eyes flew open, and with a sudden jolt he was looking deep into another soul. Darkness and mystery were there, the hint of something he had never seen before. Just as quickly it was gone, and she was in his arms sobbing.

'Sophie darling, what is it?'

'Oh thank God you're here,' she murmured. 'It's that same dream. Oh David, I felt as if I was there this time. It's so real, so,' she searched for the words, 'so desolate.'

'Come,' he said, thrusting the sheets aside, 'let's go for a swim and you can tell me about it later.' Her long dark hair splashed over the pillow; she smiled wanly.

'You'll never leave me David? We've got so much,' she paused, looking away when he didn't answer. 'I'm frightened it could all . . .'

But he was already gone, whistling as he went. Suddenly everything in her life seemed so transient. Wrapping herself in a white towelling robe, she walked out through the French windows onto a wide and graceful lanai overlooking the pool. Beyond it, the silvery blue ocean shone pearl-like in the early morning light.

Frangipani hung in thick clusters, creamy white against the velvety dark green foliage, and their perfume wafted across the water as Sophie lay, floating on her back. David churned through the water past her, swimming lap after lap, leaving a trail of wash that rocked her gently as she floated. His energy and zest for life was what she had most liked about him. It complemented her more passive nature, but without fulfilling the wistful expectations of her world, for it did not make up for the uneasy promptings that goaded her from within. With David at the helm, ostensibly she could float in blissful inertia, but with an uneasy conscience and sense of foreboding. For his hunger for life went far beyond his need for her.

Tiny fragments of the dream intruded on her thoughts. The sun was getting hotter and she could hear the clink of china and voices from the kitchen. Lalana, who when she wasn't working for Hiroko now kept house for Sophie, appeared and arranged a cane table and chairs beneath a large banyan tree, preparing it for breakfast. David, glistening like a seal, hauled himself from the pool, chatting easily about his plans to Lalana for the day ahead. Sophie joined him at the table, feeling refreshed, but still in the other world of her dream. Lalana had prepared slices of golden papaya spiked with limes from their tree, along with newly baked brioche and filtered Kona coffee—freshly brewed and strong, the way he liked it.

They ate in silence, David reading the paper. She looked across his shoulder at the alarming headline news from Vietnam. 'Why do people abuse one another the way they do?'

'We are all victims of abuse,' he answered, 'to a greater or lesser degree.' It sounded trite, she thought, but probably true. We are abused and we abuse in so many ways, from the subtle to the explicit.

'It's how we handle it,' he continued. 'If we go under or not. It's all in the mind's eye.'

With David it was pictures that counted, not words. As a photo-journalist, his world was confined essentially to what emerged from the eye of his camera. Now there were these new images of someone else's war through the eyes of another country.

'What does it really matter in the final outcome, anyway?' she heard herself saying.

David looked at her, surprised. The note of cynicism was unlike her. He was silent a moment, then said, 'Well that depends upon which hill we stand, eh honey?' He smiled at her, and without waiting for an answer went back to his paper.

Everything is coloured by our expectations, our disappointments, she thought, looking out across the water. As for words, we throw them at each other, they hang there, then slip off and away, often without trace or any real effect. But the images of her dream had triggered a response to a voice within, which was speaking to her in words that as yet she could not hear. They were trying to tell her something, leading her to what or where, she wasn't sure. She knew she would have to follow it.

David stirred his coffee, knocking the spoon noisily against the side of his cup, and kept on stirring absently.

'Why do you abuse our china so?' she asked sweetly. He paused, looked at her, then laughed. She loved the way he threw his head back and laughed with such gusto, but this morning it grated. She smiled back at him, and thought, thank God for laughter, it's a great camouflage for what is really happening.

43

HIROKO'S WISH—HONOLULU

Hiroko sent for Sophie directly, which was unusual as it was only days since she had last seen her. Usually she heard through Hiroko's nurse or through Jill. But this time it was Hiroko's voice, thin and wavery on the line, that summoned her to her home in Honolulu.

As she sat opposite the frail woman, propped up in a bed that seemed far too large for her, Sophie experienced a newfound sense of warmth and belonging, a lessening in her grandmother's habitual aloofness, and she chatted easily to her in Japanese about many of the things she had been doing.

Sophie had so many of Gina's qualities, Hiroko thought, watching the bright animated face, but there was a greater strength and steadfastness here than Gina had possessed. And she was pleased that in the past year she had finally made a real effort to get to know her granddaughter.

Within Sophie there was an innate Japanese quality that the older woman now leaned toward, a clinging to her birthright as she felt her own grasp on life ebbing. She hadn't approved of Sophie's marriage to David, and had quietly observed her growing unhappiness. Sophie had not confided in her, but she picked up things here and there, and Jill had filled her in with the rest. All the girl really needed now, she thought, was a sense of direction.

'Sophie-chan, I want you to do something for me.'

'Of course, Oba-san, whatever you want,' Sophie answered automatically.

'I want you to take something to Satoshi for me.'

'Satoshi? But where? Is he still in Japan?'

Her grandmother held up her hand. 'I know where he is,' Hiroko said. 'It's a delicate matter, and I cannot ask Gerard.' She hesitated. There were too many long-held resentments there, she thought. 'It's very important that this remains something between only you and me. No-one else must know what we discuss here today. Not Gerard or Jill, not even David. Have I your word on that, Sophie-chan?' she asked, reaching out and taking Sophie's hands in hers.

'But of course.' What on earth was coming next, Sophie wondered. She knew a little of Satoshi, but as with her grandfather Boy Baillieu, he was a shadowy figure from the past. Her grandmother had returned to Japan twice since the war, but Jill had told her that Hiroko's attempts to make any real contact with her son had been frustrated.

She held Hiroko's hands, tiny and now misshapen with the onset of her rheumatoid arthritis, and wondered about her grandmother's life before she had come to Hawaii. It's part of my heritage, and I should find out all I can, she thought with a growing sense of urgency, knowing time was running out.

In the past year since her health had declined, Hiroko played an even lesser part in the running of the Baillieu's Maui plantation, spending more time in her big beautiful house at Waikiki having treatment for her pain. After the bottom dropped out of the sugar market in the early years following the war, Gerard had converted most of their sugar holdings on Maui to growing pineapple and running cattle. He was also involved in new trading projects of which she knew little, and had brought David into them.

'I want you to see Satoshi and speak with him before I die,' Hiroko said.

'Oh darling, you've got years of life left,' Sophie hastened to asssure her.

'Maybe I have, but there's a lot to be done, and I need your help. I had hoped to go myself,' she said, 'but I'm just not well enough, not any more, and time is running away so fast. You will be the one to mediate for me . . . I will tell Gerard that you are returning the ashes of my father Yukio-san to where he wished to be finally laid to rest.'

And maybe, Sophie thought, this will open a way for me to find my own father. As yet Gerard had not been able to trace him, despite his many visits to Japan.

Hiroko talked to her at length, telling her about her great-grandfather Yukio's house in Tokyo and the other properties she still had there—'some of which I will transfer to you.'

'What about Gerard?'

'He has so much already,' her grandmother said. 'These are for you.'

She told Sophie of her time with Boy, of his death and of Michiko and her jealousy and threats, and the fear she had always carried with her that Boy had somehow been murdered by the Nakamura family.

Sophie stared. 'Murdered?'

'Yes,' Hiroko said, 'it was Michiko's way of keeping Satoshi.'

'But surely you could have done something about this earlier, told the police, accused her and brought them to trial.'

'There was no proof,' said Hiroko. 'None. We will probably never know how it happened, but I know it was their plotting that no doubt killed him, and now you know as well.'

'Does Gerard know?' Sophie asked.

'No, this is only between you and me, remember?' Hiroko's eyes were bright and commanding. She reached up to smooth Sophie's hair back from her face. Her hand shook with the effort, as any movement caused her pain. She continued. 'You will go there and be my eyes, my ears and my voice,' she said. 'Will you do this for me, Sophie-chan?'

Sophie bowed her head, then leaned forward and kissed her gently on the cheek. Hiroko's skin was like transluscent yellow parchment, with fine lines fanning out from her eyes and across her cheeks.

'I will, darling,' she replied. 'I'm so glad and proud that you asked me.'

Her grandmother acknowledged her agreement with a deep nod, then went on, 'There are letters and documents in the house at Maui. I want you to go there and look through them and bring them all to me here,' she said. 'It's better if everything is here now, so you can know as much as I can tell you, and we will organise your trip then.'

'I will go and get them this week,' said Sophie.

It wasn't until she had driven away that she remembered her dream of some months before, and felt a stirring in the shadowy recesses of her subconscious, as if a long-closed door was about to open.

44

YUKIO'S MESSAGE

Later that day, Sophie thought of the book Hiroko had given her, an old edition of *Wind in the Willows*. 'When she was sick in bed, your mother often turned to it for comfort,' Hiroko told her. 'Maybe this is a good time for you to have it, Sophie-chan.'

Sophie reached for the book now, and as she took it out of its box, a yellowed sheet of rice paper slipped out. Carefully unfolding it, she saw that it was a poem written in spidery Japanese characters. She studied it for some time, then getting a piece of paper, started to slowly translate it into English.

Titled 'Dialogue on Poverty', it read:

On the night when the rain beats,
Driven by the wind,
On the night when the snowflakes mingle
With the sleety rain,
I feel so helplessly cold.
I nibble at a lump of salt,
Sip the hot, oft-diluted dregs of sake;
And coughing, snuffling,
And stroking my scanty beard;
I say in my pride,
'There's none worthy, save I!'

*But I shiver still with cold,
I pull up my hempen bedclothes,
Wear what few sleeveless clothes I have,
But cold and bitter is the night!
As for those poorer than myself,
Their parents must be cold and hungry,
Their wives and children beg and cry.
Then, how do you struggle through life?
Wide as they call the heaven and earth,
For me they have shrunk quite small;
Bright though they call the sun and moon,
They never shine for me,
Or for me alone;
By rare chance I was born a man
And no meaner than my fellows,
But, wearing unwadded sleeveless clothes
In tatters, like weeds waving in the sea,
Hanging from my shoulders,
And under the sunken roof,
Within the leaning walls,
Here I lie on straw
Spread on bare earth,
With my parents as my pillow,
My wife and children at my feet,
All huddled in grief and tears.
No fire sends up smoke
At the cooking-place,
And in the cauldron
A spider spins its web.
With not a grain to cook,
We moan like the night thrush,
Then, 'to cut', as the saying is,
'The ends of what is already too short,'
The village headman comes,
With rod in hand, to our sleeping place,
Growling for his dues.
Must it be so hopeless—
The way of this world.*[11]

It was signed Yamanoue Okura, and dated AD 660–733. Below it, in another more flowing hand, was written:

'Let us never forget in times of plenty, the pain of hunger and deprivation. The heart of the Buddha is in my heart to help us to help those who cannot help themselves.' Yukio Sen. Tokyo, 1937.

Sophie sat for some minutes, rereading her translation of what had been written so long ago. Images of the little family huddled together in their misery filled her with a sense of such sorrow. She could visualise them quite clearly, their meagre surroundings, the threadbare clothes, 'in tatters, like weeds waving in the sea', epitomising the fragility of their grasp on life.

These were my people, she thought. Part of me has evolved from them. She thought of her conversation with Hiroko earlier in the day, and all that she had learnt. How strange, she thought, to think that all these generations later, some stray remnant from a grave long forgotten can reach out and touch me, as this has done. Images of that gaunt man still clinging to his pride and his family who depended on him, despite the relentless grasp for the headman's dues. Her eyes, hot with tears, scanned the lines again.

'Must it be so hopeless—the way of this world? . . . With not a grain to cook, We moan like the night thrush.'

Somehow, the figures had become the family she had never known. She with her mother Gina, and her father Katsura struggling to care for them both. She could hear that haunting cry of the bird that was really their voices raised to the heavens in a despairing plea. She laid her head on her arms, and wept.

'Sophie, what's wrong?' She looked up as David came into the room.

'Everything and nothing,' she answered.

'I was just looking through something of Mother's.'

'Look, if going through those old things is going to upset you, maybe you should just leave them.' He seemed put out.

'No, no,' she said, smiling at him. 'Ghosts are there to be laid.'

'And what about this one?' He looked down at her, then pulling her to her feet, kissed her long and hard so that she gasped for air. 'David, I really think that . . .'

'Let's not talk, there's not much time,' he broke in, pulling her onto the bed, his hands reaching up between her thighs.

Still feeling on the fringe of sadness, she let herself drift from the mood of that moment into this one with a growing intensity and relief. This was reality, her strong and handsome David who wanted her. She blocked out every other thought, and gave herself totally to what was here and now.

Later, as she lay warmed and secure in the after-glow of their love-making, she watched as he moved around the room looking for his cigarettes. Suddenly the cold memory of his 'there's not much time' came back to her.

'You're leaving again.' It was more a statement than a question.

'Tomorrow,' he answered, rummaging in his drawer. 'Back to Guam at twelve hundred hours.'

'Oh David, so soon?' She sat up, all the newfound sense of security slipping away.

'Let's go out for dinner, and we'll make this night together really special.'

She didn't answer.

'I have to go, Sophie—don't make it any harder.' She silently clung to him for a moment, then went into the bathroom.

Turning the shower on hot and hard, she felt the water sting her skin. This bloody, bloody war, she fumed, and his mind always anywhere but here with me.

Although not part of the active service in Vietnam and Cambodia, David was an accredited news cameraman and photographer, flying in and out of the different war zones at short notice, and usually on assignments he would never fully discuss with her. Glimpses of the horror through his photographs and film were in any case enough to make her pull back from it all. Her journalist's senses were buried in the cross-fire of her own unresolved emotions.

She was aware that David was also organising some business deals for Gerard in the market place this war had opened up. His exact involvement she had never really questioned, but suspected it had something to do with the traffic of medical supplies and drugs to and from the conflict zone. When asked, he'd shrugged it off as of no importance; just a few favours he was doing for Gerard.

I should have grown used to this see-sawing of his need for me, she thought. Maybe, as Jill had said, it was time for the balance of power to change, especially now with Hiroko's proposal. She could throw herself into that. But still, the thought of stepping completely outside his life made her uneasy. I do love him, she thought. I need him, still. Perhaps if they had a child things would be better, more secure. But not with things the way they were between them.

'You must give him space, let him breathe. You'll smother the flame if you try to contain it, Sophie,' Jill had cautioned in the early days. But how did one stand aloof from something precious, especially when so many others seemed to want what was rightfully hers?

'It's the blessing and curse of having such a handsome, sexy husband,' her friend Carol had told her. 'Every other woman wants him. But he's yours, so what are you worrying about?'

How could she explain, Sophie thought. It was like trying to hold on to jelly in sunlight. The more it melted, the harder you hung on till finally it had all drained through your fingers. In a last attempt to enjoy what had until minutes before been yours, you licked your fingers clean, but there was only the after-taste of frustration.

It's because David never really had anyone to love him as a child, she'd reassured herself. No real sense of roots, of belonging. Small segments of his boyhood had occasionally slipped out like slivers of mica, darkly reflecting only what he wanted her see—almost as if he couldn't bear to face it himself. 'What can you expect, he hasn't a clue who his parents were or where he really came from!' Jill had expostulated when she'd once tried to explain away David's detachment.

'You can't recall your mother? Or your father? Tell me about it, darling?' Sophie had asked him when he'd first told her that he'd never known his parents.

'Seems I was a love . . . or shall we say a lust child. Mom must have taken one look and got the hell out of it.' But his laugh had lacked conviction.

'Oh David, what really happened?' He'd shrugged and mentioned only that there was an old and distant aunt who'd looked after him till on her death, when he was just four, he had been put into a Catholic boys home.

'What's there to say? It was hardly Four Star, just bloody cold!' David had said with a laugh, moving quickly on to other things.

Whenever she brought it up, there was that same edge to his voice, and a withdrawing from her, so she gave up trying. But that was David, always ducking and weaving while neatly compartmentalising everything that mattered as if to contain it, or to block it out, Sophie reminded herself. Then again she recalled those fleeting insights to his vulnerability. Often he would whimper softly in his sleep, and just nights ago as he lay deeply asleep he moaned, and when she'd reached out to him his cheeks were wet with tears. Instinctively she responded to that anguish and hollow deprivation through early loss, which she knew only too well, and she'd gently wiped them away. 'What is it darling, tell me David, tell me,' she'd whispered. But as always he'd backed away, so she'd turned from him. But it hung there unanswered.

Sophie sighed, turning the shower to cold and feeling her skin tighten with the astringent effect of the sudden change in temperature.

'I've booked a table at the Royal and asked Jim and Carol to join us,' David said as she emerged refreshed from the bathroom.

'Fine,' she pretended, thinking, ah, there goes our romantic dinner for two.

'Is Jim flying out with you?'

'Yeah, it seemed a good idea, a sort of double celebration and send off,' avoiding her eyes.

She dressed carefully, her slim cotton dress clinging to all the right places. She had put on her uplift bra, wired and padded underneath to push her breasts up high and round above the lowcut top so that her nipples were barely covered. She teased her short hair until it stood up in a high swirl of blue-black curls around her face, accentuating her delicate bones and large brown eyes. In contrast, her skin glowed pale and fine. She had given up trying to get a tan. She highlighted her lips with a frosted gloss.

Dinner was a somewhat strained affair. Amid the steady stream of conversation and laughter along with the others, Sophie routinely noted David's eyes on a striking blonde sitting only tables away. Later as she watched him dancing with the woman, their every touch like a knife through her heart, she thought of the family in the poem she'd discovered in her mother's book that afternoon.

She could imagine them as the people in that poem, the woman's red dress and David's suit now faded and shredded, 'in tatters, like weeds waving in the sea', their skin roughened and aged from poverty and hardship, rather than the glow of sexual promise that bonded them now.

'Dance, Sophie?' She looked up to see Jim's beaming face.

'Why so glum chum, we'll soon be back,' he laughed as she moved into his arms and across the dance floor. She watched David and the blonde over Jim's shoulder. David had set up a meeting—she had seen that look before.

'Jim, this is probably not the best of times to say anything, but I've decided to leave David.'

'What?' as though he'd misheard. She could hardly believe that she was saying it either.

'I just wanted to tell you,' she went on. He looked at her for some time, then said, 'Are you sure that's what you want, Sophie?'

'Yes.' She had said it now, and there was no going back. She looked up at his big, good-natured face, now troubled and reflective, then across to David escorting the woman back to her table, their every movement confirming an assignation.

Sophie hesitated. 'I just want to be my own person again, and somehow telling you makes it seem possible.' She put her fingers to his lips, 'But not a word to anyone, promise? Please Jim.' As she smiled up at him, it seemed the hardest thing she'd ever had to do.

'Jim and I are going on to try our luck at the tables,' David said later, when he drove her home, 'so keep the bed warm.' He grinned at her, giving her a pat on the bottom as she got out of the car.

'Do you really have to, David? You may lose out again.' She wanted to hurt him for this.

'Come on, Sophie, it's our last night here for a while.'

'Our last night too, David,' she said quietly, steeling herself not to break down.

'I'll be back before you know it.' His grin brooked no change of course, she knew from old.

After he left, she waited until she heard him gun his car down onto the road below their gate before she hurried to the garage and drove out after him. She kept a fair distance behind until she saw him drive into the Royal Hawaiian. She parked outside, a little way down the street, and waited. Minutes later she saw him emerge with the woman and they both got into his old Porsche and drove off down Kalakaua Avenue.

She made no attempt to follow him immediately. She knew where they were going, to his studio downtown. Sitting there feeling cold and angry with an ache in her heart, she thought about their life together. How could he do this to her. They had just made love, earlier that night. How could he?

Her hands shook as she lit a cigarette and started up the engine and drove after them towards the Kapiolani Boulevard.

Anyway, I've told Jim I'm leaving him and I am. She flicked on the radio to hear the Beatles' 'All you need is love, all you need is love, all you need is love, love, love is all you need'. Their repetition of the words jarred her and she flicked it off. Love!

Her keys dangled on the dashboard. There was one to his studio. Should she go in and confront them hot in the act, if only for the satisfaction of seeing the look on his face. But instinct told her to bide her time. Why drive the knife in any deeper? She knew what was happening, so why bare her feelings in this humiliating way?

She parked below the building that housed his studio. They had gone up and the lights were on. She sat shivering in the cold, thinking of the little family freezing on that night in Japan so long ago, and of David and Jim flying back tomorrow to the madness and turmoil of a country at war. And not even our war, she reminded herself.

Her heart ached, for his going away then, rather than for what was happening now. She looked up at the lights in his window.

'Let the winds of heaven dance between you,' Jill had said. 'Winds maybe, but this was more like a gale,' she said aloud, and laughed at the thought with a sense of release.

Suddenly as if a mist was lifting, she felt she was emerging from a long dark night of bondage. Let the winds of heaven dance between you, she thought. So David wanted to go his way, well she would go hers.

Starting up the car, Sophie resolved that she would say nothing till he came back from Guam. In the meantime, she would get involved in her grandmother's project and at the same time try to re-establish her haphazard career in journalism, and pick up on all the old contacts. There was lots she could do.

'Let us never forget in times of plenty', the words of her great grandfather Yukio Sen reminded her. He must have suffered; so had they all, if in different ways. She felt a sense of belonging and strength in becoming part of a shared injustice, as if emerging from a chrysalis of her own making.

45

LETTERS AND PHOTOGRAPHS—MAUI

As Sophie searched deep in the back of her grandmother's desk, she pushed at the side of a smooth panel of cedar and it slid back to reveal a flat drawer, cleverly disguised within the panelling. Inside lay a bundle of letters, neatly stacked and tied with a faded vermilion ribbon, its once rich velvet pile now creased and flattened. She felt a thrill of anticipation: she had been given the key to reach out and bridge the span of years that lay between the writer of the letters and herself.

Taking them out to the lanai overlooking the ocean, she hesitated a moment before opening them. Despite Hiroko's agreement, she still felt an intruder. Closing her eyes, she said a silent prayer. 'Darling Oba-San, forgive me for reading what was once so private and precious to you.' She paused, looking out across the sea to where the turquoise waters met the wide expanse of sky, then went on. 'But I do it with love and a wish to understand all that went before, and so help in our quest. Who knows, maybe it will also help me cope with what's happening now.'

She thought of the pre-occupied expression on David's face when she had driven him to the airport early that morning, his mind already a thousand kilometres away.

She had hardly spoken, except to say that she was flying to Maui later in the afternoon for a couple of days to pack some things for Hiroko.

She untied the ribbon and parted the letters gently, as they were thin and frail to the touch, some in yellowed envelopes but many merely the written pages. As she did, a small posy of dried flowers fell from where it had lain for so long. A faint musky perfume still hung in the air, rather like the smell of sandalwood. She inhaled them deeply to recapture the moment when they had first been placed there.

The top letter was in a childish scrawl and was only a fragment. She had trouble reading the clumsily worked Japanese characters, but on rereading they became clearer.

. . . she won't let me see you. I miss you. Please come and take me away, Aunt-Michiko-san is awful. They said you were still away and you don't want to see me. Is that true? Please come and get me. I miss you Mamma. I love you and will try and be . . .

The page ended, and she quickly opened the next folded page, hoping the letter would throw some light on where it was from, but it merely contained some childish drawings of two stick people, one with pants and a moustache and the other a woman in flowing robes like a kimono. Carefully printed under it was 'Mamma and Boy-san by Toshi'. The man had a yellow thatch of hair and round blue dots for eyes, with a mouth that turned down. The woman had no expression, just big black eyes and a carefully drawn cupid's bow mouth. The young artist had put all his energies into making her beautiful. A fall of black hair swirled around her shoulders. Her gown had large pink and red flowers drawn in a childish hand.

Carefully Sophie folded the letter then opened another. It was headed 'Fujiya Hotel, Miyanoshita. August 23rd, 1921', and was written in English in a strong open hand which had barely faded with time.

My darling,
As I lie here in this dreadful heat from which there has been no relief today, I think of you and long for your sweet presence. It's as though when you left and I watched you being carried away like a princess in that palanquin down into the valley, all the freshness and beauty, indeed life's very breath, left with you.

The clouds hang heavy and reflect my mood without you and everything seems in a leaden wash of grey.

My love, take heart, we will work things out you will see. If you have no luck with the N. family, I will follow another lead as to his whereabouts, and will clear the way for you and the boy, have no fears. Then we three shall leave these shores.
Yours for ever and a day,
Boy.

My grandfather, part of my flesh and blood, she thought, wishing he was there so she could speak with him. She had seen photos of him before, faded smiling little snaps, maddening in that they didn't clearly convey enough of the man or the occasion. If only David and his camera had been there, she smiled. But they had captured a little of Boy's open-faced vitality. She could see he possesssed a vibrant spirit, a golden personae, and to have died so young. She sighed as she thought of his death and Hiroko's words. 'There's a hidden link here somewhere,' she said aloud, 'please help me find it, Grandfather.'

Another letter was also from Miyanoshita, written the day after. She read slowly.

My darling,
A sudden if short-lived relief after the intense heat of yesterday, with last night the arrival of monsoon rains. I was wishing you were here with me to ride the wildness of the storm from our bed of love.

It arrived with surprising swiftness like a band of galloping horses rushing down into the valley and riding roughshod over our hotel. I could hear the wind screaming through the pine trees on the hill as if all the spirits there had taken wing in some vengeful reckoning.

Some of the downstairs rooms were badly damaged and water everywhere. The proprietor, Nakata-san, was very upset. Rain fell like sheets of water at first cooling the air, but now when all is still, the heat creeps back in a steaming mist. A message from 'D' that all is ready to get the boy, if you don't have any luck.

Take heart, my love. We will have him. The N. family have no knowledge of my plan, and when they do, we will be gone.

Be brave. It's not long now.

Yours,

Boy.

P.S. A strange dream last night that I was running naked with you into the pine forest and we took shelter on a deep bed of pine needles as the storm howled about us. You lay light as a leaf on top of our soft green bed, but I sank deep, deep into the needles and had to call out to you to try and catch hold of my hand to stop me from disappearing altogether.

I miss you, miss you. But only days to go now.

A shiver went through Sophie as she read the postscript, wondering who the 'D' referred to. The phone rang in the next room, and she heard Hiroko's old houseboy Malo, answer it, then his footsteps padding across the marble tiles.

Damn! thought Sophie, I should have told him I didn't want to see or speak to anyone.

'It's Mr David,' said Malo, putting his head around the door.

'I'll take it,' Sophie answered, scooping up the letters and bringing them inside with her.

'David, I thought you'd left ages ago.'

'We've been held up.' He paused. 'Sophie, we really

didn't get a chance to talk after last night,' he said. She waited, wondering if Jim had told him anything. Surely he wouldn't. David seemed to be waiting for her to fill the gap, but she didn't.

'Sophie?'

'Yes,' she answered, part of her still with the letter she had been reading.

'I'll miss you,' was all he said. 'I have to go now, write to me, darling.'

A click of the receiver, and he was gone. She felt herself falling into the void of loneliness and nagging regret his going invariably evoked. She should have said something, talked to him. All the anger and decision of the previous night dissolved into a frantic feeling of loss. He was gone and may never come back.

'Oh David, David . . .' She threw herself face down onto the window seat and tears of long repressed hurt rolled over her outstretched arms and onto the letters beneath.

'Miss Sophie?' It was Malo coming into the room, his gentle face furrowed in concern. Sophie sat up, wiping her eyes. 'It's all right, don't worry,' she said, then, catching sight of the bowl massed with hibiscus Malo was carrying, she drew in her breath.

The flowers lay clustered in soft perfect shapes of intense colour, their velvety petals glowing deepest pink on the outer edges, fading towards a warm apricot in the centre, their stamen projecting a burst of golden and scarlet antennae. On the petals, trembling drops of water caught and reflected facets of silver light. Sophie thought, this is the true gift of beauty. It gives us a brief and pleasing respite from the weighty world of self. For in that instant we are aware only of the beauty of the thing itself and are free to float for an intense moment in the delight of perfection that gives balm to the soul.

She looked up, smiling at Malo. 'They're wonderful.' She gathered up the letters, and decided to make arrangements to leave for Japan as soon as possible.

That night Sophie relaxed, watching a television

interview, at first half-heartedly, then with growing interest. A woman was talking about the mystique of the photograph album, saying that it was 'like pieces to a jigsaw of life . . . as though trying to freeze a life in a moment of time'.

Is this then our fascination with photographs? Sophie thought. That through them we are trying to capture segments of our life as it moves relentlessly on? The small pile of Hiroko's photographs that had fallen into her lap were largely unknown faces, fashions and places—masked representations of moments.

In one, Hiroko, her tiny heart-shaped face a pale blur, was standing beside Boy, fair-haired but displaying none of the golden gaiety that had won the heart of his bride. Her elaborate kimono and the sense of another world and time gave no indication that she was soon to leave it. Another shot showed Hiroko and a young Japanese soldier. A tiny shape lay in Hiroko's arms, still little more than a baby, yet there was her whole life, the nucleus of her being. Sophie reflected on what the woman was saying, that there is no ultimate truth in a photograph. You see the surface only, and behind the surface there can be all kinds of interpretations. So while the photograph can show surface detail well, it does not show what lies beneath that surface.

She noticed for the first time a face and figure behind and to the side of Hiroko and Noboru, a Japanese woman, plain, but looking at the baby with an intense expression. Michiko, no doubt, she mused. She picked up another shot of Hiroko and the same woman, both smiling demurely for the camera. However Michiko's expression was not for the photographer, but for someone out of shot, and this time it was she who was carrying the baby. Sophie stared at it, and thought of the woman on the television saying that there is often hidden information, even just one piece of information, that could alter one's whole perception of the photograph. Who was standing out of range of the camera that day? Would Hiroko remember after all this time? She would ask her about that picture.

The woman was remarking that losing family pictures was like losing the person again. 'It's as though that delicate link of kinship hangs by the one thread of that photograph. We look at photos and try to glean things from the past. This is our way in. The key to past existence.'

It was a kind of visual revisiting of our own history, she said. 'We underestimate the power of our parents' images. One needs to learn to act in relation to our history in a positive way, and not be haunted by parental ghosts.'

Sophie thought of David, his constant grasping at others' lives through his camera, and his infidelities. It was like a compulsive devouring of other people's experiences, their histories, their bodies. Was it to compensate for his early years in that boy's home with no family photographs and linking thread of kinship? Is this to replace the blank canvas of his early life, the empty photo album? Not that the reality of a happy family, with a mummy and a daddy and the children, necessarily existed. Within families there were always the tensions and often violence that no-one seemed to want to face.

The woman on the screen was talking about her own history. 'My father,' she went on, 'was a very violent man. I lived my entire early life in fear of my father. Yet there he was forever putting us in happy family situations for the photograph, like this one where we all posed with our bikes. It was to establish a reality that just wasn't there,' she added. 'Part of our way of surviving was not to let it show. There are some moments in my childhood I just can't bear to think about, they were so horrific.'

Sophie thought of the only photo she'd ever seen of her own father, Katsura, taken dining out with Gina not long before he'd left Honolulu. Gina had been radiant with eyes only for him, but he looked so contained, she remembered, as if he was there but not there. As a child, she had been worried by his expression. Later when

Gerard had explained what happened, she realised that she'd long sensed in that look his imminent departure from their lives.

The words of her old scripture teacher came back to her: 'Nothing in life is to be feared, rather it's to be understood.' Now thinking of the unnamed fears of childhood and of her own youth in relation to that one image she had of a father soon to disappear, she thought, I am only just beginning a voyage of discovery as to why.

46

LOSS

'If you go in directly, you'll find out nothing,' Gerard cautioned. 'You'll need a cover, so why not as someone doing business for one of our subsidiary companies?'

'Why, it's becoming quite a covert operation,' Sophie said.

'And so what isn't?' her uncle quipped.

'I'd research for a story I want to do, anyway,' she went on. 'I can organise some of the interviews, and if you give me the contacts, a whole lot more.'

'I must tell you that with the Baillieu name you'll most probably not get far in finding him,' Gerard said. 'He will duck that every time. He has to date.'

'Maybe he wonders about me,' she said. 'He must wonder about this child he never knew.'

Gerard did not have the heart to disillusion her. He was not surprised when she told him she was returning Yukio's ashes for Hiroko. He knew that his mother would have set the whole thing up, and most probably asked her to make contact with Satoshi. He felt the stab of bitterness which still gnawed like some long-hidden ulcer.

So Hiroko still mourned for her long-lost son. Hadn't he, Gerard, always supported and stood by her? It was Satoshi, the one who had turned his back on her, who had never in all this time bothered to find out about her or make any contact at all, to whom she still turned in her heart. While Gerard, who had always given her his full filial backing and interest, who had turned their whole business around and built it into what it was today, was only given second place in her affections.

His bitterness mounted. He had even brought up his dead sister's child, Sophie, as his own, then steered her husband into the family business, quietly giving him a key role in the network of trading interests and investments that had been built up in the islands, across to the mainland and now into Vietnam and Cambodia. Yet despite all of this, to him his mother gave only a token interest.

His face gave no indication of his grim thoughts. Perhaps it wouldn't hurt for her to make contact with Satoshi after all—what could he, Satoshi, do to me or my family now that could be any worse than what he has already done? But there was a niggling doubt, especially in relation to Katsura. Someone who had managed to disappear so completely as he had done must carry some clout. To go without trace took some organising, and that meant money. Either that or he had to be someone of absolutely no consequence. But that he doubted. Gerard would have to keep close tabs on Sophie's movements while she was in Japan, but that wouldn't be hard to organise. He'd built up enough strategic alliances and contacts with Matsuhiro and his boys to see to that.

His mind went back to that night at the Royal Hawaiian six years ago, when he'd first met Matsuhiro's uncle, Atsuo Isawa, to set up their initial trading links with the Isawa-*gumi*. Their meeting had been brief; he was an enigmatic bastard, Gerard recalled, who gave nothing away . . . a bit of an odd-ball, yet a tough negotiator. He'd steered clear of him since then, dealing mostly through Hiro with Matsuhiro. He smiled to himself; money, and the good things that came with it, was Matsuhiro's bag, so he could always be bought off.

He still wanted to confront Katsura and hand out his own brand of rough justice. Maybe Sophie would be able to unearth him.

'It will be good for you to go now,' Gerard said. 'With David away so often, you might get too lonely if you stayed here.'

'Oh Gera, I'm so glad you agree. I was worried that you might be annoyed,' Sophie said. She looked up at him, her face serious. 'It's really important for me to find out more. I just have to try and establish that lost contact, maybe more for Gina's sake.' Somehow she had never grown accustomed to calling her 'mother'. Gina was a figure who had never played a real part in her life, except to give birth and then leave her in the most final way possible.

She had always carried a strong resentment at her mother's untimely desertion of her. Why hadn't she lived? What kind of a wimp died in childbirth anyway, she'd said angrily to the mirror as she travelled the bumpy road of adolescence.

Sophie's relationship to Jill had early developed into that of the younger sister, looking for advice, for a sounding board. With the birth of William and Louise, Jill's full maternal energies had been directed to them. To compete with this, and ensure her place within the family circle, Sophie had taken on the role of a back-up mother, helping Jill to care for them. So it was as one who'd always had to work for her rightful place in the family rather than just accepting it as her due that gave her the fragility and over-sensitivity to issues that might otherwise have passed unnoticed. At the same time, it imparted an aloofness, a holding back in giving her full alliance to anyone. Despite her feelings for David, she was still very much intact and could relate to his apparent emotional self-sufficiency, if never to his infidelities.

As a young child, one feels like the centre of the universe, far more so if there are natural parents to feed the myth, Sophie had often thought. So does one ever get over the early loss of a parent? It's almost as if there's a shadowy presence forever there, tugging at your throat, your heart, in your every waking moment.

'It's the ultimate loss of what might have been and wasn't,' Jill had said to her when Sophie expressed some of these fears. 'Remember, we all have to come to terms with loss. Look at me, I had to,' she added, as if in final proof of what she was advising. 'It's just too easy to go off the rails if you become morbid about things. Look forward, not back on the past.'

Well that's exactly what I'm doing now, Sophie thought with a renewed sense of confidence in her impending journey. As she drove back to her apartment, the question she'd asked herself a thousand times still hovered. Why, why in all this time had her father never come to find her?

'Papa-san,' she whispered. 'Please dear God, help me find him this time.'

47

DAIHACHI INTERVIEW—JAPAN

As she waited for him to arrive, Sophie looked out at the little boats skimming Lake Hakone and thought of the words of a song from her school days.

Row row row your boat gently down the stream,
Merrily, merrily, merrily, merrily, life is but a dream.

Memories returned of sitting in the school bus singing this same verse over and over as they harmonised in the round, then all collapsing in a wave of giggling as they missed the beat, or sang the wrong word or simply repeated the same thing again and again until it was just too ridiculous. For the first time, as she gazed at the boats, she thought of the actual words. How strange that I've sung them so many times without ever thinking of their meaning, and yet, they seemed to reflect her own feelings.

'Gently down the stream,' she murmured. Not just drifting, but actually rowing. 'Life is but a dream.' Yes, it's a mirage, a mere moving shadow, she thought. So is it our yearning for a sense of spiritual completeness and belonging or simply one of survival that keeps us moving forward, knowing that the dream must end and there's a goal to reach?

She looked up as Daihachi Isawa came into the room. A very old man, he moved slowly, but was surprisingly upright and didn't need a stick to help him. Gerard had given her his name as someone who might put her in touch with the events surrounding Katsura's movements after he returned to Japan. 'We were able to establish that he may be a distant relative,' he said. 'Anyway, it's worth following as he may open a door for you.'

Shortly after she arrived in Japan, she rang the number Gerard had given her and eventually got on to Daihachi. She introduced herself and mentioned that she was doing a story, from the Japanese point of view, regarding their entry into the Second World War for a book she was compiling. Would he oblige her with a meeting? He had agreed. He had been advised by the *oyabun* that she had important Japanese and American connections, and it could be in their interest to see her. And something in the sweetness of her voice had evoked a long-lost memory.

After he was seated and they were served tea, Sophie at first just chatted, telling him how she had a fascination with certain aspects of time and of death, of what appeared to be almost predestined meetings and missed meetings, of opportunities seized and of those missed.

'As it played a vital part in my early childhood,' she said looking directly at him now, 'I have long had an interest in the Second World War . . . in war itself, when the most extraordinary events took place in everyday, often mundane settings.'

Daihachi waited for her to go on, knowing they still hadn't reached what it was really all about. And it amused him to listen as she seemed to be almost thinking aloud.

'It's as though suddenly everything was turned upside down,' Sophie continued, 'as if some capricious giant took a toy box of the world and tipped it up just to see what happened. Suddenly vast numbers of men and women and children were transported from home, family and loved ones, and sent at random to places they never thought they'd see, and to events they'd never normally be called upon to handle. Often to face a horrifying death or internment. And more often than not, to discover along the way new insights, compassion, sometimes even joy when least expected.'

She had a way with words, Daihachi thought, but her philosophising and playing with words didn't amount to much as yet, so he waited quietly.

'Now, Daihachi-san,' Sophie looked at him appraisingly. She lowered her eyes when his gaze met hers, more out of politeness and discretion than a sense of shyness.

'I'm not going to ask you a lot of questions, your time is valuable, I know.' And he wouldn't answer them all, anyway. If only I can get some small lead, I'll be lucky, she thought. She continued, 'If you don't mind, I'd like to record our conversation as we go.'

The elderly Japanese nodded his agreement and settled back, seemingly relaxed, but ever watchful. On earlier investigation, he'd discovered that the girl's Japanese grandmother, who had married into the Nakamura family, had later after the death of her hero husband married a *gaijin*. It was an unspeakable act in Daihachi's code that had come at a price, but at the same time his curiosity was aroused and he felt in a tolerant mood. He well remembered the Nakamura family, and smiled to himself; their pride had not taken kindly to the whole thing.

'Are you familiar with the attack on Pearl Harbor?' Sophie asked.

'Ah yes, but what . . .'

'I would like to play you something,' she said quickly, 'and maybe you would be gracious enough to tell me of some of your associations, your thoughts or memories which come to mind.'

She pressed the recorder and the plaintive sounds of '*Umi Yukaba*' ('Going Out To Sea'), telling of the bravery and loyalty of the soldiers and sailors fighting for their Emperor, rose quietly in the air.

Surprised by the unexpectedness of this turn, Daihachi tried to veil his feelings as the notes reached out to him.

An expression of painful reflection passed over his face and he leaned forward, lowering his head as he listened to the old warrior's song.

> *If I go away to sea*
> *I shall return a corpse awash.*
> *If duty calls me to the mountain,*
> *A verdant sward will be my pall;*
> *For the sake of the Emperor I will not die*
> *Peacefully at home.*[12]

He heard the notes—a cleansing balm to memories that lay locked in his heart, the pain of which he would take to his grave.

The face of Yukio Seki, leader of the first suicide campaign, flashed before him, its intense expression merging with that of his own son Hiroshi's sweet face, anxious and expectant, his white *hachimaki* symbolising his resolve. The eighteen-year-old's eyes had looked to his father for reassurance and approval on the night before that last flight, when he first told him he was to be part of the special *Yamazakura* (Wild Cherry) *Tokkotai* or *Kamikaze* unit.

Suddenly that long-loved face disappeared in a sheet of flame and a terrifying confusion of exploding shells and fire that even now resounded in his brain. It was a sound he had heard replayed many times in the months and years that followed his son's death. And what of the hateful irony of it all? But on that point he didn't wish to dwell, not now. Close to tears, he spoke thickly. 'That will do, that will do.' He sat with his head bowed a minute.

'I do not wish to talk of the past. It is gone. We cannot go back, but must move on, always forward,' he said with difficulty.

Sophie could see he had been shaken by the song, but felt she must pursue it. 'But surely Daihachi-san, we are the product of all that has gone before us, and so the sum total of our experience.'

But he was not to be so easily drawn. 'The past is the past,' he said. 'What is to be gained by going over it?'

She broke in. 'Do you believe that the *Tokko* pilots had no hope of possible return? Did they really believe that they were flying to a certain death?'

He paled slightly as he answered, 'It was their wish. It was the Emperor's wish. And it was long ago.'

'But it has been said, in fact often said, that Emperor Hirohito truly regretted the whole event. He even conveyed these feelings of grief and regret to Admiral Koshiro Oikawa in Tokyo at the time. Maybe then it was not his wish and should not have been acted upon at the time?' She could see he was wrestling with how best to answer her.

At last he spoke in a voice now deep with emotion. '*Hakko Ichi-u, Hakko, Ichi-u* (To cover the eight corners of the world under one roof). It is done,' he added.

'Or only just begun?' Sophie queried. But he ignored her. She changed tack. 'Then how would you define bravery, Daihachi-san?'

He looked at her reflectively, then spoke at first almost in a whisper, but gaining intensity with each word.

'Ah bravery. It is to be young, to have the lifeblood pumping through your veins and all the wonder and joy of life ahead of you. It is to be handsome and clever and above all to be just starting on a journey which could achieve great things for many people, and . . .'

'And?' she prompted.

'And then to trade this for a long, cold flight into the unknown only to face a certain searing, agonising death through fire.' Daihachi stopped, his face a pale mask as he relived what had so many times been imprinted on his mind.

To ease his anguish, Sophie said gently, 'But the soul takes flight, is free.'

He seemed unaware of her presence, seeing only Hiroshi, his son's eyes brimming with tears, desperately trying not to break down completely.

'Father, is this for the best? Is this truly the way? Will I never come back?'

Daihachi had looked at his youngest son's face, and with his own resolute gaze tried to will the fear from Hiroshi's eyes. How could he answer him when the boy's wish to live was so strong? Yet to die a glorious death for their Emperor, the Son of Heaven, was an honourable thing. Yes, it was an honourable, an heroic act, was it not? He had said nothing, then gripping his son by the shoulder, handed him three shining sen.

'For your journey into the next world,' he'd hesitated, 'if you should need them my son.'

Hiroshi had taken the coins, his fare across the sacred river Styx, looking at them in silence. Then father and son embraced.

His mother, who had been standing back from them both, came forward, her face wet with tears as she looked up at him, then bowed low.

'Hiroshi-chan. *Konichi wa aka-chan. Konichi wa aka-chan.*' She bowed deeply again, repeating the words of the song she had sung to him as a baby. As if to stave off any fears of never seeing him again, it was with words of greeting that she had addressed him then. She handed him a *senninbari*, the thousand stitches stomach wrap, her carefully worked talisman to gird her son from the dangers that lay ahead. The boy had held it to him as he bowed his obeisance.

Daihachi pushed these memories from him, and with an effort returned to the present and Sophie's questions.

'Only the dead have seen an end to war.'

'Ah, Plato,' she murmured.

He looked faintly surprised that she should recognise his quote.

'When all the seas, I deem, are our brethren/Why do the winds and waves so noisily rise?' she quoted the words of the Emperor Meiji. She decided to ask outright. 'There is someone I would like to interview. Maybe you can help me?'

Daihachi looked at her, waiting, his every sense alert.

So this was why she had come. 'If I can,' he bowed slightly.

'Katsura Kurosawa,' she said.

Thankful his eyes were hidden from her, he stayed as if frozen for a moment, then raised his head. 'I did not catch the name.'

'Katsura Kurosawa,' Sophie repeated.

'Ah, yes,' he paused. 'But why do you ask me?'

'I was told you were distantly related and might know of his whereabouts,' she added, as if to head off any denials.

'I did hear something of him, some time ago,' he answered slowly, 'but I will have to enquire further. Perhaps we can meet again and I will tell you then.' He rose, firmly bringing their meeting to a close.

She replied hopefully, 'Thank you, Isawa-san, I will call you.'

He bowed and left.

Sophie looked after him, thinking of the expression on Daihachi's face when she first mentioned Katsura's name. Yes, he knew something. From her handbag, she removed the only photograph she had of Katsura with her mother, noting how the players in this game, if game it was, stared back at her. She read into them the limitations of her own small world of knowledge and understanding. So the limits are already set, within our own finite sphere and grasp of time, where 'life is but a dream'.

* * *

Sophie collected her key from the dozing clerk at the hotel desk. The room was cold when she entered, and she had a sudden sense that someone had been there not long ago. The lights were on as she had left them, the bed turned back by the night maid and some fresh fruit placed in a bowl. It wasn't the maid's presence that had left its shadow, but something else.

Crossing quickly to the bathroom she looked inside,

then walked back to the wardrobe, pushing aside her few clothes and looking behind them. The balcony's heavy glass sliding doors were pushed partly back just as she had left them. There was no sign of anyone outside, only the reassuring shine of lights and noise from the traffic below. Then it came to her, the faint fruity smell of cigar smoke. So there had been someone there.

Shaking slightly, Sophie reached for her cigarettes, lighting one and inhaling deeply. She picked up the phone and rang down to the night clerk. 'It's Sophie Chapman, room 270—has anyone called for me?' She heard the rustle of papers then, 'Yes madam, someone called but left no name or message, madam.'

'How long ago?'

The clerk hesitated. 'Some hours ago, not long after you left. He rang up to your room. He didn't leave his name, but said he'd call back. That was all.' He hung up before she had a chance to question him further.

Crossing to the cupboard, she searched for her bag of tapes. The bag was there but lying on its side. She opened it, quickly counting the cassettes inside. Two were missing. She tipped them all onto the bed and counted again. Yes, there were two gone. She checked through the tapes again to see which ones, then stopped with a sense of dismay. They were the two she had taped with Hiroko before leaving Honolulu, giving names of people to contact and her grandmother's conversations about Satoshi. Damn, damn! she fumed. Maybe she'd mislaid them somewhere. But no, she had seen them only yesterday. But how could he have known which ones to take, if they were stolen, and why? Then she remembered that they were clearly labelled, so whoever it was had known what they were looking for.

Sophie felt apprehensive, then her fears began to dissipate as she remembered that she had wiped most of the first tape with Hiroko's names and addresses. She had transferred them along with the names Gerard had given her into her notebook. She smiled with relief, thinking of the surprise they'd get when they played that one. Her sense of elation was short-lived when she thought of the second tape. That was intact and contained many of her grandmother's innermost thoughts and fears regarding her son. It was on this tape that Hiroko had spoken of Boy's death as a probable murder.

Feeling nervous and dispirited, she thought of home with longing. She gazed at her pale reflection in the mirror. So it was *Mana,* she thought, the Hawaiian name for the spiritual power, the life force that was all about us. It seemed *Mana* had put her in touch with her destiny, and now there was no turning back.

48

BATH HOUSE—HAKONE, JAPAN

Still upset by all that had passed the night before, Sophie walked towards the bath house. She loved this part of Hakone, the gentle curve of the hills now clad in their fresh spring mantle of green shoots and early blossom. There was an expectancy in the air, and the pall of the night before dissolved in a quickening sense of optimism. A warm breeze tinged with the smell of sulphur wafted around her, fluttering her cotton *yukata* in teasing bursts.

Once inside the bath house, she was pleased to see that there were no other bathers. She looked fondly around her at the wooden walls and ceiling polished to a soft patina, glowing in the morning light that filtered through high screened windows. It was a comforting place, she thought as she reached out to touch the wood, well worn over the years to a satiny smoothness. A familiar pine scent enveloped her and there was a warmth, almost womb-like, in its sense of safe harbour. Today it was her own haven, her chosen place.

A *Yuna* removed her *yukata* and Sophie sat on the wooden stool provided at the side of the long hot tub, sipping warmed sake the *Yuna* had brought her, while she washed her down with pitchers of hot water, then massaged her with a sweet-smelling soap, her tiny fingers touching all the right spots, dissolving her tensions.

Sophie closed her eyes, lost in the sensual delight of the massage, recalling David's vivid descriptions of the *awa-odori*, or lather dance, and body-body massage where a naked girl, or girls, covered in creamy suds, would massage with her body every part of her male client, using her breasts, her thighs, her pubic hair, her whole body in a skilful foreplay, before further arousing him with prolonged oral and manual sex.

She looked at her own body, her small rounded breasts thrusting into erect nipples as the *Yuna* splashed water over them. She felt stimulated, the water here was especially invigorating, charged with an erotic, almost electric, quality that started to revive her and she felt the fatigue of the months of worry with David start to fall away.

Her massage over, the girl left after refilling Sophie's cup. Sipping her warmed *sake*, Sophie slipped into the deep water of the bath. It was hot, almost too hot to bear. Steam rose in lazy meandering vapours, and she laid her head back on the wooden railing, her hair caught up in a white turbanned towel, a stray tendril curling wetly around her neck.

Slowly she floated up moving her legs in a languorous circular movement, spreading them wide then letting them fall through the water, curving them in together as they touched bottom, then pushing up to the top again. As she opened them, a current of water like a hot rush of semen entered deep into her. She closed her eyes, lost in the erotic sensation as she spread her legs apart again and again, till the muscle walls of her vagina started to ache and throb with a life of their own in her dream world of *sake* and sensuality.

She felt someone move beside her, and opening her eyes saw a man standing only feet away deep in the water watching her with an intensity and aroused awareness. Close to climax and not wanting the sensation to stop, she paused, closing her eyes to shut out his face. Before she had time to think her next move, Sophie felt the water swirl beside her and a strong arm go under her back, cradling her beside him as his other hand started to caress her. Startled, she opened her eyes, and he smiled at her with a sweetness that made her fears of the unknown stranger dissolve. She felt a hazy reassurance in his strength, and her first desire to pull away from him receded as his hands expertly worked on her, slow and sure, then gathering momentum, building the vibrations in her body to hot spears of shock deep within her. She turned towards him, reaching for him as he bent his mouth to hers. His fingers never stopped, and she felt his penis grow hard as it thrust in and out of her cupped hands. Her whole body seemed to vibrate to his touch as she guided him into her and she moaned, all inhibitions laid aside as she came with a hunger and intensity matched only by his.

In that moment his arms went tight around her, and holding her close to him, his mouth still working hers, he pulled her under the water. It rose hot above them, like drowning in a sea of their desire. Just as quickly he released his hold and was gone, shooting away in one powerful movement as she rose gasping to the surface in time to see him emerge from the other side of the bath.

He turned, facing her, and drew his taut body to its full height.

She drew in her breath as the sun bounced off what appeared to be a panorama of swirling flowers, birds and dragons, glistening in multi-coloured profusion from his shoulders down his arms and torso to just above his knees. It was like beholding a tattooed warrior from a bygone age.

He looked steadily at her, then with a small bow and smile, turned and silently disappeared behind the *shoji* screened walls.

* * *

When she returned to the hotel, there was a message from Daihachi to call him. 'I have arranged a meeting for you,' he said. 'It's with someone who may be able to give you information on Katsura Kurosawa. He will meet you at the Teikoku Hotel at eight this evening. Can you be there?'

'Yes, that's fine,' Sophie answered, 'how will I . . . ?' But he had already rung off.

She wished that David was with her. Since her interlude in the bath house, she'd experienced a heightened awareness of her sexuality, a physical need for him which was not helped now by her solitary state. Lying back, she closed her eyes and thought of the jagged peaks of the West Maui mountains rising in dark contrast to the sharp green of the canefields spread out below them. David was in her arms, and the scent of *awapuhi*, the yellow ginger blossom that grew wild all over the island, lent an exotic dimension to their love-making. Whatever happens, I will always love him, she thought.

The intrusive wailing of a passing ambulance jolted her back to the present. She sat up, thinking about the coming meeting that evening. She would arrange a hire car to drive her there and make Tokyo her base for the next few days. It was time she started to make contact with Satoshi, and do some of Hiroko's bidding.

The missing tapes were still worrying her. Somehow she couldn't quite shake off the feeling that maybe it was linked to her meeting with Daihachi. There was something about him. What was it? she wondered. There was a gentleness there, almost an old-world graciousness in his manner that was masking an anger and sense of desperation. When she had played back the tape of their conversation, she had been touched by his obvious love for his son, Hiroshi. Then she remembered there was something he'd said that had struck an odd note, and she couldn't quite place it. She would have to play it through again.

* * *

Daihachi awoke wet with perspiration, and the overlapping fear of yet another bad dream. He lay looking at the moonlight sifting through the shutters, reliving his phantoms of the night, their images replaying as reality.

He was in a small boat, rowing down the Sumida river. The current was swift and it carried him effortlessly in a most pleasing way. All along the banks were families picnicking in the park. It was the *Sakura Ohanami*, and everywhere the trees were heavy with blossom. Letting the current do the work for him, he lay back resting on a cushion, feeling warmed by the sun and secure in the gentle rocking motion of his little boat. A light wind had sprung up, and as it did, the blossom began to lift from the trees like a swarm of pink butterflies and float across the water. With them came the plaintive sounds of a *koto* and a voice singing pure and clear.

Sakura, sakura
Yayoi no sorawa
Miwatasu kagiri
Kasumi ka? Kumo ka?
Asahi ni ni o o,
Izaya! Izaya!
Mini yukan.[13]
Sakura! Sakura!
Cherry blossoms everywhere.
In the mountains and meadows,
Misty and so beautiful.
Come with me! Let's go and see
Cherry blossom time.

As he listened the wind grew stronger, and the blossom in the air above him became thicker and thicker. Anxiety gripped him, and he sat up and started to turn his boat towards the bank where he could see his wife and children. His youngest son Hiroshi was smiling at him, and calling 'Father! Father!'

The sky was darkening, and the wind had become a gale as the blossom grew thicker and thicker, filling his boat as desperately he tried to row towards them. But the current was far stronger now and the blossoms swirling around him were turning into a maelstrom.

He tried to brush the blossom from his arms and as he did, he saw to his horror that they had turned to drops of blood, and the heavens were raining blossoms of blood. He could hear Hiroshi's voice still calling 'Father! Father!' but getting fainter and fainter. In anguish he called back to him but his voice was lost in the howling of the winds. Desperately he tried to brush the blossom aside, but they were sticking in bloodied heaps to his arms and legs. Scooping water from the river, he washed them away, and watched as the churning waters turned red.

Now wide awake and feverish, Daihachi was aware that he was still rubbing his arms as if to wipe away the blood of his dream. Turning on the light, he looked across the sparsely furnished ten-mat room to where his wife would have lain beside him. She too was gone, long gone with their original house in the terrible fires that followed the bombings in the war. All he treasured most was now gone. His mind dwelt on his dream and he thought of the young men in the Cherry Blossom Squadron who had chosen to sacrifice their lives in their final glorious death dives on the enemy. He had heard them leave the Usa navy base, their Betty aircraft loaded with the winged blue *Oka* bombs, their nose cones painted with the cherry blossom symbol, in which these young gods would fly their final deadly mission.

It was only later he had heard that their attempts to reach the enemy had failed. Would they have worn the same haunted expression beneath their white *hachimaki* which Hiroshi had carried with him to his death at Pearl Harbor early in the war? He whispered,

If only we might fall
Like cherry blossoms in the spring
So pure and radiant.[14]

The girl Sophie's face floated into his mind and he

thought of her. She exuded familiarity. He wondered about her real reason for seeking out Katsura Kurosawa. The false name his older son had used in Hawaii before the war was known to only a very few. What was his link with this girl?

His son's attempt to cover his reaction had not hidden the note of fear Daihachi detected in his voice when he'd told him of her request. What was hidden in that chapter of his son's life that he didn't want uncovered? Daihachi recalled how, in the early years of the occupation, the Americans had searched for this Katsura Kurosawa, a 'Class A' war criminal they had called him. Hah! To them, maybe. Still, he wondered what Atsuo had done in those years away to merit their continuing search and desire for retribution. He decided then that for his wife and Hiroshi's sake, he would find out. As if to pay Daihachi back for loving Hiroshi and mourning him so deeply, Atsuo had not made his life any easier in the past years. There was always that steel edge to his politeness, and the strength of the Isawa-*gumi* to back his every wish.

Maybe through this girl he could find out the things he wanted to know, but he would have to move carefully. His son must never know.

49

AT THE TEIKOKU HOTEL—TOKYO

As the car drove into the Teikoku (Imperial) Hotel, Sophie noticed that the irises were in full bloom in a large lily pond at the entranceway. They gave her fresh heart as she went in through the immense swinging doors to the foyer, then up the steps into the hotel mezzanine. It was packed with people, and she wondered how she would ever know this stranger without any helpful description from Daihachi Isawa.

A bellboy approached her, and with a small bow, asked, 'Sophie Chapman-san?'

She nodded in surprise. 'Please come with me,' he requested. She followed him as he threaded his way to a table at the far corner of the Grill room, softly lit and secluded from the surrounding hubbub.

A tall distinguished Japanese man, his hair silvery white, rose to greet her, using his stick to help him. His face was partly hidden by heavy-framed dark glasses, and she noticed his skin stretched taut and shiny as though from old scar tissue. His suit was impeccably tailored.

'Mrs Chapman?' His English was without the usual American accent, which surprised her, in fact with very little traceable accent at all.

She could feel his eyes studying her as he introduced

himself. Strangely enough, she had none of the nervousness that often accompanied a first-time meeting.

'I hope you didn't find the trip here tiring.'

She smiled and said, 'No.'

'I thought we'd dine a little later, but first a drink?' he asked.

'A dry martini, please.' She waited for him to speak again, then when he didn't, she said, 'Daihachi-san said that you may have news regarding a Mr Katsura Kurosawa?'

He didn't answer her at once, just studied her quite deliberately, so she rushed on to fill the silence. 'Perhaps he mentioned to you that I'm researching for a book I'm writing.'

He gave a slow nod, and she went on. 'I only plan to be here a short while, and Katsura-san's name was given to me as someone who may be of help.'

'Who gave you his name?'

She hadn't expected this, and wondered whether to give Gerard's name or not. She decided not to and said, 'My grandmother actually.'

'Your grandmother?'

'Yes, she is Japanese herself, and knew him.'

'And your grandmother's name?' he asked.

'Hiroko-san,' she answered, 'Hiroko Sen,' she added, using her grandmother's maiden name, remembering Gerard's advice to keep the Baillieu name out of any conversation regarding Katsura.

'Ah so,' he said. He paused a long time, looking at her.

Sophie sipped her drink, nervously now. She sensed he was not a man to be trifled with. She now felt at once acutely aware of his every reaction. Although his movements were studied and quite restrained, this somehow made her all the more aware of them. Her early feeling of comparative ease had now been replaced by one of wariness.

Guile would be of little use here, she decided. Gerard had advised that 'attack is often the best form of defence', and she decided to get straight to the point. She smiled at him and said, 'There seems to be some mystery surrounding Katsura-san. Whenever his name is mentioned, I don't seem to get very far. Can you tell me why?' She looked at him expectantly, awaiting his answer.

It was surprising, he thought, what a shrinking world we live in. Despite all the care he had taken, he was now to be confronted with a past life, and one he thought he had long laid to rest. His first inkling of its re-emergence was when his father Daihachi had contacted him the night before.

'That name has come up again. Someone is looking for Katsura Kurosawa,' Daihachi said.

'Ah, and who is it this time?' he asked, the anxiety in his voice barely veiled.

'A young woman. She wanted to see me, and naturally I checked on her first.'

'Who is she?'

'Mrs Sophie Chapman, an American-born Japanese.'

'And what did you tell her?'

'Nothing really.' The old man hesitated. He resented the way this son always got straight to the point. There was never any subtlety, no softening nuance within which to pause while gathering one's thoughts. It had always been the same way with him. A feeling of resentment rose as Daihachi's thoughts went back to Hiroshi, and the sadness he'd experienced when the notes of the *Umi Yukaba* washed over him once more.

'Father.' The voice had a steely note now. 'What did you say to her?'

'Oh, just that I knew someone who may be able to help her,' Daihachi replied.

'Ahhhhh!'

'I mean, it was all so sudden, I got quite a surprise,' the old man hurried on as if to compensate for what he could now see had been a foolish mistake. His son's drawn out 'ah' had put him at once at a disadvantage.

'She's writing a book on the war and wanted to

include the Japanese point of view, and this name had been given to her.'

'By whom?' his son cut in.

'She didn't say. What was I to do?'

Atsuo ignored the plea in his father's voice, and his words took on a harshness now.

'Ring her back and make sure she's at the Teikoku Hotel tomorrow evening at eight,' and he'd rung off.

His first glimpse of her as she walked across the room to his table from the mezzanine had confirmed his worst fears. It was one of them, that family who still occasionally haunted his dreams. She carried herself with the same confidence, and moved with a fluid grace for one so small. It wasn't until she was nearer his table that he suddenly felt a shiver run through him, and he braced himself for the confrontation.

At first he thought it was Gina, that mouth and tilt of her head. No, she was too young. But there was a strong likeness, that cool assessment when she looked at him, with large eyes as dark as his own. He felt somehow drawn to her, but at the same time his mind raced. Who was she really, and how best to sidetrack her? It was all so long ago, yet as he looked at her it seemed as if it was only yesterday, and memories moved across his inner eye as sharply defined as if he was just seeing them.

He had ordered a whisky, and as he raised his glass, she noticed that the top digit of the little finger on his left hand was missing. It made the other fingers look too long, she thought. His stout walking stick was beside his chair and she wondered if he had been in a bad accident at some time. It would explain the burn scars on his face.

When Sophie told him Hiroko's name, he gazed at her as if suddenly a veil had been lifted. Yes, it was Gina's mouth, Gina's delicacy, he thought, and so this must be her daughter. As he looked at her again, taking her all in with a new intensity, he felt his heart start to pound.

This must be her child; then she must be his. He could see that now. The hands, the way she held herself, there was a hint of his late mother's mannerisms. He steeled himself to give nothing away and to continue his questioning.

He wondered about Gina and what her life would be like now. It was but a passing thought, as she had long been swept aside by others, most of all his own wife, Mariko.

As he looked at Sophie, he thought, she would be twenty-five or twenty-six. That would make her two years older than his son, Yasunari. She was asking him a direct question again, and he frowned, thinking how unlike his younger daughter Sumiko she was, who would never have dared to be so bold. It was the girl's American side, he thought with distaste. He would have to somehow cover his father Daihachi's indiscretion, and make sure she had no way of discovering who he really was. He would need to keep a close watch on her, and direct her search as he wanted.

Sophie was smiling at him, waiting. He had a sudden flash of Gina's face with just such an expression. Memories long dormant of that last morning they had spent together arose to confront him. He had awakened, he recalled, to find Gina in a sarong with a *lei* of *lliahi* and plumeria strung across her shoulders, smiling at him as she came into the room with steaming coffee. The memory of her sweetly perfumed *lei* and the promise of that full mouth, even now, rekindled a faint reminder of the passion of their love-making. He knew it to be their last, so it had had an intensity, he remembered, that had surprised and delighted her but left him with a bitter after-taste. He could hear her voice, 'Oh darling, to think we can do this for a whole lifetime,' and recalled his own cold withdrawal at her words and presumption. Quite deliberately, he now held onto that coldness as he looked at the girl.

He hadn't answered her at once, but Sophie felt the chill that had descended.

'Do you know anything that might help me?' she repeated.

Any answer was precluded by the waiter arriving with

their meal, and the ensuing bustle swept aside her question for the moment. Sophie noticed the waiter treated her host with almost fearful deference.

In a warmer tone, Atsuo turned to her and said, 'I took the liberty of ordering before you arrived, I hope it's to your liking.'

How interesting, she thought with pleasure, that he should have chosen a *Kaiseki-ryori* meal, as she watched the superbly presented dishes arrive. It was traditionally the light repast served with the tea ceremony during the *Ashikawa* period, she remembered, to provide a delicate sustenance to the stomach before drinking the often harsh green tea. Aesthetically it was the ultimate in Japanese preparation of food, and she ate with relish and a sense of homecoming.

The *Zensai* or hors d'oeuvres were a *Takara-yaki Tamago* and a delicate *Ikura-no-Yuzugama*, and she savoured their sharp freshness and the harmony of presentation of each course as it arrived on the shining lacquer ware.

She decided a change of tactics was called for and so began to chat and warm up this strangely remote man. To hell with Gerard's ploy she thought, you catch more flies with honey. However, it wasn't until they'd nearly finished their meal that she realised he had cleverly controlled the whole direction of their conversation, and that she was talking of Hawaii and her early life there quite freely now.

'Your mother is a writer too?' he asked.

Sophie hesitated a moment, then thought, well he doesn't know our family name, so it won't hurt to tell him.

'Actually she died when I was born,' she said, looking away from him.

He felt a momentary stilling of his senses.

'I'm sorry,' he murmured.

Remembering why she had come, and thinking a twist of the knife wouldn't go amiss, she added, 'Strangely enough, I was born the day your countrymen bombed Pearl Harbor.'

'Ah, I see,' he said. He bowed his head, and seemed lost in his own thoughts.

'And now,' she continued, 'maybe we can talk again of Katsura-san.'

'Of course,' he said, collecting himself. 'It seems you will have to do your research elsewhere.'

'Really?'

'Yes,' he said as if it had only just occurred to him. 'Katsura-san died over five years ago. My father was not sure of the dates and didn't like to disappoint you.'

He watched her face grow pale, and went on quickly to circumvent the questions he could see would be forthcoming.

'It seemed he had been suffering from a form of tuberculosis, and was ill for many years. No doubt his end was a blessed relief,' he added, to soften the blow.

'Where? Where did he . . .?' she paused, shrinking from the finality of that word.

She was like a young salmon smoult, he thought, viewing her dispassionately, who swims up the current of scent to seek out its birthplace, the spawning grounds where it was born. It's as if some magical signal of smell is locked within their senses to enable them to find their own stream, despite the obstacles they encounter. But this, he decided, was to be her final attempt.

The full force of Gina's death had momentarily taken him aback. The irony of her dying while giving birth to his child at almost the same time his brother Hiroshi had gallantly died, and all partly as a result of his own involvement in the Islands, only added to his bitterness. To him, the whole debacle was felt as something still unresolved. What had started out so well, had ended in the humiliation of his nation with the signing of their unconditional surrender aboard the USS *Missouri*. The battle was lost, but the war was far from finished, he brooded. It would never be over in his mind until they were truly victors once more and the red sun flew proudly over all.

But this girl had opened a door he wished to remain closed. Nothing was to be gained by rekindling that relationship, only certain danger to himself and his family. Katsura's death would surely signify a severance in her search, he decided.

'He must have other relatives here I could speak to,' Sophie was saying.

'But how would that help in your research?' he asked.

She was jolted back to her supposed reason for finding him.

'Oh,' she answered, 'there may be papers or . . .'

He came in quickly, 'I'm sure there are many others who could probably help further your work even better, Mrs Chapman.'

'No doubt,' she murmured, still upset by her discovery and wanting only to end their meeting now.

She thanked him, and as she rose to go, with a backwards glance said, 'I just don't feel as though he's dead. I just don't feel it.'

Atsuo stayed on for some time after she had gone. He would have to organise a back-dated funeral notice, and even a shrine to satisfy her, he thought with a grim smile.

50

HIROKO'S LETTER—TOKYO

Satoshi had agreed to meet her.

Memories of his Aunt Michiko's meanderings during the last days of her illness had spurred him on to find out more, to fill in the spaces of his life that were still a mystery. Maybe this was his chance to dispel once and for all some of those unknown nightly spectres that had haunted his dreams as a child.

One phrase of his aunt's in particular had remained with him, offering a promise that could overcome many of the financial problems that beset him now.

'Hiroko has taken your inheritance,' Michiko had whispered. 'She has great treasure that is rightfully yours.'

'What treasure?' he'd asked. But she went on as if not heeding him.

'You must get it back, Satoshi, promise me, you owe it to your father, Noboru.' She reached out to him with the cold hands of a dying person, knowing full well that this would be the emotional lever he would respond to.

Michiko had seen to it that Noboru had become the guiding light in Satoshi's life, regaling him with inflated stories of his father's prowess and achievements from an early age. That they related only in passing to the actual truth mattered little. With the onset of multiple sclerosis, this often cruel, angry figure of his childhood had withered to a gaunt wreck of a woman he found extremely distasteful. The stale smell of impending death already pervaded her room.

'And I'll tell you something else,' she had added, leaning towards him, 'but it's for your ears only, 'Toshi-chan. Her American husband's death was no accident.' He recoiled from the fetid breath that rose towards him.

'What do you mean, Aunt?'

She had looked at him, her head shaking in the perpetual rhythm of her disease, her eyes like polished boot buttons with a brightness that conveyed no depths. He remembered that same expression when he was only five, as she had held his hand to a flame to sear into his consciousness forever that fires were not to be played with.

'Just that,' she said. She looked away from him, closing her eyes, and was silent.

He rose to go, and as he reached the door she suddenly called out to him, her voice warm and wheedling.

'Satoshi-chan.' He turned to her. 'You may need help to get what you want.' She was silenced by a fit of coughing. He waited impatiently for her to stop. From a side table, she took a card and held it out to him. 'Here, take it,' she wheezed. 'When the time comes, just tell him what you want.' She paused. 'His grandfather handled the other job for me, very well, and from what I hear the grandson is just like him. He'll help you—he owes me that.'

* * *

Sophie looked at the man who was her long-lost uncle, Hiroko's beloved son and the half-brother of her late mother Gina and Uncle Gerard. It was hard to reconcile this neat middle-aged man with the person who had been the hub of her grandmother's longing and anguish all these years. Every now and then she could catch a glimpse of a faint family likeness to Gerard, but in reality they were like chalk and cheese, she thought. He held himself with a military bearing, and she sensed an immense pride and ego beneath his veneer of politeness. He had refused her offer of a drink, and sat quite still, waiting for what she had to say. She had set aside an hour for their meeting, and was going on to a party at the American Embassy afterwards, which Gerard had arranged for her to attend before she'd left Hawaii.

Sophie felt an antagonism towards this self-contained man which she tried not to show. How could he have never wanted to seek out his mother? What had caused such a resentment that in all these years he had made no contact with her at all? Since learning of Katsura, she had had only one desire and that was to find her father. As she thought of him, a sadness filled her when she remembered the words of that strange man, telling her that Katsura was dead. She still couldn't reconcile herself to the thought. Not until she could see proof with her own eyes.

Forcing a smile, Sophie said to Satoshi, 'I have brought a letter for you from . . . from Hiroko-san, my grandmother.' She emphasised the 'my' with a tilt of her chin. 'She's very ill,' she paused, lowering her voice, 'in fact, she may not have very long at all,' skirting any direct reference to the word 'dying'. 'Hiroko-san asked me to give you this, and she requested if you could please let me have your answer before I leave.'

'And when is that?' Satoshi asked, taking the letter from her.

'I fly out tomorrow afternoon.'

'Then I shall read it now,' he said to her surprise, quickly unsealing the envelope and taking out the single sheet.

Sitting opposite him, Sophie tried unobtrusively to observe him as he read. His face gave no hint of reaction to what he saw, and if anything seemed completely devoid of emotion. He was a handsome man, but she sensed his coldness towards her.

So, his mother was dying. She had died for him so

long ago. This was not his mother, but some stranger from another land, and the young girl sitting opposite him was not of his blood. Not to him. His mother may be her grandmother but they were part of a life that wasn't his and never would be. He felt the corrosive bitterness of rejection as he always had.

Shadowy memories floated across his mind, then one stayed with him. There it was, a face smiling down at him and saying 'Toshi-chan, Toshi-chan,' then picking him up and swirling him around as she chanted 'Toshi-chan, Toshi-chan, po po po po, Toshi-chan!'

Behind her was a tall man with hair the same colour as the golden tendrils encircling the heads of the fierce-looking *kami* he had seen on the giant floats at the *Nebute Matsuri* at *Hirosaki*. His surge of happiness was stilled in that instant. The man was holding out his cupped hands to him with a look of expectation on his face. They had a strange smell, and he didn't like the smell of him, and he stepped back until he felt the softness of his mother's skirts envelop him from behind.

The man had opened his fingers a little and a faint whirring sound came from within. Satoshi looked up in surprise. A *kirigirisu*!! He hoped it was a *suzumushi* or bell cricket with its wonderful sound, to add to his collection. He reached up for it and looked at the big hands with their funny yellow hairs on the back as they transferred the insect into his. But it had only been an ordinary *kirigirisu,* his disappointment momentary, as he was still pleased to have it.

Satoshi remembered he had looked up at him with new interest, then back to his mother, and she was smiling at this man in a way he wanted for himself alone. He resented her smiling that way at this stranger, and even now could feel that sudden stab of jealousy.

Sophie's voice cut through his memories. He looked across at her.

'So what can I tell my grandmother?' she asked.

Satoshi's thoughts went back to the letter. It contained a lot of sentimental statements that were lost on him and which he pushed aside for the one line which meant anything.

'There are some business matters of mutual interest which we should discuss,' Hiroko had written. He smiled grimly, of more than interest to me, he thought. He rose. 'I will book a flight for next week,' he said.

'Hiroko-san will be pleased, it has been a very long time,' Sophie couldn't resist adding, then went on, 'Anyway, let me know your time of arrival and I'll pick you up. You'll be our guest and . . .'

'No,' he said quickly. 'I'll stay at an hotel.'

'If you wish,' she answered with a sense of relief. If that was how he wanted to play it, well then let him, she thought.

'I will contact you with the details before you leave tomorrow,' he said, and with a slight inclination of his head, he left.

* * *

Later that evening, as she dressed for the party, Sophie reflected on her meeting with Satoshi and wondered why he had agreed to come to Hawaii. His manner had indicated no softening towards his mother, no anxiety for her welfare.

She thought of Hiroko's longings for her son, her memories still tied to a child who had clung to her heart from the past. A child who had been wrenched away before they had lived through the natural course of their shared destiny. What did those past memories have to do with the man her grandmother would have to face now?

Sophie had read somewhere that 'we possess nothing but the past', but it was one thing to possess, another to be possessed. And yet these fleeting figures from the past were like a summoning to Gethsemane for a reckoning in the areas of light and shade, the black and white which lodged within one's soul. Vainly she had fed in a mass of new experiences, facts and figures, yet there were these old ghosts, laughing on the sidelines in the recesses of her mind.

Sophie picked up her ivory elephant necklace and thought of those ancient creatures of the wild which had so captured her imagination.

Amongst the piles of David's press photographs, she had seen a shot of a rhino lying on its side beside a waterhole, its horn hacked from its head. She could almost hear the sound of sawing through living tissue of densely massed hair compressed to form this handsome horn of potency, so desired by many, yet preserved by so few.

She wondered if this ancient creature—clothed in a skin tough to the touch yet tender enough to burn beneath an African sun—was aware as it stumbled to that muddy waterhole that it was moving into the final phase of its ponderous journey. And all for the price of a horn.

'Why do they do it?' she'd asked David, looking at the piles of elephant tusks and rhino horns in his photographs.

'Black magic,' he said. 'The horns become aphrodisiacs, mostly for the Eastern market,' he grinned at her, 'or for whoever thinks it will work,' he'd said.

Could so much wishful magic be vested in that one clown's hat of compressed hair? Would mere rendering to a powder or potion give a promise to prolong the ecstasy of an act that at its best was a fleeting voyage into the mysteries of the flesh, at its worst a loveless copulation which was done almost before it had begun? Was it mere mockery, a bad joke devised by a few to rip off the many in a base and soulless search? Surely it harboured a taste that would turn all sweetness into soured regret, just as the creamy up-thrusting tusks of a kindred creature, the mammoth king of the forest, promised untold riches through an illusion of beauty.

She could see the herds of elephant moving in majestic slow motion towards the waiting weaponry in stealthy poachers' hands ready to hack and wrench the prize from its proper place, leaving behind only tears of blood.

Sophie fingered the creamy beauty of the ivory now lying cool and smooth against her skin. It had been Jill's present to her on her seventeenth birthday. 'It's a really special piece,' Jill had assured her.

Carved and polished to its present pleasing facsimile of the creature from which it came, it was a far cry from its home place, the savannah of the mighty *Ruwenzori*, the Mountains of the Moon. Yet there were no wisps of skin, no rotting flesh, no tears and frantic trumpetings of the tiny calf running around its mother still ensnared by steel biting into flesh. She looked and thought, I know, I remember from where and how you came. One glacial diamond eye studding her elephant's head winked in unseeing complicity.

51

A MEETING WITH THE *OYABUN*

Matsuhiro looked across the room at the girl Hiro had indicated to him. She was chatting and laughing with a tall American, one of the consular staff, he noted. She was pretty, very pretty. Not pure Japanese he could see, and there was something about her he couldn't quite place.

'She had a meeting with my uncle, you say?' Matsuhiro asked. 'What was it about?'

'I don't know,' Hiro answered. 'Only that they met at the Teikoku Hotel and had dinner.'

'Maybe he fancies her,' Matsuhiro smiled.

Hiro looked surprised. 'No, I'm sure it's nothing like that.'

'Well, let's find out what it was about.'

Sophie had felt the dark eyes studying her so was not surprised when he was introduced to her.

'I believe you have already met my uncle,' he began, 'Atsuo Isawa-san.'

'Why yes,' she answered, wondering how he knew.

'He mentioned you to me,' he said with a smile.

'Really? Regarding my father?' she asked, without thinking, her mind still on the news of Katsura's death.

'Yes,' he said, hoping she would supply him with further details.

'Are you able to tell me any more about him then?' She turned her full attention to him now, biting her lip at her indiscretion, but thinking, maybe he knows something.

'What in particular did you want to know?' he parried.

'Whatever you can tell me,' she answered. 'About his illness, his death, anything you can.' What game was he playing?

He studied her.

'When did you last see your father?'

Sophie looked at him, pretending surprise. 'I can see your uncle hasn't told you very much at all.'

'You're right,' Matsuhiro went on, 'our conversation was very brief, so maybe you had better fill me in, and then we'll see if I can be of any assistance.' He took her by the arm and started to move towards the door. 'But let's go where it's a little quieter.' Expertly, he steered her through the crowd and out into the large courtyard.

It was a truly lovely building, Sophie thought, looking back at the colonnaded room that ran the length of the raked pebble courtyard. Her eyes wandered over its graceful lines, the floor-length windows overflowing with light and music. Matsuhiro had motioned to the waiter with his tray of drinks, and taken command of the situation quite naturally, she noted. Clearly he was accustomed to a position of authority.

As he raised his glass, she saw that the upper digit of the little finger on his right hand, too, was missing. She felt slightly uncomfortable with him, but pushed aside her sense of unease. She hadn't got far with his uncle, and what did it matter if they knew now that Katsura was her father.

'You were saying?' he prompted her.

'Actually I have never met my father,' Sophie turned to him. 'He left Hawaii before I was born.'

'His name?'

'Why, Katsura Kurosawa,' she said, 'surely your uncle must have mentioned him.' Her words trailed away; she was suddenly aware of his sudden reptilian stillness.

'He didn't mention it?' she repeated.

He looked at her and with a slow smile and slight bow, said, 'Why yes, of course. It had just momentarily slipped my mind.'

She thought, he was not a person who would easily forget a name, any name.

Matsuhiro noticed her hands nervously reaching for her necklace, and scrutinised her more closely. The flash of the ivory elephant's eye offset the big square-cut diamonds in her ears. She had an expensive air, he thought, there was no shortage of money there. And yes, there was something of his uncle in her. The old dog had kept his secret well. He wondered if his father Akira had ever been told. But no, he was sure he hadn't. Akira had told him of Atsuo's magnificent surveillance operation in Hawaii before the Pearl Harbor bombing as the double agent, Katsura Kurosawa, but never any mention of this. He wondered if Atsuo had been supporting the girl and her mother all these years. No, he discounted that idea. His father would surely have known. Maybe she was as much of a surprise to his Uncle Atsuo as she was to himself. He could barely stop from laughing out loud at the thought.

'So what can you tell me about him?' Sophie asked.

'Probably not much more than what he has already told you,' he said, his mind racing with his newfound knowledge. So his mealy mouthed old uncle had a daughter, and a *gaijin*! He wondered about the mother, no doubt American, he surmised. Then just as quickly he thought that Atsuo must not know that he knew his secret. Not yet.

'Will you be seeing my uncle again?' he asked.

'No,' she answered, 'I fly home tomorrow, and he said he'd send me the documentation regarding my father's death.'

'To you or your mother?' Matsuhiro asked, his fingers lightly steepled.

Sophie smiled wistfully at him. 'My mother died when I was born.'

'Ahhh,' was all he said.

'You knew my father?'

'It's many years since we met.'

'He was ill then?' she continued.

'Yes, and had been for a long time.'

To cut short their meeting, Matsuhiro rose to his feet and, bowing slightly, said, 'It appears I can't add much more to what my uncle has already told you. And now I won't keep you from the party.' He seemed anxious to get away, she thought. And there was something he'd said that didn't quite correlate with what she had already been told.

'I must be going anyway, I have a long day tomorrow.' She hesitated then added, 'What was the illness my father had for so long?'

'You didn't know? My uncle didn't tell you?'

She shook her head, her face open, waiting.

'It was a disease,' he paused, 'of the blood.'

'Of the blood?'

'Yes, leukemia and very bad.' Matsuhiro shook his head, clicking his tongue in sympathy.

Sophie stood, feeling suddenly very tired.

'It was nice meeting you,' she said, extending her hand, 'and thank you.'

With a brief bow, he left.

'I want you to find out all you can about her,' Matsuhiro said to Hiro on his way to the car. 'Everything. Also about her family in Hawaii, everything there is to know. And that goes right back till before her birth.'

'That far?' asked Hiro.

'As far as it takes,' said Matsuhiro. 'And no hint of this must reach my uncle, or the girl.'

What a bonus, he thought. He wasn't sure yet how he would use it against Atsuo, but use it he would, when the time came.

'Information is the second most valuable commodity you can have,' his father Akira had once told him.

'And the first?'

'Come, you tell me,' Akira had quipped. Matsuhiro

thought rapidly, then replied, 'The power to act upon it.' His father had laughed his explosive laugh, and nodded, gazing fondly at his son.

Matsuhiro mulled over what his father had told him about his Uncle Atsuo's part in the undercover work in Hawaii before the war, and the name he'd used—Katsura Kurosawa. It seemed he'd dallied in a trifle more than mere politics, with a *gaijin* daughter to show for it . . . *ne*! Even Akira hadn't known that juicy piece of information, or he surely would have told his only son.

Later that evening, as he thrust his way into the soft wet flesh of the young girl he'd had brought to his room, thoughts of the information he'd just received spun through his brain. He pushed his way into her, thrusting harder and harder as though seeking the knowledge that he needed to know. She cried out in pain but he took no notice. Before she was brought to his room, he had asked that they insert the tiny silver *rin-no-tama* balls deep into her vagina and now he could feel them tickling the tip of his penis and hear the faint high-pitched hum of their vibration as he swayed them to action.

She was on a bed kneeling on all fours as he stood and came into her from behind, and he could see that her slender arms were beginning to tremble. With a grunt of disgust, he stood up, working his penis with his hands as if willing the elusive climax to come. She had turned to face him, still on her knees, her head bowed in shame. Dressed in only the frilly crotchless panties she'd been told he liked, and with the up-thrust of her tiny breasts, she seemed younger than her fourteen years, but this *yakuza oyabun* preferred his girls and boys young. As *oyabun* of the powerful Isawa-*gumi*, the numerous *mizu shobai* clubs, love hotels and gay bars he owned provided an endless stream of *pan-pan* girls and *bishonen* for his pleasure.

Lately it had been long-lashed, willowy Filipino boys, some as young as ten, brought in to feed his sexual appetite. An avid reader of the more sado-masochistic and *ero manga*, Matsuhiro would have his loyal *koban* set up some of the wilder scenarios for him to play out his sexual fantasies. It lent a certain spice. Tonight his walls were alive with giant television screens playing the erotic videos that currently turned him on.

The girl looked up, fearful of his reaction. She recalled how earlier his servant with her large fingers had oiled her in preparation for the *oyabun*, and the sharp pain as the woman roughly tried to insert the two *rin-no-tama* balls into her tightly resisting vagina. Then the woman's oiled hands were massaging her nipples and her breath was hot on her as she sucked at them to arouse her to relax and open up, and her obvious excitement as she felt the girl resist, then writhe as the balls slid into her. She did not want to go through that again.

With a shy smile, she reached up and placed tentative fingers around his large wet organ, now erect and engorged, the blue veins standing out on its rigid shaft like writhing serpents, and she started to give the *fingaa sabisu* she had been taught. Roughly he pushed her hands aside, and moving close in to her face, pushed his penis into her mouth. He felt her draw back, then lacing her long hair tight between his fingers, he held her head in hard, and her tongue started slowly to work on him, only stopping when he sensed the gagging motion of her throat.

Ah, that was better, he thought. This was more like it. His thoughts of the evening started to recede as with grunts and cries he thrust his way into her throat, feeling his slow passion mount as he roughly worked her towards his climax.

* * *

From the entrance of the consulate, Sophie had seen Matsuhiro driven away in the long black Cadillac, its darkened windows somehow adding to the effect of threat and mystery. But not before she noticed a black-tinted window glide down on a following car, and a very beautiful young girl, little more than a child, peering out anxiously. A nuggety chauffeur standing waiting in dark sunglasses at the side of the car quickly motioned her to raise the window. Sophie noticed another older man also in a dark suit and glasses appear at the side of the limo and get in beside the girl.

They had the air of hoods, of bodyguards, she thought. Matsuhiro Isawa seemed to travel with quite an entourage, but he alone had come to the party. Then she recalled that the second older bodyguard had also been there lurking in the background. She had a sudden feeling that she had seen him before, in another place.

Later that night as she relaxed in the bath, letting all the tensions of the day slide away in its warmth, her mind went back to their conversation earlier in the evening. It was strange that her father seemed to have died from two quite different diseases. Either Matsuhiro was pretending he knew more than he did to see what she could tell him, or he or his uncle was lying. Or, she hesitated, maybe they were both lying and there was something they didn't want her to know about her father. At least now she had something more tangible for Gerard to work with. He'd know what to do, she thought with relief. All she wanted to do now was to get back home, and see David.

PART FIVE

52

HIROKO'S WISH—HONOLULU

'Do you want me to stay when he comes, Oba-San?' Sophie asked. 'Malo is picking him up from the Moana, and he should be here in twenty minutes.'

She looked at her grandmother, so tiny and frail, like a small dove settling back against the cushions. The dark blue rings beneath her eyes somehow gave her pale skin an almost translucent look.

Hiroko was propped up on the velvet chaise longue in her lovely room overlooking the gardens that fell in a luxuriant mass of greenery and flowers down to the sea. She had insisted on being fully dressed, and at the last moment decided to wear a silvery-blue silk kimono which somehow accentuated her slight frame. Her small feet encased in white *tabi* were propped up on the cushions. Sophie had brushed her hair and coiled it tightly into the nape of her neck.

'Will you pass me my mirror, Sophie-chan?' Gazing into it, Hiroko sighed deeply.

'Let me put some colour on your cheeks.' Sophie deftly brushed the high cheek bones with rouge, and gave a little smile.

'I remember Hattie-san saying "it's like putting on the war paint after . . ."' Hiroko paused as a spasm of pain passed through her chest, '". . . after the war is over",' she whispered.

Sophie felt quick tears come to her eyes and said quickly, 'Don't be silly darling. There!' Sophie stood back, her head to one side, appraising her handiwork. 'Now, what about the pearls?'

Hiroko nodded and Sophie slipped a long string of perfectly matched creamy pearls around her grandmother's neck, offsetting the pearl and diamond earrings she always wore. As she felt them lying cool against her skin, Hiroko looked up and said, 'After today they are yours, Sophie-chan.'

Sophie gave her a quick hug then said, 'I think a little colour is needed,' and she took two of the deep pink rose buds from a vase and pinned them to her grandmother's shoulder.

'If you don't mind Sophie-chan, I think I will see him alone,' Hiroko whispered. 'He might prefer that.'

No doubt, thought Sophie to herself, wondering if her uncle would warm up a little when he actually met his mother.

'I'll be just outside anyway, if you need me. Maybe I'll have a swim.'

Hiroko had drifted off to a light sleep, and didn't hear him arrive. She awoke with a start, conscious of eyes staring at her. At first she lay there just looking back, then slowly she reached out to him.

'Satoshi-chan,' she said, her voice thick with emotion. 'Satoshi-chan.'

He held himself erect, then bowed deeply.

'I have come,' he said, 'as you requested.'

This painted old lady was not the figure of his dreams, he thought. She was not the smiling young woman with her smooth cheeks, whose skirts he had clung to as a child. He felt disappointment like a leaden shroud envelop his heart.

She was like a shrunken effigy of all that he had imagined, almost as bad as his Aunt Michiko in her last days. It was almost impossible to believe that he had sprung from such a faded and spent thing. Thank goodness his father had not lived to see what she had become. He waited for her to speak again.

Hiroko tried to raise herself a little, but found it too difficult without help, so settled back, panting with the effort. 'Please,' she said, motioning him to the chair nearby. He sat down stiffly.

'You must excuse me,' she said, 'but it's difficult to move or talk easily,' she paused, gathering breath. 'My strength is not what it was.' She gave a tentative smile, and he drew back from it, seeing it more as a garish death mask. It's to be hoped she can hold on till whatever business she's proposing is completed and settled between us, he thought. To hasten the discussion, he said, 'You wrote that there were things we must talk about,' he said.

'Oh,' she answered vaguely, 'there's time for that, but first, some refreshments.' Hiroko rang the little bell beside her. 'We'll talk while we take tea.'

'As you wish,' he said.

He walked over to the French windows and out onto the lanai, staring out to the ocean beyond the gardens. He saw a figure swimming in the large pool at the far end of the lanai, with long graceful strokes propelling her effortlessly through the water. He could swim, he thought enviously, but not well—remembering those dreaded days when he was tossed over the side of the little boat by his *sensei* into the cold waters of the lake. His fear then prevented him ever mastering the art, and the sense of shame at failing to do so still stayed with him.

His only child, his seventeen-year-old son, Takeo, had more than made up for his father's lack of ability with an innate love of the water. He thought of Takeo and his heart warmed. The boy would have his rightful inheritance from this old woman, the grandmother he thought was already dead. He'd make sure of that. He must stifle his dislike of her, and tread carefully.

This place must be worth a fortune, Satoshi thought,

looking around at the sprawling buildings and vast gardens, and comparing it all to the small flat he had in Shibuya. He felt his resentment grow for this woman who claimed to be his mother. What had she ever done but shame him by marrying a *gaijin*, and then abandon him to the care of his hateful aunt. The injustice of it knifed through his heart as he walked back into the room where the maid was serving tea from a large trolley.

He felt out of place here, and stared at the old woman he couldn't even bring himself to call mother. He noticed that she neither ate nor drank, apart from a slice of peach and a few sips of tonic water.

''Toshi-chan, this must seem as strange to you as it does to me,' she said. 'There's so much to catch up with and . . .'

'I will not be staying long,' he cut across her. 'I have business elsewhere, so if we can discuss the matters now that you wished to bring up with me, I would appreciate it.'

She detected the harsh note in his voice and the inflexible look in his eye, and felt she saw the implacable ghost of Michiko. Her heart sank, and she thought, I must be brave, it will take time, but if I persist, maybe, maybe . . .

As if she hadn't heard him, she went on, 'Do you remember our happy summers spent at Lake Ashimoko?' She smiled up at him feebly. 'The time when you hid from Ume and me?' She went on and on, pausing occasionally to rest, panting a little, gathering strength.

He listened, matching her every endearing story in his mind with one of equal coldness and his sense of abandonment. He sat, gazing at her, letting her go on till his smouldering resentment flared up. 'Is this what you asked me to come and hear?' he asked, his voice full of repressed anger when eventually her reminiscing seemed to stop. He stood and started pacing the room, looking down at her, waiting for an answer. Hiroko returned his glance and knew that the steel edge of vengefulness had entered his heart. She closed her eyes and willed her failing strength not to desert her now.

'Satoshi,' she said, 'what of your Aunt Michiko?'

He stopped his pacing. 'She died some months ago,' he answered briefly.

'So!' Hiroko paused, feeling a vast sense of relief and release at the news. She crossed herself and murmured a prayer, asking forgiveness for her uncharitable thoughts. He looked at her in open rejection now.

There was a silence in the room, and she could hear the breakers rolling in from the *Waikiki* channel and, in the distance, Sophie's voice talking with Malo, who was now getting old like herself. A sudden coldness had gripped her heart as she gazed at this stern young man, sitting so still nearby. He sat as if poised for instant flight and a quick get-away, she thought. Was it too late now, to reach his heart?

Heavenly Father, please help me do what is right, she prayed. She felt she was looking at a stranger. Where was the little boy from so long ago? No hint of him was left in the implacable face of the man sitting opposite her. Rather than her own or Noboru's stamp, she saw more of the look and mannerisms of Michiko lurking there.

''Toshi-chan,' she whispered.

He looked at her coldly. This clinging old woman filled him with shame. 'Yes,' he said, waiting.

'Tell me a little of your life now. What of your wife and . . .'

He broke in. 'I understand you had business matters to discuss with me,' he reiterated. He had never learnt the power of charm. To him, it was a time-wasting exercise he wasn't going to indulge in now.

When she said nothing, he went on, anxious to bring their discussion to some kind of fruitful conclusion. 'Aunt Michiko said you have family money which is part of my inheritance,' he said. 'And that's what I am here to discuss.' He looked at her, waiting, but she didn't answer.

'She mentioned that there were some valuable things that must be rightfully passed on to me,' he went on, 'and I would like to talk about that now.'

Mustering her strength, Hiroko at length spoke, her voice silky. 'Did she say what they were?'

'Just that they were very valuable and were to be passed on to me,' he said, wishing he'd gleaned more from his aunt at the time.

'Ah, I see,' said Hiroko. Then changing direction, she went on, her voice gathering strength. 'Satoshi, did you receive your grandfather's sword?'

'Well of course, but that was years ago,' he said.

'And did you pay homage at his shrine?' she persisted.

'What has that got to do with now?' he said, getting up and starting to pace the floor again.

Hiroko sat up as straight as she could manage, a slow anger starting to feed her failing strength. So, Michiko had worked her poison on her son. She could see now how deeply it had eaten into him. He was here only for what he could get out of her. That was all. She felt cold with a growing anger for the injustice that had been done to her all those years ago, and now she was looking at the result of it. So it was too late, too late, but she would try just once more.

'Satoshi-chan,' she said, 'it seems your Aunt Michiko has misinformed you. It must have been the Sen family sword given to you after your grandfather died that she was thinking of. Let us talk now of each other, there's so much to catch up on.'

'Just who do you think you are?' he broke in, his voice falling like ice upon hot coals. 'I am Noboru Nakamura's only son, and Yukio Sen's grandson, and any of the family inheritance you took from them—*stole* from them—is rightfully mine now when you die.' He stared at her in open dislike. 'You abandoned me as a child; I owe you nothing.'

'Well, well,' Hiroko said, and her voice was light and cool. 'It seems you have made this long trip to no avail. As you can see, all I have now, which of course is not inconsiderable, is part of my Baillieu family. No doubt, Satoshi Nakamura,' she said emphasising his family name, 'as your Aunt Michiko would have told you many times, I am sure, the Baillieu family has nothing to do with you, or your inheritance.'

He could see now that he had underestimated this woman. He still couldn't bear to think of her as his mother, and now least of all. He stood over her, his face white with anger.

'So what are you telling me?' he said.

'As for your family treasure,' she went on, 'I have no idea what she was speaking about.'

'You lie!' he spat at her.

As he spoke, there was a light knock. Sophie entered the room, still wet from her swim, a towel slipped hastily around her hips.

She took in the scene at a glance, Satoshi in a threatening stance over her grandmother, and Hiroko sitting straight, her face so white that the rouge stood out like clown's spots.

'What's going on?' she asked, moving swiftly to her grandmother's side, and putting her arm around the frail shoulders.

'I'm taking my leave,' Satoshi said curtly. Sophie looked to her grandmother, who made no acknowledgement, then she got up and followed him from the room. He turned at the door, and looking back at Hiroko said, his voice cold and measured, 'This matter is not at an end and you have not heard the last of it.'

Sophie felt like hitting out at him, but controlling herself she rang for Malo to bring the car around and drive him back to his hotel. With a glance neither to left nor right, Satoshi strode from the house.

Sophie hurried back to her grandmother. Hiroko was lying back on the couch, drained of all energy, like a heap of blue silk weighed down by her pearls.

'You should have called me,' Sophie said.

Hiroko didn't reply. She was so still, Sophie felt frightened.

'Oba-san!' she said.

Hiroko turned to her.

'I've been very foolish,' she murmured.

To her surprise, Sophie saw that rather than upset, her grandmother was angry.

'What is it?' she asked gently. 'Or would you rather speak later?'

'There's nothing to speak about,' Hiroko answered, her voice flat. 'Things are as they are.'

> *Kazu no kokoro no*
> *Kizahashi wo*
> *Hata futatsu mitsu*
> *Kare ya noborishi.*[15]
> Of the numberless steps
> Up to my heart
> He climbed perhaps
> Only two or three.

Sophie waited for her grandmother to go on, and when she didn't, she said, 'Would you like to go back to bed now?' Hiroko turned to her and nodded, tears on her cheeks, but her eyes bright and clear. She clasped Sophie's hands and said, 'Sophie-chan, always remember to live for the moment. It's a great mistake to cling to the past. When it finally catches up to us, what was there is gone.'

It wasn't until the following day that Hiroko told her of what had happened. It was then, too, that she spoke of her father Yukio's last words to her before his death in Tokyo, and his showing her the rare Sesshu scrolls. She gave Sophie the key and had her bring them out from the lacquered chest, and carefully unroll them one by one on the long oak dining table, delighting in the girl's excited reaction to their beauty. She recounted a little of their history, then added, 'In monetary value, they are the most precious things we have. In fact they are part of the national treasure.'

'Well, shouldn't they be for everyone to enjoy then?' Sophie asked.

'Be that as it may,' her grandmother answered, 'they have been in our family, carefully safeguarded for many, many generations now, and by my bringing them here, they survived even the last war. So it's important that only the right people have them to care for.'

After safely storing them away again, Hiroko called the family lawyer to organise to have the bulk of her estate that had not already been transferred to Gerard, including the scrolls and the property in Tokyo, to be given to Sophie.

'No-one can take it away from me now,' she told Sophie the next day. 'It belongs to you.'

'Shouldn't you tell Gerard about the scrolls?' Sophie asked.

'He already owns so much here that he inherited from Hattie and Gare-san,' Hiroko answered. 'He's a very wealthy man, and I hardly think he would deny you this. After all, it's what would have come to your mother Gina, and now you have become more like a daughter to me.'

As Sophie left her grandmother later that evening, Hiroko said, 'Remember, Sophie-chan, the scrolls are very precious, in fact priceless—they are irreplaceable. So be careful to guard them well.'

'With my life,' Sophie smiled at her.

53

SATOSHI'S MISSION—JAPAN

Satoshi remembered someone telling him that the bonds made in one lifetime last for three. Then this must be the fourth time around for my mother and me, he mused.

He had detected the flinty look in her eye as soon as he brought up the business of his inheritance. She was hard. There was no real feeling for him there. But he wouldn't let things end this way. She had abandoned him as a child, and now owed it to him to at least give him what was rightfully his.

He wished that Michiko had given him fuller details of the inheritance his mother was supposed to have taken with her. Then he would have been in a stronger position to demand it back. Being unable to specify what it actually entailed made it that much harder.

A sudden thought struck him. His grandfather's servant. What was her name now? Ume, yes Ume. She may still be alive, and she would know. And she had no reason not to trust him, unless—his face darkened—that woman had warned her never to say anything. But he could get around that.

His spirits started to lighten with the prospect and he stared out the aircraft window at the expanse of sunlit sea that stretched in a silver wash below them as far as the eye could see. He shivered a little and closed his eyes. The thought of all that water made him feel nervous, and whenever the plane hit an air pocket and suddenly sank, he had visions of their plummeting into those unwelcome depths.

He took a long gulp of whisky, his hand shaking a little as he pushed such thoughts from his mind.

Why did he fear death as such? Death by one's own hand, the act of *seppuku*, that he could accept. But at the hands of someone else, or even by mischance before one was ready . . . He remembered how his *samurai* ancestors had regarded death as 'lighter than a feather', but it was the manner in which one met this final encounter and how well it was handled that finally decided one's courage.

He warmed as he thought of his son Takeo's face, shining with effort as he practised his *kendo,* already handling his stave like a champion. The boy showed such promise; he was quick and bright and seemed to easily master whatever he did. If some of that fat life he had just seen in Hawaii could be transferred to him, what a difference it would make to his son's future. Hiroko owed him that, and he would make sure he got it. That woman, his own mother, had humiliated him and that was unforgivable; it must be wiped out. In this instance, revenge would taste very sweet.

Remembering the old trick of *muga,* Satoshi completely emptied his mind and settled back, drifting into a light sleep. The sound of flutes, whistles and drums beating out a rhythm became louder and louder and, spirit fashion, he was floating in and out of the merrymakers at the *Awa Odori* dance festival . . .

How gently the *geisha* moved towards him, like exotic tropical fish, their arms and legs undulating in the perfectly timed rhythm of their age-old dance, their deep-brimmed hats like closed petals, sweeping low over their faces to lend an air of mystery. As they moved, the flash of their black and white kimono contrasted with the gentle movements of their hands, languorously swaying like reeds in water, their feet in white *tabi* balanced precariously on high wooden *geta*, as if forever dancing on their toes.

Satoshi felt himself being carried aloft in the fond familiarity of their dance as he hung suspended, unseen, delighting in the happiness of the moment. A new sound was intruding, the drums beating faster now with an overriding rattling of percussion as the whistles became shriller. He floated higher as the dancers with their fast stylised movements followed on after the *geisha*, and his heart beat faster as he watched them whirl through the fool's dance with all the spontaneity and madness of their mood. He wished he could join them leaping and dancing like athletes, using their small fans in expressive whirling arcs as if to punctuate each perfectly timed step.

For a brief instant, he became one of them and he could feel his body young and lithe once more as he joined in the dance. As they moved past the crowds of onlookers, he could see their faces staring at him, admiring him, and he felt puffed up in one glorious moment of achievement, as he swirled his fan and feet with the others.

Then he was floating again, looking down at the dancers, and now he could see his son Takeo leading them, dancing and whirling with magnificent leaps into the air. Just behind them came the enormous floats of the *nabuta kami*, fierce, giant-sized effigies of dragons and demons. The dancers had now reached the top of a hill, and were making their way towards a large black lake at the bottom. He tried to float above Takeo, calling to him, and once the boy looked up at him, laughing and excited, but his eyes gazed straight through his father, and with a sinking heart, Satoshi realised that he must indeed be a spirit, invisible to the human eye and that his son couldn't see him.

The dancers increased their pace now as they started down the hill towards the lake. The tempo of the drums was getting faster and faster and the whistles and flutes had become an almost frenzied cacophony. Above them, the sky was growing darker and a wind had started to howl and blow all about them, and he could see the lake below being whipped into large waves. The floats of the *Nabuta* figures were picking up speed as they moved downhill, and the dancers were now running, straining not to be overtaken by the fierce-looking monsters racing along behind them.

'Takeo! Takeo!' he called out, reaching down towards the boy, trying to lift him away from the now frenzied mob. He could see the fear on his son's face as he looked behind at the monstrous green dragon float that was almost upon him.

They had reached the waters of the lake, and Satoshi watched as the dancers threw themselves into the water to avoid being squashed by the floats of monsters. He could see Takeo's head bobbing amongst the waves as he tried desperately to swim away while the largest of the *Nabuta* dragons came down on top of him. Then as if by magic, all the dancers disappeared beneath the lake and all he could see was the darkened shape of the dragon as it floated out to sea, its eyes alight with candles that burned from within.

The waves had died down and wreaths of flowers and small paper lanterns glowing with candle light floated where the dancers had once been. A terrible sense of anguish filled him, and he tried to force himself down into the darkening depths of the lake to search for his son, but he was fixed in space . . .

A gentle pressure on his shoulder awakened him, and Satoshi looked up as the air hostess indicated to him to fasten his seatbelt for landing. The dream still hung around him, and he felt a leaden sense of foreboding. When he got home he decided he would make a special offering to *Kannon,* the goddess of mercy.

* * *

'Ah 'Toshi-chan!' Ume's broad face wrinkled into a wide smile of greeting. She ushered him into the tiny six-mat room where she now lived, bowing apologetically before him and clicking her teeth in a mixture of nervousness and delight at seeing him. She was still comparatively sprightly for her eighty-odd years, although stooped.

He handed her a cloth-wrapped gift.

'My mother sent you this with her warmest greetings,' Satoshi said.

'*So desu ka*, you have seen her?' she asked in surprise.

'I have just returned from Honolulu,' he said, telling her of Hiroko and making it sound quite the joy-filled reunion between mother and son it had never been.

Ume listened quietly, her old face shining with delight at this news, drinking in every scrap of information of her once-loved young mistress. He went on to describe Hiroko's failing health and the grand house and beautiful gardens in which she now lived.

'Actually, Hiroko-san has sent me to you on a mission of mercy,' he went on.

Ume looked at him expectantly. 'Mission of mercy?' she repeated.

'Yes, she has grave worries and is hoping you can clear this matter up,' he went on. 'She asked me to come and see you especially as you are the last one she can think of to turn to in this matter.'

By now he had Ume's full attention. And he paused, letting the moment build.

'*Hai, Hai!*' she said, as if to hasten what he had to tell her.

Satoshi continued slowly, deliberately choosing each word.

'It seems that when her father and my grandfather Yukio Sen died, he left her many things.'

'Ah yes, that is so,' Ume broke in, 'but she arrived in time for them to discuss it all and organise everything before he was taken.'

'Everything?' prompted Satoshi.

'Yes, you know, the properties here, all his furniture and books, and the things in the big lacquered chest,' she said.

'Actually it's the things in the chest she is most

anxious about now,' he went on, hoping she would fill him in.

Ume looked at him perplexed. 'But it all went as she planned. I helped her pack everything, so carefully into the big tea chests. To be shipped to Hawaii.'

'But not all went into the tea chests?' he prompted.

'No, that is so,' she answered, pleased to be talking about an event she remembered so clearly.

'And what happened to those things?' Satoshi asked.

Ume looked at him in surprise. 'Why, she took them with her on the plane,' she answered. 'For safe-keeping, so they didn't get lost.'

He smiled and nodded, waiting for her to go on. She giggled suddenly, remembering. 'You should have seen us! We had such trouble finding a bag to fit those long boxes.'

'Long boxes?' he asked, casually.

'*Hai*, for the scrolls. They were very long. I said she should put them in the tea chests, but she said, "No, Ume, they are very special, and it's better they stay with me."'

He felt an excitement grow within him.

'Did you see them, these special scrolls?' he asked.

'Only once, long ago. They are very old and so beautiful, I saw the master looking at them many years ago,' she added, drifting off into a reverie, remembering the day.

She had been a young girl then, only fifteen, she recalled, and her mistress, Hiroko's mother, had been alive with a tiny bundle that was baby Hiroko strapped to her back.

Both Hiroko's mother and her husband were bending over something on the floor, she remembered. Not knowing that they were there and thinking that she would dust the room and shake out the *tatami* mats, she had looked in, and kneeling at the doorway had bowed, waiting for their orders. She had stared fascinated by the delicate colours and images of the scrolls unrolled on the floor. It was a fishing village scene, she recalled, and the early morning light filtering through the *shoji* screens caught and heightened the colours, bringing the scene to life as if they were viewing it through a window. She could hardly tear her eyes away. Then they had looked up and saw her gazing at the vista on the floor, and she remembered the anxious expression that had passed between them.

'Later! Come back later!' her master Yukio had called out impatiently, motioning her from the room. But she would always remember their stillness and reverence as they had sat poring over the magnificent scrolls that covered the whole floor.

Satoshi's voice broke across her reverie.

'How many?' he was saying.

She gazed at him from the distance of years, not quite comprehending.

'How many?' she repeated.

'Scrolls?' he asked.

'There were two boxes that went with Hiroko-san,' she said, wondering now about his interest in these things. Surely he must have seen them when he visited his mother.

He questioned her for a while longer, then abruptly took his leave.

It was not until after he'd gone that Ume remembered Satoshi's words, that he'd come to her on a 'mission of mercy'. Nothing they'd talked about seemed to indicate any such thing. But even as she thought about it, her memory was starting to play tricks with her, as it always did. She knelt on the *tatami* listening to the bean curd man crying his wares in the street outside, and she thought of the little boy, always so quiet and keeping to himself. She remembered how Satoshi had clung to his mother's skirt when worried. Even now she could see the tiny hands clutching tight on the folds of Hiroko's kimono, as if hanging onto it was his hold on life itself. She could still hear his sobs when Michiko Nakamura had called to take him out with her. He had run back, his face so white, clinging to his mother while his Aunt

Michiko waited at the door. He hadn't wanted to go. I wonder why, she thought now. She could still see his tear-stained cheeks, and Hiroko-san smiling as she tried to disengage his grip on her, and bowing her apologies while she had led him over to his Aunt Michiko. The Nakamuras were not an honourable family, she remembered.

The mournful cry of the bean curd man stirred another memory of the night she had taken his grandfather's ancestral sword to Satoshi at the home where he had been boarding. She had felt so sad as everything seemed to be changing. A servant girl had taken the precious sword from her quite rudely, and Satoshi hadn't wanted to see her then, she recalled. She'd heard that he was married with a young son now, and wondered whether Hiroko had seen the boy. She remembered hearing that his name was Takeo. Ah yes, Takeo. So, there was yet another grandchild to bless Hiroko-san. She sighed, thinking if only her master Yukio-san was here to enjoy the fruits of his family. And a hollow sense of loneliness made her long to still be an active part of their lives. She could help care for the boy, Takeo. Hiroko-san would like that.

54

YAKUZA

'It sounds like the *yakuza*,' Gerard said, having listened to Sophie's description of her meeting with Matsuhiro. He stared out the window, deep in thought. So it seemed the wheel was slowly turning full circle, he mused.

'*Yakuza*?' Sophie prompted.

'They go back many years,' he said, 'to the early *bakuto* gangs in the *Tokugawa* era during the early seventeenth century.' Gerard paused, recalling what he knew about them. 'They would travel the Great Tokaido highway between Edo, now Tokyo, and Kyoto, visiting the numerous inns and mostly gambling their way. Loyalty to their *oyabun* or leader was paramount and they adhered to pretty strict rules and secret codes within their *yakuza* gang or *kobun*.'

'Why the title *yakuza*?' Sophie asked.

'Their name came from the *Hanafuda* flower card game they would play. We had an old pack of the cards, remember?'

She shook her head, and he went on.

'Actually yakuza stood for the lowest score anyone could make in the game.'

'How come?' she asked.

'Well three cards were dealt, and the last digit in their

total value was the one which counted as the player's score.' He smiled at her.

'So a losing combination of say 8–9–3 or as we say "ya-ku-za", which amounts to twenty, would have zero as its total score. So "yakuza" became a kind of catch-cry.'

'Hardly a complimentary title then,' Sophie laughed.

'Well it stuck,' he said. 'Originally the *yakuza* were seen as gamblers and drifters, but later as their power increased, the name became synonymous with various powerful underworld families.'

'And Matsuhiro Isawa?' she asked.

'Since his father Akira died, Matsuhiro is the *oyabun* and heads a very powerful family *yakuza* clique,' Gerard said, wondering what Matsuhiro was up to.

'He's only young,' Sophie said, recalling their meeting.

'But don't underestimate him.'

'*Yakuza* . . . born to lose,' she murmured.

'Hardly!' He gave a laugh. 'Not that one.' And he wondered how she had come to meet up with him. That was one contact he hadn't given her, but he'd find out.

Matsuhiro had the air of someone from the underworld, Sophie thought, remembering the darkened limo and the bodyguards, and that waiting flower face at the car window.

'The top of his little finger was missing,' she said, suddenly remembering.

'Ah, *yubitsume*,' Gerard said, and added, 'it's all part of their ritual. The top joint of their little finger is often ceremoniously severed, then wrapped in a fine cloth and handed to the *oyabun* as a mark of obedience and total commitment.' He paused, and looked at her with an arch expression. 'If the second joint is missing, then you worry.'

She gazed at him inquiringly.

'It's considered the greatest punishment to bear, and usually happens only before expulsion from the *oyabun-kobun*. And you can forget joining a rival gang,' he went on. 'They would already have been notified by open postcard of the miscreant's deeds, so expulsion is total and all doors closed.'

'Matsuhiro was dressed very conservatively,' she said, recalling his dark suit.

'If you had met in a bath house you might have thought differently.'

'Really?'

'I heard his father Akira carried a psychedelic art exhibition around on his body, and maybe he does, too.'

She looked surprised.

'Tattoos,' he said. 'Some of them are amazing and are the signature of many of the *yakuza gumi*.'

Sophie remembered the young man rising from the water at the Hakone bath house with a sense of dismay. Gerard noticed the flush that spread across her neck and cheeks, and wondered.

At his bidding, Sophie talked to him of her meetings, filling him in with all the detail she could. Gerard listened, his face impassive as he took it all in. He was more interested in her description of her encounter with Atsuo, recalling his one meeting with him at the Royal Hawaiian. Now she recounted her discussions with Daihachi, and his reactions to her.

'And it was he who put you in touch with Atsuo?' he questioned.

'Yes, but he was very strange and vague about that too,' she went on.

Whoever would have thought, Gerard reflected, that this Daihachi would have led her to the one person that he, Gerard, had been doing business with all these years. The odd-ball he'd avoided, preferring to deal with his nephew, Matsuhiro.

'I wouldn't be surprised if they are not all part of the one *yakuza* gang, the Isawa-*gumi*,' he said. 'And do you know something, Sophie-chan—after all you have told me, I still don't believe that Katsura is dead.'

She stared at him, and felt relief rise up and fill her with new hope.

'Oh Gera, so you feel that way too. I've felt it all along. My sixth sense just tells me that he's alive.'

Gerard gazed at her, troubled now. 'Is finding him still so important to you?' he asked. 'I mean, he obviously doesn't want to be found. It might be very hard for you,' he hesitated, 'when eventually you do.'

'I'll face that when the time comes,' she said.

He wondered if she fully realised the conflict of interests she'd have to face, if and when that time arrived. And his mother, how would she cope, knowing they'd made contact with the person she saw as largely responsible for causing Gina's death. To him there was no conflict. Just to get his hands on that devious bastard, and put him where he belonged. Maybe, he thought, it would be better if she had remained thinking he was dead. Still there was no going back. Not now.

'I'll see what I can do then,' Gerard finished.

55

DAVID'S WAR

That night as she lay pressed against David's back, her arms encircling him, Sophie thought about her conversation with Gerard.

Already David was deep in sleep. She envied the way he could so effortlessly float into unconsciousness with none of the nagging doubts that often hung around her, ensuring a state of mild discontent.

He had returned that afternoon from Saigon, with more stories and stills of the conflict there. Looking at these images of a war that was taking place, somehow the events of her Japanese journey into the past had seemed trivial by comparison.

There was one shot in particular of a young Vietnamese woman taken just after she had survived the horrors of water torture. Sophie had stared at it, sickened, thinking that the woman could have been me, born in another place, at another time.

The woman was barely alive, the horror of her experience etched on a face which was hollow-eyed and haunted and, like her body, still in shock from her forced drownings.

'Oh God, why do they do it?' she had said.

'It's war,' David answered.

'What the hell has that got to do with it?' she snapped back.

He said nothing, and went on sorting out his equipment. He looked dispirited and tired, and she wondered how she ever could have thought she would leave him. She reached out and touched him. 'They are wonderful shots, darling,' she said.

When he didn't answer, she continued, 'I read once about a Buddhist woman who would say to her son that those who have done evil in their past life will be reborn as horses or oxen and their masters will beat them, and when they are no longer capable of work, they will be slaughtered.' She stared at a photograph of a Buddhist monk, sitting calmly in lotus position while the flames of self-immolation carried his soul in protest to a higher state. 'And she taught her son that other evil spirits would come back in human shape, but it was so arranged that their new life on earth would be as cruel and heavy to bear as that of the beasts of burden.'

She turned to him. 'What on earth can these people have done that . . .'

David broke in. 'Bloody hell, Sophie, you over-rationalise everything. Things are as they are. They just exist and that is that.'

He felt the old resentments rise as they always did as her words washed over him. He felt like shouting, 'For Christ's sake Sophie, get real!' stripping away her words which sprang from a cushioned perspective. Real? The word resonated and anguished shame rose within him, threatening to unbalance him as it always did. He closed his eyes. A low child's moan rose within him as he felt the hot breath on his neck and the large hands of the Brother's Brennan pulling him down onto his lap and the quiver of excitment as the man held him close, the beads and cross of the Brother's crucifix biting into the back of his head. 'Hold tight now laddie, it's only for a moment now . . . just a little harmless fun eh?' And those big hands that suddenly softened, sliding and pulling at his penis, and a sort of sweet sensation as it grew large and his body melted a little, offsetting the fear of what he knew was to follow. Then just as he felt he'd burst, as quickly the man had turned him around, pushing his head down into that shadowy stinking place which had become an oft-repeated hell as he was forced to suck hard on the cock that filled his mouth. He choked and fought for air, trying to suck, to be finished and away from the acrid fluid he knew would soon shoot deep into his throat.

'There now, give it a real good suck laddie . . . a real good suck . . . and then we'll see what I can do for you.'

Sophie sensed David's withdrawal and going over to him, pressed her body against his, now rigid and resisting. She looked into his eyes and whispered, 'Well thank God we are as we are, and this is real,' as her hands and lips reached for him.

It had been raining heavily, and she lay now looking at the silver drops of rain trembling on the rim of the window frame, poised ready to take flight down the long expanse of glass, and she thought of the shiny little steel balls as they fell through a maze of metal pins in the Pachinko parlours. A bell would ring to announce a win and a silver shower of balls would shoot up and out to start the game all over again, like a never-ending game of chance, and for such tawdry prizes.

Her arm had gone to sleep under the weight of David's body, and she withdrew it gently so as not to disturb him. She sat up looking at him, feeling suddenly very alone. The restlessness that was always with her precluded any real sense of belonging to anything or anyone for very long. It reminded her that at its best, happiness and that feeling of belonging were but fleeting things. And for her, the still of the night was their favourite dwelling place.

Sophie drew on her robe, slipped quietly from the room and went downstairs into the large space they had set aside for David's studio. She loved this room with its spacious work area and the wall of books at one end leading off to a glassed-in atrium.

She had furnished it with big comfortable leather couches and chairs, and on every available piece of wall space were David's photographs, filling the room with a thousand faces of human emotion. She didn't have to go to war, she thought, looking at his latest batch of shots from Vietnam. It was all there for her to see and experience in her imagination. Looking at his images of Saigon's streets now choked with a never-ending stream of pedicabs, Lambrettas and bicycles dodging the continuous flow of military traffic from the *Tan Son Nhut* airfield, she could almost smell the dirt and heat of war in the former 'Paris of the Orient'.

Here were people living out their day-to-day lives in a country largely sustained by a centuries-old technology, while an almost surreal quality of hi-tech intruded into the world around them.

In sharp focus a mother suckled her child, while behind her in ruins lay a once thriving village now napalmed to non-existence. Sophie could see that David had worked to build the contrasts between normality and extremes, so that after a while one wondered what was normal and what was extreme.

A GI off duty, complete with 50-gallon hat and pearl-handled sharp shooters, laconically sipped cocktails at the Bar Imperiale with a pretty Vietnamese girl, looking at the camera rather than to her date. In another shot taken from the cockpit of a domestic airliner, he had filmed a pilot relaxing and drinking coffee while looking out at two F-100s making an air strike on a group of huts, with flashes of flame and white smoke shooting from guns nestled under their wings.

And everywhere there were children, living through a war-torn landscape as though it was the most natural place in the world in which to play. She noticed how children seemed to outnumber the soldiers, their lotus faces and wide clear eyes peopling his photographs with their compelling innocence. A small boy, his stick-thin legs scarred from ankle to knee with a gaping shrapnel wound, smiled brightly for the camera, a can of Coke held tightly in his hand. Had that Coke been the price of his smile?

Sophie saw a people bent on surviving their lot, no matter what. Now rape, pillage and plunder had taken on a new dimension, encapsulated in the clarity and cleanliness of neat black-and-white or colour photographs and film, spewing out world-wide from the UPI files, ready to assuage the social conscience of the lucky ones watching from the comfort of our homes, she thought.

She moved away from his war to the corner of the room where she had placed her own special couch and roll-top desk, and above them a blow-up shot of Gina and Katsura. David had enlarged the only small precious shot she had of them taken together years ago.

'I want a life-size enlargement,' she had said.

'It will be too grainy and diffused, you'll hardly recognise them,' he had argued.

'As I never saw them in my life, it won't make any difference. I wouldn't recognise them anyway,' she had replied. 'Please, David, make it really big.'

He had enlarged it almost to life size, and the two shadowy figures stared out at her, phantoms from the past. Gina was laughing up into the face of the handsome young man as he stared away at some other distant horizon. This said it all, Sophie reflected. Her mother full of warmth for the man and the moment, the man beside her there only in body, his spirit already taken flight.

As she stared at the photograph, she felt a faint twinge of recognition. Pulling her silk robe tightly around her, she peered closely at his face. But it remained impassive, frozen in that moment of time. She reached up and ran her fingers around the outline of his head.

'You are still alive,' she said softly, 'I just know it. At least if I find one real parent, I'll have roots then. Do you know what it's like not to have parents?' she asked the image above her. 'It's as if . . . there's always an emptiness and it never goes away. I need to really belong to somebody to be complete. Please help me to find you,

Papa-san,' she whispered, tears of self-pity washing her cheeks.

'Sophie, what the hell are you doing? Who are you talking to?' David had come up behind her.

She turned with a start. 'What's the matter, Sophie?' he went on more softly, noticing the tears.

'Oh nothing, I just couldn't sleep.' Somehow she couldn't talk to him about it.

'I thought you must have been sleepwalking,' he said.

She smiled at him. 'It's almost as though one's asleep, this searching in a world of half-perceived images.' She was looking at the face of Katsura as she spoke.

'I'll get us a drink, and you can tell me about it,' David said. 'I want to hear how the whole thing went.'

As they sat sipping the cold Beaujolais, she told him of her meetings in Tokyo and her discussions with Gerard later. He listened intently.

'Maybe you have seen him,' he said when she stopped speaking.

'Who?'

'Katsura.'

'Seen him? How do you mean?'

'Maybe he was at that party, in the street, at the hotel, anywhere you may have been, and you had a passing glimpse.'

'I would have known,' she said.

'Would you? How?' he asked. 'You've got an image printed on your brain from a photograph taken over twenty-five years ago,' he said looking up at the shot above them, 'and a hell of a lot can happen to a face in that time. Even that isn't a clear representation,' he went on, looking critically at the enlargement. 'It's diffused and shadowy. I said at the time not to enlarge it so much, but you insisted.'

'Oh David, but the size was important. It somehow made them seem real to me.'

'I wonder,' he went on, staring critically at the photograph.

'Wonder what?'

'If I kept them, the smaller shots that I enlarged to get this one. They were far clearer, remember?'

'You didn't show them to me.'

'You've forgotten,' he replied. 'It could help you now.' He was silent, staring at the photograph.

'Uh huh!' he exclaimed. 'I've got an idea.'

'What is it?'

He didn't answer but got up and started searching through the drawers of his desk.

'Never mind,' he said. 'I'll have to find those shots first.'

'David, tell me what it is?'

He looked up with a smile. 'I don't want to spoil it,' he answered. 'You'll just have to be patient.'

Sophie sank back onto the couch, letting the wine warm its way to her brain, and soften the sharper edges of anxiety as she drifted into sleep.

David gazed at her sleeping, as he finished off the wine. Her slight figure seemed lost on the couch, and there was a flush accenting her high cheek bones. She really was beautiful, he thought with a surge of pride, but her energies were so scattered. She looked too far beneath the surface of things, and you couldn't do that, it only screwed things up. Better to skim along, in life, in relationships. But of all the women he'd known, Sophie had that something extra. He related to her feeling of parental rejection and her search for roots and sense of belonging. But as for delving beneath the surface . . . he'd long forgotten his early anguished desire to try and find his own mother or father. Who in the hell were they and where in the hell would they be now anyway. And who the hell cared!

He yawned, feeling exhausted and dispirited. That last trip to 'Nam hadn't gone as well as it should. Gerard was expecting too much of him from these junkets. Keeping his network of drug dealers sweet was getting more difficult with every trip now. At least Sophie didn't have to worry about that, and she must never know. Jesus

Christ, she'd be trying to save them all, he thought with a grin.

He leaned back, and the darker images of his recent trip started to intrude. He sat up with a start, pushing them away. God, he needed a buzz, he thought as he got up and went into the dark room and started opening one of the sealed packages of amphetamines he hadn't shipped out as yet. At least he had a never-ending supply of 'speed' from 'Nam, and if he couldn't make good use of it, well who the hell could!

He extracted a pack of Methedrine, and after downing some capsules with the remaining wine, he went back to take Sophie to bed.

David glanced at the waif-like figure sleeping beneath the shadowy images on the wall above her. They seemed to have taken on another dimension, and getting out his camera he started to shoot her and the photograph behind, adjusting his lens to give greater emphasis first to one, then the other. With a surge of excitement, he began to see the images take shape as he worked with a cool professionalism, so that it was neither his wife nor her parents he saw, but mere props to the final layout.

Sophie stirred as the noise of his camera and its flash started to impinge on her sleep. She moved to one side, her gown falling away so that her naked body emerged. He took shot after shot of her as she was, the long curve of her thigh accentuated as it hung over the edge of the couch, her small breasts rising and falling as she lay in the trusting abandonment of sleep.

The mix of wine and 'speed' was beginning to have its required effect. He could see and experience things with a new intensity. Laying aside his camera, David knelt over her, kissing her breasts and open mouth, then down the gentle curve of her stomach to the soft brush of dark hair below, now hot with his desire to take her. She opened her eyes and reached out for him, and even as he entered her with a fierceness and hunger to explode within her, a part of his mind was operating with a white light clarity, and kept thinking if only he was filming this now. He could see how it would look, the parents above and the child below, living out the desire in her mother's eyes. He cursed himself that he hadn't left his camera on automatic.

56

GERARD'S DECISION

'Why didn't you tell me?' Jill asked, her voice rising.

'Tell you what?' he answered, wondering what she would accuse him of now.

'About that whole business with Satoshi and your mother. Really Gerard, the first I heard of it was from Sophie this afternoon, and it happened over a week ago,' she went on heatedly. 'Hiroko's probably wondering why I haven't been in touch about it.'

'Well you know now,' he replied. 'Look honey, I've got to dash to an early meeting at the office, we'll talk later,' he said, giving her a quick kiss on the forehead as he hurried downstairs to the car.

He's ducking this one, Jill thought, watching him go. She leaned out over the balcony and saw him stop to talk briefly with William and Louise, who were still getting ready for school. He must have sensed her watching, because he turned just before getting into his car and looked up at her, raising his hand in a mock salute.

She smiled. That was Gerard, always tuned in. Somehow she couldn't feel sorry for what had happened with Satoshi. Hiroko had put all her emotional investment into that little bastard, and now look how he had repaid her. Whereas Gerard, with only token warmth from his mother, had always done so much for her, she thought resentfully. God, wasn't it always the way!

Maybe Gerard doesn't know what really happened, she thought suddenly. It would be hardly like Hiroko to tell him, and Sophie would know only the half of it. Now if it had been Hattie, she would have told us everything in full psychedelic colour, she smiled to herself. Perhaps I can dig out all the details from Hiroko, and fill Gerard in later. He would like that. He needs to know, and Hiroko will never tell him what really happened. But she might confide in me.

'Tell me about Satoshi,' Jill said later that morning to Hiroko, who was resting in the big wicker chair under a jacaranda tree where she could get some relief from the heat with a breeze that came in across the water. Jill had decided to get straight to the point, and not waste time working around to it. Instinctively she felt Hiroko would know what she was on about, anyway.

Hiroko looked across at her and smiled, but Jill could see it was an effort. She looked so frail, though she was holding on well. 'What's there to say?' Hiroko sighed.

'Well, Sophie only told me a little about it, and I thought it might be a lot easier for you to talk now and see where we go from here,' Jill replied.

'We?' Hiroko asked.

'Why not? We can all be of help. I mean if there's any further discussion to have with Satoshi, Gerard will be going to Tokyo in a few weeks' time on business, and maybe he could take up the matter with Satoshi for you then,' Jill went on. She'd resented Hiroko's ambivalence towards Gerard but, in some ways she thought, we are really birds of a feather as we both go after what we want.

Hiroko gazed at Jill's face, and felt a surge of fondness for her. There was something disarming in the way she approached things head-on. It somehow made her seem more vulnerable even than Sophie, with her more innate wisdom. Jill sailed purely by the seat of her pants, she thought, recalling one of Gare's favourite phrases. She sighed—she had learnt so much from him and Hattie, and her life here on the Island. It had been a good life; if only, if only Boy and her little son had been part of it. Despite their meeting, she still saw Satoshi as the small boy she had left behind in Japan, her mind shutting out the angry middle-aged man she had encountered.

'Jill-san, I've been a silly sentimental woman, and it's a closed door now,' she said, speaking her thoughts aloud.

Jill reached across and took her hand. 'What did he do that so disappointed you?' she asked, ignoring Hiroko's last remark.

Hiroko looked away and didn't answer her.

'What did he want from you?' Jill went on, not to be pushed away now. 'Mamma,' she said, her voice becoming softer, 'we only want to help you, and how can we if you only tell half the story?'

So, Hiroko thought, Sophie had not told Jill about the scrolls. That was good. Better to keep things quiet a little longer, until the transfer had finally gone through.

'He is interested in property I have,' she answered, 'property my father left me in Tokyo, and to which he feels he's entitled.'

'How ridiculous!' Jill interjected. 'If anyone should be entitled, it's Gerard,' she couldn't help saying, then wished she hadn't, when she saw the expression on Hiroko's face.

To forestall any further questions, Hiroko said, 'Gerard and I must speak on these matters. Will you ask him to ring me tomorrow, Jill-san? And now, if you don't mind, I must go and rest, I'm very tired.' She smiled wanly at her daughter-in-law.

Jill could see the matter was closed, and she helped Malo take the tiny figure inside.

As Jill drove back along the Lunalilo freeway and past the Moanalua gardens with their huge monkeypod trees and white hibiscus, a phrase from a movie she had once seen sprang to mind. 'In one wasted moment a door may close forever.' She thought with regret of all those wasted moments when she could have been getting closer to Hiroko, and which were now gone.

'She's not saying anything, not to me, anyway,' Jill said to Gerard later that night as they lay together in their large bed. 'She asked for you to ring her tomorrow, so maybe you'll be able to find out just what is going on with Satoshi.'

He didn't answer.

'He sounds dangerous, Gerard,' she went on. 'Evidently he's simply out for what he can get from her. He's been sniffing around trying to find out about her inheritance from Yukio, *your* grandfather. But as I said to your mother, if anyone's entitled to anything, it's you, darling.'

She went on chatting a while longer, and he lay looking out at the night sky, wondering about this half-brother who had suddenly surfaced after all these years. Looking embarrassed, Sophie had told him that her grandmother had decided to transfer the Tokyo properties to her, and some other personal items she had inherited from her father.

'Oba-san said they would have gone to Gina, anyway. I hope you don't mind, Gera.'

'Of course not honey,' he said, taking control as always. 'I'll do what I can to set it all in order,' he added, looking at her anxious face.

He hadn't told Jill, leaving that to Sophie when the matter was all settled. So Hiroko's darling little son Satoshi had turned out to be only out for what he could get. What a turn-around! Gerard experienced a strong sense of vindication. Maybe now Hiroko would see things in their true perspective. His long-felt sense of injury and injustice were assuaged as the image of this shadowy half-brother, who had dominated his mother's emotions all his life, emerged somewhat tarnished. He hadn't quite risen to the occasion, so could now be banished to a back seat in his mind forever. At the same time a sixth sense warned him that Satoshi could be dangerous. If he had come this far to find out what he could get, he wasn't going to lie down easily now. What did he really want? It was essential that he find that out from his mother tomorrow, so he could diffuse the situation before it harmed any of them. Then he'd get on to Satoshi in Tokyo when he went there.

Meanwhile he'd had word from his Japanese connection that a top man from the Isawa-*gumi* was arriving in Honolulu in two days, and had requested a meeting with him. Gerard wondered about this. It was not like the *oyabun*, if that's who it was, to deal directly. Gerard had mostly been meeting with his representatives over the years, ever since Hiro had first helped set up the connection. He wondered if he would be seeing Matsuhiro. His curiosity about him was roused, especially after Sophie's encounter. Although they had spoken, and done business many times, they had never actually met. He'd heard numerous stories about him and his father Akira, and had even met up with Akira briefly in Japan during the MacArthur occupation when Matsuhiro was just a boy. Akira was busy doing favours then, he recalled, and ingratiating himself with the new powers. He was doing very well even in those lean times, controlling the *tekkiya,* the thriving *yami ichi* and *mjizu shobai* business. Hastily setting up bars and brothels with *pan-pan* girls, booze and drugs, whose money like water just washes away, he was soon catering specially to the American GIs, loaded with PX goodies, silk stockings, cigarettes, gum, food and dollars, arriving by the jeepload at Funabashi and wherever the world of feeling and pleasure was served.

He remembered Akira as a charming man with an infectious laugh and a great sense of fun, who went out of his way to provide services for the MacArthur administration. He was a master in the art of Japanese '*wa*', or love of order and smoothing out difficulties while presenting a bland face to prevent any loss of face. Old Akira, he recalled, liked to be thought of as a promulgator of the ancient *bushido,* or spirit of the *Samurai*, rather than as a racketeer, and before he died had built up quite a standing in the community, not to mention a business infrastructure that stretched right across the world.

Gerard had soon sensed that under Akira's mask of affability lay a smart and serious operator, who had only just managed to dodge any war crime charges, while at the same time proving invaluable as a supplier and link man. Akira had been one of the contacts he had turned to when trying to trace Katsura. He had provided leads, but none of them had come up with anything at all. It would be more than interesting to meet his son Matsuhiro at last, if it were he who was arriving.

Perhaps this business with Satoshi was a matter for Matsuhiro to handle, he thought. But then he wondered if he should talk of it to Matsuhiro; the less he had on our family, the better. But then again, Sophie would have mentioned her grandmother Hiroko's background, no doubt, in discussing her search for Katsura, so there was little to lose and maybe a lot to gain. He'd put that bastard Satoshi in his place. What right had he to come here and start making demands on his mother? There must be something they could pin on him, and if anyone could make it stick, it would be the Isawa-*gumi*. It would cost a bundle, but would be cheap at half the price, he thought with grim satisfaction. But his mother must never know.

There was a rustling of leaves in the camphor trees outside his window as cold air from the trade winds blowing in from the Akua Lapu channel sprang up and swept across the garden, bringing with it the perfume of the sirius flowers, which bloomed only at night. He could hear the tinkling of the shell chimes in the hakoa trees below rising to a sudden frenzy.

He got out of bed and, walking out onto the balcony, looked up at the velvety sky, and there shining like a beacon was Polaris, the northern star, and for the first time in months he thought of Iman.

With the passing of the years details of her face had become veiled, but the feel of her skin, silky fine and always cool to touch, and the faint musky smell of mimosa, had stayed as clear as day. He recalled the softness of her mouth and their kisses that seemed to melt and merge as had their bodies in those all too fleeting days and nights of love.

'Iman, Iman,' he whispered, as he stood there aching for her, cursing this memory which had emotionally trapped him in the indigo blue of a Moroccan wasteland, always waiting for the time of their reunion.

57

SUNDAY'S CHILD

As she looked around the studio, Sophie felt quite sure that it was on that night here with David just three months ago that she had become pregnant. The sleepy warmth and security provided by the wine they had drunk that night, then waking to David's love-making—that was the moment of conception, she knew. It was as if all those faces looking on, even my own parents, she remembered with a smile, were giving their blessing to the event.

She felt the thrill of the quickening of a life within her. David's child and hers. As she let her mind dwell on it, wondering which day it would be born, the chill of fear intruded. What if things went terribly wrong as they had with her mother, Gina? She pushed such thoughts away, starting to sing the old nursery rhyme, the notes of the plaintive melody filling the room.

Monday's child is fair of face,
Tuesday's child is full of grace,
Wednesday's child is full of woe,
Thursday's child has far to go.
Friday's child is loving and giving,
Saturday's child works hard for his living.
But the child who is born on the sabbath day,
Is bonny and blithe and good and gay.[16]

I was a Sunday's child, Sophie recalled, taking a childish pleasure in having inherited the better part of the rhyme and its predictions. But what a time to have been born—in the middle of a bombing attack on a day 'which will live on in infamy'.[17] I was a war baby, and this little one will also be a child born at a time of conflict. Its father is involved in a war that has little meaning, she thought. Maybe it would be over by then, but she wondered if it would, her mind slipping back to the comfort of the verse.

Gerard must be a Saturday's child, as he never stops working. And David? She couldn't quite decide. Maybe a Monday, as he's certainly good looking. But he's a ladies' man too, she thought with a pang, so Tuesday would be nearer the mark. Tuesday's child is full of grace, she hummed. No, grace denoted a purity of spirit, an enlightenment. And that wasn't quite David, so he must be a Monday's child.

And what of my own father, would the same rhyme count for him? Maybe like Satoshi, he was a Wednesday's child and full of woe, she decided, the feeling of hostility towards Satoshi and his treatment of her grandmother still fresh in her mind.

Katsura was probably a . . . she ran through them all, but couldn't decide. She knew so little about him. Her reason for finding him now seemed to take on a new urgency with the coming of this baby. Gerard was going to Tokyo next month, and she would try to go too. There was no reason not to; she felt well enough and it would be better to go now than later in the pregnancy. He could help her with her search.

'I'll have a surprise for you when I get back,' David had said before returning to Saigon some weeks ago.

'Tell me now,' she'd asked.

'No, it's not quite ready yet,' he said with a grin.

'Oh go on David, I can't wait weeks for it, I'll die of curiosity. Tell me what it is,' she had pleaded.

'I can't,' he answered. 'It might spoil it if you see it

too soon. Just be patient.' And he had kissed her with an air of finality, and she knew that the subject was closed.

She hated waiting for anything, and now the months before the birth of their child seemed to stretch ahead forever. At least David would be back next week. He didn't know about the baby yet, and she couldn't wait to tell him. She would plan a really romantic night and tell him just at the right moment. Would having sex affect the baby? Luckily David would be here before she started to look fat. If anything, being pregnant made her look sexier. Her waist had barely started to thicken, though her breasts were already much fuller and her nipples larger, an overall voluptuousness that would go down well with David. He liked his women curvy, she recalled with a stab of jealousy.

'It's an act of faith to love and be loved,' Jill had said to her in the early days of her relationship, when she was deciding whether to leave David or not. 'But remember, men don't hold on to love as we do. For them it's a tremendous burning up, a sort of turbulence, and then they move on.'

'So how do I cope with that?' Sophie had asked, thinking that already she had broken all the rules, as she loved David far more than he did her, of that she was sure.

'Do not quite let yourself go. Keep half of your heart with you, then, when you have to break your heart, it's only half-broken. You know,' Jill warming to her subject, went on, 'it's a marvellous sort of freeing up to be in control, instead of being totally obsessed and just completely dragged along.'

Sophie had laughed at this, and she smiled now, thinking, well, what's new! She had brought down some bundles of photographs that David had left upstairs, to be put away in his cupboards. As she pulled out a bottom drawer, she was surprised to see a face that looked vaguely familiar staring up at her. She lifted it out and saw that it was an enlarged shot of a Japanese man, which someone had been retouching. There had been lines added to the mouth and brow as if to age it.

She suddenly realised that she was looking at the head shot of her father, Katsura. David must have taken it from the earlier, clearer shots he'd found and was working on it. So this was his surprise!

As she gazed at it, Sophie had a feeling that she had seen the face somewhere else, but where? Anxiety gripped her, and she took the photograph and laid it on his work desk, switching on the bright lamp overhead. Pouring herself a Coke from the studio fridge, she perched on his high stool, peering down at the photograph.

David had been trying to subtly age the face, and that made sense, she thought. She searched through his desk and found a silver felt pen. Carefully she worked some silver onto the hair-line of the photograph, at first just a few strokes here and there, adding silver to the temples and through the black thatch at the crown. Lightly she brushed darkened rings under his eyes, and with a small tingle of excitement, she started to see something there that pulled at the recesses of her memory.

Sophie worked away, darkening the lines near his eyes. She looked at it critically, but it still wasn't right and somehow the image was beginning to look really screwed up. With a growing sense of frustration, she continued to darken and smudge the lines under his eyes, then thought, well I may as well go full tilt now, and she continued tinting over the eyes, like large sunglasses.

Reaching across for another pen, she accidentally spilled some of the Coke across his nose and chin, and as she blotted the liquid away, it lent a strange stretched look to the face. I've really wrecked it now, she thought.

Tired of the futility of what she'd been doing, Sophie switched off the desk lamp. As she did her eyes glimpsed the face now in the softer, more diffused light. With a sharp intake of breath, she looked again. It was Atsuo, the man she had dined with at the Teikoku Hotel. Atsuo Isawa was her father?

Her surprise, then joy, of discovery was quickly replaced by one of rejection. That strange man, her father? He must have known who she was. She went over every detail of their meeting, straining to remember his words, his reactions, his every nuance. There had been no warm and loving parent who would greet her with glad cries of wonderment and relief of rediscovery. Just emptiness.

Sophie lit a cigarette, drawing deeply on it, then remembering the baby, quickly stubbed it out. Yes, for all the clumsiness of her retouching, it was definitely him, Atsuo Isawa. Sophie Isawa, she said aloud to herself, nursing a cushion to her as she'd often done as a small child, rocking slightly from side to side. So, he had quite coldly and deliberately chosen to ignore her. Am I so unimportant, she wondered, that even my own father felt nothing? Nothing at all? Maybe, just maybe he hadn't realised who I was, a small voice of hope intruded, only to be quickly squashed by her more rational thought.

58

NINJA

When reflecting on the ebb and flow of a war on her and David's emotional shores, Sophie had often thought of how we dream of violence and fear it. Like an intermittent intruder on our waking moments it lies there, forever lurking in our subconscious, ready to present itself when least expected.

She arrived home to an empty house late that Sunday night. Lalana was not due to return till the following morning. It had been a somewhat tedious night, a party given by Gerard for business friends, and she had made a last-minute decision to go. She hadn't as yet told him of her discovery with the photograph, wanting to hug these findings to herself, at least until David returned.

But she could confront Atsuo, if she went to Japan with Gerard.

'He's got an important meeting tomorrow, with some big wigs from Tokyo,' Jill had told her. 'So at the moment his mind's on anything but us.'

Apart from a few brief spells mingling with his guests, he'd hardly appeared, and she decided that the time wasn't right to bring up anything.

It was a relief to be home, and Sophie kicked off her high-heeled sandals and unzipped her dress. It really was too tight to wear any more, she thought, slipping into a loose cotton muu-muu. She could hardly wait to lie down. In the past few days she had been exhausted, the pregnancy starting to make itself felt. When she complained of the never-ending tiredness, Jill had replied somewhat tartly, 'Honestly Sophie, you're so lucky you've never had morning sickness. You haven't thrown up once. I spent the first three months with my head over a basin.'

Sophie warmed some milk, then took it out onto the lanai, sipping as she listened to the sea rolling in against the retaining wall below. She hated going to bed when David wasn't there. While he was away, she often slept on the couch in their living room. The night didn't seem quite so long there. Bolting the glass French doors, and putting on a Dylan tape, she lay on the couch looking out into the garden as the sound of his voice and guitar filled the empty spaces.

As she settled back, she thought she saw a movement through the wiliwili trees. Just a fleeting shadow. She stared into the darkness, but all was still. No doubt a night owl. There was a family of owls nestling in the garden, Lalana had told her only that morning. They had flown in from the rainbow valley of *Manoa,* from the home of the owl god *Pueno,* and it was very auspicious, she said.

Sophie felt uneasy and wished Lalana, who had come across for the day, was still there, as she hated being alone. Since her pregnancy, Lalana had made a point of spending more time in the house with her, laboriously making her way from Hiroko's house to be with her, almost like an old guard dog Sophie thought with fondness.

A sudden sound roused her and she sat up, every sense alert. Quietly she moved towards the arched doorway. She could hear the soft, careful movements of someone in the next room and see an occasional flash of a torch piercing the darkness as it bounced off the wall. She paused for a moment, the sound of her heart pounding in her ears as, with a sinking sensation, she realised she would have to walk through that room to get to the phone.

Slowly she moved across the room and through to the adjacent hallway. It was then she saw him, a dark shadowy figure as he got up from taking something from a chest. It was the lacquered chest Hiroko had sent to the house only two days before, the one in which she had placed the precious scrolls. Panic assailed her. He was taking the scrolls, the *Sesshu* scrolls.

Sophie stood, frozen, as he turned and moved towards her, seeming to fly like a Ninja. She must get to the phone quickly. She ran, knocking over a chair, and then everything moved at lightning speed. He leapt and was upon her. She was aware of the strange vaguely familiar smell and strength of the body now grappling with her. She screamed and a hand clamped across her mouth, jerking her head back so she felt as if her neck would snap. She bit into his hand, and he grunted but still held on, his fingers like iron across her lips as he dragged her to the floor, her arms across her stomach as if to ward off any blows to the child within.

The scrolls had fallen to the floor, but now his energies were concentrated on her. She saw a curve of torchlight on the wall as it arced up, then down, and with the force of rock hit her head. Then she was falling, falling through an explosion of lights into a black well of oblivion.

How many hours, days, years had passed till she opened her eyes? Her body seemed to belong to someone else as she floated, looking down at it. She couldn't move, all co-ordination had left her. She lay there as the sun's first golden pink rays spilled across the early morning sky.

She was flying, like Apollo's son, in a chariot across the sky, but her strength had gone and she couldn't hold the horses, as with a heady bid for freedom within their slackened reins they charged across the heavens towards the sun. That must be why she felt so hot, Sophie thought, and why her eyes and head throbbed with a pain so intense that she cried out. Without warning she was vomiting, the bile liquid forming a pool around her hair. As her retching ceased, she felt a slow trickle of fluid between her legs, and she cried out with all her strength. 'No, the baby, the baby! David!' But she couldn't move and lay back as pain and darkness engulfed her once more.

59

MATSUHIRO'S REQUEST

As Atsuo drove towards Nihonbashi, he imagined himself in a flying suit, on the deck of a carrier as it ploughed through the Coral Sea. He was preparing to join the other men, little more than boys, the daring in their eyes barely concealing dark shadows of fear. Like Icarus, they would be borne aloft, the soul of *Kamikaze*, the divine wind carrying them across the Pacific only to fly too close to a sun that was their island nation, rising from a China sea.

Matsuhiro had sent for him, and talked generally of business matters.

'I would like you to look into something for me, Uncle,' he said. 'It requires a specific knowledge and you would be best suited to handle it.' He then spoke of some problems he was having with their drug links into the American market.

'It needs someone with real authority to look into it, and should only take a few days.' Atsuo waited.

'That is not all, I have been approached on a somewhat sensitive matter, and it requires someone who has the right contacts to handle it,' his nephew continued, remembering his father Akira's words. Careful planning and preparation is what really counts, he'd said. A weak foundation and the whole structure falls. He smiled to himself, thinking how proud his father would be of him now.

Atsuo said nothing. He knew how his nephew's mind worked, and waited for him to eventually get around to what he really wanted.

Matsuhiro went on. 'It's regarding a family in Hawaii. I understand they have taken what should rightfully have stayed here. It concerns some valuable artworks that are now residing with this family in Hawaii.' He then told Atsuo about Satoshi's request for assistance in the matter.

'Surely Hiro can handle this for you,' responded Atsuo, guardedly.

'Unfortunately not completely, Uncle, as it seems you have already met at least one of the participants,' Matsuhiro answered, his voice smooth, giving no hint of his thoughts. 'A Mrs Sophie Chapman.'

'Ahhh,' Atsuo thought, so he knows. But does he? He scrutinised the younger man. Without giving him time to reply, Matsuhiro went on. 'She is the granddaughter of a Japanese-born woman, Hiroko Sen, who took these artworks to Honolulu, among other things, in the late thirties just before we were at war. Hiroko is dying, yet she refuses to acknowledge her son Satoshi Nakamura's claim to them.'

And there was still the debt of *giri* to the Nakamura family for the Isawa clan to repay, Atsuo recalled. Favours extended to Daihachi and Akira Isawa in black market dealings during the Manchukuo war, and still not fully repaid.

'It could be unsafe for me to go to Hawaii again,' Atsuo said, playing for time. 'I could be recognised, and I'm too old to stand trial now.' The Pearl Harbor attack was still fresh in the minds of many. He'd risked that brief trip back in 1960, at Hiro's request, but to risk it again, especially now with all that was emerging . . . Did Matsuhiro know his real link with the Baillieu family? He must have found out, he thought, and Matsuhiro's next words confirmed it.

'I have been advised that they are scrolls worth many

millions, Uncle,' he said, 'and as our payment for getting them back, I have agreed to a third of the selling price, and that you will agree is too large a sum to be ignored. And another thing,' his voice barely above a whisper now, 'you will no doubt agree that it would be in your interest, as well as our family's, for there to be no scandal, no ghosts from the past to spoil this, *ne?*'

When Atsuo didn't answer, he added, 'Being recognised will be the very least of your worries, Uncle. Anyway I have already sent Hiro ahead to set things up for you, and clear the way in retrieving the scrolls, but it will be up to you to finally negotiate with the Baillieu family. And knowing Sophie Chapman as you do will make all the difference I'm sure.' Matsuhiro bowed slightly, to hide his smile.

Atsuo listened to his nephew unfolding his plans. This business with Matsuhiro was getting out of hand, as he knew it would one day. Matsuhiro had established an unassailable position for himself now as the powerful *oyabun* within the Isawa-*gumi*.

Despite his undertaking to his dying brother Akira, he could see that it was now time for him, Atsuo, to step completely aside. This would be on his own terms, but he sensed that there could well be a threat to his life if he openly opposed his nephew now. Matsuhiro was hell-bent on acquiring total power, and would not tolerate opposition from an uncle he saw as part of an outdated hierarchy.

As Matsuhiro had spoken of his and the Nakamura interest in retrieving the scrolls, Atsuo couldn't help but think that his nephew lacked the spirit of *satori*. His vanity and personal desires for easy wealth seemed to over-ride any real sense of greater obligation, and as such he was a dangerous man. Whereas he, Atsuo, was a man who was not self-seeking but self-disciplined and free of selfish passion. He thought of the maxim he'd taught Matsuhiro as a boy, 'behold the frog who when he opens his mouth displays his whole inside', but they were lessons in humility he'd long forgotten. Atsuo listened quietly while formulating his own plans.

Matsuhiro watched his uncle as he spoke. He could see that the threat of exposure of his American-born daughter had hit the mark. His uncle had become very quiet, and was going along with his plan. That was good. As usual, everything seemed to be progressing just as he'd planned.

On his way home, Atsuo wondered about the art works. If these scrolls were so valuable, they must be very old and maybe of historic importance. He felt a sense of anticipation that here was something that could be retrieved and brought back to its country of origin, as part of the nation's rightful heritage. Matsuhiro was only interested in their monetary value and a quick sale, but if they were truly of historic importance they must not be lost again.

He thought of this other daughter who, despite his turning his back on her, had intruded into his life yet again. Gina's presence was only a shadowy memory now. Like the lion cat, she had laid her scent well on her young, he reflected, recalling how the lioness rubbed her head against her mate, then against her cubs, laying her scent and that of her mate's on the pride so that he didn't harm them in any way.

That night, back at his home, he made an offering of rice and persimmon, then prayed before the simple altar to his brother Akira's spirit, asking for wisdom and guidance in this matter with his son.

Afterwards he went to a box of papers he had long kept secret from Matsuhiro, and carefully went through them, looking for a letter his brother had given him many years before his death, the one that would help him now. Maybe it was time to lay certain cards on the table, he thought. He would fly to Honolulu, but not do as Matsuhiro expected. He would plot his own course on his appointment with destiny, and nothing his nephew could do would change his course this time.

* * *

Gerard was twenty minutes late in arriving for their meeting at the Moana Hotel. He had come from the hospital, the white heat of anger still upon him. It was simply unbelievable; Sophie attacked within her own home.

Her gynaecologist had beckoned Gerard outside. 'It's still touch and go,' he said. 'She has lost blood and her waters have partly broken, but with rest, we may still be able to save the pregnancy.'

When Gerard first saw her after she'd been raced to hospital, she was still partly sedated and only able to say a few words.

'The scrolls, he took the scrolls,' she whispered.

'What scrolls?' he'd asked, thinking she was delirious.

'Oba-san knows about them,' she said.

The whole thing was incredible, he fumed. She was so white and still badly concussed. Her pallor accentuated the dark bruise spreading down one side of her face, and her blackened eyes.

Later he had rung his mother from the hospital, without telling her the extent of Sophie's involvement or condition. He had broken the news to her gently, so as not to upset her, simply telling her that someone had broken into Sophie's house and stolen some scrolls.

'What scrolls are they, Mamma?' he asked.

'Is Sophie-chan all right?' Hiroko questioned. 'She wasn't hurt? Can I speak to her?' she went on as if not hearing what he had said.

'It has been a shock for her, Mamma, and she's resting.'

He didn't mention the hospital. Not yet; he would go and see her after this meeting, and tell her a little of what had happened then. But in the meantime, he needed to know what had been stolen.

'I asked Jill for you to ring me about it all,' Hiroko said with a note of exasperation in her voice.

'I'm sorry, I've been busy,' he replied.

'There's so much to say. Do we have to discuss it now on the phone?' she asked.

'Mamma,' he said, trying to keep his voice calm so as not to alert her, 'the scrolls have gone.'

'What do you mean, gone?' she asked.

'Stolen, gone, taken from the house.'

'Oh my God!' she said, panic in her voice. 'Have you told the police?'

'Yes, but it's important you tell me all about them now,' he said.

'But Sophie knows, ask her.'

'She's resting and I don't want to disturb her,' he answered.

'There's something wrong that you haven't told me,' his mother persisted. 'Where's Sophie, I want to speak to her now,' she said, her voice rising.

'She's asleep, but I'll get her to speak to you as soon as possible,' he said. 'Now tell me about the scrolls.'

She heard the steely note in his voice, and with long pauses for breath as she spoke, she had complied.

* * *

He was in no mood for this meeting. He felt angry with his mother and Sophie for not confiding in him in the beginning. With art works of such value in the family, he should have been told years ago so that adequate precautions could have been taken.

Who would have known of their value? Admittedly Sophie had disturbed the intruder, but he could have taken anything else of value after he'd knocked her unconscious. But only the scrolls had gone. Whoever it was knew the full value of the *Sesshu* artworks, he thought grimly.

After arriving at the Moana, to his surprise, rather than being ushered to the private room where he had usually conducted business with the Isawa *kobun*, he was taken through the foyer and out to the banyan court and to a corner table, set apart from the other guests.

At first he didn't recognise the figure sitting at the table, then as he turned, realised it was that odd guy he'd briefly negotiated with through Hiro Miyaji at the Royal Hawaiian seven or so years ago. It certainly wasn't Matsuhiro Isawa—so it was not to be a meeting with the *oyabun* this time.

A further surprise, too, was that the man rising to greet him was alone. A quick look around the room revealed none of the usual group of *yakuza* henchmen lolling in the background. After their initial greeting, and his apology for being late, Gerard said, 'We have met before?'

With a small bow, the other man extended his hand and replied, 'Atsuo Isawa, Mr Baillieu, and as you will recall, we have met. Now what will you have to drink?' he asked, beckoning the waiter.

Gerard was quietly regarding him as Atsuo sat and gave their order, feeling a faint sense of recognition, but from where and when?

He reached for his whisky. 'I thought it might have been Matsuhiro Isawa I would be meeting this time,' he remarked, looking closely at the man opposite him, trying to piece together all that Sophie had told him regarding their meeting. There was something about him, and Atsuo's next words confirmed it.

'I have come at my nephew Matsuhiro Isawa's request, but that's not only why I'm here. We have met, many times, but long ago and that is why I am here today instead of my nephew Matsuhiro,' he said.

He gazed steadily at Gerard's face now, as he continued.

'Atsuo Isawa is my name, but,' he paused, steeling himself for what was to come, 'but you know me as Katsura Kurosawa.'

Gerard stared at him as if everything had stopped, then half rose as if to strike out.

'No theatrics now, Mr Baillieu,' Atsuo said smoothly, speaking softly in Japanese. 'It would not be in my interest, and certainly not in yours. We have much to talk about, and very little time, so let us do it in a civilised manner.'

'Just who the hell do you think you are, coming in and telling me what you want. We've got enough on you to lock you away forever!' Gerard spoke softly now but each word was measured for its impact. 'You bastard!' he hissed. 'How many years have I been looking for you, and now you just turn up and . . .' then stopped as he realised for the first time that this man, Atsuo Isawa, who Sophie had mentioned she had dined with in Japan, was not only part of the group he'd been dealing with all these years but the same man who, when faced by his own daughter, had tricked her into thinking her father was dead.

Atsuo coolly watched him, knowing what he was thinking. 'Yes,' he said, 'I believe you had some dealings with my late brother Akira, and for some years now with his son, Matsuhiro. My daughter and I have already met in Tokyo.'

Mentally Gerard pictured the acts of violence he'd like to inflict on the man. The clever, cunning bastard, he'd set up this meeting in a public place to sidestep any threat of attack, and now he was even quick to pre-empt the obvious questions. So what did the double-dealing son of a bitch really want, and why had he come here? He ordered another whisky, and sat quietly observing Atsuo's face and taking in the many changes, as the other man told him a little, but only what he wished to reveal, of his life in the past years and of his involvement with the Isawa-*gumi*. He deliberately touched on the key part Gerard had played in initially aiding and abetting the Isawa-*gumi*'s money-laundering activities on the Island and into the mainland, and now his involvement with their channelling of drugs from Vietnam into America and Japan.

For Gerard, it was an effort to fully take in what Atsuo was saying. He could think only of the morning he had flown back into Honolulu after the bombing, and first seen Jill's face as she stood there to greet him with baby

Sophie in her arms. Then as she'd told him of Gina, he recalled the pain of that knife cutting through his other natal half, severing his twin sister from his life forever.

'You son of a bitch!' he said, breaking in across Atsuo's voice. 'You murdered my sister.'

'Murdered her?' Atsuo looked at him, startled.

'As good as,' Gerard leaned in close to him, 'as good as if you'd dropped the bloody bomb on her yourself.'

'She was killed in the bombing?'

'When you left, you killed her,' said Gerard.

Atsuo paused a moment. 'It's about that I wish to speak now.'

Gerard's mind, starting to clear, leapt ahead. The bastard was here for a pay-off of some kind. He sensed the *junkatsuyu* used to smooth things over. And it wasn't just their mutual interest in the Isawa *yakuza* money-laundering network that he'd just been on about either. Not this time. Gerard stared at him, his eyes like bullets.

'Cut the crap, Atsuo, and tell me what you really want,' he sneered, 'then I'll tell you!'

The other man stiffened, and Gerard could see he had difficulty in curbing his anger.

'The Isawa-*gumi* have been approached by, I believe, your half-brother, Satoshi Nakamura.'

Gerard tensed, and waited for Atsuo to continue.

'He is concerned about certain property that was brought here many years ago by his mother, and which he now wishes to lay claim to as his rightful inheritance.'

As he spoke, Gerard's mind had moved into overdrive, and he rose to his feet, pushing back the table.

'The scrolls!' he hissed.

People at the other tables were staring openly at them now. Atsuo half rose, and said quietly in Japanese, 'Sit down and listen.'

But Gerard stayed standing, towering over the other man, then leaning forward and thrusting his face towards Atsuo, he snarled, 'She was bloody near killed!'

'Who? What are you talking about?'

'Sophie,' Gerard said, 'your daughter.'

'When? What do you mean?' A note of alarm had crept in.

'Last night someone broke into her house and bludgeoned her about the head and stole the *Sesshu* scrolls.' Gerard's voice was cold and measured. He saw the quick look of surprise, then anger, pass over Atsuo's face.

So, Atsuo thought, Matsuhiro couldn't wait for him to act. His nephew had got his hoods to get in first before he'd had half a chance to negotiate. He felt cold with anger and humiliation. But his nephew would keep, he thought.

'I knew nothing about that,' he said. 'It seems Matsuhiro has gone ahead with his plans and not informed me.'

Gerard sat down and stared at him, as the light started to dawn. So things weren't going well at the Isawa corral, he thought, and there's a falling-out among thieves. The light was becoming bright as day.

So that was what Atsuo was really on about. No doubt Matsuhiro, being a true son of his father Akira, had got wind of his uncle's relationship to Sophie and the Baillieu family, and had sent his uncle to negotiate a deal, while he set about his own dirty work behind his uncle's back. While Atsuo, he thought, hoping to defuse any threat his nephew could hold over him regarding his relationship to our family, had decided to come out in the open. After all, what did he have to lose? He knows too much about my dealings with the Isawa-*gumi* to know I couldn't pull the plug on him now.

Gerard gave a bitter laugh and said, 'I guess this is what you'd call a *Yakuza*-Yankee stand-off.' Then looking hard into Atsuo's eyes, he leaned across the table.

'I'll never forgive you for what you did to my sister, and despite what you think you can hang on me, if those scrolls aren't returned fast, and Sophie's safety ensured, I'll see to it that you're handed over to a bunch of people who'll take the greatest delight in seeing you, and yours, die slowly.'

With that he rose to his feet, and without a backward glance strode from the hotel.

Atsuo sat for some minutes without moving, then he quickly downed the last of his whisky and ordered another. He looked across at the spreading banyan tree, winking with tiny white lights threaded through its boughs, ready to greet the festive season. A breeze wafting in across Waikiki beach from the sea brought with it the warm smell of coconut oil, and memories of the night he and Gina had last sat here.

He'd hoped to achieve so much for his revered Emperor and country then, and this place, still beautiful but changing, had been his springboard.

He thought of his children Yasunari and Sumiko, and their place in this new order of things. Then his mind turned to Sophie.

60

AWAKENING

Sophie opened her eyes and saw him standing there. He was looking out through the floor-length windows, watching something in the grounds below. Sunlight streamed in across her bed and myriad flecks of dust magnified by light suspended in the air above her. She followed one particular shining speck as it floated this way and that, at the mercy of every fleeting air current, moving with it in her thoughts. Everything seemed so sharp and clearly defined, like the acid trips David had described to her, where even the most simple things exploded into an hallucinogenic surreality, so enlarged and intense that often the solace of death seemed preferable to this overwhelming mirage of the mind.

The harshness of the light pained her eyes and she raised her hands as if to ward off its intensity, moaning as she did. He turned, and it was then she saw who it was. He moved across to her bed and sat beside her. She saw concern in his eyes that were now without their usual screen of darkened glasses, and there seemed a softening in his strangely taut face. He sat upright and proud beside her bed.

'How are you feeling now, Sophie-chan?'

Chan—child? He had said chan! That one word was illuminated by all its associations.

She couldn't bring herself to speak, her eyes taking in every detail of this man who was her father. He seemed so different, sitting here in the morning light, the formality of that night at the Teikoku Hotel replaced by his more casual appearance. She sensed the separateness, the monk-like control she had seen in the temples and shrines, where the spiritual flame of belief fuelled the promise that Earth was but a temporary staging post in the pursuit of karma.

Where had he come from, she wondered. Wasn't that how it had always been, recalling the stories and myths that had peopled her dreaming where, when a child was in danger, the parent appeared as if by magic to save it? It was a little late this time, but he had come now.

'Sophie-chan,' Atsuo repeated, 'are you all right?' This time he spoke in English and she sighed, a deep drawn-out expression of journey's end, and speaking in little more than a whisper she replied, 'You knew, but didn't tell me.'

He said nothing, and she knew in that moment that accusations and past disappointments would have no place in their relationship, if there was to be one now. There were too many lost moments to recall. Once raised, their bridge would never span the tears and shadows of recrimination. This was to be like Day One, a rebirth, she decided, and as she looked at him, the tears she'd tried to hold back for a lifetime brimmed up and over in a gentle wash of relief and release.

'Thank you for coming,' she whispered, 'Papa.'

They were silent awhile, then he handed her a small package.

'This belongs to you. Do not lose it,' he said. Then with a small bow, he stood to go.

She watched him leave, but knew he wasn't going from her life, not now. The link had been established, and she would take it from there. As he turned at the door and looked back once more, half raising his hand in farewell to her, it was as if she was seeing him for the first time. It was later when the nurse told her that for over two hours he had sat by her bedside, waiting for her to wake.

She looked at the packet for some minutes. It was as

if everything in her life was still on hold and any movement came gradually. Slowly she unwrapped it, and a key fell out. Attached to it was a ticket and on it was written the name and address of a downtown Honolulu bank, and a number. What did it all mean? She suddenly felt very tired, and with the key clasped tightly in her hand fell asleep.

As Atsuo drove away in the darkened limo, he recalled how, watching that small figure in the hospital bed as she slept, he'd thought of his daughter Sumiko, and how alike they were in sleep. Their childlike defencelessness in repose gave them a sisterly bond.

His inital fury at Matsuhiro's act of deception, a move that had knowingly threatened the life of his own flesh and blood, had given way to some rapid thinking. He would break right away from his nephew's organisation. It was beyond his control, and he was not about to spend the rest of his life faction fighting to change it. He had wealth enough to achieve what he wanted without that.

He had taken two copies of the letter that would help effect the change he desired, and now carefully refolded the yellowing pages of the original, he placed it within an envelope. He wrote Gerard's name upon it, and directed his driver to Gerard's office. His thoughts on what should become of the scrolls could keep till later.

Gerard saw the key still clasped in her hand when he looked in on her, on his way to the office. There was a trace of colour in her face, and for the first time he felt that things would be fine.

Her eyes flew open as he approached the bed, and she murmured, 'Papa?'

'What, honey?' He gave her a light kiss and sat down beside her.

'Oh, it's you, Gera. I thought it was . . .'

'Was who?' he prompted.

'Katsura, I mean Atsuo, was here,' she said, as if the old name was to be replaced forever.

Gerard stood up, looking agitated. 'When, what did he say?' he asked.

'He gave me this.' She opened her hand, revealing the key. 'He said it belongs to me, and not to lose it,' she added, remembering his words.

He took the key from her outstretched palm, and read the attached tag.

'He came, when he knew I needed him.'

Gerard stared. So she knew who Atsuo was.

'Look honey . . .' he started to say.

'Yes, I know who he is,' she interrupted. 'I was going to ask you to take me to Japan to see if I could find him, but now there's no need.'

Gerard thought of a thousand words of warning he'd like to pour out, but didn't. She must not be upset, not now while there was still a chance to save the child.

As if reading his thoughts, Sophie suddenly remembered.

'The baby!' she cried, her eyes widening.

'Everything's fine,' he said, 'just fine with your baby. But you'll have to rest for some time yet.'

She ran her hands across her stomach. Yes, everything felt as it had before, still the fullness and the same sense of growth within.

'Thank God, thank God,' she murmured, crossing herself and closing her eyes, praying with a fervour she could never recall before. 'Thank you heavenly Father for your blessing on this new life and for safeguarding our child. And I thank you for returning my father to me.'

There was a pause, then Gerard's voice, firm and reassuring, 'David's flying in this afternoon.'

'David . . .' she murmured.

'In the meantime is there anything you want, honey?'

She shook her head, her mind still on his news.

'I will call you later then,' he said. At the door he turned and, holding up the key, said, 'I think we may have our scrolls back, Sophie.' He grinned. 'So keep your fingers crossed!' He was gone before she could ask why or how.

61

REDEMPTION

'Gerard, can't you talk her out of it, the whole idea is crazy. It's not just the value of the scrolls, but they belong to the family, our family,' Jill added significantly.

Ignoring her point, he sighed. 'After what we've just been through, they could be a bloody headache, and it's better that . . .'

'You could always sell them,' Jill broke in.

'No,' he said, 'they are not mine to sell. They are Sophie's now, and it's her decision.'

'Anyway,' Jill changed course, 'if anyone should have them, it should be the American people. When you think of what they went through at the hands of those bastards, not to mention you and Bill and Tom and all the others back home. I feel mad about the whole bloody thing,' she exclaimed, feeling tears of frustration as the thought of Tom touched a long-forgotten chord.

'So what are we going to do, Gerard?' she went on. 'I just don't really feel part of any of your decision making any more.' Lately, despite attempts at being her usual positive self, she'd started to feel as if she was just moving from one day to the next, not really knowing when or where anything was leading.

Her thoughts went back to their discussion yesterday.

'I'm going to bequeath them to the Japanese nation,' Sophie had informed them.

'Bequeath what?' Jill had asked.

'The scrolls of course,' Sophie said. 'That is where they belong. They've been hidden away far too long. They should be out for everyone to enjoy.'

'Atsuo's idea, no doubt,' Jill said tartly.

Sophie flushed in anger. 'No, not at all,' she replied. 'I haven't spoken to him since that day at the hospital.'

Jill was silent, curbing the resentment she felt towards this man who had suddenly resurfaced in their lives. Gerard didn't seem to want to talk about him, and she felt shut out of the whole process.

'Well, what about giving them to the gallery or museum right here, and we can all enjoy them?'

'It's not the same, Jilly. I've been reading about Sesshu, the man who painted them, and he is one of Japan's most famous artists, and part of their cultural heritage. He belongs there,' Sophie insisted.

An idea was gradually forming and taking shape in her mind, and as it grew she could see that everything had in its way led to this moment she now envisaged.

'Anyway art is international, or should be, so why does it have to belong there or anywhere?' Jill persisted.

'It has to have a home, the right home,' Sophie answered.

Sophie did not mention the note Atsuo had sent her. Jill would only have misconstrued it. She had written to him, thanking him for coming to the hospital and for retrieving the scrolls. She added that she was wondering now what would be best to do with them; also that she hoped she would see him again soon. It was then that her plan had started to form, and a small note had arrived from him. On it was written simply a *haiku* verse.

Guntai no
Chikazuku oto ya
Shufuri
Banryoku no

Uchi ya ako no ha
Haesomuru
Sora wa taisho no
Aosa Tsuma yori
Ringo uku.[18]
The tramping sound
of troops approaching
In autumn wind.
In the midst of
All things verdant, my baby
Has begun to teethe.
The sky is blue
Of the world's beginning from my wife
I accept an apple.

It was almost as if he had read Sophie's thoughts, and was giving approval to what she was planning to do.

She had spoken to her grandmother about the idea when she first devised it, and Hiroko, after some initial doubts, had also given her blessing.

Maybe this was the only thing to do now, Hiroko reflected, and her father Yukio-san would no doubt have approved. Although Gerard hadn't spelled anything out, she knew in her bones that there had been something more than just a break-in. She feared what could happen in the future.

'The time has come to let go, you're right,' she smiled at Sophie, her bruises just the faintest shadowy reminder of that night. 'Are you feeling better Sophie-chan?'

'I feel fine, Oba-san. Don't worry, everything's going to be just as it should be.'

Gerard had informed his mother of his meeting with Atsuo and the discovery of Katsura's true identity.

'Does Sophie know?' Hiroko asked.

'She does,' he replied, and explained what had happened.

Hiroko sat quietly listening. It was as if everything had turned full circle, she thought, without surprise. Gerard told her that it was Satoshi who had instigated the theft of the scrolls, and set the whole thing in motion. As Gerard spoke, she thought of Satoshi, the small boy, and the resentful angry man he had become, staring accusingly at her before he left.

She held up her hand, to stem the flow of Gerard's words. 'I have misjudged him,' Hiroko began.

'What do you mean?'

She didn't answer for a moment, trying to calm the sense of sadness that had suddenly risen like a wave to engulf her. 'I haven't really looked at this whole thing through his eyes,' she announced.

Gerard stared at her, too exasperated to speak. She'll never stop forgiving the little bastard, he thought bitterly.

'We'll have to do something about him before he does any more damage,' he said grimly.

'I know,' she answered. 'I just want a little time to think about it. Can we speak later?'

Stifling his hurt and disappointment, Gerard got up to go. 'Of course,' he answered briefly. He then handed her the letter Atsuo had left in his office.

'Read it later, after I've gone,' he said. 'It will solve a lot of your unanswered questions from the past, things that are better known than not. Don't be sad for him Mamma,' he added, turning to go.

As he left, she called out to him, an urgent appeal in her voice.

'Gerard!'

'Yes?' he looked back at her, as she sat holding the envelope, still unopened.

'I have been very foolish about so many things. You have been a good son to me, Gerard-chan, and if I haven't always shown it, you are always there, firmly planted in my heart,' she added, smiling tentatively. He nodded and turned abruptly so she would not see the quick tears that had sprung to his eyes.

Hiroko sat for some time looking at the envelope, addressed to Daihachi Isawa. She recalled the name from her days in the Nakamura household. He had visited them there once, she suddenly recalled, the day she had been photographed with Noboru before he left for Manchukuo. Michiko had insisted on being in the photo too, and holding Satoshi, who was only a baby then. That Michiko, always forcing her way into everything. She had even been making eyes at Daihachi Isawa that day too, she remembered. And now it seemed from what Gerard had just told her, that his son Akira was the older brother of Gina's husband, Katsura, or should she call him Atsuo now? How strange that he should come back into their lives like this. But her Gina would never return, she thought, the bitterness rising. It was like circles within circles, she mused, remembering how, as a child, she had cast small stones into a pond of carp near their home, and watched as the circular ripples widened and spread, getting fainter and fainter as they moved from the central point where the stone had landed and sunk without trace.

A rustling in the plumbago bushes nearby made her turn in time to see two Nene geese who had made their home in her garden. They mate for life, she thought, just as Boy and I had hoped, but our union was broken too soon to fulfil its promise.

The geese, their rich cream and grey-brown markings catching the morning sun, stopped and stared, suddenly aware of her. Their gentle eyes were without reproach or fear of danger, calmly accepting with equanimity their rightful place here in her domain.

Hiroko saw that the letter she held was in Michiko's bold hand. So she had even written to this Daihachi Isawa, she thought with a quickening of interest. With trembling fingers, she drew out the yellowing rice paper sheets. She could almost hear Michiko's harsh voice speaking the words as she read them. After a flowery introduction, full of over-solicitous greetings and apologies for troubling him, Michiko had got straight to the point, referring to how happy it had made the Nakamura family to have been of service, in extending assistance to Daihachi Isawa-san in certain land deals and in the transporting of copper and nickel out of Manchukuo. She then went on to say that in the name of her now deceased brother Noboru and the Nakamura family, she was requesting a favour, and felt confident that with his many contacts in his thriving organisation, he would be the person best equipped to assist them in this matter.

'We have a snake in our midst,' she had written, 'who threatens to destroy our young, the rightful heir of our family and my late brother's only son, and so tarnish our family's honour.'

As Hiroko read these words, a cold stab of suspicion began to surface. Was she referring to herself or to Boy?

Michiko had then worked herself into a near frenzy of descriptive phrases, about the American threat that had entered their lives and of the shameful marriage of her brother's widow to this foreign usurper who, not content with bringing disgrace to the family name, was now threatening to remove their rightful heir, her brother's child, to America.

'I implore you,' she wrote, 'to see the vital importance of this whole matter. Immediate and decisive action is called for, as time is of the essence, and he could be abducted from us at any time.'

She again referred to the Nakamuras being happy to have been of service to him, and then closed the letter, which she was having hand delivered, saying she would contact him that night to discuss a way to remove this stain that threatened to darken their family's, as well as their national, honour. 'A stain that must be finally eradicated, and with haste,' she said. Then with profuse salutations, the letter had ended.

Hiroko recalled the love letter Boy had sent to her from Miyanoshita referring to a 'D' who was going to help him retrieve Satoshi. So Boy's death *had* been a premeditated murder, and the instigator had been her former sister-in-law, Michiko Nakamura. A sudden flame of anger shot through her and she wished she was young again with the power of *Pele* to grasp this evil woman by her throat and squeeze and squeeze until not a breath of air was left. She imagined herself throwing the body into the crater of *Halemaumau* and watching as it bounced and bounded on its way into the molten depths.

'Oh Boy,' she whispered, remembering the stories he had told her of *Pele*, the fiery goddess of many volcanoes from which the Hawaiian islands had sprung, and how as an old woman in sleep she could, on waking, throw off the mantle of age and, rising from the shell of her old body, become young and beautiful again to ride upon the crest of the curling waves, sometimes with *Kamohoalii* the great shark god as her surfboard.

But the myth had no reality, and Michiko had gone to join her ancestors. She crossed herself and asked for forgiveness for her vengeful thoughts. But she couldn't bring herself to ask for forgiveness for Michiko.

She marvelled at the letter's malicious intent, then carefully folding it, replaced it in its envelope and sat quietly, deciding what best to do.

Later she had Malo drive her downtown to Communion and evening mass at Our Lady of Peace cathedral. She craved the sustenance of the sacrificial meal, the solace of redemption. 'Whom do we receive in Holy Communion,' she murmured, then answered, 'in Holy Communion we receive Jesus Christ, Body and Blood, Soul and Divinity under the appearance of bread and wine.' She chose communion 'under both kinds', the bread and wine, for full participation in the Sacrifice and heavenly banquet.

'Unless you eat the flesh of the Son of Man, and drink his blood, you have no life in you. He who eats my flesh and drinks my blood has eternal life, and I will raise him up on the last day. For my flesh is food indeed and my blood is drink indeed. He who eats my flesh and drinks my blood abides in me and I in him.'[19]

In the church's dim peace, she sought the strength of the Holy Father, and the absolution of her sins for being too unyielding in the matter of Satoshi. It was not a mother's right to cast judgement on her child, no matter what disappointments he bestowed.

Malo assisted her, frail and shaking, to the Baillieu

pew, and she sat enveloped in the heavenly comfort of this sacred place that had given such succour to her spirit all these years. Soon she would go to meet her Boy, and sit at the feet of their holy Father, and all would be perfect again. As she had tasted the wine and the wafer and heard the intonation of the blessing, she knew in that moment what she planned to do. It filled her with a radiance and sense of freedom that comes with the act of bestowing total forgiveness. Gerard was going to Japan in a few days, and he could organise it all for her then.

62

SEPPUKU

Hiroko had given three letters to Gerard, with explicit instructions as to how she wished them to be delivered. Michiko's two letters first, and then her own letter later in the day.

'I wish Satoshi to have time to reflect,' she said. 'It is better you simply deliver them rather than getting involved in seeing him.'

When he objected to not confronting him, his mother spoke with surprising strength. 'I know you, Gerard. There would only be harsh words between you. Please do it my way, otherwise nothing will be gained.'

As Satoshi read through the two letters, the web of mutual obligation that had long bound him to a mental path he had tried to follow was suddenly stripped of all its interconnecting links.

He felt as if the ground on which he had stood all these years had crumbled from under him, and he was left suspended in a limbo largely of his own making. With this new realisation came a sense of shame and recrimination such as he'd never before experienced. Laying his head on the table, he gave way to deep wrenching sobs.

If all he had read was true, and how could he doubt it, his life with his Aunt Michiko had been based on a lie, a myth fed by the evil machinations of a woman who had set up the murder of his mother's husband, and worse, then by threat of death and forcible restraint of her child, had prevented his mother taking and keeping him with her. It was his Aunt Michiko, not his mother, who had betrayed him. The harsh cry of a black bird in the garden outside seemed to mirror the cry from his soul.

As he reread of his aunt's planned murder of Boy-san in the first letter, and her subsequent threat to his own and his mother's life in the second, voices and shadows from the past now came to haunt and humiliate him, and all the more because of his recent actions.

Mercifully, Kaori-san his wife and son Takeo were out of town visiting her family, and he was thankful he had been spared the added humiliation of their seeing him like this.

How many hours had elapsed since the letters first arrived? Now with them cast aside, Satoshi looked up at the night sky outside, the stars emerging in pin-pricks of twinkling light. He saw only the stars, his eyes drawn to their light as if to shun the blackness that surrounded them, the frightening darkness of death.

Tonight the stars reminded him of a summer in his youth when a myriad fireflies had descended in a cloud of light and settled in the hedges, turning them for a few brief minutes into a magic place of tiny lights. He and some friends had rushed out from the house, with hands outstretched to gather the shining booty, and they'd watched as the fireflies ascended into the sky, darting hither and thither in a burst of brilliance. He had managed to catch some and hastily put them into the sleeves of his *yukata*. He had caught twelve in all, he remembered with a flicker of pride. Later, his Aunt Michiko had screamed, then summoned him to her room, angry at finding them in her clothes cupboard. Accusingly she had flung open the cupboard door where they glowed like eyes looking out from the neatly stacked kimono. They seemed so pretty as they nestled amongst the folded fabrics, and he could never imagine why she had made such a fuss.

It was in that same cupboard, behind her clothes, that he had found a bundle of papers and letters after her death. He had put them aside with other papers to be looked at later. He sat up now, every sense alert. Those letters, where were they?

He went over to his wife's sandalwood chest, and after removing numerous articles from the top there, neatly contained in a *furoshiki,* he saw what he was looking for. Taking it to his desk, he carefully unfolded the cotton cloth that had long kept the letters safe.

A faint scent of the creamy flowers he had seen in his mother's garden in Honolulu—plumeria, she had called them—was released, and now yellowed with age, some petals scattered as he unfolded the pages in which they had been pressed. There was letter after letter she had sent to him, written over many years—not one of which he had ever received. He read them now, and a part of his life he had never experienced unfolded for him that night, with all the long-denied reassurances of a mother's love. Neatly tied in a separate bundle were the few anguished letters he had sent to her, carefully written in an unformed childish hand, imploring her to return. They had never been sent.

The rage and disappointment he'd long felt for his mother was now fully transferred to his aunt. Michiko had lied to him for all those years, and no doubt had lied about his inheritance, too. With a heightened feeling of remorse, he thought of how he had added to the shame by his recent demands. He'd had no word from Matsuhiro regarding the scrolls. Perhaps there was still time to prevent the whole thing. He must try and put everything right.

With growing urgency, Satoshi rang Matsuhiro's number, only to find that he was out of town and could not be contacted. He replaced the receiver with a sense of hopelessness, and a feeling that things were now out of his control. Later after he had bathed, he sat motionless on the *tatami*, his grandfather's ancestral sword in his arms, holding it as one would a lover, and thinking, 'You will become part of me, another arm to deliver me from the trials of this life.' Thoughts of *seppuku* intruded with their seductive glimpses of this final act of courage, tempting him with an offer of total atonement.

Would it not be more honourable, he thought, to put an end to his shame and restore the family's high standing which had been only further tainted by his recent action against his mother? He remembered his *sensei* teaching him many years ago that the way of the warrior was the way of death: to fight to the death, devoid of all fear, and so be immune from death. Such valour in combat encased one in the impenetrable shield of the victor. It was an act of total commitment, and so bound to succeed in a safe victory. But only, he added, if the enticing and weakening thought of victory remained outside the act of battle. A state of *'munen muso de aru'*, 'to be free of all worldly cares' must exist. The mind must be of no mind, *'munen'*, he recalled.

Satoshi unsheathed the sword, and took in the perfection of the silver-blue blade, curved and tempered to its finest point, the spirit of its master swordsmith essential in its substance. Slowly he looked around him. It was not all as it should be. There was no white-edged *tatami*, and no white cushion on which to kneel with the body resting back on its heels. Nor was there kneeling just behind him and to his left his chosen *kishaku-nin*, with this ancestral sword drawn and held aloft in both hands, ready to decapitate him at the moment they had agreed upon, to watch his face form the most subtle sign of deep-felt agony or a turning back, ready in that instant to deal his merciful blow.

Would that have been at the moment after he had removed the smaller sword from the tray and plunged it into his *hara*? Or would his courage have lasted through the complete ritual, slicing his abdomen from left to right, and then with a slight upwards tilt, the *jumonji*, then and only then drawing out and replacing the dirk, and leaning forward to present his neck for the final blow. He sat back, his face composed as if his mental re-enactment of this honourable act in greeting 'death as lighter than a feather' had calmed and restored his long-lost *samurai* spirit. He had arrived at this point almost by accident, rather than as a planned route. It was as if in playing out the fantasy of final self-sacrifice it had become a reality.

A sudden knocking on the door downstairs drew him from his trance. A cold shiver ran through him, and he laid aside the sword and waited for whoever it was to go away. There was an insistent knocking again; then he heard a swish of paper as something was pushed under the door, and the sound of footsteps retreating.

The spell of *muga* was broken, and he shook himself from its mantle, rose to his feet and went down to see what had been left. There was a long flat envelope, and on it in his mother's hand an informal message, 'for Satoshi'. Inside on ivory paper, she had written:

Satoshi-chan,
By the time you receive this, you will have read the two letters I sent ahead to you, and I hope have revised some of your previous thoughts and actions. Just as certain events in the past weeks have given me cause to look to my own attitudes.

You are perfectly right in the supposition that as my first-born son you are entitled to an inheritance, and I wish to settle that matter with you, I hope satisfactorily now. My lawyers will be transferring a sum of $250,000 to your bank, and I would also like to make a settlement on your only child, I believe, and my grandson, Takeo. However, I have just one request, and that is that Takeo comes himself to Hawaii, so we may meet at last, and I can personally hand it to him then.

Naturally, you and your wife are welcome as our guests, too.

Now there is another matter which will be of interest to you. The Sesshu scrolls have been returned to my grand-daughter Sophie by her father Atsuo Isawa, uncle of Matsuhiro Isawa. I am sure you will be pleased to know, that despite the break-in to her home, she was not badly harmed. But no more talk of that, it is well behind us now.

Let us not dwell on the shadows of the past, but look towards the brightness of the future, my son. There is much we can still do and enjoy, and our strength lies in our children.

My health is a little better, but time moves on. If you give your permission, I would like Takeo to be here for a special ceremony Sophie is arranging for early next month. Please let me know your decision, soon.

Mamma.

He put the letter aside. So, it was too late to stop the theft of the scrolls. It had already happened, and been thwarted. But if she knew of the extent of his involvement, his mother had had the grace not to openly implicate him in her words. And Atsuo Isawa, her grand-daughter's father!

The whole thing seemed like a nightmare, but his mother's willingness to start afresh filled him with a sense of release. She had offered a generous settlement, and Takeo was to benefit also. His long-felt sense of grievance seemed to be lifting, and in its place came a renewed hope.

Now he felt his allegiance lay with his mother, not the aunt who had cruelly usurped her place in his life, if not his affections, he thought. Hiroko had once more become central to his circle of *ko*.

63

DISCOVERY

Jill opened the letter that had arrived that morning from Maria. She had put off reading it, but maybe, she sighed, she had better look at it now before going downstairs to join the others. It was in Maria's usual scrawl, and read:

'Winganna',
November 1970

Darling Jilly,
It's one of those still hot days where I've spent every spare moment lying in the hammock under the big peppercorn tree, hoping for a breeze while listening to the hum of cicadas. The sound has been almost overwhelming! Long bursts of incessant whirring that every now and then changes beat to a faster more intensified sound that's quite deafening. Remember?? But I love it. It's like our first Christmas beetles which have just arrived, shiny incandescent bodies flying in through the broken screens and falling about everywhere, more often than not on their backs with legs waving hopelessly in the air, their reappearance assuring us that Chrissy's just around the corner, and everything's O.K. Thank God for that, AND our full water tanks!

Anyway, this is not just to chat on about insects

and the weather, but to talk about Jack and 'Winganna'.

The steam seems to have finally gone out of him, Jill, and since that whole business of transferring the property finally went through, Jack has dropped his bundle, and is barely keeping up with the work that has to be done. I've been here the last few days as with Tommy still away at school, I've been able to spend more time helping out. But things are in a mess. The new manager you put on hits the bottle more than he should, so we have a problem there.

You will really have to decide what's to be done, as it can't go on like this. Bill just won't have a bar of any of it now, and I seem to be the only one aware of what's happening. It's a pity, as it's a beautiful property, and Molly would turn in her grave if she could see the state it's in.

We had such good times here, remember? Is there any point in keeping it, if it's not being run properly? Our kids are too young as yet, and anyway you're mostly on the other side of the world with your life there. Bill is away flying most of the time, and I can't do it alone. Really Jilly, when it's all boiled down, it's your baby. So what about it??

Do be in touch as soon as possible.
With love from us all,
Maria XXXXX
p.s. Tommy will be twelve next month. Can you believe it? Why not be a true fairy godmother and fly down for his birthday—he'd love that.

Jill skimmed through the letter, impatiently. Really, it was just like Maria to dramatise everything rather than doing something effective. She was always intimating that she was taking on the weight of the world, and was such a martyr at times. Surely things couldn't be as bad as she said. The last thing Jill wanted to do now was to fly to Australia, and take on that whole business. God, Bill was a wash-out, she mused, transferring her impatience from

Maria. Just because he didn't have a stake there any more, he'd been completely selfish. At least he could give Maria some back-up.

As for Jack, it seemed he couldn't give a damn either, now that he didn't own 'Winganna'. Was it her fault he'd left that whole legal thing in such a mess? After all, it had been Jack's decision to stay on after she'd bought him out, she reassured herself. He'd agreed to carry on and had invested his money into some property on the coast down south somewhere.

Maybe it would be better if Jack finally left 'Winganna', she thought. Yes, she would have to replan it all. But in the meantime, it seemed she needed someone there who could take proper control of the running of the place, until she decided what was to be done. She would have to talk to Gerard; he would know what to do.

One thing was certain though, she didn't want to sell it, not yet. Ownership of all that land gave one such a sense of security. She would always have 'Winganna' to fall back on, and no-one could take it from her. If things ever went really wrong here, she mused, it was her safe haven, her escape hatch. She smiled as she tightened the belt on her jeans. She could still fit the buckle into the last notch, and she looked appraisingly at her image. Her tailored white shirt was tucked neatly into her Levis, under a handworked leather belt Gerard had brought back from Mexico last year. It was studded with silver and turquoise, but discreetly—understated, with just that touch of the exotic to set it apart.

She still had the slimness of a girl, and apart from a brief weight gain after the birth of baby Louise, which she had assiduously exercised away, her figure had maintained its spare look. She was wearing her hair longer now, smoothed back into a sleek shoulder-length bob, a la Grace Kelly. Any white hairs that appeared were soon blonded to a platinum perfection.

Carefully, Jill tightened the screws of her pearl and turquoise earrings fashioned from part of a brooch

Granny May had given her years ago. She thought of that sharp old woman now, and Molly, always busy keeping 'Winganna' the show place it had been, and sighed. She would have to take that all in hand, and soon. A spray of 'Joy', then a quick appraisal of the final effect and she was ready to go downstairs and greet their first guests.

She saw Gerard mixing with the early arrivals and felt a surge of pride. This handsome husband of hers had learnt well the distancing of charm, she observed, and used it to maximise most situations where he needed either time to think or the space in which to extricate himself from a situation he wanted to abandon. He had invited guests for a mid-morning brunch, not close friends, mostly business associates. It all looked so elegant, she reassured herself. They had put up the white marquee over the lanai as the day was promising to be hot. It threw a soft light which seemed to intensify the setting in a distillation of shapes and colours.

Sophie had brought over masses of roses from Maui, and they glowed amongst her silver and glassware and her white linen napery, their perfume pervading the house. She looked across to Sophie chatting animatedly with a tall fair man. David hadn't come after all. He had lots to do, Sophie informed her, but she wondered if this included chatting up some little piece at one of his favoured trysting places. As always when Jill thought of David, she felt uneasy. He and Gerard seemed to have established a fairly close working relationship, but she wondered about him and didn't trust him. And he certainly wasn't good enough for Sophie. Hopefully, he'd do the right thing by her and turn up to the ceremony Sophie was organising at the Memorial, but she wouldn't hold her breath. God knows why Sophie was so insistent on doing this whole thing with the scrolls anyway, but it was out of her hands, so she would just have to go along with it.

Jill looked over to Gerard in his white shirt and linen

pants and suddenly thought of the white rabbit in *Alice* and the rhyme,

> *How doth the little crocodile*
> *Improve his shining tail,*
> *And pour the waters of the Nile*
> *On every golden scale!*
> *How cheerfully he seems to grin,*
> *How neatly spreads his claws,*
> *And welcomes little fishes in,*
> *With gently smiling jaws!*[20]

She contemplated Gerard momentarily as he circulated amongst his 'little fishes'.

She recalled how she would beg her mother to read *Alice in Wonderland* to her at night, and for years afterwards how she'd felt she was Alice and that this was her story. After the accident when Freida was gone and she cried herself to sleep at night, she imagined that she would fall into this magic dream and change shape at will and, like Alice, swim in the pool of her own tears. Visions of Alice, her long hair floating behind her, still in her dress and apron and buttoned-strap shoes, swimming past the mouse who had fallen into the pool of tears along with her, had brought a sense of comfort in their familiarity.

'Ou est ma chatte?' she would whisper to herself, and laugh at the thought of the mouse leaping from the pool in fright. Feeling smart and sophisticated she would casually toss off her one French phrase for anyone near enough to hear.

She noticed Gerard as he circled the room, carefully working his way to a side door for his escape to the private sanctum of his study, no doubt to start making and receiving the interminable phone calls which seemed to punctuate his life at home. She could see he needed a breather from the demands of playing host, and smiled as she caught his eye on the way out. He gave her a quick wink as if to say, I can always rely on you to take over, Jilly.

It wasn't until later that she remembered the bony face of her hated English mistress from fifth form, her nasal voice intoning, 'Pride goes before a fall, Jill Ferris. Pride goes before a fall.' It was just after that she had missed out on gaining the coveted senior literature award, after widely boasting it was hers for the taking. She remembered to this day the bitter sting of defeat.

Reflecting on her feeling of confidence that morning with her guests, how could she have known that only four hours later there would be the hateful discovery? After everyone had left, she had asked her houseboy Eleio to lift Gerard's old suitcase down from the top of his bureau, as she'd decided to throw out old things that weren't used any more. It wasn't empty as she had expected, and in the sleeve of the lid were the letters.

Was the pain of finding a lover in your husband's past life any better or worse than the discovery that he had a current mistress? At least, a mistress would be someone tangible to deal with. Jill thought back on their life together. He'd always seemed rather indifferent to the charms of other women.

Holding the letters, her heart hurting, she realised that there was a side to Gerard she had never known. She had put it down to his preoccupation with work and his single-mindedness. But now after reading of his anguish in those early days after Iman had gone, and his hungering for her all these years, she knew in that instant that she had indeed only ever possessed a part of him.

He'd had everything she could give—absolutely all her love. But she couldn't say the same for Gerard, and now she knew why. She felt a searing anger well up at his betrayal as she paced the room, wanting to hit out at whatever came in her way. If he had been there now, she would have killed him without hesitation and without compunction. She looked again at the pages spread out on her dressing table, letters from Iman, and the many he'd written in reply over the years but never sent. It was almost as if in writing them he had found a confessional, an outlet for his built-up passion for this woman, this bloody Iman.

When she'd found them tucked into the lid of his case, she'd thought how unlike Gerard it was, not to have got rid of such evidence years ago. But even as she reflected on this, she realised that it was not Gerard who would be harmed by such a discovery, only herself. After all, it was a passion of the past, ostensibly over before she had become part of his life. There was nothing here that could be used in a divorce to sweeten the way for her. He was quite safe with this kind of evidence, she thought bitterly.

Only she, who realised now its real bearing on their life together, only she would be aware of its full impact. This was a cheating that went way back, and had a reality that only she could understand.

The bastard! bastard! she fumed, her resentment fuelled not so much by the affair, but the fact that, as a result of it, he'd only ever given her a part measure of what she really deserved. Worse still, Gerard, her husband, was still emotionally and mentally tied to this woman from the past. His precious Iman.

Jill couldn't bring herself to cry. There was to be no pool of tears here to wash away her sorrows, she thought.

Feeling drained, she replaced the letters, then sent Eleio to return the case from where they'd taken it. 'We'll keep it after all,' she said. 'It could be useful some time. But don't worry my husband with any of this,' she cautioned him. 'He has enough to think about.'

She wouldn't confront Gerard, she decided, but would distance herself for a while, until she knew how best to handle it.

64

PEACE CEREMONY

Professor Takei from the National Museum, Tokyo, had arrived on board the shuttle boat, carefully carrying the box containing the scrolls, and was ferried away from the simple white shell sitting on the waters of Pearl Harbor, where once a naval fleet had lain at anchor. With him was his associate, Dr Nakajima, curator of antiquities from the Ashigaka and Muromachi periods at the museum. They sat, each enveloped in his own thoughts, taking in the beauty of that shining Hawaiian afternoon, the sky clear blue with only a feathery crown of cirrus circling the peak of the Waianae Mountains rising beyond Ford Island.

Takei looked with covert appreciation at the small Wran piloting their boat. He noticed the sun glancing off the golden hairs on her arm, so gold, as was the long hair neatly coiled into a roll behind her cap. Occasionally she turned and smiled at her passengers, and he was taken with the whiteness of her teeth, and wondered if she was as easily accessible as her open friendly manner suggested. He could picture her hair falling in a golden curtain across his arm as she lay naked beside him. He had never had a blonde *gaijin* woman, and wondered what it would be like. He looked across at Nakajima, saw that he too was looking at the blonde, and turned away quickly so that his colleague was unaware he'd been observed.

It had been a strange little ceremony; yet another untoward ritual they had to endure to obtain what was rightfully theirs. For many years now, he'd noticed the assorted artworks creeping back onto the walls and into the glass cases of their museum. Looking out across the harbour, he reflected on the ceremony. Such a fuss for the handing over of these scrolls which were simply finding their way back to their rightful home. It was as if the temporary caretakers of such things always felt compelled to make a big song and dance about it, he reflected. Well, if it meant more trips like this one, who was he to complain?

That the scrolls had resided with Sophie Chapman's family for generations meant little to Professor Takei. When one thought in terms of millennia, centuries had a way of being concertinaed into a brief passing of time. Time was a relative force of nature which had little to do with the paremeters humans had placed upon it. Rather, it was tied to the natural rhythm of the sun's cycle and demands of nature, and he for one didn't encapsulate his thinking and reactions according to artificially apportioned spans.

Sophie Chapman-san, a *Nisei* and very pretty, he reflected, seemed to be fixed in a time that had become irrelevant to him. It was as if she and people like her were still mentally rooted in that day in early December, when those brave young men had swooped in and attacked the American forces here. He had seen it on newsreels as a young boy, and at the time it had excited him and his heart had soared with them.

He found it extraordinary that today, he and his colleague should have been subjected to an American film of the actual attack on Pearl Harbor on that December morning. He had sat through it unmoved, except to remember those newsreels where as a boy, in the comforting darkness of the theatre, he had taken flight with the young heroes as they winged their way to their victorious deeds of glory in the name of the Emperor.

He wondered at the intensity of feeling such a shameful loss on that day seemed to invoke in these people. It was well behind them, so why did they keep going back as if to further castigate themselves and open old wounds?

Afterwards Sophie Chapman-san had read a poem in both Japanese and English, often glancing towards a man his colleague informed him was Atsuo Isawa, the uncle of Matsuhiro Isawa, the *kobun* of the powerful Isawa-*gumi* and he wondered what part the *yakuza* had played in today's events, and on the relevance of her poem. As long as there had been history, there had been conflict, he mused, and there would be wars again, for whatever reason. The only reality of the ceremony today were the two scrolls which were going back to where they rightfully belonged. Nothing else.

Professor Takei suddenly felt hungry, and longed to hear the sounds of the *yaki-imoya*, the sweet potato vendor's mournful horn and cry of '*yaki moohh*!' as he pushed his cart through the streets, and to taste his hot sweet offerings. Ah, such simple pleasures, but the things most missed when far away from home.

There was to be a celebration party at the Baillieu home in Honolulu, and he hoped there would be plenty of whisky, and blondes. He looked up and noticed Atsuo Isawa looking at him and the scrolls at his feet, and he inclined his head in a small bow of recognition, but not before seeing the expression in the older man's eyes. It reminded him of a haiku verse from his youth.

Hebe nigeta ware,
wo nishi me-no,
kusa-ni nokoru.[21]
A snake! Though it passes,
eyes that had glared at me
stay in the grasses.

* * *

When Takeo Nakamura arrived back at the big house with the others after the ceremony, Hiroko looked at him and her heart turned over. It was Satoshi just as she had seen him that day at her father's funeral, the same strong face and steady eye. It was not too late. Some of those lost years with her own son could be recaptured with this boy, her grandson. He bowed deeply before her, and she reached out and, taking him by the hand, drew him close to her.

'Takeo-chan,' she said, her eyes alight with love. 'Oh Takeo-chan, it has been so long.'

He was touched and moved by the expression of joy on the face of this frail old woman in her wheelchair. She held herself erect like a tiny queen, and he could see the effort she mustered to maintain this. He had often wondered about her, this grandmother far away, and now at last his father had allowed him to come here and meet her. There had been a misunderstanding that went back many years his father had told him, and now he owed her a great deal; they all did. 'Your future will be more than assured,' his father told him. 'Your grandmother has made a generous financial settlement on our family, and she wishes to give you something as well.'

Takeo had been excited by this, his first flight to America, a place that beckoned like a dream country of abundance and opportunity. Hawaii was so beautiful, and his grandmother's home and lifestyle seemed so opulent and grand compared to anything he had ever known.

Aunt Jill-san had picked him up at the airport, and he'd arrived only just in time for the special ceremony at Pearl Harbor. Jill-san gave him a brief explanation as to what it involved, but she seemed more anxious to learn about him. Smiling shyly, he told her how he had fulfilled a promise to his father Satoshi, gaining entrance to the prestigious Todai or Tokyo university, and his dreams of passing through the main gates alongside the *Aka Mon*, the Red Gate of Hongo Avenue, had been realised. He had managed to get through the *jigoku shiken*, or examination hell, for entry into this university of his choice. His fears of joining the unlucky graduates or *ronin* who had failed to make the grade—and like their namesakes, the *ronin* or masterless *Samurai* before them, were fated to the limbo land of waiting till they tried again—were now well behind him. And now—provided he did well—his future acceptance into one of the top companies in the commercial world after graduation would be assured.

'So how long do you have until you go back?' Jill asked.

There was a month's holiday before he began at Todai, he answered, so this trip had come at an opportune time.

'You should go back via Australia,' Jill suggested. Takeo's interest was roused, especially as two of his friends were already there exploring the Great Barrier Reef. He had promised his friend Hideyoshi that he would do his best to join them there. Hideyoshi would be expecting him, and as the son of his father Satoshi's old friend General Hideyoshi Ueda, it was an obligation he felt he must keep.

'It's perfect then,' Jill said when he mentioned this. 'You can have a few days at "Winganna" with me when I go, then continue out to the Reef for a couple of days with your friends, and I'll organise connecting flights for you to get back to Tokyo in plenty of time.' He hesitated in answering.

'You must see as much as you can,' she urged him, 'before you start your studies, as you will be too busy then.' And she thought quietly to herself, at least Jack won't be there to cast any looks at the boy and embarrass him with his racist remarks as he had done so often now when speaking with Hiroko or Gerard. Rather than diminishing with time, Jack's bitterness from his wartime experiences had increased. He constantly dwelt on the hardship he'd suffered and Bill's recounting of some of the kindnesses of his Japanese captors on the farm in Nagasaki only further fuelled his sense of injustice and anger at the loss of Tom. Bill had really laid down the sword she thought. But from what Maria told her, Jack was getting worse, particularly now with the steady increase of tourists from Japan and Asia. But then again he'd always been so parochial she reminded herself. Really it was a bore, but at least not one she'd have to deal with this time.

Later Takeo thought of how, when he'd stepped aboard the floating white memorial, he'd had a strong sense that this was indeed a shrine of lost souls and that the *kami* or gods dwelt there. Passing by the large brass ship's bell, he had stared down through the observatory hole in the deck to the murky green waters washing over the rusted battlements of all that remained of the USS *Arizona*. As he looked, a bubble of oil rose to the surface and spread its multicoloured slick across the water, and a shiver ran through him. He could almost see the glimmering of bodies stripped back to their whitened bones, floating like rags upon the currents.

It was not until he filed with the others into the third room of the memorial, and stood gazing at the marble wall with its list of over one thousand names of navy and marine corps men lost on that fateful day, that he had a disconcerting feeling—some magnetic pull from below was holding his feet fixed to where he stood. He closed his eyes momentarily, feeling rooted to the floor while at the same time experiencing a sense of vertigo, of being pulled into a vortex of a bad dream, wanting to run from it but unable to move. He had a sense of ghostly arms reaching up to clasp him, and only him, and his throat felt dry with a fear that went beyond rational thought.

'Takeo-chan?' He opened his eyes and Sophie's face swam into view.

'Are you all right?' she asked anxiously. He nodded, unable to tell anyone what he'd just experienced.

'I think I'll go outside and get some air,' he mumbled.

She smiled. 'We're all coming out for the handing over ceremony. You must be tired after the flight. Don't worry about anything, we'll talk later. Come on, let's go,' she said, taking him by the arm.

Takeo felt as if a door had opened and he'd found a whole new family. His own small self-contained world had been enlarged beyond his dreams. There were now uncles, aunts and cousins he'd never known existed, and he felt quite heady with a newfound comfort that belonging to such an extended family gave. He was particularly drawn to Sophie-san. Her sweet manner and infectious gaiety often gave way to a more reflective repose that he could identify with.

'There will soon be yet another one of us for you to meet,' she had said to him, patting her rounded abdomen. He'd laughed with a lack of restraint he hadn't felt in ages, lightheaded with all the champagne and the over-sweet perfume of the leis.

He hadn't fully taken in what the ceremony was all about. Why hadn't she handed the scrolls over privately to the curators? he wondered. Sophie-san had read a poem and talked a lot about peace and understanding while they had stood in the central open area of the memorial. Then an American admiral friend of his Uncle Gerard's had spoken at some length about what he termed 'that day of infamy', and Takeo noticed how the two curators from the museum had exchanged glances and looked uncomfortable. Sophie-san's father, Atsuo Isawa-san, had stood proud and tall and looked hard at nothing at all.

Sophie had then handed over a long box containing some scrolls to the curators who had bowed low, while one of the servants had set some white doves free from a cage. He smiled, recalling how they hadn't seemed to want to fly away, and had circled and circled above them as if wanting to land on the shrine. Then Uncle Gerard-san had stepped in and brought it all to a fairly quick close.

He'd noticed during the ceremony how Sophie-san had cast many anxious glances towards her father, a proud and strangely withdrawn man who had stood apart from the others with his son and daughter.

Later, before leaving his grandmother's house to go on to Jill-san's where he was staying, his grandmother had called him aside.

'Takeo-chan, I mentioned to your father that I wish to help you now,' Hiroko said. 'And as I don't have much time left to do all the things I'd like, we'll just have to get on with it.' She then told him that she had arranged to invest $50,000 in a trust account for him. She waved aside his thanks.

'From what I've heard you're going far, and this will help. Now,' Hiroko added, 'I would like you to do something for me.'

'Of course,' he answered, with a bow, 'anything, Oba-san.'

She handed him a small leather box. He opened it and there, on the black velvet, was a simple golden cross and chain.

'I want you to have this,' she told him, 'and I would like you to wear it for me. In time I hope you will want to know its full significance.'

Takeo took the cross out of its box and held it up.

'Put it on,' Hiroko said, and she crossed herself as he did.

'It's the symbol of Jesus our Lord—the cross on which he died. Will you always wear it for me, Takeo-chan? Promise?'

'Of course, Oba-san,' he said, bowing deeply.

It looked good against his golden skin, he decided later, and if it pleased his newfound mentor, he would wear it. His girlfriend, Suki, had one too, and he would ask her all about it. It could become their lovers' talisman. As he lay beside the big unfamiliar bed that night on the carefully folded blankets he had transferred to the floor in a sort of makeshift *futon*, his mind dwelt on the events and people of the past day. As an observer of life he'd felt a kinship with Sophie-san, if not with her husband David, who spent much of his time photographing and recording the day's events. He'd noticed how David-san had taken many photographs on the launch out to the memorial, concentrating on the expressions of the two museum curators and Atsuo-san, then photographing them all on the white memorial and the stars and stripes flag flying overhead.

It would all symbolise something, Takeo imagined, but how well? David-san's kind of observation, he felt, was rather like a charade. It was as if he was recording his life rather than living it, Takeo reflected. He had seemed very hyped-up, not really part of anything that was going on around him. He gave Sophie-san the occasional abstracted smile, and once he saw her go up and put her arms around him and hold him to her, but David-san had barely seemed to respond.

David-san's elaborate recording of events wasn't what he, Takeo, was on about. The science studies he was about to embark upon would be used in a constructive way, and he felt excited about what lay ahead of him. Marine biology would be his chosen specialty. He loved the sea, and the study of it would be his life.

He had spoken a little about to it to his Aunt Jill-san. She naturally drew people to her and seemed to shine, with her bright face and hair. Although she talked a lot and bustled about keeping things going, she didn't seem happy. Uncle Gerard-san didn't respond to her much, but still managed to appear at just the right moment, and didn't miss anything that mattered. Jill-san had had a long chat with him later in the evening, and he wondered now about taking this trip to Australia.

He thought of his grandmother's generous gifts and reached up to touch the cross. As he drifted off to sleep, he wondered what his mother was doing now in their small apartment in Shibuya, and what she would think about all this.

65

FLIGHT

'Well everything's organised,' said Jill.

Gerard looked at her and waited for her to continue.

'Takeo's coming with me. Now don't say anything against it Gerard. It will be nice for me to have company on the flight there, for a change. Wouldn't you like to know where we're going?' she asked, a little too sweetly.

He glanced at her. She hadn't been herself in the past week. Something was bugging her, but he didn't feel like taking on whatever it was tonight.

'You tell me,' he said.

'Why to the moon, of course.' He waited, then said, 'Don't you think Australia is rather a long way round for him to go back to Tokyo? I take it that's what you intend when you leave next week.'

She turned to him, her face set.

'Why shouldn't I?' she said. 'He can spend a few days at the homestead and see a bit of the life there, then he's dying to get a look at the Reef. Evidently a group of his friends are in the Whitsundays, so he may even catch up with them and spend a few days there. I've organised a connecting flight out of Sydney and he's really looking forward to it. It's only a pity that Will and Louise will be at school or they could have come too.'

'It seems you've got it all pretty well set up then,' he said.

'Somebody has to,' she answered shortly. 'I may stay on at "Winganna" for a while. There's a lot to be sorted out there. You know Gerard, it wouldn't have hurt you to have given some real support there,' she added.

He sighed. 'I will,' he said, 'but not tonight, I'm well and truly tuckered out after today.'

He lay on the bed gazing at her as she brushed her hair. She was wearing it longer, and the lamp caught its golden lights as she leaned forward brushing in long strokes from the nape of her neck. She wore only a brief satin nightie that clung to the willowy lines of her body. She was still beautiful, he thought, with the sort of grace that never ages. Her more subdued manner in the past days wasn't unattractive, he reflected with a smile, and far more restful for a change. He wondered what was on her mind, but he knew from experience with Jill that she would take her time in revealing what it was. And he wasn't over-anxious to find out just now.

'How do you think the ceremony went today?' he asked, hoping to move on to safer ground. She shrugged.

'Who knows.' It was her turn to be evasive. Then: 'That Atsuo still gives me the creeps, but Sophie seems happy with it all. His son and daughter are so very Japanese, aren't they?'

'Well, what did you expect?'

'Oh I don't know. They seemed overly formal, somehow. Far more so than Takeo,' Jill observed. 'And the girl is very quiet. Submissive, I guess would be a better word,' she added. 'And as for the son, somehow he didn't seem too pleased with things. Pretty stand-offish and sulky, if you ask me.'

They hadn't really seemed at ease or wanted to be there, Gerard recalled. But the girl Sumiko had responded well to Sophie, he'd noticed, and she had an appealing way with her. He could see them being friends. But the boy, Yasunari, that was another matter, remembering the tense haughty expression on the young man's face. He acted as if he wanted no part of any of it, he recalled.

'It seems your mother's playing lady bountiful,' Jill said suddenly, pleased when she saw the shadow that crossed his face. 'She and Takeo seem to have really taken to each other. He's got a lot more life in him that his father Satoshi, thank God,' she couldn't resist adding.

Jill continued to chat about the day, and he drifted into sleep, half listening to her. The sudden silence woke him, and he realised she was waiting for an answer.

'Incidentally, what's happening with David?'

'Why, what do you mean?'

'He doesn't seem himself. He's so jittery and up in the air about everything. Sophie tells me he hardly sleeps when he's home, it's just go, go, go all the time. It's got worse since he's been flying in and out of Saigon. He's really changing, and not for the better. Is he drinking too much or what?'

Gerard knew, but didn't tell her. David's spaciness had not escaped his attention. 'You're getting hooked,' he'd said to him some time back. 'For Christ's sake, we're flogging the stuff, not getting off on it ourselves. You'll have to put a stop to it, or you'll be in a bad way.'

'Sure, sure, it's nothing to worry about. I can handle it, don't worry,' David had assured him. But clearly he couldn't. He'd have to ease him out of the business, Gerard decided, and replace him with someone else before he really slipped up and threw the whole network into jeopardy. He'd get right on to it tomorrow.

'I'll talk to him.'

'Thank God you can talk to someone,' Jill answered tartly. She sighed and turned away from him, her mind churning. How could she get back at Gerard for his indifference, and his long-held secret infatuation for that bloody woman, Iman, or whatever her name was?

Gerard's mind drifted back to the events of the day, and Jill's decision to show Takeo 'Winganna' and the Reef. He liked that boy. He had a brightness and a natural friendliness that his father Satoshi lacked. It was good that Hiroko had brought him into the family and that the whole thing was working out, at last. But like everything else it had had its price, he thought grimly. She'd had to pay off that little bastard Satoshi to get him on side. No matter what his mother might like to think, and he wasn't about to disillusion her, it wasn't those letters that had done the trick. It had been the dollars that had eventually won Satoshi over, he thought with some satisfaction.

* * *

David didn't come in until late. Sophie could hear him moving about heavily in the kitchen below. He'd been drinking, she could tell from the sounds. She had waited up for him, but then decided to go to bed and read and reflect on the day's events.

She must have dozed off when the baby's kicking awakened her and she turned and saw that the bed beside her was still empty. It was becoming a familiar sight, even when David was at home. He was becoming harder to get through to, fluctuating between the highs which she often found hard to handle, and the follow-up depressions which were worse. She'd hoped he would be home early as he'd promised, as he was flying out to Saigon tomorrow, and she wanted to tell him her news over dinner. But it wasn't to be.

'Two heart-beats,' her doctor had told her when she had her check-up in the morning. 'It looks like twins.'

'Twins seem to run in our family,' she'd said, wanly returning his smile.

'Now don't you worry about it,' he assured her. 'Everything's coming along just fine, but I'll want to see you every week from now on until the big day.'

She had spoken to Jill about David, without spelling out all the details, and knew that Gerard had planned to see him during the day. Maybe he'd be able to get him off those bloody pills. She'd tried, but got nowhere apart from the many rows they'd had. And it wasn't only the pills, she thought. She tried to stifle an anger that rose in her. It wasn't good for the baby, babies, she corrected herself. She lay doing the deep breathing they had shown her at the pre-natal clinic.

The noises in the kitchen downstairs had stopped, and she could hear the door into his studio close, and then the voice of Jimi Hendrix, barely muffled by the closed doors. She followed the words, moving in her mind with the pulsating beat.

> *'There must be some way out of here,' said the joker to the thief,*
> *There's too much confusion, I can't get no relief.*
> *Businessmen they drink my wine, plowmen dig my earth,*
> *None of them along the line know what any of it is worth.'*
> *'No reason to get excited,' the thief, he kindly spoke,*
> *'There are many here among us who feel that life is but a joke.*
> *But you and I, we've been through that, and this is not our fate,*
> *So let us not talk falsely now, the hour is getting late.'*
> *All along the watchtower, princes kept the view*
> *While all the women came and went, barefoot servants, too.*
> *Outside in the distance a wildcat did growl,*
> *Two riders were approaching, the wind began to howl.*[22]

Was David like the joker seeking some way out of here, she wondered. Was he, too, feeling that life was but a joke . . . while 'all the women came and went.'

God, how she'd come to resent that song. She associated it now with David's playing it either when he was in a drug-induced fantasy world, or wanting to be alone after being with one of the many women she knew still were part of his life. Her earlier heartbreak had given way to a rationalisation of his infidelities. Somehow, after her initial angry reactions and decision to leave him, she had now fallen in with his life while making one of her own. She could see that, like the pills, the women were little more than fuel to an almost manic energy he had for his work, and that they were consumed and cast aside with only passing interest. She, Sophie, was his mainstay, she knew. She didn't doubt that he loved her. But it was a love tempered by this other side of him.

Maybe, she reasoned, it was because of his lack of love during his early years in that orphanage. As if to make up for all the deprivation then, he was now like a child, a spoilt child who wasn't to be deprived of any of the toys he wanted, when he wanted them. Sophie lived divided between loving him and hoping things would change and get better. But the business with the pills was getting worse, and he needed help. If anyone could help him, she reassured herself, it would be Gerard.

She lay troubled, waiting for him to come up to bed, but he didn't and she knew he must have fallen asleep on the couch in the studio. She reached out and drew his pillow to her, longing for his warmth. The infrequent sex between them now was not the love-making of old, and often ended with his crying in her arms like a child and her nurturing and comforting him, while yet again being reassured by his need for her. She would tell him about the twins in the morning, before he left. Maybe when the babies arrived, he'd settle down.

The words of that song came back to her, and she sang them softly to herself.

> *'But you and I, we've been through that, and this is not our fate,*
> *So let us not talk falsely now, the hour is getting late.'*

Fearing for what lay ahead, she felt tears flow down her cheeks and into his pillow. Then with the weight of the babies pressing on her bladder, she got up awkwardly and went to the bathroom.

Her mind wandered to her father Atsuo as she sat at the window seat, staring out across the garden to the moonlit sea. She had seen him only briefly when he arrived at the memorial, and later after the ceremony, but this time he seemed to be more preoccupied with his son Yasunari and daughter Sumiko than with her. She had invited them to dinner the following day before they flew back to Tokyo, but Atsuo had declined, suggesting that perhaps instead she and Sumiko might like to meet the next morning as he had business to attend to that evening. She sensed it was a brush-off and had been troubled by it. But then he had reassured her by saying he'd like to see her beforehand for a drink.

They met at the Royal Hawaiian Surf Room, looking out at the board riders catching the rolling waves into the beach. The Kona winds had whipped up a heavy surf, and the sound of the waves almost drowned out Bill Akamulou's Hawaiian orchestra playing in the adjacent dining-room.

Sophie gazed at her father, thinking what a strange sequence of events had brought them together, and sensed the spirit of her mother Gina, hovering, as if trying to tell her something. Listening to the romantic sounds of the sea and music combined, she imagined her mother sitting with him in just such a setting. Without warning, she blurted out the question before she knew it, regretting it immediately when she saw the expression in his eyes.

'Did you love my mother?'

He hesitated, looking away from her.

'Your mother was a fine person,' he answered, 'full of life. We were close,' he said. And she knew in that moment that he hadn't.

'Forgive me,' she murmured, stifling her anger. 'I didn't mean to bring it up.' But she was thankful she had, and felt a sense of doubt and a distancing from him.

The waiter brought their drinks. Raising his glass, Atsuo complimented her on the ceremony and for handing over the scrolls, and expressed interest and concern in the whole event. Sophie listened to his words of praise, but sensed his mind was elsewhere, with the same preoccupation she'd felt the first time they had met at the

Teikoku Hotel in Tokyo. Somehow his more formal manner now precluded her from saying any of the warm and loving things she would like to have poured out. So instead, she sat mostly listening to him speak, then merely outlining what she planned to do with Sumiko the next day.

'I liked your poem,' Atsuo said suddenly.

'Oh did you?' she said, clinging to the compliment, as a child might to a pet blanket.

'You must come to Tokyo again soon,' he said, summoning the waiter for their bill.

'I'd love to,' she answered, 'but it will have to wait now until after the birth.' She somehow couldn't bring herself to speak of his first grandchild. His manner didn't invite such intimacies.

'I hope Yasunari wasn't bored during the ceremony,' Sophie said, recalling the unsmiling face of her half-brother.

'Not at all,' Atsuo answered quickly. 'He's a serious young man, and maybe next time you'll get to know each other better.'

But she wondered now, as she got up from the window seat and went back to bed, if they ever would. There had been no warming sense of kinship there, unlike the spontaneous friendliness extended by his sister, Sumiko. They'd had a girls' morning out, doing the shops and local sights. 'There's so much more for you to see here, we've hardly even started yet,' Sophie told her. 'You'll just have to stay longer next time.'

'I hope so, if my father agrees,' Sumiko had answered shyly.

Our father, thought Sophie to herself.

'It would be nice if you could be here after the baby arrives,' she said. Suddenly Sumiko turned to her, her eyes widening. 'Oh my goodness,' she exclaimed, 'I'll be Aunt Sumiko-san soon!'

'And your father, a grandfather,' Sophie couldn't help adding, and they'd both laughed, then chatted about her plans for the baby, and she'd felt a sisterly bond with the younger woman.

But thinking back on it now, there was something in her father's attitude to her this time that she couldn't quite fathom. And it worried her.

* * *

She'd given him a copy of the poem she had read at the peace ceremony, and he perused it again with a wry sense of irony regarding that whole event. He recalled Sophie's expression, and the look of hope she had cast his way as she read it.

> *How do we explain away guilt?*
> *Is it the uneasy pang the conqueror feels for the fallen after the event?*
> *Is it the cooling restraint that often tempers sudden anger, after the event?*
> *Is it the heavy heart and questing brain which ruminates and forever seeks a palliative answer, after the event?*
> *Is it the sharp reminder of pain and suffering?*
> *Is it a reaching out for a serenity and peace to blanket memories and still thoughts, after the event?*
> *Is it the face of a fatherless child, a woman without her man, a man whose family has ceased to exist, after the event?*
> *Is it the personal pain and collective conscience,*
> *Is it too late, after the event?'*

There was a universality in her message, Atsuo reflected, but like most collective feelings, they soon took on an amorphous quality that threatened to engulf the original truth, which became yet another idealistic truism that got lost along the way.

Nonetheless, she had played her part well in what he wanted to achieve, and the scrolls were now safely back where they belonged. He smiled at this, but his smile vanished as he thought of his son Yasunari. The boy wore his heart on his sleeve, he thought irritably, and that just wouldn't do. Not when there was so much to plan and achieve in these early stages. He would have to talk to him and make him fully aware of the role he must fulfil. The boy was too proud, and his pride would trip him up one day. He would have to learn to channel his resentments into more productive areas. This was not something that was going to be achieved overnight, but a reward that would come with years, perhaps even generations and decades of effort, he mused. There was still much groundwork to be done, and Yasunari must be made aware of that. He recalled the stories of the frog and the pomegranate that he'd told Matsuhiro long ago. Little notice he'd taken, Atsuo recalled now with regret, and it would be his undoing. But Yasunari had a different mind, and he would respond, Atsuo thought confidently. The boy had been accepted to do his MBA at Harvard, and that would be a valuable step along the way.

His thoughts went back to Hiro, and how his old wartime colleague seemed to have switched allegiance from himself to his nephew Matsuhiro. It had been Hiro who had set up the whole bungled operation to steal the scrolls from Sophie's house, and yet had not forewarned Atsuo of the plan. Yet Hiro must have been aware of his relationship to her. Hiro had never had the larger picture in mind, he reflected, always out only to get a quick reward, the immediate gain. 'The roar of a thousand golden tigers!' He well remembered their call to arms, but Hiro had lost sight of its purpose. He and his *oyabun* were birds of a feather, he thought with disdain. His brother Akira's spirit was no doubt much troubled to see just how his son was now operating the Isawa-*gumi*. Gone was any sense of aspiring to the greater glory for one's country and emperor, and a desire to forge the national way. Never would he forget the events of 7 December 1941 which he, Atsuo, had helped set up, and his late brother, Hiroshi, together with that gallant band of men, had put into action. Their temporary defeat at war's end was well behind them now, and there they were rising once more like the mythical phoenix.

His thoughts moved from Hiroshi to his father, who still idolised his lost son's memory. Daihachi could come and live in the house he intended to set up here in Honolulu. He would be well away from Matsuhiro's influence, and the more temperate climate would be good for his failing health. Yasunari would also spend some of his holiday time from his studies in the States here, and Sumiko could live with her grandfather until her marriage. Her husband had been chosen, and it could well be in his interest to set up an arm of his business here. He would see to it all.

Sophie's husband David sprang to mind. They had met briefly and he'd noted his photographic foray at the ceremony. He was a disturbing personality. It seemed he was playing his part in the network of drug supplies which Matsuhiro was shipping through Gerard Baillieu to the US and Japan from Vietnam and South East Asia, and his nephew's eyes no doubt were already on plans to expand this lucrative market. That had its place, he thought with a grim smile, but not for him at this time, and he wanted his daughter Sophie well out of it too. Something would have to be done about David, he decided, and soon. Through her association with David she could be hurt, as well as her child, his grandchild, he thought with mixed feelings, and that would not fit in with his plans for her. Maybe here was a chance for Hiro to regain favour and re-establish himself in his old friend's eyes. Either that or be shamed into *Seppuku*.

The sound of a distant church bell reminded Atsuo of the deep reverberating notes carried on the early morning air from the massive bronze bell in the Buddhist *Chion-in* temple in Kyoto. It was one of the earliest sounds he could remember as a boy, ringing out across the countryside, summoning the faithful to prayer. He recalled once watching the team of men pulling on the long thick ropes which rang the seventy-four-ton bell, one hundred and eight times on New Year's Eve to absolve every person of man's one hundred and eight sins. And the faithful would be rewarded with their rebirth in *Jodo*, the pure land that promised enlightenment and happiness.

'*Namu-amida-butsu*,' he murmured, recalling the one Sutra chanted continuously day and night by the disciples of *Jodo*. But it was not the Buddhist *Jodo* he saw as nirvana, but the blessed islands of Japan, born of the gods who had thrown the jewelled spear from the floating Bridge of Heaven, from whence sprang the mighty mountains, plains, valleys, the rivers, lakes and bubbling springs, all part of the Great Eight Island Land that emerged from the sea of tears of *Amaterasu-o-mikami*. And rising above it in majestic splendour was the sacred Fuji-yama, guardian of the islands. While from the Sun Goddess, *Amaterasu-o-mikami*, *kami* of the High Plain of Heaven, came *Jimmu*, the first Emperor of Japan, and whose red orb was the symbol of this land of the rising sun.

Atsuo's pragmatic nature sat quite comfortably in the mist-shrouded mythology of the past. Hadn't he seen his country emerge from the ruins of 1945 to become in 1970 the world's third largest economy—fast emerging as an industrial and economic force to be reckoned with? He and others like him, generation after generation, would restore it to its rightful place of honour. For they were the one family, the children of the gods.

Emperor Hirohito had renounced his divinity in 1946 purely for political reasons, Atsuo reasoned. He and his descendants would still symbolise the evolution of their mighty nation. They were a chosen people, and the imperialistic policies of old still existed, if in a different guise.

He felt the peace that comes with knowing that he was playing his small part for the nation he revered. He knew what he must do now, and his flight out of Hawaii tomorrow marked a new phase in his quest.

PART SIX

66

'A LAND OF FLOODS AND RAINS'—QUEENSLAND, 1971

His knee had been giving him curry all week, so he wasn't surprised when the cyclone warning came in over his car radio. This old body of his knew, Sid Carpenter reasoned. It was the best weather forecaster he could think of. Soon as that knee of his played up, it meant a change was on the way. He should hire it out, he thought with a chuckle, it would give those boys at the weather bureau something a little more tangible to work with.

But he'd better put a call through to his old lady to batten down the hatches. She'd know what to do, he thought with satisfaction, picturing his wife boarding up the windows, and securing anything that was likely to let fly in the expected eighty to one hundred knot cyclonic winds which swept in at this time of the year. Still, he'd call her, just to make sure. She'd better get the kids out of school, anyway.

'Sounds like it's shaping up to be a little beauty,' Sid said cheerfully to the youth who walked out of the small general store to fill up his tank for him.

'Yeah, I reckon,' the gas attendant, his face lined and weather-beaten beyond his twenty-odd years, looked out to the darkening horizon stretching away to the distance.

'We could do with the rain,' Sid shook his head, 'but they can keep their bloody cyclones. Look at the damage cyclone Ada did last year. What have they called her this time?' he asked.

'Cyclone Althea,' said the boy. 'I've got a cousin Althea, and if she's anything to go by, this one promises to be a real little bitch!' he smirked. 'Heading far?'

'Fifty miles up the Reef near the old Henderson place.'

The boy continued to stare. 'What's up?'

'An accident, another croc attack,' Sid answered briefly.

His questioner wasn't to be shaken off so easily.

'One of the locals?'

'Nope, a foreigner this time, one of the tourists.'

'They never bloody learn, eh? Bloody dick-heads!' The boy gave a short laugh and banged the side of Sid's car as it roared off, then headed back to his shop and the telephone to set the bush telegraph in motion.

Why did these things always have to happen around Christmas, Sid wondered, as he drove away. It was a time when all you wanted was to be with your family, enjoying the safety and comfort of home, and not worried about what was happening in the world outside, and that was for sure. Well, one poor bugger wouldn't have to worry about his Christmas shopping, he thought, as his mind went to the victim. I wonder if those Japs celebrate Christmas.

The young gas attendant's sneering expression when he'd mentioned the croc attack still hung before him. It reminded Sid of that same look on the faces of the men at the hotel when he'd been called in to break up a barney between some visiting Japanese and the locals. It was the same group of Japs who had gone off snorkelling out of Orpheus despite storm warnings, Sid recalled.

That big bruiser son of Bert Henderson's had been the instigator of the brawl, they'd said. But he was always spoiling for a fight! The boy hated the Japanese. And any wonder. His old man's brother Jim had more than suffered at the hands of that lot in the war. After years of imprisonment in PNG he'd been executed . . . beheaded by them. Bert had never got over it and his bitterness had fuelled the boy's hatred.

But somehow these same racist resentments hadn't rubbed off on himself, Sid reflected. And it was a small miracle considering what his own dad had been through. But what was the use of hanging on to hate? It only ate into those who harboured it. He'd seen that well enough, first hand.

Sid had just missed out on the war. He'd been too young to be called up. But he well remembered the dancing in the streets of Brisbane the day peace was declared. He smiled, recalling how they'd been let out of school early, and he and some kids had donned cowboy hats with his mate Tony in full Indian headdress, and how they'd ridden around the streets on their bikes, yelling and yahooing. It had been a great day.

But it was not so good some months later when his old man had finally got his discharge papers from the AIF and arrived home unexpectedly, hollow-eyed and all tuckered out. He'd lain about like a wet rag for days, then the shouting had begun, and the terrible fights with his mother. It was as if all the fears and frustrations of his years of suffering at the hands of his Japanese captors while in the notorious Changi prison camp had been stored up to hurl at the very ones he'd fought for.

His father's hatred was immense, Sid remembered now with a shiver, and he'd hit out at anything or anyone who came near him. And his mother, as if filled with a guilt for not having been part of his father's privations, had bowed down to his abuse, as if accepting it as the price she had to pay, though God knows she'd had enough hardships of her own. That was till one day he'd arrived home to the sounds of his father's shouts and his mother's screams. He had rushed inside in time to see her cowering in a corner, and his father hitting her repeatedly across her back and neck with the heavy stick he used to hobble around with.

Suffused with an intense rage, Sid had run towards them, and wresting the stick from his father's hands had turned it on him. He shuddered now as he recalled the soft thuds it made as it hit the older man, and his surprise when he fell to his knees after just a few blows, and how easy it had been. He'd often had nightmares about it later, knowing he would have continued the blows till he'd killed him if his sister hadn't arrived and, with his mother, had stopped him. His father had gone into a psychiatric clinic not long after that. They had never spoken about the incident again, but it still lay between them. He pushed it aside now, his mind switched to seeing his way through the deluge of rain that had started to hit the windscreen in opaque sheets.

* * *

The rain had been thundering down all afternoon, and Jill had listened to the cyclone warnings throughout the morning. She had noticed last night that Jack's old barometer was falling. In the early hours the south-westerly monsoon winds had sprung up, swooping in from the north in spasmodic bursts and bringing the heavy rains that often heralded Christmas and the New Year. It was a change from the morning, when she'd been awakened by the screeching of white cockatoos feasting in the flowering fire-wheel trees, in full sunshine, promising a hot day ahead, and now this, she thought, looking out at the deluge.

She wondered about Takeo. He had left for the Reef days ago, and she worried that his stay would be a wash-out. She recalled Bill years ago explaining these tropical cyclones to Maria and herself. 'See, there's nothing to it,' he'd said cheerfully, trying to lessen Maria's fears of storms. But it hadn't worked—these things never did, she thought. If you were scared of storms, that was it.

She thought of Maria's letter. She certainly hadn't exaggerated. The house had the air of months of neglect, and she'd set about organising the clean-up. There was major work to be done, and she could see it would take ages. Jack had gone down south before she arrived, no doubt to avoid any confrontation, and only the manager and his family were there.

Takeo had thrown himself into helping out with some of the work, and in between she'd shown him around the inner areas of the property, amused by his amazement at its size.

'And these are only the homestead paddocks,' she told him with a laugh.

'So much land, Jill-san,' he said, his eyes alight with interest, as yet another vista opened up before him.

The heat had been intense, and they'd swum in the cool of the dam, drying off in minutes in the sparse shade of the tall gums that surrounded it. She had made him billy tea, swinging the blackened billy can in a wide circle just before pouring, and serving hot freshly baked damper with butter and some of Maria's plum preserves she'd unearthed in the pantry.

'Australian tea ceremony!' she'd said, and they'd laughed.

'Let me try,' Takeo had asked, swinging the billy at first apprehensively, then delighted with his success when not a drop spilt.

Afterwards he'd managed to make contact with his friends, and had left for the Reef four days later.

'Next time you'll have to stay much longer when Will and Louise are here,' she'd said, giving him a little hug as he left, and he'd enthusiastically agreed.

No, she wouldn't sell 'Winganna', she decided. Her earlier ambivalent feelings were being fast replaced, seduced as she was by its rugged beauty and the space of the spreading landscape. It lacked the lushness and intimacy of Hawaii, but instead had a simple reality which helped put one in touch with things as they were.

It would take time to bring it back to what it was, but she would, and make it better than ever before. She had the money and the will to do it. She would put in a first-rate manager and a good staff to start with, then spend a lot more time here, and commute to and from Hawaii. Maybe that was what was needed, she decided.

Gerard would soon notice that things didn't run as smoothly without her being there all the time.

A sudden ringing of the phone resounded through the empty house, and Jill hurried to answer it. It could be Gerard, missing her already. She listened to the slow drawl on the other end.

'Yes, this is Jill Baillieu. Takeo Nakamura? Yes, he has been staying here, he's my husband's nephew. Why? Is anything wrong?' she asked with a sense of apprehension.

She listened, then sat limply on Jack's old leather chair.

'What do you mean? How do you know it was him?' her voice rose.

The voice at the other end was hesitant.

'Don't screw around. Tell me now,' she said, heatedly.

She listened, then broke in. 'It's not possible, he was off to the Reef with friends. He just couldn't have been there,' she said, as the voice went on.

'How? When?' she paused. 'Where are you ringing from?' She listened, feeling suddenly chilled. 'I'll come up now,' she said. The voice at the other end held a note of warning.

'Look cyclone or no cyclone, I'm coming,' she said.

She was shivering as she hung up, and automatically went about turning off the switches, getting together the few things she would need. She rang through to the manager's cottage and told him she had to go north urgently.

'You'd better not,' he said. 'We're in for a real blow.'

'I'll take the Land Rover,' Jill said, ignoring him. 'You just get over here fast and make sure everything's battened down.'

He started to remonstrate, but she slammed the receiver down. She'd fire that bastard as soon as she could replace him, she fumed. Then the full reality of what she'd just heard struck home. Takeo attacked, maybe gone? It couldn't be, just couldn't be. He was so alive, only days ago. She could still see him laughing at their tea ceremony as she'd swung the billy.

She hardly noticed the rain pelting down like a wall of water as she backed the Land Rover and headed down the homestead driveway, only stopping to open then close the numerous gates before she finally hit the Great Northern Highway ten kilometres later.

She felt like an insect, suspended now in a web of frightening ramifications of such an event. Oh God, what would Gerard think? She'd been the one who had insisted that Takeo come here on his way home. It just couldn't be true, her more rational mind reasoned. A crocodile! Such things just didn't happen to people you knew. They were the stuff of horror stories, full of shivers of morbid fascination, always happening far away, and to someone else. It just wasn't possible. Takeo would still be there, somewhere. They'd got the whole thing wrong, she tried to reassure herself. But what if they hadn't? a small voice persisted.

The wind hurling rain against her windscreen was building up. At times her Land Rover went into a skid, and she only just managed to pull out of it. She was a good driver, and automatically controlled the heavy four-wheel-drive vehicle over potholes and fallen branches which were starting to pile up along the road, while the powerful headlights pierced the rain. She thought of Hiroko—what if the news were true. Oh God, please don't let this happen to me, please don't let this happen to me, she prayed as she drove through the afternoon, heading for the small police station further north.

Suddenly all the things she had been escaping from when she flew out of Hawaii assumed a new importance. If Gerard didn't really love her, would this be the final thing to drive him away from her completely? A cold panic filled her. Oh please God, don't let him be dead, she prayed, as if willing Takeo to re-emerge from the maw of the crocodile. Let it all be a terrible mistake. Let it be someone else, anyone but him, she pleaded.

Jill had visions of Satoshi, and his anger. She had seen that coldness on his face, and hastily pushed this thought from her mind. She wouldn't ring Gerard until she knew exactly what had happened. At the thought of ringing him, she felt numbed, and sick with apprehension. She had worked so hard to establish her place in his family, and now this one terrible event threatened to turn everything upside down. Hiroko would never forgive her for the loss of her newfound grandson. As for Gerard, her anger and disappointment in him over the past weeks now gave way to this new fear of final loss.

Takeo gone? It just couldn't be happening, she reassured herself. She would find out that the whole thing was a ghastly mistake when she got there.

Townsville was like a ghost town as she drove through its outskirts and across the Ross River, its waters swirling and already rising fast. The cyclonic winds rushing down through the Coral Sea were building up waves she could now hear beating against the long arm of the breakwater which sheltered the harbour. She recalled Bill telling them how there could be a stormwater surge in a cyclone, sometimes rising nine feet or more above the tidal level.

As she drove away from the town and saw the coastal palms, some bending nearly to the road from the strength of the winds, she dodged the occasional sheets of roofing iron that flew towards her, untethered by the winds. For the first time, she became aware of the severity of the storm. But any fears for her own safety were over-ridden by the enormity of what lay ahead and her fears for what she might find when she arrived at Lucinda, still over sixty kilometres away. Although it was only four o'clock in the afternoon, she had turned the headlights on to high beam, peering through the deluge the wipers were failing to clear away, and driving as fast as she dared through this no-man's land of howling winds and rain.

She was only three kilometres from her destination and desperately tired. The last thing she remembered was giving in to the seductive promise of sleep, then the Land Rover skidding and turning over and over, as if in slow motion, while she clung to the wheel and screamed her mother's name, returning to that fateful day with Freida so long ago.

67

LAYING THE GHOST

She would have seen the letters. He knew Jill. There'd be no way she could resist reading a pile of letters and a diary, no matter who they belonged to.

Eleio had mentioned that she'd been sorting through things in that room, and he'd suddenly remembered the case and its contents. 'Did she throw out that old case on top of the wardrobe?' he'd asked casually. Eleio had looked uncomfortable. 'No, she left that one, I think.'

Ah, so she had been through it and asked Eleio not to mention it to him, Gerard mused. It explained her attitude towards him during the weeks before she'd left for Australia. Bloody hell, he should have burnt them!

Now as the cab sped towards the Mater Hospital, he fingered the golden cross Hiroko had given her grandson, and felt a cold hand clutch at his heart. Sid, the police officer, had handed it over along with Takeo's passport and jacket when he met him at the airport earlier in the day.

'She's a plucky little thing, that wife of yours,' were almost his first words to Gerard. 'She drove all the way up here in the height of the cyclone, and almost made it,' he said. 'She must have been pretty upset about it all.'

Jill was still under sedation when Sid had taken him

to the hospital from the airport. Gerard gazed at her face, so smooth and childlike in its deep sleep, a bruising around her eye and cheek the only mark marring its beauty. Thank God for that, he thought, knowing how she clung to perfection with a tenacity deep within her psyche. Her left leg had been fractured, but would be fine, the doctor had assured him. She was still in shock, and needed plenty of rest. She seemed deeply troubled, he'd added. And well she might be, thought Gerard.

'This is a bloody dreadful business,' Sid Carpenter had said as he handed over Takeo's few possessions they had retrieved.

'I want to see where it happened,' Gerard insisted. 'And where's the body?'

'You gotta be joking mate!' Sid answered, without a trace of a smile. 'There's not much left when those blighters get their teeth into you.' He regretted his candour when he saw the expression that crossed Gerard's face.

'We brought back what there was left of him,' he added by way of explanation. 'We're lucky we got anything, and if he hadn't taken off his jacket, we wouldn't even have this to help trace him. You might not realise it, but when a croc sinks his teeth in, he sort of plays with you, so to speak. I mean, they move like bloody lightning, grab you, then take you down under the water and do the death roll, once, twice, three or more times,' he finished with relish.

Oh Christ, Gerard thought as he listened to Sid's gory saga. Takeo taken that way? It just wasn't possible.

Sid's voice droned on. 'They've got this sort of underwater pantry where they store their food, alive if possible—they like it fresh, see? If he'd stored the body there, chances are we never would have retrieved even the few bits we did.'

Gerard now stared out through the windscreen across the sodden landscape, battered after Althea's onslaught, as Sid's four-wheel-drive bumped its way deeper into the mangroves. It was like another world, he thought, with its almost primeval vegetation and overpowering sense of isolation. What the hell was Takeo doing in a place like this? Surely sheer instinct would have warned him not to go through this way. It just wasn't like him to have done so, he had far too much innate good sense. That was what he'd liked about the boy, Satoshi's son or not.

For the first time the full impact of confronting Satoshi, and worse still Hiroko, with the news hit him, and he felt weakened at the thought. Until now, his concern with Jill's welfare had obliterated almost everything else. He hadn't as yet really taken in or thought through the full ramifications of this whole unbelievable event.

'It's a short cut through here,' Sid explained to him, 'from the beach to the motel. We think he must have rested along the way, where we picked up his jacket later on. You'd think he would have known better.' He paused, extracting a couple of menthols from a battered packet and offering one to Gerard. The sharp mentholated taste and smell as he sucked it shot him right back to his days at 'Winganna', as he lay face down with Bill and Tom gazing deep into the dark green waters of the dam for the first signs of tadpoles while sucking on the Butter Menthols Molly had handed out before they'd left.

Sid's laid-back drawl meandered on. 'You'd think he would have known better,' he said. 'The sight of one of those brutes, and I'd be off like a goanna up a tree. You wouldn't see me for dust.'

'Maybe he dropped off to sleep,' Gerard suggested.

'Yeah, that could have been it,' Sid agreed wearily. 'Either that or he thought he was in a fun park, and the crocs had come out to play. These tourists, they just don't have a clue,' he said, ignoring the fact that his passenger hadn't long flown in. 'Someone should warn them,' he went on. 'I mean they should find out a bit about the place before they go traipsing all over it. They act as if they're in bloody fairy land. I don't know.' He pulled up with a sudden jerk. 'Well, there she is,' he said, pointing to the melaleuca tree where they'd found Takeo's jacket.

* * *

Jill lay still, the weight of the cast on her leg pinning her to the bed. A slow deep ache seemed to travel all the way up her thigh and into her hip. She thought she'd heard Gerard's voice in her dreams, and the sister told her, yes, he had been here, but she was asleep, so he was coming back later. The Sisters of Mercy, she thought, reflecting on the nursing nuns at the hospital, and smiled, thinking Hiroko would like this place.

She could still feel herself turning over and over in the car when she closed her eyes, and groaned as she tried to move her head on the pillow. Her cheek felt sore and swollen, but she couldn't summon enough energy to lift her hand to touch it. It was as if everything in her life was on hold, and she floated in the warmth of a drug-induced world. Like David, she thought. No wonder he . . . she broke off. There was something about David, David, David, the name reverberated in her mind. What was it about him? Never mind, later will do, she thought as she drifted off into sleep.

She awoke to see Gerard sitting at the side of her bed, and behind him the shelf was covered with bowls of roses and orchids, their profusion of colour lighting up the room. He moved closer, his eyes gazing deep into hers.

'Hi honey, how are you feeling now?'

'A bit clearer, I think,' she whispered. 'I'm so glad you're here.' Her smile vanished as the memories came rushing back.

'Oh Gerard, Takeo . . . he . . .'

'I know, I know,' he answered, 'don't worry about it, I'll handle everything now.'

'But it's all my fault, I should never have . . .'

'Don't be bloody silly,' he broke in. 'He wanted to come. It's no-one's fault, and least of all yours.' He leaned down and kissed her lightly on the forehead. 'All you've got to do now is get strong again,' he said. 'We've got a lot to discuss and work out.'

She looked up at him, searching his face. He got up and walked over to the window, then turned to her. 'I know you saw those letters,' he said, 'and I won't deny anything I wrote or felt. It was a very big part of my life. One day—not now—I'll tell you about it, but for now it's important that you know it all happened long ago. I loved her then, but I love you now . . . I've only fully realised just how much,' he added softly, and looked away from her, fearing what she might say.

There was a silence between them, then as she tried to sit up, she said in a voice perplexed yet clear, 'What letters? What are you talking about, Gerard?'

He turned and stared at her in surprise, then burst out laughing when he saw the expression on her face.

'God Jill, you must be getting better,' he exclaimed as he moved over to the bed, and gently took her in his arms.

'I need you,' he murmured, his voice deep with emotion, 'you just don't know how much, Jilly. Don't ever move away again.'

'You can count on that,' she whispered, cradled in the warmth and comfort of his embrace.

'I'll always love you,' he said.

'Is that a threat or a promise?' she murmured sleepily, as he kissed her.

He looked at her and wondered, thinking of the fragility of one's hold on love and life.

68

HOUSE OF THE SUN
HONOLULU, 1971

There's always the emphasis on man's totality, including his failings, Gerard thought, recalling the words of Jung. When he'd first read them in the early days after Iman had left, they'd made a sense he had clung to, as had Jung's assertions that 'we are always looking for wholes' and that 'there's always an opposite to fit what is missing'. He related especially to the Jungian idea that 'man must always live in a world of his biological truth. That he is born into a specific historical setting and is only complete when he has a specific historical relationship to it'.

The assorted phrases he'd committed to memory came back to him now as he gazed at his sleeping wife. They had assailed him, too, in David's studio in Honolulu before he'd left, looking around the walls at the faces staring out at him wherever he turned. It was as if he was looking into a kaleidoscope of human emotions and events, created from this bitter little war which seemed to have no end, no easy solution. Vietnam had become a nightmare in more ways than one.

The message out of Saigon, telling of David's death in a car bombing, had unnerved him. Every fibre in his body warned him that this was no accident, no misplaced target, but premeditated murder.

It seemed that yet another element had been introduced, and he had to think carefully on what to do next. He would fly to Saigon and see what he could track down, if anything, then follow through from there. He'd have to set up a replacement in the network or get out of it completely. But the time for that, he knew, wasn't now. He had far too much riding on the drug shipments as it was. He couldn't completely dismiss a strong suspicion that Matsuhiro and the Isawa-*gumi* were at the bottom of it, somewhere. There was a hell of a lot going on with them that he would never be privy to. That bastard Atsuo being part of the set-up, no matter what he claimed, hadn't helped matters.

Gerard had carefully gone through David's papers and belongings for a clue to his death, but found nothing. Somehow he hadn't expected to. This, he felt sure, was something that had come completely out of the blue for David, an eventuality he neither expected nor feared. He had looked up at the shot David had taken of the young GI, the John Wayne look-alike and his companion, a bar girl, little more than a child, but already sucked into the tawdry world of prostitution and survival, the hint of vulnerability in her face soon to be replaced by a knowing bitterness—if she survived that long. The boy had a studied sophistication, no doubt a buffer to the confusion around and within him.

'The personal shadow is the bridge to the collective shadow,' he reflected, taking in the full impact of this photograph. And this was the shot that had flashed around the world. Gazing from the pages of *Life*, *Time*, *Newsweek*, it had run the gamut of the international media big time, and David had had his moment of glory.

As he had moved around the studio, taking in the sheer bulk of David's photographic records, it was clear that his compulsive addiction to his work was doubtless to assuage something that even he was probably not fully aware of. Gerard thought of Jung again, and his premise that 'man is not complete if he is not in touch with that inner mystical part, the soul'.

It appeared that David was in touch, too closely in touch: recording, recapturing, distilling in time-frames the joy and mostly misery around him. His sensibilities and mystic awareness were there. But his soul? It seemed that the self-destructive course David was travelling, particularly through his drug addiction, had no doubt led, if indirectly, to his death.

Sophie must never know her husband's full involvement in their drug dealings, Gerard mused. If David had lived, it would have been only a matter of time until she'd found out, so maybe his death was a blessing in disguise. There was something here, though. It didn't have Matsuhiro's stamp, but it was almost as if some other unseen person was quietly pulling the strings. He'd get to the bottom of it in time. He always did, he thought with grim satisfaction.

* * *

Is one's body a mere divining rod, Sophie wondered, an antennae attuned to all the messages that sweep past, often invisible to the human eye? She recalled a stick insect that had landed fleetingly on her desk at school long ago. The initial horror of its intrusion had given way to her interest in this frail creature, quivering in the still heat, alive to even the faintest stirring of the air around it. She had stared, fascinated by its fragility, unmindful of the teacher's voice, imagining herself in that brittle hair-like body. What were its thoughts, its purpose? How could such a delicate thing survive in such a threatening environment?

Her answer came swiftly in the action of Miss Dean, towering over her desk, her eyes lighting on the cause of her pupil's distraction, and sweeping it aside with the rolled-up maths sheets clenched in her hand. The insect's awkward body lay stilled and broken under a desk nearby.

She looked down now at her own spare body lying in

the hospital bed, and felt assaulted like that creature of long ago.

Gerard had come to her apartment six days ago, his face tense, and far more preoccupied than she could ever remember. He'd poured himself a whisky, and her one glass of wine that she allowed herself for the day, then without looking directly at her had told her the news. David's car had been blown up near Saigon airport by a bomb they suspected was planted there just before he drove away.

But how? Why? Why? she'd asked, her voice trembling, unbelieving. She had seen such things in movies, but to David? It wasn't possible.

Perhaps it wasn't David's car. Was he sure?

Yes, he was quite sure.

How did it happen? What time? What did the police say? Did anyone see it? The trained journalist's questions poured out. It was as though she were interviewing someone about a stranger, not her husband, her David.

Gerard hadn't wanted to talk about the details, but realised that she had to know. It had probably happened when he turned the key in the ignition.

Oh God, she could see it all now—the key going in, then turning, and then the fatal flash of light and terrible heat. A burning, searing heat together with the deafening roar and blast that tore one's body as if it were a bag of rags, shattering it into millions of tiny particles to take flight on the wind and light anywhere in that war-torn landscape, only to merge with all the other spent remnants of human life.

'The body?' she whispered.

Gerard had shaken his head, his dark eyes like oil slicks, moving yet impenetrable. He reached out for her hand and held it tight.

'Who did it?' she asked, her voice rising. 'Who would want to . . . ?'

'We don't know yet, but we're going to find out, Sophie honey. But it's a war zone, and anything's possible.' He was silent, then as if placating a small child said, 'Come on, drink that down and then we're going back to my house. It's better you stay there.'

'Maybe it wasn't David in that car,' she'd repeated on the way out, her body numb, not fully comprehending. But it was, Gerard had said, and added that it was a terrible shock and that she must be calm and just think of the baby.

'Babies,' she had corrected him, her voice so distant it sounded as if it were coming from way off through a hollow tube.

He'd insisted that she come back with him then, and she had gone with her case already packed and ready for the hospital. His house when they arrived had seemed empty and resounding with William and Louise away at school, and without Jill's presence reaching out to fill every corner. Gerard had organised for Hiroko to be there too, knowing how close Sophie was now to her grandmother. The old lady's health seemed to be holding up well, even better than they'd ever envisaged. Six months ago he'd wondered if she would see the year out, but since Satoshi and Takeo's re-emergence, she seemed to have taken on a new lease of life. Before she had left, Jill had even set about planning a special *luau* for *Tutu*, to celebrate Hiroko's seventy-second birthday in February.

Now as she lay on her bed, looking out the hospital windows to the garden below, Sophie ran her hands down her body with a sense of relief. Apart from the swelling and hardness in her breasts, and a soreness from the few stitches, it was her very own body once more, freed from the small lives that had been part of it for eight months, and who were now sleeping in their cribs beside her.

The contractions had started that first night after hearing of David's death, and Malo had driven her sedately to hospital, still numbed from the news, her body's endorphins hastening to protect it from life's ill-fated 'slings and arrows'.

To compensate for her long-held fears of repeating her mother Gina's fatal journey into childbirth, Sophie had summoned all the meditation exercises she had been practising for months, and in just two hours after her arrival at the hospital her first son had arrived, then five minutes later his brother. They were three weeks ahead of time, almost as if hastening to fill the void left by their father.

Her sons were both perfectly formed, if a little underweight, at four and five pounds respectively, and had announced their arrival in loud and healthy cries. Sophie had looked at the large clock in the labour ward, noting each time of arrival to the minute, so that later she could have their horoscopes cast. It was only then she realised that it was Thursday. 'Thursday's child has far to go,' she whispered, suddenly remembering her night of love with David in his studio. It was then the full realisation that he had indeed gone from her life swept in on a first wave of grief to wash away any sense of shared joy in the arrival of their first-born. But the milk flowed, and the babies drank as if her body was there for their sustenance alone. And she nursed and nurtured them with the tears of loss still wet on her cheeks.

David's voice and last words to her the morning before he left still hung in the air. After a sleepless night, she'd awakened late to see him standing at the foot of her bed all ready to go.

'You came home so late,' she said reproachfully. 'Surely you can't be going away again so soon. I feel dreadful, what time is it?'

'Well you still look bloody good first thing,' he said, bending over and kissing her. 'We'll talk about it all when I get back.'

'Oh David, do you have to go?' she'd pleaded, sensing somehow that he shouldn't.

'I've got a feeling it could well be for the last time,' he'd replied, smiling at her.

Those fateful words lingered, as she heard him drive off and felt the emptiness that always followed his going rushing in to confront her yet again. It seemed another lifetime away now. Was it only a week ago?

Hiroko sat at the end of Sophie's bed, resting in her chair. Malo had wheeled her there ten minutes before, and she sat quietly watching her granddaughter as she slept, thinking what a blessing was the gentle curtaining of sleep. It gave one space to pause and recover, finding comfort in the hall of dreams.

She turned and looked at the two rounded bundles lying side by side in their cribs, joining their mother in the sweet solace of sleep. What a blessing it was, she thought, that if one life was to go, then two lives should arrive to replace it, the extra one a bonus.

She had been shocked by the violence of David's death when Gerard first told her, but somehow not grieved, except by what she knew Sophie would now feel and experience. Two babies and no father. It was becoming a familiar occurrence in our household, she thought, her mind regressing to her own loss at a time of birth. Maybe our family is cursed, she thought, then crossed herself for having such ungodly ideas, as well as for tempting fate. She looked at the two babies, only their tiny heads emerging from the white cocooning of their shawls, one so dark and the other golden haired, just like her Boy. Then after some minutes, as if following their example, her head fell back against her chair, and she drifted into one of the many cat naps that punctuated her day.

As so often in her dreams, Hiroko saw the laughing face of Boy, smiling and beckoning to her, and she felt a surge of excitement as he reached out his hand to her. They were on the floating plains of Hara, and she was running towards him, so young and free again and able to move with the effortless ease of youth, and getting a little closer to him this time. 'Wait for me Boy-san!' she called out.

A baby's cry awakened her, and Sophie was out of bed and picking up her golden-haired son, to bring him across to her grandmother.

'Here's Boy-chan, Oba-san,' gently placing the baby in the old woman's arms. 'Do you mind,' she said, looking at her grandmother, her eyes wide with appeal, 'if I call him Boy?'

Quick tears sprang to her grandmother's eyes, and she nodded, then bowed her head.

'I would like that—very much, Sophie-chan,' she whispered, her voice low with emotion.

Sophie gave her grandmother a hug as she took the baby from her and put him back in his crib.

'Well it's twins again. Seems like history's repeating itself,' she smiled wanly across the babies to her grandmother. 'You'll have to help me—show me how to cope.'

Hiroko nodded and smiled at her. 'We've been doubly blessed,' she said, unknowingly repeating Hattie's words from many years ago. 'I'll be there to help you, for a long while yet,' she added with a laugh.

'Is Gera coming later?' Sophie asked her. 'I haven't seen him yet.'

'No, he has had to take a flight to Australia. He had a call from Jill-san. There's urgent business at "Winganna" to attend to, and she needed him there.'

'Really? What business?' Sophie sat up. 'Did he have to go now?'

'Evidently yes,' Hiroko said. 'He told me not to worry,' she went on repeating her son's words. 'It's a legal matter, and he must be there to help Jill-san. It will only be for a few days.'

'And Takeo?' Sophie asked.

'I suppose he has gone on home to Tokyo by now. We're not to worry, Gerard will be ringing, and he'll tell us all about it when he gets back,' said Hiroko, more to reassure herself. She would like to have spoken to Takeo again.

After her grandmother had gone, wheeled out by the faithful Malo, Sophie thought about Gerard and his sudden trip to Australia. It wasn't like Jill not to be able to handle whatever legal matter had come up. There must be something more to it than that. A sense of apprehension filled her. Could it have anything to do with David? No, she couldn't see how. Whatever it was, Gera would handle it, she reassured herself, as she tried to push away the worrying thoughts which threatened to engulf her again.

But there was something going on, she mused. Jill had seemed very tense in the week or so before she left. When Sophie had asked her if anything was wrong, she'd brushed it aside with a quick, 'Nothing that hasn't been around for a long time. Anyway you've got enough to contend with, with your own problems, and I've spoken to Gerard about David.'

That was so like Jilly, she thought. Always presenting a strong front and making out that everyone else was in need, but never herself.

When she had first mentioned her fears about David and the drugs, Jill had stared at her, then answered in her flip way, 'Darling Sophie, when are you going to realise that all men are bastards?' and she'd laughed.

Sophie felt a softening towards the older woman who'd always been more like a big sister to her, and a sudden desire to get herself together so she could help Jill with whatever it was. Slowly, the strength that had deserted her with the news of David's death was starting to creep back. Perhaps their past few years together, with all the hurt of his infidelities and their long weeks spent apart, had somehow prepared her for his going. It seemed to lessen the loneliness she now felt, if not the sting of her loss.

Sophie gazed out at the evening sky fused with a crimson light from the last rays of the sun before it sank into Haleakala, the House of the Sun. She recalled the many happy times she had spent watching this wondrous spectacle on Maui, as the sun hastened to its home in that mystical crater, lighting up the exotic *Akina Akina* or Silverswords along its way.

The last time she had visited Haleakala was in the evening with David as he set up a photographic shoot. She remembered looking down upon the snowy carpet of clouds that filled the crater beneath them, with the sun behind her shining through a misty rain which had started to fall. As she looked, she saw a rainbow appear, springing up out of the mist, and there reflected in its opalescent arc was a ghostly figure, her shadow. 'You have seen *Mana*, your spiritual power, your soul,' Lalana told her later. 'It's a sign of good fortune. You have been specially chosen.'

Sophie recalled the early mornings spent on the mountain as a child with Jill and Gerard, sitting with their kites close to the rim, waiting for the winds that swept in from the waters of Hilo Bay, then towards the mountains through the gorges of the Wailuku River, and up the ten thousand foot climb to the cinder-coned rim.

'Oh winds, the winds of Hilo/Come to the mountains, come!'[23] she whispered now, remembering the words of the god Maui, as he summoned the winds in across the island to lift his mighty kite.

The first time she could recall being there they had taken the horses from the plantation and ridden up the narrow, winding track with rests along the way, until they arrived near the crater's edge. Jill had forged on ahead, as always, wanting to take the lead and looking for a suitable picnic spot, while Gerard had fallen behind to check on Sophie, who was watching the clouds gathering in the valley below them even as they climbed.

'Your mother loved this place, and came often,' he told her. It had comforted her, knowing they shared the same mystical sense of belonging to Haleakala's wild moonscape and majesty.

They had left early to catch the *Ukiukiu* trade winds that swept in from the north-east and bounced off the mighty mountain, only to meet headlong the *Naulu* winds blowing in from the leeward side of the mountain. And it was there, sitting near the crater's rim in the playground of *Ukiukiu* and *Naulu*, before the winds got too intense in their final assault on Haleakala, battling for the bands of cloud which gathered around its summit, that they flew their graceful Japanese kites, the red and white bird-shapes soaring and swooping, her spirit flying with them in moments of intense joy, a happiness only ever to be fleetingly recaptured.

Such precious moments Sophie knew now as balm to the restless spirits within each of us, roaming the world at will, seeking and searching for their spiritual home. She sat up and looked proudly at her baby sons with a feeling that everything in her life was starting anew. She would take the boys to that same magic place to fly their kites, and once more experience the wonder of those moments.

'Boy-chan, David-chan,' she whispered, gazing at the sleeping twins as they started to stir. 'We're going to make it all happen,' she said, laughing delightedly as Boy opened his dark blue eyes, trying to focus on the sounds of his mother's laughter, which was to become a touchstone in his life.

And in that moment lay the stirring of hope, for no story really ends but merely links our past with the future.

AFTERMATH

You know he's gone and your mates are gone, when you come home and run all over the place looking for your brother in your dreams. Then you know he's gone.

Bert Henderson drew long and deep on his pipe, as if to put new fire in his veins and rekindle old memories. He looked at the five bedraggled young men crowded into the front of his open launch as he steered it towards the distant Lucinda Point.

They were all quiet now, their initial laughter and good humour when he had first picked them up replaced by silence, each man submerged in his own world of thoughts.

Their impassive expressions made him think of a group of Japanese prisoners they'd taken captive at war's end, young boys little more than kids, their faces wiped of all emotion, silent and lost in the sudden reversal of power.

This lot were more like the sons of the others, and no doubt with a different world of experience behind and ahead of them. The message telling of their whereabouts had come through only that morning, out of Palm Island, the first in four days since cyclone Althea had done her dash. It appeared they'd been snorkelling off Orpheus, and had engine trouble and couldn't get back, then old lady Althea had struck and they'd been washed up on North East Bay, and the rest was history.

They were bloody lucky they hadn't all drowned or

been dashed to death on the coral reefs, he thought. Or worse still, like that other crazy bugger the whole place was yakking on about, who'd been wiped out by that croc. But he, Bert, wouldn't be wasting his tears on him, or any of them.

He sat staring through the haze that had started to rise above the distant shoreline as the heat of midday and smoke from the cane fires bounced off the Great Dividing Range, and rushed to meet the moist air blowing in from the Pacific Ocean. A sweet cloying smell of burnt sugar drifted across the water to meet them.

He felt a surge of pride as his eye followed the shape of the shoreline which seemed to stretch away forever. Mount Spec, the highest point in the Paluma Range, rose like a silent sentinel above the purple-shrouded mountains and lush rainforests that came down to meet the chain of white coral beaches that ran north all the way to Cape Tribulation. God almighty, it was a bloody big place this country of his, riding the ocean like a giant old whale. It was as if she was floating and waiting, just there for the taking, he thought, remembering the fight they'd put up to keep her safe all those years ago.

Is it true then, he wondered, that we are only temporary caretakers of the land we love? He and his brother Jim had had such big plans and dreams. The things they weren't going to do! His thoughts went to the memorial in Lae. He and Vi had left the kids at home and gone to New Guinea only last year to visit Jim in his sacred final resting place. It was the most beautiful bloody place he'd ever seen, just one vast stretch of mown grass surrounded by towering trees and gardens, the simple white crosses mute testimony to the fallen. It was a hallowed place, and everything so green, a deep vivid green. It was like being in the heart of an emerald, Vi had said.

He could almost feel the spirit of Jim rising to greet him. There was no-one there but him and Vi, so he'd lain down in the grass, his tears sinking into the earth as if to meet those of his brother. It was the first time he'd cried for Jim. Everything was so silent there, he remembered now, with just the occasional sound of a distant bird. He was glad he'd gone, but it didn't take away his feeling of loss. Nothing ever would.

Bert observed his passengers now with a sense of the old resentment. Memories of Jim and what had happened to him fuelled his bitterness. He stared at them, his anger rising at the injustice of it all. Jim should have been there with him, not this washed-out bunch of Japanese kids. He wondered what the hell they were on about anyway, coming all this way just to do a spot of fishing. But then again, when he thought of the bloody good fishing there was to be had around here, you could hardly blame them. Hadn't he hauled in a beauty to end all beauties only last week? A coral trout that tipped the scales at ten kilograms! She'd given him a real run for his money, he recalled, hitting the bait hard, then racing away with it down into the coral grotto before he'd had a chance to haul her in. He'd let the line slacken and waited till he felt her move out of her convoluted coral world, then reeled in fast before she had a chance to get away. His eyes shone with the memory.

Bert nosed his boat towards Dungeness jetty, sighting the long arm of the sugar-loading wharf spearing out from Lucinda. The usual translucent calm of clear blue and aquamarine waters above the shadowy other-world shapes of coral below were still churned up and littered with debris.

As they came in closer, the destructive sting of Althea's tail could be clearly seen. His passengers started pointing and talking excitedly amongst themselves, except for one, who stood apart from the others with the air of someone who knew his way around. He seemed detached from his mates, and was staring expectantly at the jetty and people standing on it, as it came into sight.

What was he on about now, Bert wondered. Only a short while ago the boy seemed to be looking for something, and had come up and asked him if he'd seen a gold cross on a chain, a crucifix his grandmother had given him, he said. They'd had a bit of a search, and then later he'd come back and said it was OK now. It seemed he'd just remembered he'd probably left it behind on the mainland in his jacket with his mate, before he'd gone off in the boat with the others days ago.

Come to think of it, what would he, a Jap, want with a gold cross, a crucifix of all things?

The way they were silently staring at the results of Althea's handiwork, you'd think they'd never seen the aftermath of a storm before. Then again nothing would surprise him. Not any more. After all, when it came to the unexpected, who'd ever have thought he'd end up ferrying a bunch of Japanese, the sons of his and his brother's tormentors, across these waters. He sucked on his pipe with more than usual force. You had to hand it to the old boy up there, he reflected, his eyes following the trail of smoke as it curled heavenwards. He certainly moved in a mysterious way. And no doubt, he mused, he still had plenty more wonders to hand out.

The sun hung, a golden-red orb suspended in a washed-out sky, as he nosed his boat towards Dungeness. He noted with surprise Sid Carpenter and a small group of people, strangers too, waiting for them on the jetty. They were waving excitedly to the boy who'd lost his crucifix, and he wondered what that was all about.

* * *

'Goodbye,' said the fox. 'And now here is my secret, a very simple secret: It is only with the heart that one can see rightly; what is essential is invisible to the eye.'[24]

GLOSSARY

bishonen	pretty boys (young male prostitutes)
ero manga	erotic comic books
fingaa sabisu	finger service
fundoshi	loincloth
giri-to-on	obligation
go-yo	official business
gumi	clan
haboku	broken ink
hachimaki	headband
hai, hai!	yes, yes!
hara	abdomen
hikyaku	flying legs (messengers)
hiragana	Japanese orthography
ichiya-zuma	one-night wives
ie, ie!	no, no!
ikura-no-yuzugama	salmon roe in citron
jumonji	crosswise cut
junkatsuyu	lubricating oil
kachi guri	victory chestnuts

kami	a god
kenjutsu	swordsmanship
kiku	chrysanthemum
kishaku-nin	assistant
ko	parental obligation
kokusaika	internationalism
lliahi	sandalwood
mizu shobai	the water business
mushin on shin	mind and no mind
ninjo	chivalry
nisei	second-generation Japanese American
noren	trade mark—entrance curtain
omiai	arranged marriage
pan-pan	female prostitutes
plumeria	frangipani
renai	love marriage
sakoku	closed-door policy
Sakura Ohanami	Festival of Cherry Blossom
sansui chokan	long landscape scroll
satori	enlightenment
sensei	teacher
shakuhachi	Japanese bamboo flute
shunga	erotic pictures
suki	unguarded weakness
takara-yaki tamago	egg omelette
Tango No Sekku	the annual festival for boys in early May
tekkiya	barrow boys and food peddlers
torii	entrance arch to Shinto shrine
tutu	grandparent
wa	great peace
wabi	a taste for simplicity

Yakuza	the Underworld—gangsters
Yamato	old Japan
yami ichi	black market
yu-jo	play girls
yuna	bath-house girl
zuda-bukuro	pilgrim's bag

NOTES

1. Anon.
2. Retold by W.D. Westervelt. Edited by A. Grove Day 'Lei Mauna Loa', an ancient Hawaiian chant, *Myths and Legends of Hawaii*, Mutual Publishing of Honolulu.
3. Chikafusa Kitabatake, *Jinnoh Shotoki*, published 1339.
4. Denis and Peggy Warner with Sado Seno, *Kamikaze—The Sacred Warriors 1944–45*, Oxford University Press, 1983.
5. Thomas Kempis, *Of the Imitation of Christ*, Oxford University Press, London.
6. Chikafusa Kitabatake, *Jinnoh Shotoki*.
7. Ishikawa Takuboku, *Modern Japanese Literature*, editor Donald Keene, rev edn., Penguin Books, 1968.
8. Robert Jung, *Children of the Ashes*, Heinemann, London, 1961.
9. Masamune, the famous Japanese swordsmith (1264–1344), whose nobility of spirit was said to have pervaded his blades. Richard Storry and Werner Forman, *The Way of the Samurai*, Orbus Publishing Limited, London, 1978.
10. Islam, origin unknown.
11. 'A Dialogue on Poverty', from the Manyoshu or *Collection of Ten Thousand Leaves*, compiled around AD 750.
12. Denis and Peggy Warner with Sado Seno, *Kamikaze—the Sacred Warriors 1944–45*, Oxford University Press, 1983.
13. Taoao Taguchi, *Beautiful Japanese Children's Song*, Tokyo International Academy Press, Japan.
14. unknown.

15. Yosano Akiko.
16. Nursery rhyme, England.
17. Franklin D. Roosevelt
18. Haiku, origin unknown.
19. John 6: 53:56.
20. Lewis Carroll, *Alice in Wonderland*, Anderson Press, London, 1993.
21. Haiku, by Kyoshi.
22. 'All Along the Watchtower', by Bob Dylan. Copyright © 1968, by Dwarf Music. All rights reserved. International copyright secured. Reprinted by permission.
23. W.D. Westervelt, *Myths and Legends of Hawaii*, Mutual Publishing Co., Hawaii, 1987.
24. Antoine de Saint-Exupery, *The Little Prince*, Pan Books Ltd, London, 1974.